Just Willa

HELEN SHEEHY

ALSO BY HELEN SHEEHY

All About Theatre

Margo: The Life and Theatre of Margo Jones

Eva Le Gallienne: A Biography

Eleonora Duse: A Biography

Just Willa

HELEN SHEEHY

A Cave Hollow Press Book

Warrensburg, Missouri 2025

Cave Hollow Press
304 Grover Street
Warrensburg, MO 64093

Copyright 2025 by Helen Sheehy
Cover Design by Sue Rollins
Author Photo by Alison Sheehy, used with permission
Formatting by Stephanie Flint

Library of Congress Control Number: 2024946542

Paperback ISBN: 978-1-7342678-3-9
Hardcover ISBN: 978-1-7342678-4-6

cavehollowpress.com

For Rocky, Dena, Buddy, Bill, and Roger
In loving memory of our parents

Art is our chief means of breaking bread with the dead.
— W. H. Auden

Table of Contents

Prologue
Stirring the Ashes

I CAME TO DREAD HER calls. I knew it meant bad news. A relative had died or had a stroke or gotten divorced or mangled in a car wreck or mice had overrun her kitchen. It's the shits, she would say.

And then there was the saga of the stray cat. A year or so before Mama died, a feral tomcat had shown up. Instead of running him off, Mama let him stay in the barn. He was skin and bones, so she fed him milk and table scraps. He would follow her back and forth to the mail box and "talk" to her all the way. Suddenly, one Sunday she announced, "The cat's dead."

"What happened?" I'd grown fond of that mangy vocal cat.

"Well, Huck's dog got loose and just ripped him apart. Came right into our yard and that cat didn't have a chance. I heard him screaming but by the time I got there it was too late. You know there aren't any trees to climb."

"Stop, stop! Don't tell me anymore."

"Well, it's what happened. I drove over to Huck's and let him have it about his goddamn dog."

"Stop! Just stop!"

"Well, you need to know."

My mother believed I knew nothing about death when, the truth is, death has haunted me since I was five years old. But I couldn't tell her that. I couldn't tell her anything.

My first memory of conscious writing has to do with the fear of death and the need to record a life. I must have been about five because we were living on the Boyce place. A tornado threatened, and before I ran down to the cellar with my family, I scribbled a sentence on a scrap of paper, put it in a matchbox, and buried it. I remember the four words I wrote— "Ellie Hardesty lived here." When I was eleven, I stood on a dirt road in Freedom, Oklahoma, and watched as a girl, about my age, slipped from the horse she was riding and fell to the ground. Blood gushed from her left ear. Someone put a pink towel under her head. Her eyes were closed and her face turned deep red and then to purple. When her gasping breath stopped, although no one said so, I knew that she was dead.

No, I didn't want to hear Mama talk about death. I preferred to write her letters and to call her, every few months, at random times. Because I only called my mother with good news. When she answered the phone and I said, "Hi Mama, it's me," I loved hearing the delight in her nicer voice, the rising inflection of pleasure. We had lived together for almost eighteen years. I was her baby, the last of six. I knew she loved me, and I loved her too, although we never said so. I lived sixteen hundred miles away, and she had no idea who I was. And it was her fault. She raised me to live in a different world. An urban world of theatre and books as far away from the farm as I could get.

Just Willa

Mama has been dead for years, yet she's more alive to me now than she ever was. I worked in the theatre, taught acting, and wrote biographies. I realized I knew more about complete strangers than I did about my own mother.

It became an obsession. I wanted to know her. Why did she raise me to live in another world? Did she ever want a different life? Questions I could have asked when she was alive, but I didn't. Who was she? What did she want? She didn't keep a diary, but she wrote lots of letters. They would let me right inside her head. I interviewed my siblings and cousins and neighbors, her older sister, her nieces and nephews, and her grandchildren. I had her wooden document box and the family photos and the memorabilia she packed up for me when I got married. I knew the clothes she liked, the perfume she wore, and the cigarettes she smoked. I claimed her silver compact, her Indian pouch, and her special egg-shaped rock.

Of course, I had my own memories. The sound of her voice. The rhythms of her speech. Her constant work. She never seemed to rest. She was always doing something, and I grew up believing that Mama could do almost anything if she set her mind to it. She plowed ground, baled hay, and raised cattle, pigs, and chickens. She baked bread, made soap from lard, planted a garden, and canned sand plum jelly. She fixed the clutch on the tractor, built fences, castrated cattle, cleaned copper and metal for resale, and clipped coupons. She quilted, tatted, embroidered, sewed, and tailored. She played the piano by ear, could pick up a dance step after seeing it once, and cooked meals that make my mouth water just thinking about them. Ham and beans, chicken and noodles, cherry pies and cinnamon rolls, fried chicken and mashed potatoes and gravy. I make those dishes all the time, but they don't taste the same as hers.

Mama and Daddy, Willa and Jake, were formed by the Great Depression and the Dust Bowl. They were the Okies who stayed. How could Mama leave? She was the proud daughter of Doc Sharpe, a homesteader who founded Freedom, Oklahoma. The furthest distance she ever traveled from her home was some three hundred fifty miles away to visit a half-sister in Blue Springs, Missouri. And there was Daddy, Mama's second husband, who outlived her. He started out as a cowboy, a boxer, a bootlegger, and he told lots of stories, which Mama called his damn lies. She knew she was fighting a losing battle, but she tried to clean up his bullshit just like she cleaned up the cow manure he was always tracking in on her fresh-mopped kitchen floor. Daddy was good-looking and fun, and he worked as hard as she did. She chose to spend forty-seven years of her life with him.

She had secrets, too. Secrets I uncovered while stirring the ashes of our family history. I've asked myself, why does any of this matter? Mama was just a nobody living in the middle of nowhere. But as Mama would say, that's a damn lie. She thought she was somebody. And everybody's got a story. Maybe that's what it is. Just words on a page that tell a story. Or maybe what I really wanted was to spend more time with Mama. And this time round, listen to what she had to say.

PART ONE

Burning in Hell

1964

Willa Hardesty lit a cigarette and tossed the burning match into the barrel. The bone dry stacks of the *Enid Morning News* and the *Freedom Call* caught first and fueled the rest. Flames and smoke filled the barrel and poured over the top. She took a deep drag on her cigarette and then another. She stared into the inferno and imagined the flames leaping out of the rusted barrel, igniting the twine-wrapped bundles of newspaper and the stacks of cardboard boxes filled with things that nobody wanted, and then, unsatisfied, the flames would devour the shed and, still hungry, would lap up the dry yellow grass in the yard, explode the gas cans in the garage, engulf Annie's Dodge Dart, and then roar onto the porch of Aunt Mattie's house, eat through the walls and doors and floors consuming everything, and then race across the pastures, and into the plowed fields, burning deep into the soil and charring the fresh drilled wheat, then gobbling every fence post, every weed and thistle along the way, burst to the top of Sugar Loaf hill until all four hundred acres was a wasteland of dry black powder. And the ravenous fire wouldn't stop there;

it would blaze east to Protection and Coldwater and beyond to Wichita and Topeka until there was nothing left of the whole goddamn state of Kansas. Nothing but ashes.

Ashes. Her mouth tasted like ashes. Willa sucked smoke deep into her chest. Searching for some kind of comfort. She stubbed out the spent cigarette in the dirt and lit another. Her stomach burned. Her ulcer was acting up again. The new medicine wasn't worth a damn. She picked up another bundle of papers and threw them into the fire. The flames leapt. Hell. She was in hell.

She had gone over it so many times in her mind she was sick of it. Still the outcome was always the same. She knew something was up when Jake ran off to Kansas without her. He had said yes immediately to all of Aunt Mattie's terms. They would farm on a 2/3-1/3 share, giving Mattie a third. "We should have talked it over," Willa said. "Gotten a better deal."

"What's to talk about?" Jake said. "We'll put cattle on wheat pasture, pay off our loan, and soon we'll buy her out."

"But without a contract, something in writing," Willa argued, "what's to stop Mattie from just selling it to somebody else or giving it to the church if you piss her off."

Jake shrugged. "You don't have contracts with family. We shook hands on it."

"That's bullshit and you know it," Willa countered. "She hasn't cared a thing about us all these years."

Jake walked away. He hated arguing. He'd made up his mind, done what he wanted, and there was nothing she could do about it except start packing.

Just Willa

She should have known, when the President was shot and that bastard in Protection spit on her Kennedy bumper sticker, that the whole world had turned dark.

She stared at the fire. Her heart pounded, and her face was hot. Maybe if she got lucky, she'd have a stroke and end it all right here. But then who would take care of Annie? No one, that's who. Not Jake. The boys had their own lives. Not Ellie. Where the hell was she? Ellie was supposed to help her clean out this shed, and then she disappeared. She was always disappearing, always finding some excuse to get away from home. Away from work.

Willa stubbed out her cigarette in the dirt and lit another. It dangled from her lip as she picked up a box to toss into the barrel. Why did she have to do every goddamn thing herself?

"Mama!"

"Ellie! You scared the shit out of me! Don't sneak up like that. You made me drop my cigarette." Willa placed the box in the barrel. She picked up her cigarette and brushed off the dirt.

She took a drag and stared at her fifteen-year-old daughter. As bright and shiny as a new penny. And about as useless.

"What are you doing, Mama? You look all sweaty and weird."

"What does it look like I'm doing? I'm working. Which is more than you're doing."

"You don't have to bite my head off."

Willa added a stack of newspapers to the barrel. Ellie was up to something. Seemed like the only time Ellie ever said two words to her was when she wanted something.

"Well, don't just stand there, missy. Hand me one of those boxes."

"No. I'll get all dirty and sweaty like you. Stewart's picking me up. We're going to town. Daddy said I could."

"Oh no you're not!" But Ellie pretended not to hear. She'd already run off. Back to the house to put her head in a book while she waited for Stewart.

Oh, forget it, Willa thought. Maybe Jake's right. Let her do what she wants if it makes her happy.

And more than anything Willa wanted her baby girl to be happy. To have a happy life. Not a life like hers, filled with unhappiness and despair and grief. Willa lit a cigarette, savoring the familiar calming taste. She filled her mouth with smoke and blew a perfect smoke ring. At least she could still do that. She envied Ellie running toward her future. All Ellie wanted to do was get out, and Willa was doing her best to make sure she did. Nothing would stop Ellie from getting an education. Unless she got pregnant. Willa worried about that. Flicking the porch light on and off when Ellie stayed in Stewart's car too long. It made Ellie furious, but Willa didn't care. Everybody said that Ellie looked just like her. That they were two peas in a pod. But as soon as Ellie was born, Willa vowed that her daughter wouldn't follow in her footsteps. And so far she hadn't. No. Ellie took after Jake. Always spilling over with enthusiasm and optimism, never thinking of anyone but herself. But at least Ellie was happy. And that was all that mattered.

Willa picked up another box to add to the fire. A big boot box tied with rawhide string. No, it couldn't be. She hadn't seen this box in years. She put the box on the ground, kneeled down, and unknotted the string. She lifted the lid. Inside were dozens of calendar notebooks, all different sizes and different colors. So many years. She sorted through them until she found the first one. A small spiral notebook with a faded blue cover. A stubby pencil still stuck in the wire coils.

She took a deep drag on her cigarette and then buried the butt in the dirt. She flipped open the notebook. As she read, she remembered something. A long time ago she had been happy. She hadn't started out in hell. She had started out in Freedom.

Freedom
1927

"MUG. TAKE THIS WITH YOU." Her father handed her a bright blue calendar notebook with a pencil stuck in the coils.

"What's it for?"

"Writing things down so you won't forget. What you spend your money on."

"I don't have any money." He stared at her. Willa was looking up at him and right into the sun so she couldn't tell if his blue eyes were frowning or laughing. He'd warned her never to lie to him. Did he know about the cigar box she hid in the root cellar filled with pennies, nickels, dimes, quarters, and one dollar bill?

She decided to hedge. "I mean I don't have any money *with* me."

"Uh-huh. That's what I thought." He reached into his pocket and gave her three crumpled one-dollar bills, one five, and four tens.

She ironed the bills with her hands. She'd never held so much money.

"Forty-eight dollars!"

"That's right. You'll need to buy two round-trip tickets to Kansas City. Your mother's will be eleven dollars each way and yours five dollars. How much is left?"

Willa didn't hesitate. "Sixteen dollars."

"That's for the tickets to Blue Springs. Whatever's left over is for you. Don't lose it. And keep an eye on your mother. Where is your mother, anyway? We need to get a move on."

"Yes sir."

Willa knew exactly where her mother was. She was in the bedroom deciding which hat to wear. Or scribbling one of her stories for the newspaper. Damn fool waste of time, Daddy called it.

Willa folded the bills and put them in her pocket. She climbed into the bed of the 1925 Ford Model A Truck; her younger brother Heck had washed off the dried red mud, and the black paint gleamed. Her father had been the first in Woods County to own one of Ford's factory-produced trucks. He paid three hundred dollars in cash for it at a time when their house had peeling paint and lacked indoor plumbing. With seven children to feed, he didn't see how a flush toilet put more money in the bank.

Willa's father's name was Luther, but everyone called him Doc. Everybody said Willa took after him although she didn't look a thing like him. Willa inherited Lizzy's silky smooth olive skin, high broad cheekbones, dark brown eyes and black hair; Doc was tall, with fair skin, blue eyes, and light brown hair. He kept a wooden box filled with tools and medicine and tended to his children with a calm, healing touch.

When Luther was fourteen, he left his parents' farm in Jewel County, Kansas, and found work as a freighter, piloting ox teams to Oregon and then back again. Along the way, he learned the art of bread making and healing from Sugar, an old Black cook. Sugar made a fine-textured white bread with everlasting yeast that he carried in a sealed fruit jar. When something more than healing bread was needed, Sugar opened his wooden box filled with herbs and bottles of medicine.

During an ill-advised river crossing, Sugar and his team of mules drowned. Doc rescued the cook's medicine box, took over his healing duties, and earned his name. Doc was fond of his nickname and gave each of his seven children a special handle. To Willa, his youngest and favorite daughter, he gave the name Mug.

Willa sat down on her mother Lizzie's brown tin suitcase, opened her new notebook and printed WILLA'S NOTEBOOK 1927 on the cover. On the inside she printed "MONEY $48.00 from Daddy." It was the first time he'd trusted her with money. Money had to be earned, he always said.

She was eleven years old and this was her first trip. Her mother had wanted to take all the girls to Blue Springs to visit her adult daughter Effie and her twins, but Doc said he could only afford a trip for two. They had drawn straws, and Willa, to the dismay of her older sisters, had picked the short straw.

Willa tucked the notebook in her pocket and smoothed the skirt of her blue-checked cotton slip-on dress with the dropped waist. This was the first time she'd worn a dress made just for her instead of one of her sisters' hand-medowns. She inspected the hem which she had sewn using an ornamental cross-stitch. Willa could embroider and was an expert hand sewer. When Willa turned twelve, her mother promised she could use the treadle sewing machine.

Willa ran down the list she had made in her head. Heck promised to sneak milk to the kittens in the barn when he gathered the eggs. Cissie would do the bread baking. Ro and Dilly would do Willa's share of the milking and washing and ironing. Willa prided herself on all she could hold in her head. At school, she always won the ciphering contests because she silently added up the numbers as soon as they were announced. All the other kids just wrote down the numbers and then added them together at the end. She had come up with this system herself, and the more she practiced the faster she got. When they checked out at the Square Deal in Old Freedom, her mother always looked at her to make sure the amount was right before she paid the bill.

Where was her mother? She heard car horns honking and looked down the hill toward Old Freedom. Someone must have hit a home run. They were playing Farry today. Willa's shoulders slumped. She wished she were there eating ice cream and sitting with her best friend Annie Shaw. What if they missed the train? What if something happened on the way to Waynoka? What if they had a blowout? The sky was clear now, but what if they got caught in a hailstorm or a tornado? What if she lost the money or even worse lost her mother? Willa gnawed the inside of her cheek, consumed with all that could possibly go wrong.

Her father had given her an enormous responsibility. She couldn't let him down. Her brothers and sisters teased her about being Daddy's girl, but she didn't care. She adored her father. Doc was an important man, one of the founders of Freedom, Oklahoma, who owned a section of land, six hundred forty acres. He had shown her the document, his homestead claim, and taught her to understand what it meant. According to the paper, Luther Richard "Doc" Sharpe had filed his claim on the Southeast Quarter of Section 2 in Township 27, North of Range 18, West of Indian Meridian in the Cherokee Outlet of Oklahoma Territory. The land was part of the Great Plains, an area twenty-five hundred miles long and six hundred miles wide, nine hundred sixty million acres encompassing ten states. His original one hundred sixty acres, one six-millionth of the Great Plains, was a tiny crumb on the vast prairie table.

Willa liked visiting the original dugout, which was now the root cellar. From the doorway, Doc pointed out a landscape that hadn't changed in thousands of years. You looked five miles south down into a wide valley and saw the red clay bluffs of the Cimarron River fringed with cottonwood trees, tamarack, and sand plum thickets. Further south were rough canyons, spring- fed streams, and deep carved gorges. Hidden in the canyons were caves lined with alabaster and fantastic formations of crystals. Turning to the north and then to the east, more rolling prairies dotted with cedar trees that made fine fence posts. Miles to the southwest, a torrent of rushing white water, about three miles wide and twelve miles long, cut through the red earth. But Willa knew that was only an illusion. The white stripe was actually a barren salt plain, fed by deep underground brine pools. Doc told her how years ago he harvested salt there in big slabs and then hauled it to Alva and Coldwater and sold it for cash money. Eight to ten dollars a load. It was a farmer's dream, he said, no plowing, no planting, no cultivating, all harvest.

Doc made the run into Oklahoma in 1889, but tragedy struck, and he hauled his wagon back to Kansas. When Willa asked what had happened, her mother shook her head. When Willa persisted, Doc promised to tell her when she was older. In 1893 when the Cherokee Outlet opened, Doc decided to try the run again. He collected his last paycheck from the Comanche Cattle Company. And when he pulled the tarp off his old wagon, he found everything just as he had left it in the '89 land rush; one axe, one spade, a sod plow, a water barrel, a tin bucket, a cast iron skillet, a butcher knife, some rope. He wouldn't need much else. He added two wool blankets, his clothes and a razor, coffee pot and grub sacks, and his medicine box. He filled the water barrel, hitched up the mule team, tossed in a saddle and bridle, and with his horse Buck trotting behind, Doc left Kansas to start his new life in Oklahoma territory.

Doc unloaded his wagon and staked out his homestead on treeless high pasture. Some of the wild grasses stood three and four feet tall, all green and silvery, sweet-smelling, and blooming. He taught Willa their names. Bluestem bunch grass, milkweed and lamb's quarters. Western yarrow with its five white flowers and spicy smell. Prairie clover with its purple spike. The bushy-branched broom weed with its yellow flowers and the feathery tickle grass. And scraggly bull nettle with its delicate white blossoms, each holding a blazing yellow sun at its tiny center. Indian paintbrush and cowboy roses and sagebrush, with its soft gray-green bristles, all flourished in the good sandy loam.

The land had sweet, clean water, unfouled by gyp rock, and drawn up by bucket from his hand-dug well. The weather was temperate and moderate most of the time with a steady wind, but it could turn in an instant when hot and cold air collided overhead and formed tornados and thunderstorms or hailstorms and blizzards.

"Mug!" her father said, "Stop day dreaming!

Willa rubbed her eyes and stood up in the truck bed. "Can I ride back here, Mama?"

"No!" Lizzie held the truck door open. "You'll get filthy back there."

Doc swung her to the ground and ruffled Willa's bobbed black hair. "Don't be such a worry-wart, Mug. Old Freedom will still be here when you get back."

They drove through Old Freedom in less than a minute. It wasn't much of a town now, just the baseball field, the one-room Houston Valley School, and the Square Deal store where they got blocks of ice and picked up anything they had forgotten to buy in Alva or the new town of Freedom. Doc and two other homesteaders had wearied of hauling their wheat to Alva to sell and raised money for a railroad through the

Just Willa

Cimarron River valley, linking the towns of Buffalo and Waynoka. In 1917 they sold out to Santa Fe, and the following year businesses in Old Freedom moved five miles south and a half-mile east to hook up with the railroad.

The new Freedom boasted a red brick schoolhouse with grades one through twelve, Freedom Hardware, Star Lumber, Kasem's General Store, the Freedom State Bank, Dr. Hunt's Drug Store, Eason Oil Company, the Farmer's Co-op and grain elevator, Alma Ritter's boarding house, Mack's Barber shop, the Liberty Theatre, two cafes, and the post office. The town wouldn't get around to building the small white wood-framed Christian Church until 1929.

The cemetery remained in Old Freedom, each year spreading further into the high prairie.

"Slow down!" Lizzie warned, as they got closer to the iron gates of the cemetery. Doc braked the truck behind a black car stopped in the road.

"Need any help, John?" he called.

A tall, rangy man with a shock of white hair got out of the car. He was dressed in khaki pants and a dark blue shirt. Two boys with thick dark brown hair, blue eyes, and square jaws, as alike as stair steps, scrambled out of the car. Both wore dirty overalls. The taller boy opened the trunk and lifted out a wooden toolbox. The second boy moved closer to the man and looked admiringly at Doc's truck.

"Nope. Thanks for asking. We're just getting things ready for Decoration Day. How's old Bill doing?"

"He's good as new. Eating up a storm."

Willa turned to look out the back window as they drove away. The second boy still stood in the road. Willa waved. The boy grinned, waved his arms over his head, and kicked up dust with his boots, doing a kind of dance. "Who was that, Daddy?"

"John Hardesty. He's a horse doctor, stone carver, too. I guess you weren't around when he pulled Old Bill's rotten tooth."

"No, the boy. The one kicking up dust."

"Well, John's got three boys. That one's the middle one. What's their names, Lizzie?"

"The biggest one is Jimmy, then Jake, and the little one is Billy. It's such a shame."

"What's a shame, Mama?"

"Those boys shouldn't be working on a Sunday. They need a mother, that's what they need."

"Where's their mother?" asked Willa.

Lizzie cut her eyes at Doc over Willa's head.

"She passed away, Mug," Doc said.

Willa wanted to ask how, but from her father's tone she knew that the subject was closed.

In fact, John Hardesty had divorced his wild, young wife, and Maybelle Hardesty died of a botched abortion. For years, whenever she ran away on a drinking or drug binge, John had brought her back home. She would promise to behave, but after she gave birth to a daughter that he believed wasn't his, John packed up and left with his boys. Since he traveled around northwestern Oklahoma working as a veterinarian and

20

a stone carver, he called on his sisters to take in his three sons.

Willa took out her notebook and pencil. She wrote "Saw Jake Hardesty by the cemetery."

The red brick Waynoka Depot bustled with activity. Willa had never seen so many people on their way to somewhere. Lizzie grabbed the suitcase, and with a wave goodbye, Doc turned the truck around and headed home. He didn't see any point in waiting around doing nothing when there were chores to be done.

Their train, the #44 eastbound Santa Fe Train, the Missionary, was right on time. There were just four wooden coach cars, a dining car, a baggage car, and one sleeping car. They were in the second coach car. Willa took the window seat, and Lizzie sat next to her on the aisle. Willa counted twenty-four rows with two seats on each side of the aisle. The air from the open window felt cool. The whistle sounded and in a cloud of oily smoke and a clatter of engines, the Missionary headed east toward Missouri.

The Train to Blue Springs
1927

WILLA PLANNED TO STAY AWAKE and see every station where they stopped, but the rocking movement and the steady noise of the engines sent her to sleep. She was barely awake at 4:00 a.m. when her mother pushed her to the toilet at the rear of the car, keeping a hand on her shoulder to steady her. "Where does it go?" Willa wondered, as she flushed a toilet for the first time in her life.

"What a question!" Lizzie said. "Well, I think it's dumped out on the track."

Willa awoke to hot sun on her face and the smell of coffee. The view from the train window transfixed her. It was a world she had seen only in pictures. A world of trees. Everywhere she looked there were leafy trees in every shade of green.

Lizzie's daughter Effie and her husband farmed eighty acres of loamy river bottomland outside of Blue Springs. First, they picnicked on the Little Blue River, and Willa, who knew only cottonwood and cedar trees, discovered sycamore, willow, elm, oak, ash, and walnut. Later, wanting time alone, Lizzie and Effie shooed the girls out of the house to play.

Just Willa

Willa didn't know how to play with the twins who seemed interested only in their dolls. To Willa, it was odd that Effie, a grown woman, was her half-sister and even odder that Willa was an aunt to girls who were eleven, just her age. They were fair complexioned, blonde and blue-eyed like Effie, and wanted to know why Willa's skin was so dark and why her hair was black. "Are you an Indian?" they asked.

"No!" Willa said. "I'm an Oklahoman. My daddy founded Freedom, Oklahoma." That was the end of the conversation, but Willa felt as if she had been criticized. While the girls undressed and dressed their stupid dolls, Willa busied herself pulling weeds. She missed her family and worried about the kittens.

She was thrilled when Lizzie decided to leave early Thursday morning and spend some time in Kansas City. They checked their suitcases at Union Station, and Lizzie took Willa to breakfast at the Muehlebach Hotel. While she waited for her mother to finish her coffee, Willa surveyed the other diners. Most of them were men wearing business suits, and many of them were smoking cigarettes. She breathed in the aroma of coffee, cigarettes, and fried ham. It was heavenly. A baldheaded Negro man, wearing doorman's livery, smiled at her from across the room.

"That old man is staring at us, Mama." She pointed to the archway.

"Don't point, Willa." Lizzie put down her coffee cup and turned her attention to the waiter who had arrived with their check. On their way out, they passed the doorman, who nodded at Willa.

"Miss Allen, it's sure good to see you."

Lizzie peered into his wrinkled dark face. He winked.

"Why Henry Lewis! It's good to see you, too. But it's Mrs. Sharpe now."

"Is this pretty little girl in the blue dress your daughter?"

"Yes. This is Willa Elizabeth. Say hello to Mr. Lewis, Willa."

"Hi," Willa said. She knew it wasn't polite to stare, but she couldn't help it. His skin was black. As black as stove coal. But the inside of his hands were lighter, sort of pink.

"Yep. I work here now," Henry Lewis said. "They tore down the Edward. That was a sad day. All the old places are gone, except the Standard Theatre is still running. They call it the Folly now. Mr. Dayton sure loved that theatre, rest his soul."

"Mr. Dayton, Wade, is . . . He's gone?"

"He died about seven years ago, Miss Allen, I mean, Mrs. Sharpe. Had a full head of hair, too. Not like me. Mine was falling out so fast I just shaved it all off. Yep, he sure was proud of his yellow-gold hair. They buried him up in Elmwood Cemetery."

Tears flooded Lizzie's eyes.

"What's the matter, Mama?" Willa could not recall ever seeing her mother cry. "Are you sad about Mr. Dayton?"

"Yes, honey, I am. He was an old friend," Lizzie said, searching for her handkerchief in her purse. "I'm just a little teary at seeing Mr. Lewis again, too."

"It was nice to see you, Mrs. Sharpe, and nice to meet you, too, Miss Willa. You're a pretty little lady. You look just like your mother."

"My half-sister Effie has blonde hair like a doll, but she's not pretty like Mama."

"Willa!"

Henry chuckled. "I'll get a cab for you."

Willa added to her mental list. Her mother had a friend Wade Dayton who had died. Mr. Lewis was another first. She had seen Negroes in pictures but she had never met one in person. Ever since the twins commented on her skin and hair, she had been wondering about all the different shades of skin and hair color.

Later, on the train, Willa asked, "Mama, why does Mr. Lewis have black skin?"

"Well, I suppose because his folks are the same color."

Willa thought for a while and decided that her mother was right. She was brown like her mother, and cows and pigs and chickens came in all different colors, too, depending upon who their parents were.

As the train pitched forward, clattering them closer to home, Willa leaned against her mother. "Tell me again, Mama, how you found Daddy." It was a story Willa and her brothers and sisters knew well. Their mother loved to read, and she loved to tell stories. Lizzie could turn anything into a story. She said she made them up in her head when she took one of her long walks. "Damnit, Lizzie," Doc would say, "get your head out of the clouds. You're not living in a book."

"Okay, Willa. It'll help pass the time." The train was still rocking onward.

"Your name was Lizzie Allen then, Mama," Willa

prompted. It delighted Willa that her mother could become a character in a story and still be her mother.

"Yes. That's right. And Lizzie Allen loved to walk. If truth be told, she was also somewhat lazy and walking was a good excuse to escape the stifling dugout with all its unfamiliar chores. She wanted to go with her father and her sister Pearl's husband to Alva for supplies, but there wasn't room in the small wagon. Pearl agreed to mind Lizzie's daughters Effie and Edith for a few hours, and Lizzie headed across the prairie. It was a warm October afternoon with blue skies and a few high white clouds. She felt free and unencumbered in her shapeless muslin dress. She coiled her long black hair and didn't bother with a hat. Her brown skin never burned."

"You, I mean, Lizzie Allen has brown skin just like mine, Mama!"

"That's right, Willa. Now, in Lizzie's pocket, she carried a fringed leather pouch, perfectly round and intricately beaded with blue, red, white, and yellow beads. For as long as she could remember, Lizzie had carried the beaded pouch. For some reason, she couldn't recall why, an old superstition perhaps, the pouch must never be empty, so she always tucked a special treasure inside, a baby tooth, a dried flower, a silver hairpin. Inside the pouch today was the last one of Lizzie's calling cards. A final reminder of a civilized life and time in Kansas City."

"A sad time when Lizzie's mother died," Willa said.

"Yes. It was a very sad time, Willa. Laura Allen, Lizzie's mother, died suddenly, of a stroke. And then Lizzie's father

John Allen slipped into depression. And Lizzie just ran wild."

"That's when you got Effie and Edith," Willa said.

"Yes. Your half-sisters. Don't interrupt, Willa, I'll lose my train of thought. Well, one day John Allen told Lizzie and her sister Pearl about free land in Oklahoma territory. It would be like the old days on Sappa Creek, he said."

"Tell again about the old days, Mama! And the Indians!"

"Well, let's see. Lizzie's parents, John Allen and his wife Laura, were the first white settlers along Sappa Creek in Decatur County, Kansas. When the Indians raided . . . "

"The last Indian raid in Kansas!"

"Stop interrupting, Willa. Lizzie's parents hid in the tall corn and they were saved."

Willa nudged her mother. "Go on, Mama. What happened next?"

"Well, the soldiers rounded up the Indians and sent them to a reservation. For years, Lizzie's parents prospered on the farm, and then they moved to a big house in Kansas City. And that was a happy time. When Laura Allen passed away, John said they would start all over and try to be happy again in Oklahoma."

"Did you like starting over, Mama?"

"Well, no. Lizzie Allen hated to leave Kansas City and all her friends, but she knew that her father wanted to start over in a new place with no reminders of Laura Allen. They had to travel light, so even though it made her very sad Lizzie sold most of her books, all her jewelry and many of the elegant New York hats she owned. She wouldn't be needing them in Oklahoma territory."

"Why did you, I mean Lizzie, have so many hats?" Willa asked, as she always did, hoping for a different answer. She hated wearing hats. They made her head itch.

"You'll understand when you're older," Lizzie said.

Willa's sister Cissie believed that their mother probably got the jewelry and hats from her lover, Effie and Edith's father. And parting with her hats was like parting with him. And that's what made her so sad.

"Go on with the story, Mama," Willa said.

"When they arrived in Oklahoma, Lizzie walked across the prairie. As far as she could see there was empty grass plain. She felt a strange sense of peace. And, she realized, the land wasn't empty at all. It sang with life. The grass sea murmured and rippled in the breeze. A bobwhite whistled his two-note song. Grasshoppers rustled and gnats buzzed.

"Lizzie walked steadily uphill and soon she found the Alva road, a hard-packed dirt track with deep wagon ruts. Up ahead she could see a small ramshackle building, part sod and part white painted wood. An enormously fat woman in a faded calico dress stood in the doorway watching her approach.

"The woman waddled forward and stuck out her hand. 'I'm Alma Ritter. I run the post office and this here store.'"

Willa loved this part of the story. "What did you say, Mama, I mean what did Lizzie say to Alma Ritter?"

"Lizzie shook Alma Ritter's hand and said, 'We just moved here from Kansas.'"

"'Your father's John Allen. A widower with a bushy black beard. Your brother-in-law's a stocky fellow named Al

Davis married to your blonde sister Pearl. And you're Lizzie, mother of Effie and Edith.'"

"'How did you know about my family?'"

"'Honey, I know everything that goes on around here. And your father and brother-in-law stopped by early this morning on their way to Alva. You sure are a beauty. Where'd you get those big brown eyes? Do you have a man?'"

"'No, ma'am.'"

"'Well, we'll soon find you one. There's lots of young fellows and not so young ones, too, scouting around looking for a woman they can work to death.'"

"'I'm not looking for a man.'"

"'Sure you are, honey. You just don't know it yet.'"

"'Well, nice meeting you, Alma. I'll get on with my walk.'"

"'Where you headed?'"

"Lizzie pointed. 'I thought I'd go up there and enjoy the view.'"

"She walked back to the road and turned to wave at Alma, who had wedged herself in the doorway. 'Alma,' she called. 'What's the name of this place?'"

"'It's just a bump in the road, but we call it Freedom.'"

Willa hugged herself. She loved this part of the story when the Old Freedom she knew was just a bump in the road.

"Lizzie walked toward a hill where she could see a field of kaffir corn. Two mules stood in a rough cedar corral. As she drew closer, she saw a well. Nearby was a sod roofed dugout built into a sandy bank. The absence of any trees made the place feel lonely.

"'Hello,' she called, knocking on the store-bought wooden door. There was no answer. She drew some water from the well with the tin cup attached to a rope. The pale gold water tasted sweet and clean.

"Lizzie had hoped she would find a congenial neighbor. She opened the door and went inside. But as she looked around the shadowy dugout with its tarp-covered floor, she realized that whoever lived here lived frugally and alone. Feeling like an intruder, she stepped back outside.

"Basking in the warm sun, Lizzie admired the view from the front door. The wind cut through the thin muslin of her dress and sent her long hair flying. Rolling grassy prairie to the north and the red bluffs of the Cimarron River to the south. Again, that odd feeling of peace swept over her. Yes, she decided, she had made a proper call and she should leave one of her calling cards. She went back inside the dugout, removed the card from her leather pouch and placed it on the nail keg in the center of the room. She left, latching the door carefully.

"Lizzie fingered the beads on her empty leather pouch. She kneeled and examined the hard-packed rocky ground. Then she spotted it. An oval stone about the size of a chicken egg and as smooth, reddish brown with flecks of black and cream. When she looked closer, she could see there were tiny pockmarks on the stone, ancient scars that had healed. When she held it in her hand, it pulsed with warmth, like a fresh-dug spring potato. Lizzie tucked the stone into her leather pouch and tied the strings.

"The sky was cobalt blue and the few drifting clouds

had disappeared. The wind rustled in the corn. The mules switched their tails at flies. Lizzie lowered the tin cup into the well for another drink; then she lifted her face up and into the sun. With swift, strong strides, she headed due west. It was downhill all the way."

"And Daddy found your card on the nail keg," Willa said. "And even though the card just said Elizabeth Allen, he knew where you lived."

"Yes, Willa, he returned my call. But that's a story for another time."

As the train picked up speed and moved deeper into Kansas and closer to Oklahoma, Willa thought about her mother's story. She knew there was a lot left out, but she knew the story was as real as the stone egg inside the beaded bag that always sat in the same place on the book shelf in the living room. Willa loved to open the bag and take out the stone, hold it for a while, and then put it back. No one was allowed to remove it from its place of honor on the book shelf without permission. Her father scoffed and said it was nothing but a damn rock and wasn't worth anything except to catch dust.

"There are some things more important than money, Luther Sharpe," Lizzie said.

Willa gazed out the open train window and saw what the pioneers saw as they headed west. The leafy trees grew scarce, the sky got bigger, and the land flattened. Willa opened her notebook and checked her figures again. She thought about asking Lizzie to double-check them, but her mother had that faraway look in her eyes. The kind of look she got before she went off on one of her long walks. Maybe she was thinking of another story. Or about her old friend Wade Dayton.

Willa turned the page of her notebook and started a new list. My first trip, my first train ride, my first flush toilet, and on and on until the page was full. Doc was always reminding her to write things down so she wouldn't forget. There was a lot to hold in her head and she didn't want to forget anything. The Blue Springs penny postcard she bought at the train station would also help her remember. Instead of sending it to her sisters, she decided to keep it. The first of many that would mark all the places she would visit.

Webb Connell
1930-1931

"ALL ABOARD! ALL ABOARD!" SHOUTED Webb Connell, as he walked through the dusty Houston Valley schoolyard, swinging the bell. Webb Connell loved trains, train tracks, train depots, train whistles; in short, he loved everything about trains. He dreamed of trains; he was obsessed with trains. He told everyone he knew that he planned to travel to every destination on his collection of Santa Fe timetables.

When Doc Sharpe, who was head of the school board, proposed to pay Webb one hundred ten dollars a month to teach from September to April, Webb accepted. He passed the certifying exams easily. He was the first male teacher at Houston Valley School. Despite the fact that he had no experience teaching and no particular fondness for children, Webb wasn't worried about succeeding in his job. How hard could it be? He had to work at something, and teaching would give him four months of freedom to indulge his obsession for trains.

Twenty-six students showed up for the first day of school, and Webb knew most of them, including two Sharpe children,

Willa, who was entering the eighth grade, and Heck, a fourth-grader.

"Webb!" Willa called. "I'm in the eighth grade!" Willa was thrilled that her brother Stub's friend was her new teacher. Except for the tie, Webb looked the same as he always looked in his dark gray pants and white shirt. His curly light brown hair had been trimmed and slicked down.

Webb greeted the two young Sharpes, who performed a kind of war dance around him. "I'm your teacher and you have to call me Mr. Connell now," he said.

"That's your father's name!" said Willa.

"Why don't you call me Mr. Webb?"

"Okay!"

"Well?"

"Mr. Webb," said Heck. "Can I ring that bell?"

Webb shocked everyone by allowing the students to select their own desks. Willa chose a seat in the front row beside her best friend Annie Shaw, who had blue eyes, a mop of dirty blonde hair, and thin legs with knobby knees. Heck, hoping that Willa would help him with arithmetic, sat behind her.

The room had changed, Willa noticed. Webb had replaced the old oaken teacher's desk with its stuck drawers with a long wooden table, which he set on the raised platform in front of the blackboard. A new bookcase crammed with books stood against the east wall. Everything else was just the same. The old piano in the corner, the American flag high above the blackboard beside portraits of George Washington and

Abraham Lincoln, the coal oil stove, the water pail and paper cups, the cloakroom with the shelves for lunch buckets, and the musty smell of dirt and ink and chalk dust.

Webb wrote TIMETABLE on the blackboard. Underneath, he wrote, 8:30 A.M. PLEDGE OF ALLEGIANCE, and then further down, 4:00 P.M. DISMISSAL. "Now, you kids," Webb said, "help me make up a timetable for the day. Who knows what a timetable is?"

Willa flung up her hand. "A train schedule."

"How many of you have been on a train?"

Willa and three others raised their hands.

"Well, this classroom is our train," said Webb, "and I need to know where to go first. Any ideas?"

At first no one spoke, confused by this radical notion of school. Finally, Annie Shaw raised her hand. "Maybe we could sing something? Willa could play for us."

"Just the chords," Willa said.

"Okay." Webb wrote 8:32 A.M. SONG. "Then what?"

"Recess!" shouted the Stewart twins.

"No," said Heck, "we should do arithmetic and get it over with."

With much bargaining and erasing, Webb and the students arrived at a timetable for the eight grades which would evolve from week to week as the classes progressed through the multiplication tables, Oklahoma history, and the diagramming of sentences. Friday afternoons were set aside for ciphering contests, spelling bees, and geography races.

Webb also took the students on field trips. Their first

outing was to the Waynoka Depot. He told them that Waynoka had been given its name by Man-on-Cloud, a chief of the Cheyenne. The Cheyenne, though, were not one of the five civilized tribes of Oklahoma. "And who are the five civilized tribes?" he asked. "Cherokee, Choctaw, Creek, Chickasaw, and Seminole," the students chanted.

"History is all around you," Webb told them, "cattle drives, the land rush, and Indian battles." Willa and most of the older students already knew the story of Dull Knife and his band of northern Cheyenne who had escaped from the reservation. Webb took the students to Turkey Creek, the site of a Dull Knife battle, and they drove north of Old Freedom and stood over the graves of the two salt haulers that Dull Knife's band had killed.

"Why did they kill them?" Willa asked.

"Well, the Cheyenne were hungry and needed supplies," Webb said. "They took their mules, too. They just wanted to get back to their home in Wyoming."

Everyone agreed that the best field trip, though, was to the Alabaster Caverns, six miles south of Freedom. The caves stayed a cool fifty degrees and the winding cave passages with their fantastical formations of alabaster were a wondrous site.

In the darkness of one dimly lit passage, a boy hugged Willa around the chest and fondled her breasts. Willa held her breath, stunned for a moment by her feelings as a hand passed over her nipples. Then, she punched him hard in the stomach with her elbow, and he stopped. She thought it was one of the Stewart twins, but she didn't tattle to Mr. Webb.

She could take care of herself. Who did he think he was to grab her like that! And, what was wrong with her that she didn't punch him right away? Ever since she had gotten her granny just after her thirteenth birthday, she had felt funny, not like herself. Sometimes she felt all grown-up, but she hated the task of boiling and washing her monthly rags made of feed sacks. Sometimes her stomach and back hurt. "It's just cramps," her sister Dilly said; "they'll go away when you have a baby." Sometimes Willa wished she could have stayed twelve years old.

After each field trip, Webb assigned a paper about what they had seen. To supplement their textbooks, he purchased a five-volume set of *The Library of Knowledge*. Another book he had brought in from his own library, *A Photographic Trip Around the World*, fascinated Willa. When she had time for free reading, she leafed through it. She lingered on the fourth picture. It was very much like one she had seen in her mother's yellow plush photograph album — a family photograph of Effie and Edith, Doc holding baby Ollie, and Lizzie standing beside him in front of their dugout home.

The State of Oklahoma required that all seventh and eighth grade girls study domestic science. Webb bought one copy of *First Course in Home Making*, by Maude Richman Calvert, and placed it in the bookcase for the girls to borrow. Willa checked it out first. After reading Chapter 1, Willa took eighty cents from her cigar box and asked Webb to buy her a copy.

Webb taught her to take notes on her reading, and Willa copied two sentences from page one in her notebook. Prepare for Emergencies. No healthy, normal individual should depend entirely upon her father, brother or anyone else for support. The textbook was filled with sensible advice. Willa never imagined that the ordinary tasks she did every day were worthy of being included in a textbook. Maybe she could even go to college and have a career as a domestic scientist. Poems and quotations were sprinkled through the book. Willa had no idea who William Morris was, but she copied his words. "Have nothing in your home that you do not know to be useful or believe to be beautiful."

Willa played "America the Beautiful" by ear on the piano, and everyone learned the words. Webb quizzed them on the meaning of amber waves of grain, fruited plain, and liberating strife. He sent them to the dictionary and then led a discussion, starting with the poetic amber waves of grain and ending with a practical analysis of wheat prices, which recently had fallen from a high of two dollars and thirty-five cents a bushel to eighty cents.

Willa knew all about wheat prices. It was Doc's favorite subject. Flush with wheat money, Doc built a new barn, bought a radio, and splurged on an eighty-acre farm in Texas. Stub bought a new Whippet Roadster. Then wheat prices dropped, so Doc built a granary to store his wheat and hold it until prices rose.

Webb added current events to the Timetable every Monday morning after the song. Students presented short items they had taken from newspapers, and then Webb led a discussion. Most told about local news of baseball scores or farm prices or automobile accidents. One day Willa shared two items she had cut from the *Freedom Call*:

"Who Wants a Boy? I have a boy eight years old, who desires a home in some good family. His father is in a state prison and his mother is incapable of supporting him as she has two smaller tots to care for. Please communicate with me at once as this child must be cared for without delay." Frank E. Severn, County Judge.

Willa's voice trembled as she read the second clipping: "A dead baby, estimated to be between four and five months old, was found early this morning by Commissioner M.S. Moreland on a road grader near the new Sand Creek bridge northwest of town. Lying beside the infant was a bottle of milk. County authorities were called, and the mystery will be investigated through the sheriff's department."

Willa waited for Webb to start the discussion about her articles. She wondered if Webb or anyone in the class might know something about the boy or the baby, but Webb wanted to discuss Annie's article about the low price of wheat. That was a subject everyone wanted to talk about. With wheat prices so low, tenant farmers struggled to get by. A few had moved on to try to find work somewhere else, and the school had dwindled to only nineteen students. Several of the children were bringing mostly empty lunch pails to school. Willa brought extra bread and butter in her lunch bucket to share with Annie, who usually brought just a piece of fried mush.

One day in early November, Webb announced, "Today

we're going to work during lunch recess and learn all about eggs." The class groaned.

"That's not on the Timetable," someone whined.

Webb laid out two dozen eggs, several loaves of bread, some butter, salt and pepper, and a skillet on the table.

"Willa, do you know how to crack an egg?"

Willa rolled her eyes.

"Now, gather round everyone."

Willa picked up an egg and rapped it sharply against the rim of the skillet. The egg split neatly in half. Willa stood holding the halves.

"Should I separate it or just dump it all in?"

"Separate it," said Webb. "Slowly. See everyone, the white pouring out is called the albumen, a-l-b-u-m-e-n, and see those two little white cords attached to the yolk? They're called chalazae. C-h-a-l-a-z-a-e. New spelling words. Does anyone know what those cords are for?" No one knew. "They hold the yolk in place in the center of the egg. Who wants to learn to separate an egg?" A first-grader and two-second graders held up their hands. "Does anyone know why some eggs' shells are brown and some are white?"

"I know," said Willa. "We have white leghorn chickens and they lay white eggs, but the Rhode Island Red hens lay brown eggs."

"Do their eggs taste the same?" asked Webb.

Willa thought for a minute about something she'd never thought about before, and decided that eggs tasted like eggs no matter what color they were.

"Ooh! There's blood in that one!" said Annie.

"A little blood vessel broke when the hen was making the egg," Webb said. "It won't hurt you."

After all the eggs were broken into the skillet, Willa put them on the stove and whipped them with a fork. She added salt and pepper. "Too bad we don't have some cream."

"Next time I'll bring some cream," Webb said.

Everyone enjoyed scrambled egg sandwiches for lunch that day. Willa pointed out that they could cook lots of things on the stove. Why not a pot of ham and beans? Or chicken and noodles?

During the winter of 1930 at the Houston Valley School, the first three grades practiced adding and subtracting and multiplying and dividing with piles of dried beans. Then they soaked, cooked, and ate their lessons. The seventh- and eighth-graders skinned a rabbit, examined its internal organs, then cleaned it, cut it up, rolled it in flour, and fried it. They repeated the process with the quail and pheasant that Willa's older brother Stub had shot.

That winter and into spring of 1931, when Webb Connell fed his students, he often told his class that he loved to teach. In fact, he thought he might love teaching as much as he loved trains.

Willa, his best student, was miserable. Four students graduated from the eighth grade in 1931. The Stewart twins, Annie Shaw, and Willa. On graduation day, three students beamed with joy, but Willa, who had earned straight A's and passed her final examination with 100% in every subject, frowned and hung her head.

After the ceremony, Webb gave Willa a package. She removed the wrapping paper. It was *A Photographic Trip Around the World.* "Thank you, Mr. Webb," she mumbled, avoiding his eyes.

Willa rode home in the pick-up between her parents. Doc and Lizzie talked about the new contour farming he was going to try. Willa sat silent.

When they arrived at the farm, Willa ran upstairs to her bedroom. "Take off your new dress, Willa," Lizzie called after her.

Willa threw the book down on the bed. She clenched her fists, trying to control her breathing so that she wouldn't cry.

"Hurry up, Mug. Get down here and help your mother," shouted Doc.

"I hate you, Daddy! I hate you!" Willa whispered, beating her fists against her thighs. Then she did cry, great sobs that shook her body. She flung herself on the bed beside her new book. She opened it and ripped out a page. "I'll show him! I'll show him!"

Betrayal
1931

Willa would never forget the exact words her father spoke the morning he betrayed her. How could she forget the most shattering event of her fourteen years of life?

Willa prepared her arguments and chose her moment carefully. On the morning of her eighth-grade graduation, she got up early. She looked over her notes, practiced her arguments, and then gathered the eggs as usual. She waited outside the barn for Doc to finish the milking and walked with him to the house.

Willa spoke in a rush, not wanting to forget any of her points.

"Daddy, Mr. Webb says that I'm so smart I could teach eighth grade. You saw. I got every answer right on the final examination."

"I know, Mug. I'm proud of you." In fact, as head of the School Board, Doc knew it was an extraordinary achievement for Willa to score 100% on the difficult exam. The final test covered U. S. History, Oklahoma History, Physiology, Geography, Agriculture, Arithmetic, Civics, Grammar and

Composition, Domestic Science, Reading, Spelling, Penmanship, Music, and Drawing.

"Mr. Webb says I should go to high school in Freedom. I asked Alma Ritter and she says that I can help her at the boarding house and walk to school, and I can stay there with Dilly and Hal, and it won't cost me anything. I'll come home on weekends and school holidays and work for you and Mama. I've saved up half of the fifty-four dollars tuition and I can earn the rest in the summer. Mr. Webb says I could be a teacher like him. And that's what I want to do."

Willa took a breath.

"Whoa! You're needed here, Mug. And before long you'll be running off and getting married like your sisters."

"I don't want to get married! Ro and Dilly and Cissie didn't like school, but I want to go to high school like Ollie and Stub did. Lots of girls go to high school!"

Doc set down the milk buckets. Willa watched as he rubbed his hands, all knobby and swollen with arthritis. Nothing he had in his medicine box seemed to help. Willa pushed her bare feet into the dirt. She clenched her hand, and the wire handle of the egg bucket dug into her palm. She waited for him to speak.

"Think about it, Mug. Your plan's no good."

Willa opened her mouth, but Doc held up a finger. "Ritter's boarding house is no place for a young girl, and Dilly and that good-for-nothing Hal will soon be moving on. You'll need fifty-four dollars tuition every year. How much is that for four years?"

"Two hundred and sixteen dollars."

"That's right. A down payment on a new tractor. Your

place is here working with us. You'll be leaving soon enough."

"But, Daddy, I want to go to high school! And college!"

"It's not about what you want. You're not going to high school and that's that." Doc glared at her. His face looked like a slammed door. Then he picked up the milk buckets and walked into the house.

Willa stood in the dirt-packed yard holding the bucket of eggs. She wanted to dump them on the ground and stomp on them until they all were crushed. She didn't move, gritting her teeth until that feeling passed. Then she just felt numb and sick. She felt like a fool. How could she have been so wrong about her father? She was his favorite. He had always praised her and she thought he admired her good grades. She had trusted him, and he thought she was worthless. Good for nothing except farm chores and getting married and making babies. What was the point of anything? School and good grades didn't matter. Nothing mattered now.

"Hurry up, Willa," her mother called through the screen door. "We need those eggs."

Willa didn't move. Already the sun felt hot in the cloudless sky. The wind swirled around her, stirring up the red dirt and blowing grit into her face. She had forgotten to feed the kittens in the barn. Well, the kittens could just go to hell. Everything could just go to hell.

"It's about time," Lizzie said, as Willa put the eggs on the table. "Wash up, now. It's graduation, a big day for you." She glanced at Willa who was rubbing her hand across her eyes. "What's the matter?"

"Nothing, Mama. Just some dirt in my eyes."

Depression
1931-1932

WILLA'S SPIRITS WERE LOW. WHEN her father accused her of spite, she didn't argue. She hung her head, did her chores, and spoke only when necessary. A layer of dust settled on the notebooks and textbooks she had shoved under her bed.

At her full height of five foot three inches, she was now taller than her older sisters, but she didn't care anymore. Even Heck couldn't cheer her up. What did it matter what she looked like? She didn't bother curling her straight black hair—which had grown past her shoulders—and set her mouth in a tight line of resignation. Willa couldn't control the tears, though, that would appear without warning in her dark eyes.

She rarely saw her best friend Annie Shaw, still thin and knobby-kneed, but pretty now with her unruly blonde hair smoothed into a short bob. Annie had moved with her parents into Freedom when their tenant farm was sold in a foreclosure sale. Annie's mother took in sewing, and her dad traded in his mules for a pair of greyhounds and spent most of his time hunting rabbits, which he used as barter at Kasem's General Store.

Just Willa

Once in a while, Lizzie urged Willa to play the piano and cheer up, but Lizzie was going through the change and often felt low herself. Whenever he could, Heck escaped the dreary house on his bicycle, coasting six miles downhill to Freedom to see his friends, drink some pop, and then if he couldn't catch a lift, he pedaled uphill, struggling to get home in time for chores or risk a whipping. Doc worked from sun-up to sun-down. His hair had turned completely white, and deep lines etched his forehead. He dosed himself with aspirin, which had little effect on the arthritis in his hands, or on the ache in his knees, hips, and back. There was no cure for the worries that assailed him. Even on clear days, the gray clouds of the Depression that shadowed the country loomed over the Sharpe farm.

Times seemed to be bad everywhere. Lizzie got a letter from her daughter Edith, who lived with her husband and three children in Beaverhouse, Canada. Her man was having a hard time finding work, and wages were low, about two dollars a day. They had a big garden, though, and they wouldn't starve.

At a time when everyone else was cutting back, Doc, who never gambled and didn't even play cards, took a chance on an investment. He got the idea from an article in the *Freedom Call* written by a fellow named McMurty, the agricultural instructor at Freedom High School. McMurty had evaluated Woods County farmland and learned that 70% of it was washing away from sheet erosion. The only way to fix the problem was to terrace.

Doc knew that the two quarters he planted to wheat, three hundred twenty acres set on high rolling land, were particularly vulnerable to run-off. Heavy rains came rarely anymore, but when they did get a downpour of an inch and a half or two inches, a lot of the water just ran off into the ditch, watering the weeds. After the 1930 harvest, Doc asked McMurty for help.

Terracing was expensive (about two dollars an acre) and time-consuming, but Doc had some money saved, and he sold a load of hogs at a good profit. In the early fall before it was time to sow winter wheat, McMurty ran level guide lines across the slope of one quarter section. Using these lines as a guide, Doc and Stub plowed the field in broad curves, so that instead of running off, the rain would sink back into the soil. They borrowed the county's road scraper and created broad, low terraces on the contour. The terraces would catch any water lost from the furrows, and the slope was gradual enough that wheat could be sowed on the terraces.

The 1932 wheat harvest proved Doc's gamble was right. His terraced wheat averaged twenty-six bushels to the acre, but wheat prices had dropped below fifty cents a bushel. Forced to sell off some of the wheat, Doc stored the rest at the Freedom elevator and in his already overstuffed granary. A wall of the granary burst, and Doc, Stub, Willa, and Heck spent several days shoveling the wheat out, repairing the wall, and then shoveling it back.

Willa's hands sprouted blisters and deep thick calluses. Although Lizzie kept to her normal routine of walking, writing her stories, reading, and paying social calls, she was still going through the change, and was moody and solitary. Without being asked, Willa took over the management of the house, doing all the cooking, cleaning, and laundry, and filled in as needed with the farm work. Working kept her mind off all that she was missing.

Things got a little better when Doc broke his ironclad rule about not allowing his wife or daughters to drive and taught Willa to drive the pick-up. Willa knew he was trying to make up with her, but she was stubborn and only spoke to him when he spoke to her. When he asked for her opinion, she didn't have one. Why should he bother? She was nothing more than an uneducated drudge. She volunteered for errands into town, and at every opportunity she fled the farm to visit her sisters.

Then, suddenly, and despite the heat and the never-ending work and the drought that followed the harvest, Willa's joy and her good looks returned.

Doc noticed that Willa had snapped out of her funk, but didn't comment, not wanting to cause a relapse. Even Lizzie, who rarely paid attention to anyone not in a story, noticed. Dilly and Cissie knew the reason for Willa's high spirits, but they kept quiet.

"What do you have to smile about?" Lizzie grumped one Saturday morning in July as Willa washed the dishes. Lizzie had torn herself away from the *Freedom Call's* new serial, *Cimarron*, to dry the dishes.

"Nothing, I guess," Willa said. She rinsed the yellow

mixing bowl and when her mouth was fixed in a firm, straight line, she said, "What do you want from town?"

Town, town, town! She wanted to scream the words and dance around the kitchen. That's where she'd first seen him, standing in front of the pool hall under one of Freedom's new electric streetlights, smoking a cigarette. It was the first week in March, and Willa was staying in town with Hal and Dilly, helping them hang wallpaper in their rental house.

"Hey, pretty thing," he'd called, "come over here and let me look at you." His name was Charles Stone. His boxing manager and the guys at the Pool Hall called him Big Charley, so Willa did, too, and he called her pretty thing, sweet stuff, little bit and baby in a deep, gravelly voice. She loved his long legs and thick, muscled arms with hands twice as big as her own and his crooked nose ("broke three times," he said) and his narrow green eyes with flecks of gold and his rough reddish-brown hair. She loved the way he rolled her a cigarette, flicking his tongue to wet the paper, and then lighting it between his lips before giving it to her.

Next January, when she was sixteen, she would be Mrs. Charley Stone. She'd written the name over and over again in her notebook, Mrs. Charles Stone. She didn't feel like Willa Sharpe anymore, the Willa who wanted to go to high school and college and become a teacher. That Willa was gone. She wasn't a daddy's girl anymore. She was Big Charley's girl now. He was all the teacher she needed.

Big Charley
1932

CHARLEY STONE BELIEVED HE WAS one-of-a-kind, destined to hit the top of the boxing game. At one hundred seventy-five pounds, six feet two inches tall, with a seventy-five-inch reach, he boxed as a light heavyweight. Actually, Charley was like hundreds of destitute young men in the 1930s with no education, no money, no skills, and no prospects, drawn to boxing by the sheer pleasure of punching and the promise of fast, easy winnings. Many of these young men ended up broke or brain damaged or both.

Born on a forty-acre chicken and egg farm west of Alva, near the tiny town of Whitehorse, Charley hated chickens, chicken feathers, chicken eggs, chicken feed, and the ever-present chicken shit, which was permanently embedded in the soles of his two pairs of shoes. When Charley was sixteen, his father died of pneumonia and his older brother ran off and joined the Army leaving Charley responsible for his mother, two younger sisters and a brother, several thousand cackling chickens, and the twice-weekly egg deliveries to customers in Alva.

Charley felt suffocated. On Sunday afternoons, he played baseball on the Whitehorse team and escaped for a while from the biting black flies that swarmed in the chicken houses, and the acrid stench that burned his eyes. When a regular egg customer, who owned several local restaurants and was a part-time boxing promoter, told Charley that "a big fellow like you ought to try boxing," Charley thought why the hell not? The promoter taught him the basic punches and advised him to watch the body not the eyes.

Charley spent most evenings and Sundays working out at the Alva gym. He picked up tips from local boxers, like Jimmy Hardesty, a gifted young welterweight noted for his quickness and intelligence in the ring. He sparred with Jimmy and his younger brother, Jake, giving them a chance to test their skills on a tall, long-armed opponent. Like most heavyweights, Charley was slow, but his attack was relentless, and he prided himself on being able to withstand multiple, punishing blows. A bruised kidney or a broken nose seemed a small price to pay if it meant he could be free of the damn chickens. He hung a punching bag in a shed on the farm, chewed the toughest of chuck steaks to harden his jaw, and by the time he was twenty-two, he had won some local matches and was breathing easy. His brother took over the duties on the chicken farm, and Charley was a free man.

When Willa first saw him that March evening in Freedom, Charley was feeling good. He had a job on a Woods County road crew and bouts lined up in Waynoka, Woodward, Enid, and Alva in the months to come.

"Hey, pretty thing," Charley called, "come over here and let me look at you."

Willa hung back, not sure what to do. She'd never seen him before. There were lots of strange young men now, drifting in and out of town, looking for work.

"Come closer, little bit, I won't bite. So, you want to play some pool?"

"No! I'm here for Hal Dixon. It's time for supper."

"You're not Hal's wife."

Willa edged closer until she stood in the circle of the streetlight. "I'm Willa Sharpe. Hal's sister-in-law. "

"I'm pleased to meet you, Willa Sharpe." Charley stubbed out his cigarette. "You're the prettiest girl I've ever seen." A line Charley had used many times, but this time he meant it. Willa's brown skin glowed, and her dark eyes were enormous with long black lashes. He wanted to touch her. In her baggy overalls smeared with wallpaper paste and her tangled black hair falling to her shoulders, Willa looked nothing like the women he'd been with, the thin, hungry women wearing high heels and red lipstick and strong perfume, the women who could always be found after the fights waiting in the parking lot or in the backrooms of pool halls eager to part a fighter from his money.

"I'm Charley Stone."

"Would you mind telling Hal supper's ready? I don't want to go in there."

"Why sure. I'll be right back."

Charley came back alone. Hal had a hot streak going and

didn't want to interrupt his run of good luck. Charley drove Willa to her sister Dilly's, who at first wanted him to go back and tell Hal that he'd better get home, but Charley calmed her down, and Dilly said, "Well, if Hal's not going to eat you might as well." After supper, while Dilly put Jessica to bed and nursed the baby, Charley helped Willa wash the dishes. When Willa walked him to his car, Charley made the move he had been thinking about ever since he'd first seen her. He cupped her face in his hands, feeling her warmth and the silky smoothness of her skin. He kissed her gently, trying not to frighten her.

Willa had never been kissed by a grown man, and a part of her calmly said, oh, this is what it feels like, and another part of her that she couldn't control opened her lips and kissed him back. She felt his tongue sliding into her mouth. The sweetness of it overwhelmed her. She pressed her body into his, and he lifted her up and held her against him. She felt his hardness against her thigh and trembled.

That night and all the nights that followed during the spring and summer of 1932, Willa learned from Charley. While her mind told her that she should stop, her body craved his with an urgency that swept away all rational thought. When he took her to Woodward to watch him box, she cringed when he was hit as if she was being hit herself, but there was something thrilling about seeing him take blow after blow and then suddenly smash his right fist into his opponent's nose until the blood spurted out and the man fell and Charley stood over him and raised his arms in triumph. Later, in the car, when she kissed him, she savored the coppery taste of blood.

Billed as The Whitehorse Wonder, Charley won all his matches that summer. At a time when men were happy to get two dollars for eight to ten hours of farm labor, he earned twenty-five to thirty dollars a night, sometimes for as little as three minutes of work. Once in a while he had to go the whole ten rounds, but he always won the decision, earning the respect of the referee and the cheering fight fans. In late August, his manager booked a series of out-of-state matches.

"Take me with you, Charley," Willa pleaded. "I won't be any trouble."

Charley tossed his duffel in the trunk of his car. He'd settled his bill with Alma Ritter and was eager to get going.

"You know I can't right now, sweet thing. Soon as you're sixteen, I'll come get you and we'll get married. How'd you like to live in California, Mrs. Charley Stone?"

"I'd love it!"

"Well, bye, baby."

"Write to me, Charley."

"Oh, now I don't know." Charley was ashamed to tell her that the most he was able to write was his own name.

"Write to me care of Dilly."

"Sure."

Then Charley was gone, heading west toward the mountains. Willa pestered Dilly every week as she waited for Charley's letter to arrive. By October, when she still hadn't heard, and Dilly and Hal went off to Kansas to shuck corn, she was getting desperate. Her granny hadn't appeared for she wasn't sure how long. She couldn't remember the last time she'd suffered from cramps. Sometime in the spring, she thought. Her body felt different. Her breasts were tender and her middle had thickened. She couldn't admit to herself that she was pregnant, so she shoved the thought away. She wore loose-fitting dresses and baggy overalls and went about her work at home as usual, but she felt like she was playing a part, that her real self was somewhere else, dreaming of Charley.

One day in late October, just before she went to sleep, she felt something move inside her, like a finger stroking her from inside her belly. She told no one. She didn't know what else to do. She couldn't face telling her mother or her sisters, who had their own families and worries. And if she didn't talk about it or think about it, maybe it would just go away. She avoided her father.

All the Sharpes gathered at the homestead on Thanksgiving Day. There hadn't been any rain for weeks. Her brother Ollie and his family drove in from Rocky Ford and reported that the drought was even worse in western Kansas and the Panhandle. Willa baked bread, made sage dressing, roasted the turkey and the duck, played with her nieces and nephews, did everything just as she always did, and no one noticed that her heart was breaking.

After dinner when everyone had gone, Willa took a bucket of scraps to the hogs. She didn't need a coat. It had been windy, but sunny and nice all day. She stopped when she saw her father leaning against the fence looking at the sunset. The whole sky to the west was lit up with glowing colors. Pale, butter-like yellow, creamy peach, rose, magenta, all melting into purple and deep blues. It was beautiful, but all Willa could see was her father, arms folded, white hair blowing in the wind, waiting for her.

Willa poured the bucket over the fence into the hog trough and watched as the snorting, squealing pigs fought for position. Doc took the bucket from her and put it on the ground.

"How many months?" he said, as if he were asking if there might be snow tomorrow.

Willa held her breath. The moment she dreaded had finally arrived.

"I don't know."

"Let me see." Doc lifted her loose shirt and placed his hand on her stomach. "You're far gone." He moved his hand, feeling and assessing, as if he was checking a bred heifer. "I'd say about seven months."

Willa hung her head. She wanted to throw herself into the hog pen and cover herself with mud and shit. She was filthy. She wanted to disappear. She couldn't bear it that her father was looking at her and seeing her for who she was.

"Keep your head up. Look at me. Who's the father?"

"Charley Stone."

"Beulah Stone's boy, over by Whitehorse?"

"Yes."

"Where is he now?"

"I don't know. Maybe Colorado. He said he'd write."

"By God, Willa, I thought you had more sense." Doc turned his attention to the sunset.

Willa was silent. What could she say? He was right. And then a terrible thought hit her. Maybe Charley wasn't coming back at all. How could she bear it?

"Don't tell Mama."

"She'll have to know."

"Not yet."

"Okay, Mug." Doc patted her head. He folded his arms around her. He cradled her close, his chin resting on the top of her head. Willa hugged herself, trying not to cry. She'd never been so ashamed. She couldn't bear that her father was seeing her like this. She tried to break free, but he kept holding her and patting her back. And then she was holding onto him and bawling like a baby. He hadn't held her like this since she was three and had fallen off Old Bill into a patch of stickers.

When she was all cried out, Doc gave her his handkerchief.

"I'll take care of it," he said.

Willa blew her nose, and they walked back to the house.

On the day after Christmas, a cloudy, cold day that threatened snow or sleet, after the chores were done and breakfast was over, Doc put his hand on Willa's arm. She had just gotten up to clear the table and do the dishes. "Get your coat, Mug. We're going to take a little drive."

"Not a very nice day for a drive," Lizzie said. "Where

are you going?"

"Never you mind. There's something we need to do."

"Well, don't be long. Looks like we're going to get some weather."

Willa put on her coat and followed her father to the truck. She'd forgotten to get a scarf, and she held her hands over her ears to keep out the icy wind. He opened the door for her and she got in. "Wait in the truck, Mug."

Doc returned with his Kentucky squirrel rifle, which he placed between them, the barrel pointing toward the floor.

They headed east on 64 toward Alva. After a while, Doc turned left onto a country road, guiding the truck between the deep frozen ruts. After a few miles, he turned right into a driveway. Willa saw a small frame house with a collapsing porch; behind the house were chicken wire fences and several long sheds. Then she knew. Charley's farm. He hated that farm and the chickens. She sneaked a glance at her father. What was he going to do?

Doc turned off the truck. "Stay here." He took the squirrel rifle and walked to the house. A woman opened the door, but Doc didn't go inside. He waited, the rifle resting in the crook of his arm. Soon Charley appeared. He nodded as Doc spoke. Then he turned to go back into the house. A moment later, he came out wearing a tweed coat.

Charley opened the truck door and sat beside Willa. His body pressed against hers, and she glanced up. She gasped. His left eye was swollen shut and his face was mottled with bruises, all greenish-blue and black and yellow. His crooked nose was twice its normal size. His lips were cracked and scabbed. He breathed deeply through his mouth, revealing several missing teeth. Charley turned his head away from her.

"Sorry," he whispered.

They drove to Alva without another word. Doc parked in front of a large brick house. A man in a suit opened the front door and motioned them inside. Willa didn't catch his name, Judge something or other, a friend of Doc's. The marriage ceremony lasted just a few minutes. The judge signed the marriage certificate and gave it to Willa. She put it in her coat pocket.

Heavy sleet was falling when Doc stopped the truck once again in the driveway of the Stone chicken farm. He left the engine running, and the three of them stared straight ahead and listened to Charley's mouth breathing and the rapping of icy sleet against the metal roof of the truck. Willa folded her arms over her swollen stomach and waited.

Finally, Doc turned to Charley. "What you do is up to you," he said, measuring every word. "Time will tell if you're a man or not."

Charley took a ragged breath, stepped out of the truck, and slammed the door shut. With his shoulders hunched against the wind and sleet, he walked to the house and went inside.

I'm married, Willa thought, and that's my husband walking away from me. The father of my baby. And he didn't look at me once.

Listening to Roosevelt
1933-1934

WILLA SAT DOWN TO DRY CHARLEY off after his bath. Every day she weighed him on the flour scale. Today he was forty days old and weighed exactly ten pounds, six ounces and was twenty-three and a half inches long.

"Let me do that, Willa," said Lizzie. "Why don't you go and take a nice long bath? Fix your hair and put on something nice."

"No. I'll dress him." Lizzie had been especially kind and loving, but her constant hovering and concern were getting on Willa's nerves. She knew her hair was stringy and greasy, and her housecoat needed washing. What did it matter what she looked like? At least Doc left her alone.

Willa lifted Charley up into a beam of sunlight. His fuzzy light brown hair had a tinge of red. Lizzie said he took after Willa, but it was hard to tell. He had long legs like his father, but he had Willa's brown skin and, so far anyway, he had her disposition, only crying when he was hungry or needed his diaper changed.

Willa watched as her mother turned her face away,

taking extra care folding dish towels to hide her hurt feelings. She was only trying to help. Willa knew she'd caused trouble between her parents. When Lizzie learned about the shotgun wedding, she lashed out at Doc in a voice loud enough to carry through the thin walls of their bedroom. "It's all your fault," she said, "Charley Stone might still be around if you hadn't interfered."

"Shut up, woman! No daughter of mine is going to have an illegitimate baby!"

"Why don't you just say it, Luther Sharpe? You don't want Willa to ruin herself like I did! Well, it seems to me you took your time making Ollie legitimate!"

Afterward, Lizzie stayed silent for days and disappeared for hours on long walks. Willa and her sisters often discussed the mystery of Edith and Effie's father. Who was he? Wade Dayton? Or someone else? And Cissie pointed out that in the family album, the picture taken at the dugout of Doc, Lizzie, Edith, Effie and baby Ollie was snapped in 1905, but their parents' marriage certificate placed in the family Bible was dated 1907. On it, Lizzie had used her maiden name, Elizabeth Allen, which proved that she hadn't been married before, so all three children were born out of wedlock.

Pictures of Lizzie's parents, John and Laura Allen, and her sister Pearl were in the family album, too. Lizzie, with her dark hair, eyes, and skin, looked like a changeling in the fair-haired blue-eyed family. When Willa asked her father if Lizzie had Indian blood, Doc said, "Hell No! That's another one of Lizzie's tall tales."

Lizzie put the folded towels in a drawer, and turned to Willa. She held out her hands. "Are you sure you don't want me to take him?"

As she looked into her mother's brown, lined face, Willa had a sudden premonition. I'll be old like that someday. Willa hugged Charley close and whispered in his ear loud enough for Lizzie to hear. "How about it, Charley? Do you want your grandma to dress you in the new blue shirt she made?"

She handed Charley to her mother. There was a deafening burst of static from the living room, and Charley started crying.

"Mug! Lizzie! Get in here. I found KOCO."

Doc had traded in his old Buckingham radio, which used three-dollar batteries, for a new 6-volt Zenith. The Zenith came with its own wind charger, which Doc hooked up to big Delco glass jar batteries. To justify his extravagant purchase, Doc told them that down the line he might upgrade to a 32-volt model and even run power out to the barn. It would be convenient to flip a switch and have light while he was milking or delivering a calf. They'd never run out of wind, and he could operate the wind charger for about fifty cents a year.

"You go ahead, Mama. Get Charley quiet and settled." Willa wrung out the dishrag and wiped down the table. She had eaten a big bowl of chicken and noodles, two slices of bread and butter with sand plum jelly, and a dish of applesauce, but she was still hungry. She cut a slice of bread and buttered it. It was good to taste her own bread again. Her mother didn't have the patience or the muscles for kneading and her bread lacked the tender crumb of Willa's. This morning, for the first time in months, Willa wanted to make bread. Her arms and hands remembered the familiar rhythm of measuring and stirring and kneading. As she patted the plump, soft dough into round, smooth loaves, her breasts leaked milk, wetting the front of her housecoat.

The radio hissed and hiccupped. "Mug!" Doc called. "Get in here."

Willa joined Doc and Lizzie in the living room. She took Charley from her mother in the rocking chair and sat on the daybed. The hissing subsided and then they heard President Roosevelt. His aristocratic accent had grown familiar to them in the months before the election when he talked on the radio about his New Deal.

"This is preeminently the time to speak the truth," Roosevelt said, "the whole truth, frankly and boldly. Nor need we shrink from honestly facing conditions in our country today. This great nation will endure as it has endured, will revive and will prosper." Wild cheering interrupted his words. When the noise died down, he continued. "So, first of all, let me assert my firm belief that the only thing we have to fear is" — Doc, Lizzie, and Willa leaned in toward the radio as President Roosevelt paused and then named the thing — "fear itself."

Willa exhaled. Without realizing it, she had been holding her breath. How did he know, she wondered? "Farmers find no markets for their produce," Roosevelt continued, "the savings of many years in thousands of families are gone."

"Damn right," Doc muttered. He hadn't told Lizzie yet but he was sure to lose the Texas farm.

"What's going on?" Heck said, banging the screen door.

Doc motioned for him to sit down. "Be quiet, boy."

Heck sat on the floor by the daybed. He tickled Charley on the stomach, and the baby started to fuss.

"Radio's stupid," he said. "There's a matinee of *Tarzan* at the Liberty."

"Shhh," said Willa.

Willa listened to Roosevelt with her whole body, and even Charley, who lay in her arms, appeared to be listening, too. Every word Roosevelt spoke seemed directed to her personally. Fear itself. She had felt that. Sure, she'd been nervous when Charley was born, right here on the daybed she was sitting on, but she wasn't afraid. She'd helped with calving, and she knew that giving birth was natural to animals. She was an animal, too, and labor was something her body was meant to do. When the contractions came, she listened to her father and mother and breathed when they told her to and then pushed when they told her to. As the cramps got more intense and sweat dripped into her eyes and she vomited, Doc wiped her face with a cool rag and said, "Steady, girl, easy does it." And that's what she tried to do. Just keep steady. Yet even at the end when she felt as if she were on fire and being ripped apart, she still wasn't afraid. But fear itself. Was this the feeling that haunted her, the fear that couldn't be relieved by a cool rag or holding onto her father's hands? I thought you had more sense, Doc said. Willa thought she was smart, too, but she was wrong. If she'd been smart, she would have found a way to defy her father and gone to high school instead of running wild with Charley. Still, spite had led to the baby she held in her arms. A baby she loved more than she loved herself. And how could she love herself? She didn't know who she was anymore. She shivered and Charley whimpered. Was that it? A fear that she had lost who she was and would never find herself again?

The radio erupted in static. Doc adjusted the tuning knob.

"Happiness lies not in the mere possession of money," Roosevelt told her, "it lies in the joy of achievement, in the thrill of creative effort." Willa knew what he was talking about, like the feeling she had this morning baking bread and the pleasure she felt when she first made a quilt all by herself. She possessed money, too, hidden under her mattress, but it had given her no pleasure.

When Charley was a week old, Mrs. Stone came by to deliver an envelope Big Charley asked her to give to Willa. Lizzie made Willa put on a clean housecoat and then left them alone at the kitchen table. After she admired the baby and drank a cup of coffee, Mrs. Stone said Charley had gone to California. When she saw the birth announcement in the *Freedom Call*, Mrs. Stone said she knew it was time to bring the envelope. "What's his name?" Mrs. Stone wanted to know, "the paper just said boy." Willa shook her head. The truth was she hadn't named him yet. Finally, Mrs. Stone ran out of coffee and conversation and excused herself. Her chickens needed her, she said.

When she left, Willa examined the bulging white envelope. What could it be? She tore open the seal. Inside was a thick sheaf of bills, mostly ones. She separated the money into neat piles of ones, fives, and tens, adding the numbers in her head. And then, just to be sure, she turned the envelope upside down and shook it. There was no letter, no note of any kind. Just one hundred fifty-seven dollars in cash. Now she knew what she was worth to Big Charley.

Never again, Willa vowed. Never again would she be so foolish and blind and trusting.

Willa looked at her week-old baby. His open eyes gazed, unfocused, at something she couldn't see. They were dark and liquid, with little white showing, like animal eyes. She could find no trace of her or Big Charley's features in his face. "You're your own pure self," she whispered, "but I'm going to call you Charles Luther Stone. After your daddy and my daddy. His name is all you'll ever have of your father, but at least you'll have that."

Now, as Willa listened to Roosevelt's buoyant voice and rocked Charley in her arms, she sensed what was underneath the President's words. Belief. Belief in the future. A belief that through effort and work a true destiny could be found. Pleasure. Perhaps someday even happiness.

The next day Willa cut out Roosevelt's photograph from the Alva newspaper. His picture and his words, "the only thing we have to fear is fear itself," comforted her.

At Roosevelt's urging Congress passed the Agricultural Adjustment Act, which gave cash to farmers who cut back on their wheat acreage. Both Doc and Stub joined the program and planted maize and corn for hog and cattle feed. But no matter how they tried, their efforts couldn't end the drought, stop the wind from blowing or the dust from rising. NBC radio put on a five-minute national program of praying for rain led by a Baptist minister, but skies remained clear and sunny. It seemed not even God could make it rain.

By the fall of 1933, Doc had lost the Texas farm. Parts of it might be in Georgia or New Mexico, he joked, but he didn't have time to look for it. Still, he had a little money saved, and with the garden, they wouldn't starve. Others who were selling out and moving on advised him to do the same. But Doc thought he could hang on in Old Freedom a while longer. The drought couldn't last forever.

Willa and Heck hauled water to the garden, but the tomato, bean, squash, and cucumber plants burned in the unrelenting sun and harsh wind. Even sand plums were scarce, and there were only a few jars of jelly left in the cellar. The chickens suffered in the heat and some stopped laying all together. Without moisture, most of the maize and corn withered and died, and there was little feed for the hogs or the cattle.

Then, one early November day, the wind blew in hard and howling from the north. Doc's arthritis flared up, and Willa took over his chores. As she walked to the barn a gust of wind blew her sideways. She looked at the darkening sky and wondered. She didn't have long to wait.

First, she saw just one lone dust devil whirling down the dirt road to Freedom. Then the wind whipped through the shriveled maize and corn stalks and their shallow roots tore through the earth, bringing the crusty red soil with it. The wind sucked the red dirt from the fields into the air to mingle with the other dust from neighboring fields and from dried-up wheat fields as far north as the Dakotas. By the time Willa got to the milk house with two brimming buckets, there was a thin layer of fine red dust settled on the top of the milk. Even when she strained the milk, twice, through clean white cloths, it still had a hint of red.

Doc's terraces kept some of his topsoil in place; other farmers who hadn't been as foresighted watched the topsoil from their flat fields blow all the way to Texas. Willa and Lizzie put damp rags on the windowsills and doorsills, but still the powdery dust crept in. They felt the grit in their teeth, in their hair, and worst of all in their eyes.

Finally, the sky turned from dirty gray to blue again, the wind calmed down to a strong breeze, and the dust settled. The Hazel Hurd Players arrived in Freedom and bragged they had brought rain to every town they had played from Nebraska to Texas. "If you want to have a good rain," the Players ad said in the *Call*, "you better show up on Saturday night for the play." Doc couldn't see spending money on a useless play, and the family stayed home and listened to the radio.

The next day it did rain. For almost an hour, the skies streamed water and then slowly stopped, trickling a drop here and there, followed by a boom of thunder, as if some shaky hand were tightening a rusty spigot.

The Hazel Hurd Players moved on to another town, and Willa longed to move on, too. On January 22, she would be seventeen, and two days later Charley would celebrate his first birthday. It was time for her to find work and make her own home with Charley. This time she would be smart, would make a plan, and trust no one but herself. But first, she had to do something about her hair.

It Takes Grit
1934-1937

"DEAR WEBB,

Thank you so much for the train picture book you sent for Charley. Your mother made me and Charley feel right at home. You asked about my job. Right now we're sewing overalls and mending work clothes. The government buys all the fabric and tells us what to make. The best part is that I can bring Charley to work with me. I fixed a little baby corral at one end of the room. I will close for now as Charley is bumping my arm with his truck, and I need to get supper started.

Sincerely yours, Willa

P.S. Your mother got all your old high school textbooks down from the attic. I'm going to try to work through them, but Charley and my job keep me pretty busy."

Only the perfect job could have lured Webb Connell away from teaching. He talked himself into a brand-new position as Special Assistant to Santa Fe's general manager. As a roving troubleshooter, his responsibilities took him around the country and into all three of the railroad's divisions.

It was Webb who suggested that Willa and Charley

move in with his widowed mother who was all alone in her big, old house in Alva. Willa insisted on paying two dollars a month in rent in addition to cooking and cleaning and errand running.

Willa addressed her letter to Webb and sealed the envelope. Charley made engine noises and gunned his truck along the bare hardwood floor. He was twenty-one months old but so tall and sturdy he could pass for a three-year-old. From the open window by the desk, Willa heard cars driving by on Locust and on Fourth Street.

Their upstairs corner room — Webb's old bedroom — was large, with faded blue striped wallpaper. Just down the hall was the bathroom with a flush toilet and a claw-footed tub big enough for her to stretch out in. No need to heat water on the stove. Hot water came right out of the faucet. Mrs. McConnell had a bum knee and couldn't climb stairs so they had the upstairs to themselves.

Because of the dust, they mostly kept the windows closed during the day, but when it was clear, Willa liked having her window open. They'd lived in Alva for nine months, but she was still discovering all the sounds of the city. Mostly she noticed the absence of familiar sounds, no roosters crowing or pigs snorting or cattle bellowing for water. The wind seemed quieter here with no maize to rattle, and the sky seemed to have gotten smaller.

On the oak desk, where Webb had carved his name surrounded by regular hatch marks that looked suspiciously like train tracks, Willa arranged her notebooks, pens, pencils, and ruler, and a large wooden box which held her stationery, postcards, and letters she had saved, and her eighth-grade final examination and her diploma. Inside the top lid of the box she glued a photograph of Roosevelt. At the bottom of the wooden box was a heavily creased tissue copy of a legal document. Willa had read the words typed there so many times she knew them by heart. Just as he had stood by her during her brief marriage ceremony, her father stood by her in court when it ended.

"Don't lose this," Doc cautioned, when the document arrived.

"The Court finds that the Plaintiff is entitled to an absolute divorce from the Defendant, and the custody and maintenance and control of their minor child, to wit: Charles Luther Stone. The Court also finds that the Plaintiff is without fault, in the premises, and gave the Defendant no excuse for his abandonment and desertion."

Without fault. Was she? She must have all kinds of faults since Big Charley ran out on her and only married her when threatened with Doc's squirrel rifle. Big Charley was a poor excuse for a man. Still, she couldn't hate him. He gave her a son she loved with a love as powerful and as solid as the ground she stood on. From the moment he was born, Charley knew her in a way that no one else did. She never talked baby talk to him. He listened and he watched with his observant green eyes. His first words were "Mama" and "ball." At nine months, he walked around his crib. She had no trouble toilet training him. Her boy was smart as a whip. He could count to ten and knew his ABC's. Even Doc noticed how quickly he caught on to things and took him around the farm showing him the stock and teaching him new words.

Willa watched Charley drive his truck around the bedroom, hauling cattle down some imaginary road. Absently, as she thought about going downstairs to make supper, Willa picked up the egg-shaped rock, which rested on a corner of the desk. The rock was reddish brown like the dirt of Old Freedom. For as long as she could remember that smooth stone sat on the bookcase in her parents' living room. Its feel and heft were as familiar to her as her own hand. It was nice of her mother to give it to her.

Willa's mind raced picturing all the things she had to do. All her work and activity kept her mind away from something she didn't want to think about. Late at night when those shadowy thoughts drifted in, she quickly pushed them aside. But the dark thoughts were always there, like the layer of dust that settled on windowsills and tabletops. No matter how hard you worked or how many rugs you shook out, the dust clung. And just when you believed the dirt might be gone for good, the sparkling blue sky would turn blackish-brown, the wind would gust, and the dust would descend in great boiling clouds of gritty filth. As much as Willa worked to wipe those black thoughts away, they whirled in, hissing that she was alone and divorced, a divorced woman. Shame. Shame. It was humiliating. And frightening.

"Keep your head up," Doc told her, "you, too, Charley," when he'd left them in their new home and driven back to

Old Freedom and the farm and everything that Willa loved. Those were the only words he spoke to her on the drive to Alva. He didn't think it was seemly for Willa, a divorced woman, to live on her own in Alva, even if it was in the house of a respectable woman like Mrs. Connell. What would people say? And how would they manage on the farm without Willa to help Lizzie cook and clean and control Dilly and her endless marital problems?

"Willa, this is a bad idea," Doc told her on the morning she left.

"My mind's made up," Willa said. "I did what you told me to do. What you made me do. Now I'm doing what I want to do." As soon as the words were out of her mouth, Willa was ashamed. Her mother wasn't well and leaving would burden her father with more work. But she had to go. She had to make her own way in the world. Her father had disappointed her, but he'd also stood by her. He hadn't told her to act like a fool with Charley Stone.

Willa lifted her chin and thought of Roosevelt's words. Nothing to fear but fear itself. It was time to get to work. She took Charley's hand, and they walked downstairs to fix supper.

During the four years she lived in Alva, Willa secretly thought of them as her college years. "You're going to college someday," she would whisper to Charley when she put him to bed. For Willa, college was the magic word, the pot of gold at the end of the rainbow, the happy ending to a story, the road to a better life. That road was closed to her, but it was an open road for Charley.

If Willa had graduated from high school and gone on to become a teacher, most likely she would have attended Northwestern State Teachers College in Alva. When school was in session, students poured into Alva's Square, sniffing the fragrant aroma that wafted from the Golden Krust Bakery on Fourth Street. They filled the wooden booths in Nall's Café and hung out at Monfort Drug. The college men shot pool and played dominoes at Snyder's Cigar Store or took their dates to a picture show at one of the three "R's," the Ranger, Ritz, or Rialto theatres. A few of the college boys competed in the boxing matches held at the Kavanaugh and Shea building, measuring themselves against Jim and Jake Hardesty, the top local fighters. The next day, the boys would head to Monfort Drug and stumble up the stairs to Dr. Simmons' office. He'd tape their ribs, set broken noses, stitch up cuts, and give them advice on their footwork or their left jab.

Every Monday through Friday at 8:15 a.m. Willa left the Connell home on Locust and pushed Charley's buggy down the sidewalk on Fourth three blocks north to the Square. The WPA sewing room was on the third floor of City Hall in the center of the Square. If it was a nice day, she let Charley admire the goldfish swimming in the pool in front of City Hall. She always carried a bottle of water and clean handkerchief to put over Charley's face in case the dust became too thick. After work, she'd take a stroll around the Square, window-shopping at Jett's, Anthony's, and Ellison's

Women's Wear. On hot days, they stopped at Beegles' Drug and sat at the long counter enjoying a dish of ice cream and the cool air.

Willa knew she stuck out in her old-fashioned cotton dresses and skirts and blouses. The college girls and the women in the department stores wore tailored dresses, elegant suits, and slim, bias-cut skirts with crisp white blouses. At her government job, Willa had nothing in common with the four other women in the sewing room, who were all in their thirties and forties, with older children and out-of-work husbands. Still, the women were kind, and they doted on Charley.

It was Charley who brought Willa out of her shyness. His green eyes, reddish brown hair and big grin charmed everyone who met him. He waved at store clerks and college girls who oohed and awed. What a beautiful boy!

One late fall afternoon, Willa had just deposited her check in the Alva State Bank (fourteen dollars and seventy-two cents for two weeks of work), when outside on the steps two girls swooped around Charley.

"Oh, he's so cute!" chirped a tall, thin brunette. "Look, Arlene, isn't he sweet?"

"He's a cutie pie," said Arlene, a pretty blonde with arching eyebrows and bright red lipstick. "How old's your little brother?"

"My son is twenty-three months," said Willa. The girls looked shocked.

"Really!" said Arlene.

"But you're so young!" the brunette said. "I thought you were a high school girl."

"I'm seventeen!" Embarrassed and ashamed, Willa grabbed the buggy handle and turned away.

"Wait!" Arlene called. "He looks thirsty. Let me buy him a Coke. Pretty please? I miss my baby brother."

Willa looked at the girls' bright faces and then down at Charley, who was laughing and holding out his arms.

"Okay."

As they sat drinking their Cokes in a booth at Nall's, the two girls chatted about their classes, the Zipper Club initiation, and Arlene's ambition to become the Rangers' Homecoming Queen. They joked with boys who walked by, and Willa marveled at their confidence and ease. She missed her sisters, and it was nice to be around girls her own age, even if they were city girls. Charley moved from lap to lap, thrilled with all the attention and the sweet cherry Coke. The tall, thin brunette was Carol Ferguson. Her father owned Ferguson Ford in Oklahoma City. The blonde was Arlene Murphy from Tulsa, whose father was an oilman. Both were studying to be teachers, but their real course of study seemed aimed at finding husbands and then having babies.

"Are you married?" asked Carol, who lacked Arlene's delicacy of manner.

"Not anymore," said Willa and felt her face turn red with shame.

"You're divorced, huh. That's tough, kid. My parents are divorced," said Carol. "And I turned out just fine."

"No, you didn't," said Arlene. "You're a mess! Anyway your room is."

Willa was amazed to find out that they were both freshmen and just eighteen. They lived in Mrs. Johnson's boarding house on Church Street just two blocks away from the Connell home. They looked so mature. It was their clothes and their make-up, Willa decided. Their red lipstick and plucked, penciled eyebrows.

"You have beautiful skin," said Arlene. "You look like Kay Francis."

"Thank you," said Willa. "Who's Kay Francis?"

"A movie star, of course!"

"She's from Oklahoma City!" said Carol.

In just a few months, with the guidance of Carol and Arlene, the inspiration of movie magazines, some cash from her savings, Mrs. Connell's sewing machine, and a hair trim and perm at Ruby's Beauty Shop in the Bell Hotel, Willa looked several years older, like a city sophisticate instead of a country girl.

When Doc picked up Willa and Charley to spend Easter Sunday on the farm, he took one look at her in her new black and white sundress, high-heeled sandals, and hat with a swooping brim, and said, "Who stole your eyebrows?"

Lizzie marveled at her daughter's transformation. Dilly shrugged and said it was about time. Maybe now Willa could get a man. Dean Williams, who had married Cissie a year after she had graduated from eighth grade, and rarely said more than a few slow, drawling words at one time, squeezed

Willa's shoulder and said that she had always been a damn pretty girl but now she was a knock-out. Heck would surely have had a comment, but he was riding the rails somewhere out west, trying to find work. No one knew where he was for certain because he hadn't called or written in weeks.

Six adults and six children sat down to Easter dinner. Cissie brought a baked ham; Willa fried chickens; Dilly contributed scalloped potatoes and fruit salad. Doc, with the help of his grandchildren and Dean, who all took turns cranking, made vanilla ice cream to go with Lizzie's angel food cake.

Lizzie ordered everyone out to the porch to eat their ice cream and cake. It was a mild spring day, sunny and warm with just a few wispy clouds.

"What was it like out here last Sunday?" Willa asked, keeping one eye on Charley, who had pulled off his shoes and was running after his cousin little Dean. "Was it like in Alva, where the whole sky just turned black? Cars had their lights on but you couldn't see a thing."

"Well, it was the damndest thing," said Doc. "I'd never seen anything like it."

"Tell about the birds," said Lizzie.

"It was not long after dinner," Doc said. "The morning had been real nice, sunny and just a little breeze. Kind of like today. What time was it, Lizzie?"

"Must have been around one or two."

"I'd gone out to the north corral to check the water in the tank. The wind picked up and there were big old black clouds to the northwest. So I thought well maybe we'll get some rain. Then these birds flew in. Hundreds and hundreds of birds. Sparrows and meadowlarks and crows and sage hens and red-winged hawks, birds that you never see flying together. Some of them perched for a while and then took off again, flying south."

"The sky and yard was just full of them," said Lizzie.

"Those black clouds from the north got closer," Doc continued, "and they weren't thunderstorms. It was rolling dirt filling up the whole sky. My hat blew off and I got back to the house and yelled at Lizzie and Dilly to close the windows and make sure the kids were in. Then all of a sudden, like someone had just thrown a switch, the sun went out. Everything just went black."

"I was in the house with little Dean and Randy," Cissie said. "It was pitch black. Took me forever to light the lamp. Dean was out fixing fence."

"Yeah," said Dean. "I couldn't tell which way was up."

"How'd you find your way home?" asked Willa.

"Followed the fence line. The static lit up the top of the fence."

"And I stood in the door," Cissie said, "and yelled as loud as I could." She rubbed a finger into Dean's ear and laughed. "Well, look at that. Dean still has some Colorado dirt in his ear."

Dean tugged on his ear. "That's a fact," he drawled. "Now I can say Pike's Peak came to see me."

The Black Sunday dust storm on April 14, 1935, hit southeastern Colorado, southwest Kansas, and the panhandles of Texas and Oklahoma, inspiring a reporter to call the wind-stripped area The Dustbowl. Woods County was lucky to be on the rim of the bowl.

That summer in Alva the temperature hit one hundred twenty degrees, the highest temperature ever recorded in Oklahoma. No one needed proof that they were living in a frying pan, but two stock boys at the Piggly Wiggly grocery fried a dozen eggs on the cement sidewalk. When grain and grass did manage to grow, grasshoppers swarmed on the fields and stripped every stalk. Cattle died from Johnson grass poisoning or from eating too much dirt. The only animals that flourished were jackrabbits and coyotes.

Some people thought the world was coming to an end and turned to prayer or just went insane; others packed up and moved out, headed toward somewhere green. Doc and Lizzie and all their family stayed put, believing that the drought and the dust wouldn't last forever. In August, 1937, Lizzie summed up her family news in the *Freedom Call*: "The dust continues to whoop it up, and if it takes grit to live here, we've got it."

"What's grit?" Charley wanted to know when Willa read the article to him. "Grandma says we've got it."

By 1938 Willa had lived in Alva for three years. Whenever she went home for a visit, someone, her mother, one of her sisters, or her brother Stub, wanted to know if she had found a man. Even Doc had pulled her aside and said that boy needs a father. As if getting married again would make everything all right and wash the dirt away. Willa ignored their entreaties. She and Charley were just fine. Willa wouldn't admit to herself that she was lonely. She rarely saw Arlene and Carol, who were busy with college life. She had no interest in men. She told herself that her life with Charley was enough. They spent Saturday nights listening to the radio, and every Sunday Charley and Willa read the *Freedom Call* and the *Alva Courier* together. While Willa read the news, Charley pored over the comics. He especially loved Little Orphan Annie and the Katzenjammer Kids. Once in a while they walked to Sunday School at the Christian Church on Fifth Street. Willa liked singing hymns, and Charley enjoyed his Sunday School class. None of the Sharpes were religious, and church-going was usually reserved for funerals, but the church was just a few blocks away, and Willa thought it wouldn't hurt Charley to learn a few Bible verses.

"Mama, tell me about grit," Charley insisted.

"Well, Charley, you know when the dust is blowing really hard and a little piece of it gets stuck in your eye? That little piece is grit. But a few tears or some water will just wash it away and you're as good as new."

"But Grandma says we've got it." Charley climbed onto Willa's lap. His green eyes fixed on Willa's brown eyes. His small hand patted her cheek. "Do you have it, Mama? Your eyes are all watery."

Willa hugged her boy.

"You bet, Charley. I've got it. And so do you."

Cloudburst
1938

ON SATURDAY, JANUARY 22, 1938, Willa was twenty-one, and two days later Charley turned five. They celebrated their birthdays on Sunday with a family dinner at Dean and Cissie's house, just a half-mile down the road from the home place in Old Freedom. Heck, who had returned at Christmas looking older and thinner, invited his girlfriend, Lucy Vance, a lively, freckled brunette from nearby Lookout, who spent summers working Midwest carnivals with her family.

For once, Willa was not allowed in the kitchen. After a dinner of chicken-fried steak and mashed potatoes and gravy, Willa and Charley blew out the twenty-six candles on a three-layer chocolate cake and Charley opened his presents. Willa wore her birthday gift, nubby blue wool tweed trousers with matching jacket, which she fashioned from fabric her sisters had given her. For women to wear pants in public was illegal in many places, but most ignored that law and no one bothered enforcing it. Doc remarked that he heard that in Denver, the police chief said if he had the guts to levy the one-hundred-dollar fine on the fifty thousand women who wore pants in his city every day, Denver could solve all their budget problems. Everyone admired Willa's new suit, and Willa promised to make a similar one for Cissie.

Now Willa sewed only for herself and Charley. Last November, she had left her WPA job to work for Dr. Simmons. She earned a few dollars less per week, but the work was interesting. She learned to keep records and do billing. On the farm, Doc did most of their doctoring and Willa knew some basics, but Dr. Simmons showed her how to give shots, check blood pressure, put on splints, and clean and treat wounds.

When Charley opened his present from Willa, everyone could see that he preferred the cowboy hat from Doc and Lizzie and the toy six-shooters from Dean and Cissie to the brown corduroy pants and plaid flannel shirt his mother had made.

Around 4:00, when Doc was ready to drive them back to Alva, Charley pitched a fit. He threw his coat on the ground and refused to get in the pick-up. Shocked and embarrassed, Willa told him to behave himself. Charley screamed in rage. He hated Alva. He wanted to stay on the farm with Papa and Grandma. He missed his cousins and riding horses and playing with the dogs. Willa spanked him, which made him ashamed and furious. He darted across the yard, down the ditch, across the frozen road and into a field of green winter wheat. When Willa started after him, Dean grabbed her and told her to get in the truck.

Dean picked up Charley's coat. He called his two coon dogs to come with him and they followed Charley across the field. The big black and tan dogs caught up with Charley first. They knocked him down and licked his face. Willa could see Charley wrap his arms around them. Dean kneeled down, said a few words, and helped Charley put on his coat. They shook hands and then walked back across the field. Charley climbed into the pick-up and sat, head hanging, between Doc and Willa.

"Sorry," Charley sniffled. Willa took her handkerchief out of her purse and wiped his nose. Charley leaned against Doc and soon fell asleep.

When they arrived at the Connell house, Doc left the pick-up running. He didn't like driving at night anymore and wanted to get home before it got dark. He carried Charley upstairs to bed and thought about what he wanted to tell Willa. He usually didn't give advice to his children unless they asked for it, but there were some things that just had to be said. So he decided to speak.

"Willa, I've told you before. That boy needs a father."

He waited. Willa just looked at him with a big-eyed expression that he couldn't read. He walked to the pick-up and drove away.

After Doc left, Willa fumed. How dare he give her orders like she was a child! She was through taking his advice. Maybe he meant well, but his words felt like a criticism. Did he think she didn't know what Charley needed? Of course, he needed a father. Well, what was she supposed to do about it? Put an ad in the *Alva Courier*? Anyway, she didn't need or want a husband.

Still, Willa had never seen Charley so upset. He was usually such a good boy and tried to act grown-up. He was only in kindergarten, but he could read the first-grade reader. He printed his name and letters, knew his numbers up to one hundred, and could add and subtract simple figures. As Mrs. Roosevelt advised, Willa showed him her budget, taught him the value of money, and Charley started saving pennies. Maybe she pushed him too hard, treated him too much like the little man of the house.

Charley must have felt pretty bad to throw a fit like that. Willa knew that he loved the farm. He shadowed Doc, Stub, and Dean, copied their behavior, and wanted to look just like them. He insisted on wearing his cowboy boots to school instead of the lace-up leather pair she'd bought him. One Sunday after dinner on the farm, Willa and Charley sat on the front porch and watched Cissie and Dean's boys wrestle in the yard. Charley whispered, "I want to live here, Mama. Maybe then I could have a brother."

Willa missed the home place, too. The rhythms of planting and harvesting, milking and feeding, canning and butchering. Mostly she missed the land itself and the open sky and the smell of fresh cut alfalfa on the wind. She watched Ro and Cissie work with their husbands and envied that closeness. Dilly and Hal fought a lot and spent more time apart than together, but still they were married and continued to have beautiful babies. When she held a baby, Willa felt her whole body ache with longing. She wanted Charley to have a brother or a sister, too, but she couldn't do it by herself.

If Willa had been a man, she could have asked Doc to let her rent a quarter of land and set herself up as a farmer and rancher. That's what Stub and Dean had done. Charley's fit forced Willa to think about how she felt about her life in Alva and about their future. Up until now, she had been reasonably content. Mrs. Connell was pleasant company when she was home, but she was often away, visiting her son's family at the ranch or traveling to see Webb. Willa's old friend Annie Shaw visited whenever she was in town. Annie played piano with the Gyp Hill Boys on weekends and still lived with her parents in Freedom. Willa saw Carol and Arlene now and again, but most of the time they were busy with classes and campus activities. Arlene had realized her ambition of becoming Rangers' Homecoming Queen and riding on a float in the big Homecoming parade, but she had yet to find a suitable, wealthy husband. Carol was engaged to an Oklahoma City man and planned to marry in the summer after she graduated. Even if Willa were interested in college boys, almost two thirds of the seven hundred Northwestern students were women, so the pickings were slim.

At Dr. Simmons' office, Willa met men, mostly married and either too old or too sick or too injured to be interested in a divorcee with a small child. Willa was not given to self-analysis, and she never admitted, even to herself, that in early 1938 she decided that Doc was right. Charley needed a father. And it was up to her to get him one. She had been raised to make the best of things. To work hard, to avoid whining or feeling sorry for herself. If something needed to be done, well, you just got it done somehow and didn't waste your time worrying and gnawing on the subject.

Just Willa

By April 1, she had begun the hunt. She paid particular attention to her appearance and to Charley's. His clothes, even his overalls, were ironed and spotless, and his shoes were polished. Willa always wore high heels and dressed in her signature colors of "Eleanor blue" or black and white with touches of red. She bought silk on sale and made beautiful dresses and blouses. She avoided the new rayon fabrics, which she thought looked cheap. As she shopped on the Square or walked to work, she smiled at the businessmen she saw along the way, and chatted about the weather and the wheat prospects with the salesmen in the hardware store, the shoe repair shop, and the drugstore.

When she deposited her check at the Alva State Bank, she always went to the window of Walt Jenkins, the only unmarried teller. Tall and slim with bland features and reddish complexion, he looked about thirty-five. He slicked his dark hair back with hair oil and parted it in the middle. His manner was serious and professional, and he treated her with courtesy. If Charley was with her, he always gave him a penny.

The third week in April there was a scarlet fever scare, and schools, churches, and civic clubs shut down. Willa sent Charley to the farm while she stayed on in town. One day when she stopped at the bank to withdraw some cash, Walt asked if she would like to see a movie with him on Friday. Willa said she'd like that. After four movie dates in two weeks (Willa's favorites were *Thunder Trail*, a Zane Grey western and *Bringing Up Baby* with Katharine Hepburn and Cary Grant), Walt invited her to supper at the Bell Hotel, which was noted for fine, expensive dining. Willa was not physically attracted to Walt, but her experience with Big Charley had taught her that her physical response might not be the best judge of a man.

Willa found Walt nice enough, if somewhat boring, and listened as he did most of the talking, primarily about his work at the bank, his plans to become a loan manager, and then bank manager. Willa felt a little uncomfortable when he talked about the overdrafts of various customers or the financial problems of local tradespeople. It wasn't any of her business, she believed, and she usually shifted the subject.

Walt didn't smoke and wouldn't let her smoke in his car, but he kept a flask of whiskey in the glove compartment, which he slipped into his pocket when they went to the movies. On their dates, as the evening progressed, Willa noticed that his sips from the flask became more frequent and his complexion a little ruddier. Except for slurring some words, however, Walt did not seem affected by liquor. He held her hand and put his arm around her in the theatre, kissed her quickly on the lips when he walked her to her door, and was a perfect gentleman.

For their supper date at the Bell Hotel, Willa wore a blue silk flowered dress with a slightly flared skirt in the new shorter length just below the knee. She added a navy blue straw beret, white gloves, and since it had been cloudy all day and looked like rain, she carried a navy three-quarter length cape. She had recently gotten a permanent and her hair fell in soft, dark waves onto her shoulders. Except for red lipstick and a dab of lipstick she rubbed on her cheekbones, she didn't wear makeup.

When Walt picked her up, he told her she looked pretty, and she could see that he had taken extra care with his appearance. He wore a gray suit she hadn't seen before. His shoes shone with polish and his hair gleamed with oil. Willa felt sophisticated and important. She had never eaten supper at the Bell Hotel, the finest hotel in town, and where Eleanor Roosevelt had stayed last year when she visited Alva.

They both ordered steaks with all the trimmings and baked Alaska for dessert. The food was delicious, and the candlelit dining room was romantic. From time to time, Walt hid his water glass under the table and poured himself a drink from his flask. By the time they finished supper and Walt asked for the check, Willa saw that his face was flushed, and he seemed agitated and nervous.

"I thought we might take a drive out to the lake," Walt said, as he pulled the car into the Kavanaugh and Shea gas station.

"It looks like it's going to rain," Willa said. "Doesn't that road get real muddy?"

Walt rolled down the window and told the attendant to fill it up. When Walt paid him, the man smiled at Willa. She studied him as he washed the windshield. She couldn't quite place him. He was good-looking and there was something about his thick brown hair and square jaw and the easy way he moved as he walked away and disappeared into the garage.

"What are you looking at?" said Walt.

"I just thought I knew that man from somewhere."

"I bet you do."

"What?"

Walt took a drink from his flask and then threw his right arm around Willa and pulled her close. He leaned down and kissed her hard on the lips with his mouth open. Willa tasted sour whiskey mixed with sticky saliva. He jerked her head back suddenly, sending a sharp pain down her neck and dislodging her hat. Walt hugged her tighter with his right arm. She felt his hot breath on her neck, and his left hand grabbed her breast and squeezed. Willa pushed his hand away. He flipped up her skirt and thrust his hand between her legs and into her crotch. Willa punched his leg with her fist and drew back, trying to free herself. Walt grunted. He's just a filthy hog, Willa thought. She was not a screamer and neither one of them spoke as they fought.

Just for a moment, Walt relaxed his grip, and Willa had enough leverage to throw her left elbow into his stomach. Shoving against the floorboards for traction, she found the door handle and flung the door open. Walt caught her dress, and Willa heard the fabric rip as she held onto the door and pulled herself outside the car. Walt leapt out of his side and tried to cut her off as she ran toward the service station.

There was a light over the restroom door, and Willa thought if she could get in there and lock it, she would be safe. Just as she was closing the door, Walt pulled it open. Suddenly, Walt cried out and stumbled backward, letting go. Willa fell back and slammed the door. She leaned against it and held onto the knob. She heard three loud slaps and groans and then some scuffling and then nothing. She listened. A car drove by and thunder rumbled in the distance. Then Willa heard a car start up and drive away. Soon after, there was a knock on the restroom door.

"Ma'am? Are you all right in there?" The voice was slow and drawling, reminding her of Dean.

Willa smoothed her dress and looked at herself in the mirror. Except for her smudged lipstick, she looked like herself. Her hat was gone, and her dress was ripped. But it could be repaired. She was still Willa. She would be all right. She took a deep breath and opened the door. When she stepped forward, her knees buckled. She would have fallen if the man hadn't caught her.

"Easy does it," he said.

Holding onto his arm, Willa walked into the small office of the gas station. The man spread a clean rag on a chair, and Willa sat down, trying to compose herself. The air smelled of gasoline and axle grease and cigarette smoke. More than anything, Willa wanted a cigarette.

"My purse!"

"Oh. Here. I got it out of his car. And here's your, what is this?"

"It's a cape." The man tucked it around her shoulders. Willa opened her purse and reached for her cigarettes and matches. She lit a cigarette and took a deep drag and then another. As the smoke entered her lungs, she felt herself grow calm.

The man chuckled. "Good thing I do my banking at National."

"I don't know what got into him," Willa said.

"Who knows why people do things. It's a mystery. So, feeling better, Willa?"

"You know me?"

"Sure. You're Willa Stone. You were married to Big Charley. You have a little boy about my son's age."

"I feel like I've met you."

"You have. Once, I think. I'm Jim Hardesty." He clenched his fists and crouched into a boxing stance.

"Yes! The Phantom of Fair Valley. I've seen you fight."

"That's me. Between working here and boxing and a little farming, I make just about enough to get by."

"I've seen your name on the flyers. And your picture was in last week's paper."

"No, that was brother Jake. He's the hero."

"That's right, now I remember."

"I told him that he should share the reward money with me since I taught him how to shoot."

"Did he?"

"Hell, Jake would give me everything he had if I asked him to."

Jim left to wait on a customer, and Willa sat smoking her cigarette and trying to make sense out of what had happened.

Jim returned and put money in the register. "I'll take you home. I just have to close up here." He lifted his grease-stained work shirt, removed a gun tucked under his belt, and locked it in a drawer next to the cash register. "We get some rough customers in here sometimes. But not Walt, he's pretty soft."

"What'd you do to him?"

"Oh just kicked his butt, slapped him a few times and then kicked his butt back to the car. I don't think he'll bother you again. But you should switch to National Bank."

"I will."

"Well, I'd better get home or Sally will eat me alive."

Jim's pick-up smelled of liniment and sweat. He had forgotten to roll up the window, and he wiped the seat with a towel.

"Do you want me to walk you to the door?" he asked, when he turned onto Locust Street.

"No reason we both should get wet," said Willa. "I'll just run in." She pulled the cape over her hair and tucked her purse under her arm.

"Thank you, Jim, for everything. I really appreciate it."

He grinned. "Anytime you want somebody's butt kicked, just holler for the Fair Valley Phantom."

Jim waited until he saw the lights go on in the house before he drove away.

Willa stretched out in the bathtub until she grew chilled in the cool water. Her right shoulder was bruised and the inside of her right thigh was sore where Walt had grabbed her. She'd have another bruise there, too. Lightning flashed and then thunder boomed making her jump. A few seconds later there was another white flash of lightning and more thunder cracking the sky.

Willa put on a robe and sat outside on the porch swing enjoying the thunder and lightning show and breathing in the smell of ozone and cool rain. The light shower had turned into a real cloudburst. The rain poured down in great blowing walls of water, slamming on the porch roof and making rippling puddles in the hard-packed dirt of the yard. Locust Street became a swift-flowing stream that surged downhill and joined the river gushing down Fourth Street. Willa thought of Charley and her mother and father. They would be awake, too, in Old Freedom, gathered on the porch, watching the rain fill the terraces, giving moisture to the growing wheat.

Willa longed to be there with them. As she swung slowly back and forth on the swing and watched the rain scrub the dirt from the front steps and the sidewalk, she didn't think about Walt Jenkins or her bruises. She made a list in her head of what she needed to do. When the school reopened in a few days, she'd call Doc to bring Charley back to Alva. Every Friday after she got off work, she and Charley would catch a ride to Old Freedom or someone could come and get them, and they would spend the weekend on the farm. On Saturday nights, she'd go hear Annie play with the Gyp Hill Boys at the Camp Houston dances. While Annie took a break, maybe Willa could chord for a few sets. Perhaps someone would ask her to dance. It might be fun to dance with a cowboy. It had been a long time since she'd danced.

First Dance
June 25, 1938

AT FIFTEEN, WILLA VOWED THAT after Charley Stone no man would make her feel like that ever again. Weak, helpless, humiliated and lost. If that was love she didn't want it. So what was she feeling six years later (she never forgot the date), Saturday, June 25, 1938 at the Camp Houston Dance when she danced with Jake Anthony Hardesty. So many things — love, lust, power, delight — and there was something else that she couldn't name, a kind of yearning. Or was it just the urging of time?

Like every other Saturday night that June, Willa worked the Camp Houston dance, chording at the piano, relieving Annie when she wanted to take a break. Now she was looking around for Cissie or Dilly, thinking about finding a ride home. The dance hall stank of bootleg bourbon and lilac perfume and cow manure that stuck to the men's boots. Thunder rumbled and from time to time heat lightning flickered, but there was no rain and no breeze. One of the toilets had stopped up from the sick drunks, and shouts and whistles from a fistfight out back could be heard when the band swung into *Nobody's Darling but Mine.*

She felt him before she saw him. Three men stepped back as he walked through the open door. He stood across from her on the opposite side of the dance floor, pushed back his black hat and grinned. And kept grinning. Wondering what joke she had missed, Willa surveyed the dancers, the men in starched khakis and jeans and shirts wrinkled with sweat and the bare-armed women in bright pink, tangerine, lime, turquoise, and butter-yellow cotton print dresses. He was still grinning. What was so funny?

Then he held out his arms and slowly swiveled his hips, as if inviting her to take a good look. Like a camera that freezes the action for a moment, she saw what he was seeing. They were a portrait in black and white. He wore black and white cowboy boots, dark pants, a silver belt buckle, and a white shirt with the sleeves pushed up. Willa wore black high-heeled sling-backed pumps, a bias-cut black skirt with a white leather belt, and a sleeveless white blouse with pearl snap buttons. She took a long drag on her cigarette as he walked toward her. He stood in front of her. He reached around and lifted her hair and blew on her dripping neck. She didn't move.

"They tell me you don't dance," he said. His voice was low and rough with a kind of teasing lilt. "But I don't believe it."

She took a deep drag on her cigarette, then tossed it on the floor, and crushed it under her shoe. He wrapped his right arm around her waist, and she fit herself against his body, stretching up so that her lips grazed his neck. He took her right hand in his left. His hand was dry and hard with scabbed knuckles and thick calluses. He held her with a light touch, letting her lead and followed her easily, even though he favored his left leg. They danced fast and they danced slow; they danced until their white shirts were gray with sweat. They kept dancing while the Gyp Hill Boys packed up their instruments, and they held onto each other as the crowd straggled out to their cars and sleeping kids.

"So you're Jake Hardesty," she said, tilting her head back and looking into his blue eyes. Her sisters were right—he was the best-looking man in Woods County. And it wasn't just because of his square jaw and wide mouth with unusually white teeth. He was healthy and strong and beautiful without swaggering, like a confident young Angus bull in an ordinary herd of Herefords. Curls of dark hair strayed onto his damp forehead. A clear drop of sweat floated in the dimpled cleft of his jaw. She resisted an impulse to touch it. She knew who he was, of course, everyone knew, but she wanted to hear him say his name.

"Yeah. I'm Jake." He traced the five letters of her name tooled into the back of her leather belt. "And you're Willa. Doc's baby and Big Charley's girl."

"No. Not for a long time."

Under a black sky quilted with stars, they drove the few miles to the Sharpe homestead in Old Freedom. Jake stopped the car. A breeze had kicked up and the air smelled like wheat dust that had been scrubbed clean. Willa took a deep breath. She had to know. She moved close. His mouth was soft and salty. Before she lost herself, she moved away.

He pressed his curled left fist into her cheek. "See you tomorrow, brown eyes."

And just like that Willa knew. She could feel the sweet expanse of her life stretched out in front of her. She could feel the rightness of it. She knew it in the same way her hand knew when the oven was hot enough for her bread to bake into lofty golden loaves. "How do you do that?" her sisters asked. "I don't know. I just feel it," Willa told them. Making it sound simple when it wasn't. "You either have the feel or you don't," her father said, biting into a buttery slice.

Willa lit a cigarette and watched the Ford's red taillights until they disappeared into the darkness. She touched her cheek where his fist had pushed. She could still feel his heat. She knew where he was going and what he would do. He'd drive south of the river to the Fair Valley ranch to sleep for a time before driving back to her. She stubbed her cigarette out and covered it with a dirt clod. Doc didn't approve of women smoking.

She opened the screen door and tiptoed into the house. She lay down beside her son on the daybed where he had been born. Hard to believe that Charley was almost five and a half now. She wet her finger and rubbed away a bit of food stuck in the corner of his mouth. Cherry pie, she decided, licking her finger clean. She lifted his head and turned the pillow over to the cool side.

Am I happy? she thought. Is this what happiness feels like?

Jake
1938

Jake drove back to Fair Valley with the stars shining overhead and the windows of the Ford open to the breeze. His left hand cupped the warm, moist wind.

"Whoo—ee, Whoo-ee!" Jake shouted, his lungs filling with air, bellowing out the Hardesty cattle call. "Whoo—ee, Whoo-ee!"

Jake was a happy man. And it wasn't because he'd sold a trunk load of bourbon pints at the Camp Houston dance, had a wad of bills in his pocket and a trunk load of empties. After he dropped off Willa, he went back and collected as many empty bottles as he could find in the weedy ditches around the dance hall. Each one he found meant more money in his pocket. Jake liked money. He had money in the bank, and he could always earn more money. No, money didn't make him happy. It was necessary, but it had nothing to do with happiness. Holding Willa in his arms, though, that made him happy. Willa Sharpe was a rare woman, and he'd been around enough to recognize her value. And he was tired of being alone with no place of his own. Tired of being a hired hand, batching for himself, and taking care of somebody else's cattle.

After a few hours' sleep in the bunkhouse, just before dawn, Jake heard the screen door squeak open and then bang shut. A wet nose nuzzled his neck. He rolled over and looked into the intelligent, dark eyes of Joe Savisky. Joe wiggled in delight and jumped on top of him, licking his face. Jake scratched behind Joe's long, soft ears. No need for an alarm clock. He had reliable Joe, a four-year-old, sixty-five-pound Walker Coonhound with black and tan saddle markings on his back and a white belly and white legs. Joe Savisky was a cold trail hound Jake claimed, to anyone who admired his dog.

"One night, at the end of November, it was after Thanksgiving," Jake would tell the story, "I took Joe out south on the Cimarron. Everybody said it had been hunted clean. But they didn't know Joe. If there was a coon around, Joe would find it. Well, Joe put his nose to the ground and went tearing off. Then I heard Joe bawling away, and I knew he'd treed something. When I got there, I looked up and couldn't see anything, but still Joe kept jumping up on the tree and baying. So I put down my rifle and climbed that tree. And then I saw it, in a hole of the tree."

Jake would shake his head, remembering.

His listeners would lean in and ask, "What was it, Jake?"

"The damndest thing I'd ever seen. The skeleton of a big old coon! All curled up in the tree. Hell, it must have been there for years. Yeah, Joe Savisky's a real cold trail hound. His nose is so good he can smell out a coon in this world or the next."

Jake had raised Joe from a pup. His dad had gotten him in partial payment for some vet work for Old Man Savisky, a farmer over by Enid. Jake and Joe were hunting partners—Joe found and treed the coons, Jake shot and skinned them, and then sold the pelts for five or six dollars each. Some nights they made twenty dollars.

Joe Savisky loved hunting, and he adored Jake. But then, everybody liked Jake Hardesty. Dogs, men, women, children, cattle, horses. Even the boxers whose noses he broke and ribs he cracked liked him. Through broken teeth and split lips, they would shake his hand and say, "Helluva fight, Jake."

When Jake started boxing, he was only sixteen, but he usually won most of his fights. When he was nineteen, he was shot in his left thigh and some of the bone was blown out. Doctors fixed the bone with a steel plate, but his left leg was three-quarters of an inch shorter than his right. In the ring, he compensated by keeping his left foot forward and staying out of clinches. His right leg got stronger, and if he landed a good hard punch with his right fist, the fight was over. Still, he couldn't dance around the ring as his brother Jimmy had taught him, and Jake began to lose matches. Afterward, his opponents would grab his hand, and say, "You're slow, Jake, but you're a helluva guy," and then buy him a beer. Jake left the boxing to Jimmy now. Still, his reputation in the ring followed him, and his customers were quick to pay for their liquor, not wanting to risk a meeting with Jake's fists.

Yes, everybody liked Jake, but they feared him, too. Jimmy, two years older and a well-trained, conditioned boxer, at five feet ten inches was an inch taller than Jake and fast, but Jake was heavier, with hard muscled shoulders and arms, and a thick, broad chest. If they weren't in a ring and following the rules, Jake could whip Jimmy, and they both knew it. A fearless fighter, Jake didn't look for trouble and was slow to anger, but when pushed he had an explosive temper. Once, an Alva man stopped at the Freedom Co-op to get gas and eyed Jake limping toward his car. "Hey, ain't you that washed up peg leg boxer?" the man called.

Jake kept walking. The man shouted, "Hey, you there! Peg leg!"

Jake stopped. He looked at the man, walked over to him, and smiled. "My name's Jake. Don't call me peg leg."

"Yeah, you're the peg leg," the man said. The next thing the man knew he and his front teeth were flying, separately, across a pile of Case tractor tires.

People and animals liked Jake Hardesty because he was good-looking, with laughing blue eyes and a pleasant word for everyone he met, and they liked him because he liked them. They were drawn to Jake's energy. Perhaps it was in his genes that he woke up every morning happy to be alive.

When he was six, he didn't cry when his mother walked out the door of their New Mexico farmhouse, carrying a baby girl that his father swore wasn't his. He'd never seen much of his mother anyway. His father had tended to the boys, while Maybelle, who was twenty years younger than John, ran off with various men to drink and dance. For a time, John would fetch her back and sober her up, but the baby girl was the last straw, and he kicked her out.

When Maybelle left, John Hardesty sold his farm in New Mexico and contacted his old friend George Miller. Miller and his two brothers, Colonel Joe Miller and Zack Miller, owned the 101 Ranch along the Salt Fork River in northern Oklahoma. John knew that he and his boys needed a change and a stable home. The 101 was just the place. The Millers hired John as ranch vet and horse and mule wrangler.

For three years, from 1922 to 1925, Jake lived with his dad and two brothers in a three-room cottage on the 101 Ranch, one hundred ten thousand acres that stretched across four Oklahoma counties. The Miller brothers and their families lived in a huge white house on the ranch and acted like benevolent rulers of their mini-country, a showplace of the Southwest that attracted politicians, sports stars, and movie stars.

In 1923, when Jake was eight, he met Will Rogers, the Oklahoma cowboy star and homespun philosopher, who was a frequent visitor at the ranch. Jake noticed that Rogers treated everybody with the same gentle, teasing courtesy — from the Miller brothers, to the Ponca Indian woman who washed his clothes, to the little Hardesty boys. He took the time to talk to Jake and his brothers and show them some rope tricks. One day as they watched John Hardesty work on a horse's teeth, Rogers told the boys, the best doctor in the world is a vet. He can't ask his patients what's the matter. He's just got to know.

Perhaps because he spent so much time with animals,

John Hardesty was a man of few words. He specialized in animal dentistry, and in his spare time, he was a stone carver. His distinctive hand-carved tombstones decorated many country cemeteries. Tall, white-haired, and stoop shouldered, John seemed to have always been old. He said little about his past. His sons knew that he had gone to veterinary school in Detroit, Michigan, and that he'd once been to California. They didn't know that his name wasn't really Hardesty. John didn't know who his real parents were. When Anthony and Adelia Hardesty found him in June, 1878, he was an orphan, about five or six years old, skinny and wild, living outdoors in Erie County, Ohio, with a couple of dogs. The Hardestys gave him their name and raised him with their three daughters, Martha, Molly, and Mattie.

The three years John Hardesty gave his sons on the 101 Ranch saved them and him; and the boys got an education they would never forget. Besides Jake and his brothers learning to read and write in the ranch school, everyone had to work on the ranch, and everyone was necessary. It produced everything it needed and employed a huge workforce—cowboys to work the cattle and horses, field hands to plant and harvest fruit orchards and thousands of acres of wheat, oats, corn, and alfalfa, and workers to man the pig and poultry houses, ice plant, meatpacking house, cider mill, woodworking shops, tannery, laundry, and café. While their dad worked as a vet and wrangler, the Hardesty brothers carried mail and messages around the ranch on horseback, fed pigs and chickens, worked in the orchards and gardens, filled in as extras in the Wild West shows, and helped out with the terrapin races the ranch put on every year.

On the 101, the races mingled — Indians, Blacks, whites, Chinese. Everyone, including the Millers and their families, ate at the ranch café. The star of the 101 Wild West show was the Negro cowboy Bill Pickett, who invented bulldogging in the wild, overgrown mesquite country of Texas where using a rope to catch a steer was almost impossible. Pickett would gallop his horse alongside a steer, then slide off the horse, grab the steer around the horns, and twist its neck until it fell. If that didn't bring it down, Pickett would bite the steer in the nose and hold on until the steer finally dropped.

At the 101, the only code of conduct was the cowboy code. When the Miller brothers hired someone they didn't ask for references or credentials. You were allowed to prove yourself by your performance. Strangers were welcomed and offered food and assistance. Animals were fed and watered before anyone sat down to dinner. There were no written contracts; a man's word was his bond.

Jake liked to talk about the years he spent on the 101, but he rarely spoke about the other years of his childhood, which were brutal and lonely. He'd seen too much and grown up too fast. But on the 101, he and his brothers lived a boy's cowboy dream. In 1925, however, John Hardesty invested in a sale barn in Chetopa, Oklahoma and went on the road again as a veterinarian. He knew that his boys needed to settle in one place and get more schooling, so he asked his three sisters, the Aunt M's, to take them in. Eight-year-old

Billy got sweet, silver-haired Aunt Martha, who lived in Enid with her husband Francis, a deputy sheriff. They had one daughter, five-year-old Rebecca.

The brothers loved plump and jolly Aunt Milly, who lived outside of Woodward on a farm with her husband Wyatt, but Milly had five children of her own, and couldn't afford another mouth to feed.

So Jake, ten, and Jimmy, twelve, were sent to Aunt Mattie, who lived on a prosperous wheat farm with her German husband Herman in Clark County, Kansas, twelve miles east of Ashland, Kansas. Mattie and Herman were childless and didn't know anything about raising boys. They had a nice two-story farmhouse, and Mattie wanted to keep it nice. She didn't need any dirty boys tracking mud into her house. Boys wanted to be outside anyway, she said. When Jimmy and Jake refused to go to school, Mattie and Herman didn't insist. There was plenty to do around the farm. After a year and a half of sleeping in the barn with only one wool blanket and a dog to keep them warm in the winter and working like men in the fields, Jake and Jimmy ran away. They thought they'd have a better chance if they split up.

Jake ran west and got as far as the Hazen place twenty miles west of Ashland, where he collapsed with exhaustion and hunger. The Hazens let him sleep, then cleaned him up, fed him, and contacted John Hardesty, who said that it was okay with him if Jake stayed. On the Hazen farm, Jake worked for his board and room. He had enough to eat and a warm bed, but he was expected to work as long and as hard in the fields as Mr. Hazen and his hired man, while the Hazen kids went to school and played baseball.

Jimmy, who ran southeast, ended up in Alva, where he found a job and a bed at Kavanaugh and Shea Hardware store. On weekends Jimmy hung around the boxing matches that were held in the building and soon became a mascot of the local fighters and boxing promoters. John Hardesty checked in on his sons from time to time, and every Christmas they all gathered at Aunt Martha's in Enid for a holiday dinner.

Jake's school was life, and like a clever dog he dodged kicks and learned to please and to read people and situations. By the time he hired on at the Eden ranch south of Freedom in 1934, Jake had worked on seven farms and ranches in western Kansas and northwest Oklahoma. In the fall and winter of 1930, he, Jimmy, and his dad got a place together outside of Enid, but mostly Jake was on his own. He didn't feel sorry for himself. A lot of people were worse off, and he knew that life could end in an instant. At the sale barn in Chetopa, Jake had hung over the top rail of a corral and watched as a longhorn steer gored a cowboy in the belly. The man had screamed in agony and held onto his guts as the blood and life drained out of his body. Jake knew then that life was shadowed by death and knowing that made him love life even more. So when Joe nudged him awake every morning, Jake welcomed the day thinking something good might happen.

On this particular morning, June 26, 1938, Jake's first thoughts were of Willa, about her creamy brown skin; the clean, soapy smell of her moist hair; and the smoky taste of her mouth. His need to see her again was urgent and physical. But first he had pastures to ride. He figured he could be at the Sharpe place in Old Freedom by 11:30. Just in time for dinner.

By the time he fed the two horses and Joe Savisky and fried a couple of eggs for himself, the sun was up above Wildcat Hill. Jake oversaw the ranch home place and one hundred eighty head of cattle. He earned seventy-five dollars a month, a bed in the bunkhouse, and meals during round up. Most days he batched for himself, warming up beans, frying potatoes, and opening a can of peaches. Sometimes he ate supper at Alma Ritter's boarding house in Freedom, where his dad stayed when he came through. He got enough to eat, but Jake was always hungry for a home-cooked meal.

In addition to cowboying for the Edens, Jake hired out to do whatever needed doing, cleaning cisterns, building fence, hauling hay, breaking horses and mules, and repairing cars and tractors. Once in a while, he worked as his brother Jimmy's corner man: a job he didn't like since it reminded him of the shotgun blast to his leg, as if his aching, scarred leg weren't a reminder every morning when he woke up.

Jake saddled Fortney, a four-year-old strawberry roan gelding he'd bought from Henry Eden for fifty dollars. Eden had taken him in trade for some cattle, but the horse proved too spirited for his daughter. Jake took along a rope, a canteen, and slid his .410 shotgun into the scabbard.

With Joe Savisky trailing behind sniffing for rabbits, Jake rode out into the Edens' pasture—rolling sandy prairies, dotted with sweet-smelling sagebrush, lush tall grass, and sand plum thickets. Jake stopped and let Fortney snatch some tall grass, still moist with dew. It had been a wet summer so far and grass was abundant.

"Let's go," Jake said, urging the horse forward. Fortney pricked up his ears, snorting the south wind, happy to be out of the corral. Jake sat easily on the horse, who was sensitive to the slightest touch of the reins. Jake sometimes joked that he should just send Fortney and Joe Savisky out to ride pasture while he stayed in bed.

He checked the fence lines for breaks and made sure the windmills were working. He rode through the grazing cattle, keeping a mental count and looking for any open wounds where screwworm flies laid their eggs. Unlike maggots, screwworms feasted on living flesh. If the animal was untreated it would run a fever, go wobbly and be eaten alive in four days.

Satisfied that all the cattle were present and healthy, Jake galloped Fortney back to the ranch, eager to be on the road, on his way to Willa. After a quick shower under an open rain barrel, he pulled on a clean pair of khakis and a blue shirt, swiped the dust off his corral-stained boots, whistled for Joe Savisky, and gunned the Ford back to Old Freedom.

For as long as Jake could remember, he'd lived day to day, not thinking about the future. He'd never courted a girl or dated girls. Since he'd only attended grade school sporadically, he'd missed out on knowing girls his own age. The daughters of the farmers and ranchers he worked for were off limits to him—a hired hand—and he kept his distance.

The summer he was fourteen he had sex for the first time with a lonely farmer's wife in Coldwater, Kansas. She sneaked into his bed one night when her husband was coon hunting with his buddies. She was old, almost forty, with soft, sagging breasts and callused feet. Whenever her husband went hunting that winter, she'd come to his bed. From time to time, she'd slip him five dollars from her egg money. A year later a wealthy rancher's wife in Buffalo paid him ten dollars to stay with her all night while her husband was in Denver, a practice she continued whenever her husband went on a buying trip. Jake didn't think it was wrong. Nobody got hurt. He was happy to oblige, and the women were nice and grateful. Hell, he would have done it for nothing. When his brother Jimmy was caught by Sally Sneed and had to get married, Jake vowed he wouldn't make the same mistake. He didn't want to end up with a bitter woman like Sally Sneed, who nagged Jimmy about money all the time.

"Willa's different," he said aloud. He liked saying her name. He wouldn't mind being caught by her. With his mind on Willa, Jake didn't notice the dust-covered Cadillac glide in behind him as he drove down Freedom's main street. When he stopped at the Camp Houston stop sign three miles north of Freedom, he saw the black car in his mirror. A hand beckoned from the rear window.

Jake pulled over, got out, leaned against his car and waited while the Cadillac moved to the side of the road behind his Ford. Even caked with dirt, the huge car looked brand-new. Anyway he never had seen one like it. Again, the hand appeared and waved him closer. Jake looked around. There were no other cars on the road, and, since it was Sunday morning, the Camp Houston gas station was closed. Joe Savisky hung his head out the window and looked from Jake to the Cadillac. Well, what the hell, Jake thought, it was broad daylight. He walked over. Two men in cowboy hats sat in the front seat. The man in back waved again. Jake could see a large diamond ring on his left hand.

"Jake, how are you, boy?" the man said. The door opened and Jake slid inside.

"Hello, Senator," Jake said, shaking his hand. Silver-haired and handsome, an expensive, custom-made suit covering his enormous bulk, and sporting his trademark white carnation boutonnière, Ed Drummond smiled. Not the flashy grin he used in his campaigns for state senator, but a smile that conveyed real affection.

"What's going on?" asked Jake.

"I'm looking for Jimmy's place. Your dad said he might be able to help me out with a little temporary storage problem."

"Jimmy's working eighty acres up in Farry, north of Old Freedom. Take your third right after Old Freedom. It's down the road apiece, a white one-story house with a dead cottonwood in the yard. You can't miss it."

"Thanks, Jake. Anything I can do for you?"

"No, sir."

"Well, here's my card. I've got a new number now. You let me know if I can help you in any way, son."

Drummond must need another place to stash the liquor

his men trucked in from Illinois, Jake thought as the black Cadillac drove away. Jimmy could sure use the money. Bootlegging was just one of Jake's many jobs, and an easy one at that. Right now, Jake's mind was on Willa and a new job, a task he had never attempted. He had made up his mind. It was time he got married. He had thirteen hundred forty dollars in the bank and sixty dollars in his pocket. He owned a good horse, a fine dog, and a 1934 Ford sedan. He was good-looking, healthy, and a hard worker.

Jake knew his own worth. He wasn't worried about Willa rejecting him. But he was worried a little about Willa's father, Old Doc Sharpe, a man feared by Big Charley Stone. Sweat dripped down Jake's forehead. In his hurry to leave, he forgot his hat. Well, what the hell, he'd better get moving. The sun was high. It was almost time for dinner.

Sunday Dinner
June 26, 1938

DOC GLARED AT THE WHITE-FACED Hereford. He backed the animal into a corner of the corral. "Got you now." Just as he tossed the rope, the steer dodged away, and the loop fell empty to the ground. "Goddamn sonofabitch."

Doc felt lousy. After supper last night he'd grabbed a sheet and stomped outside. The house stewed with women and children running up and down stairs, banging in and out the screen door, bawling and hollering and laughing. Then Willa and her sisters had run off to a dance leaving Lizzie and him to watch the kids. Where were their damn husbands?

He'd made his bed in the old wagon, wheels and frame broken and useless and slowly disintegrating, just like me he thought. It was a tad cooler outside, but the sun was still hanging around and storm clouds threatened from the east. Come October, he'd be seventy. Too old to be sleeping outdoors. Hell, he was too old for almost everything, except the work still had to be done. Lying on his back in the wagon, all around him Doc could see the results of thirty-nine years of work—the house, barn, and corrals, the hog sheds, chicken house, and garden. The plows, harrows, combines, and tractors needed to work the fields of wheat and alfalfa and corn. So much to take care of and watch over, and there was always something to do. Now Lizzie wanted an indoor bathroom. Well, he could just paint the two-holer or outwait her.

He bent over to pick up the rope, and a spasm of pain shot through his back. But if he didn't rope this steer and treat it, soon he'd lose another animal.

Doc shook the dirt off the rope, ignoring the throbbing pain in his arthritic hands. Then he heard a car turn into the driveway. He walked to the fence and saw someone, who looked like one of John Hardesty's boys, emerging with a coon dog from the same black Ford sedan that Doc saw Willa get out of late last night. The young man looked around as if he didn't know what to do next.

In truth, Jake Hardesty was afraid, more afraid than he'd ever been in his life. His legs felt unsteady, his heart pounded, and he was sweating. He had no idea what he should say to Willa when he saw her. Or to Doc Sharpe, who was glaring at him from the corral. Just as he had decided to get back in his car and drive away, Doc hollered at him.

"Hey, you! Hardesty!"

Jake jumped. "Yes sir?"

"Give me a hand here."

"You bet, Doc. What can I do for you?"

"Get in here and rope this damn steer."

Jake looked at the house, wondering if he should tell Willa he was here.

"Well, get a move on!"

"Sure. Be right there."

Jake climbed the corral fence, took the rope from Doc, coiled it expertly; then in one smooth movement, he sailed the rope over the steer's head. The steer bellowed in protest as Jake tightened the noose.

"Now, hold him while I get the remedy," Doc said.

As Jake bulldogged the steer's head, Doc applied salve to a stinking wound infested with screwworms just above the animal's left eye. Then Jake released the steer, who ran to a far corner of the corral, shaking his head back and forth.

"Thanks," said Doc, wiping his hands on a rag. "You're Jake, right? The middle boy?"

"Yeah. Billy's in Enid with Aunt Martha. And Jimmy just took over the Mitchell place in Farry."

"I heard. How's your dad?"

"He's good. Mostly on the road."

The two men walked in silence back to Jake's car, where Joe Savisky waited. Jake wanted to say that he'd come to see Willa, but he couldn't get the words out. The white-haired old man looked fierce. He kept rubbing his back like he was angry at something.

"That's a nice-looking dog."

"This here's Joe Savisky." When he heard his name, Joe opened his mouth like he was smiling and woofed a greeting.

Doc fondled the dog's soft, drooping ears. "You and Willa go to the dance at Camp Houston last night?"

"We sure did."

"Well, come wash up. Willa's been cooking up a storm. You hungry?"

"I'm starving, Doc."

Jake cleaned his boots on the scraper and followed Doc into the kitchen. The aroma of fresh-baked bread and fried chicken filled the air. Jake's mouth watered. The table was piled with food. Platters of golden-brown fried chicken, mashed potatoes, cream gravy, green beans, sliced cucumbers, and onions floating in vinegar, a stack of crusty white bread, a square of yellow butter. Rosy sand plum jelly sparkled in a cut-glass dish.

Willa set a pitcher of iced tea on the table and smiled at him. She wore a yellow and white checked sundress, her brown shoulders bare except for thin ruffled straps. Her dark hair was pulled back in a ponytail. Willa wiped her forehead with a kitchen towel. "I hope you like fried chicken, Jake. I fried five thinking that Hal and Dilly and their kids were going to be here, but Hal said no he was taking them out to eat in Alva. So it's just us."

"I caught the chickens!"

A boy wearing overalls peeked out from behind Willa.

"Shake hands with Mr. Jake Hardesty," Willa said, pushing him forward. "Jake, this is Charley."

Jake looked into Charley's green eyes. He took the boy's small hand in his own and carefully squeezed. "Hey, little Charley. Pleased to meet you."

"I'm not little. I'm big! I'm almost six."

"Well, you are a tall fella. But since I called your dad Big

Charley, I thought you must be little Charley."

"You knew my daddy?"

"I sure did." Jake kneeled down to the boy's level. "We used to box a little."

"Could he beat you?"

"He was what you call a heavyweight boxer so we never had a real fight. But sure, if he'd wanted to he could have beaten me. He was a helluva fighter."

"Mama, you never told me that!"

"That's enough, Charley," said Doc. "It's time to eat."

"I want to sit next to Mr. Jake Hardesty," said Charley.

"Lizzie!" Doc called. "Dinner's on. Get your nose out of that book."

Doc and Lizzie sat at either end of the long table. Willa sat across from Jake and Charley.

"Now, Charley, how'd you catch these chickens?" Jake asked, helping himself to a chicken breast.

"With this wire Mama made. I sneak up and hook their leg. And then Mama grabs them and snaps their necks."

"Charley, pass the potatoes," Lizzie said, "and let Mr. Hardesty eat in peace. Have some gravy, Jake."

"Thanks, ma'am. This sure is delicious."

"Don't thank me. This is all Willa's doing."

"I'm afraid I got the chicken a little too brown," Willa said, frowning at the wing on her plate.

"I've never eaten chicken this good," Jake said.

"We like the small fryers," Doc said, "not even a pound and a half. They're the best. Here, try some of Willa's bread."

As she watched the bones pile up on Jake's plate, Willa worried that five chickens wouldn't be enough. She'd never seen a man eat so much. And he was so good with Charley. Willa thought her heart would burst when Jake talked to Charley about his father. Jake made everyone relax; even Doc seemed to like him, and Doc had been grumpy all morning. Having dinner with Jake sitting across from her felt right. Her sisters' husbands were regulars at Sunday dinner, but Willa never had anyone to sit across from and wait on and listen to. And she had never been filled with such longing. Her breast brushed Jake's shoulder when she leaned over to fill his glass, and he winked at her. She moved away, refilling the gravy boat, clearing chicken bones, but she wanted to reach out and touch the dark curl that had fallen onto his forehead and stroke the clean, white line across his tanned forehead where his hat had blocked the sun.

Willa listened as the others talked about the weather and the likelihood of more rain. Jake agreed with Doc that hogs would be a good investment since the wet spring and summer would bring a good fall feed crop. Lizzie asked if Jake had listened to the Joe Louis fight last week.

"I sure did, ma'am."

"That German didn't know what hit him," said Doc.

"Mama made me go to bed!" Charley complained.

Jake turned to Charley. "It was over pretty fast. Joe came out punching with his left, like this, bam, bam, bam, and then when Max let down his guard, like this, Joe hit him with the right."

Jake lightly tapped Charley in his ribs and jaw with his fist. "Pow, Pow, Pow!"

"I'd rather listen to Amos 'n' Andy," said Willa.

"Now, Willa," said Jake. "Joe Louis is the heavyweight champion of the world. It was a great fight!"

"Pow, Pow, Pow!" said Charley, jabbing at the table with his fists.

"Stop it, Charley. You're going to knock your glass over," said Willa.

"Jake, that was a nice article the *Freedom Call* ran about you catching those rustlers," said Lizzie.

"A good picture, too," Willa said. "You look a lot like your brother Jimmy."

"You know my brother?"

"I've met him."

"He never said he knew you."

Willa hesitated; all the humiliation of that night with Walt Jenkins came rushing back. "It was in Alva earlier this year."

"So they put those old boys away?" said Doc.

"Yeah," said Jake. "They had quite an operation going."

"You got a nice reward, didn't you Jake?" said Lizzie. "All those ranchers must have been grateful."

"Well, ma'am, I was just in the right place at the right time. Anybody else would have done the same thing."

"I'd like to have seen their faces when you shot out those tires," Doc said. "That must have been something."

"Yeah. They were a little put out."

"Did you shoot the rustlers?" Charley asked.

"Nah, I just scared them and shot their truck tires so they couldn't get away."

"How'd you know where they'd be?" Willa asked.

"I just got lucky. They'd hit the Shattuck ranch a few weeks before. So I worked nights for a month, just sitting up there on Wildcat Hill with Fortney and Joe Savisky watching for headlights. "

"Who's Fortney and Joe Savisky?" asked Charley.

"Fortney's my horse and Joe's my dog."

"Can I ride Fortney? Please!"

"Hush, Charley!" said Willa. "Let Jake tell the story."

"Why, sure you can ride him. So anyway, it was late and I saw the truck's headlights. They were headed to the west pasture where we had the Angus herd. I rode over there, and sure enough they backed the truck up against a steep bank and unloaded a horse. Three men. They probably threw some fresh dirt down in the truck because those cattle walked in there as easy as you please. Now the plan was if I saw them, to ride back to the ranch and call the sheriff. But as fast as they were working, I knew that I wouldn't have time to do that. So I waited until they got all the cattle loaded . . . "

"How many head?" asked Doc.

"Ten good steers. Finally, they loaded the horse and all three got in the truck. I told Joe Savisky to stay behind. I rode up closer so I could get a good shot."

"Why did Joe have to stay behind?"

"Well, Charley, I didn't want him to get excited and bark and warn them."

As Jake told the story of how he stopped the rustlers who had been raiding the ranches of northwestern Oklahoma, he told it in the same way he'd always told it, which meant he left out how afraid he'd been riding through the dark pasture holding his .410 shotgun, waiting for the right moment. When the truck started to move forward, Jake fired quickly, maneuvering Fortney into position, and shot out first the right rear tire and then the left. Three men jumped out of the truck, one holding a rifle. As he rode away on a dead run down the dirt road, Jake ducked when he heard the crack of the rifle. By the time he got back to the ranch, he was covered in sweat and shaking.

"Did you help find them?" Willa asked.

"No, but as soon as it got light, I rode over and let the steers out of the truck. Those old boys didn't get far on foot. The sheriff found them hiding in a ditch just north of Freedom."

"In the old days, they'd have just strung 'em up right there," said Doc.

"Who'd like some cherry pie?" asked Willa.

"I think I'll read a little," Lizzie said. "I want to finish the serial I started."

"Daddy?"

Doc had already moved in to the couch. "Wake me in a bit," he called.

"Jake? How about you?"

"I'd love some pie, but why don't Charley and I stretch our legs first. Let's see what Joe Savisky's up to."

"Come back in a while, Charley, and I'll give you some scraps for Joe Savisky."

"Okay, Mama. Mr. Hardesty, I want to show you my six-gun."

"I'll look at your gun on one condition."

"What?"

"That you call me Jake."

Charley sneaked a look at his mother who smiled and nodded her head.

"Okay, Jake! Let's go!"

Charley flung open the screen door and ran outside. Jake caught the door before it banged shut and stood for a moment, one boot still in the kitchen and the other on the porch. The fact was he didn't want to leave Willa, not even for a moment. Willa put down the dirty dishes she was holding and moved to him. He wrapped his arms around her, and they clung together in an embrace that left them both trembling.

"I'm right here, Jake," Willa whispered. "Go on outside. I'm not going anywhere."

Get With It
1938

THAT SUMMER OF 1938 A new wind sang through Oklahoma. The wind still whistled down the phone lines, shook the cottonwoods, rattled the wheat stubble and tossed the sagebrush into a rolling blue-green sea, but after years of blowing nothing but drought and dust and despair, the wind changed. Everyone felt the new rhythm and opened their windows and listened. The wind blew a new song of green fields and fat cattle, a song echoed by a fresh new sound, a bluesy, jazzy, red-hot music. Steel guitars and fiddles and saxophones and clarinets all swinging together with a steady, heart-pounding backbeat. It was music made for dancing the quick quick, slow slow rhythm of the Texas two-step or the triple-step, rock-step of Oklahoma swing dancing. The music set couples spinning and twirling, hands clasping and unclasping, thighs and calves brushing and touching, bodies pushing and pulling together, dancing and celebrating, saying We're alive! We survived!

The happy-even-when-it-was-sad music was created by Bob Wills and his Texas Playboys, a sound mimicked but unequalled by every country band in Oklahoma. The combination of two bands in one, a string band and a horn band, produced the Bob Wills sound, later called Western Swing. It mixed old-time frontier fiddle, Negro blues and New Orleans jazz, big band swing and rural folk music, the perfect remedy for a state and a country coming out of a depression.

Willa collected Bob Wills's records, hung up his smiling photograph next to her portrait of Roosevelt, and dreamed of seeing Wills and his Playboys in person. When she left Dr. Simmons's office and walked home for lunch, every radio along the way was tuned to Tulsa's KVOO and from the open windows she could hear *Fan It*, *Faded Love*, or *Whoa Baby*, all punctuated with Bob Wills's distinctive *Aaaah – haa*.

Get With It was her favorite Wills number, and "Get with it" became Willa and Jake's catchphrase, their exhortation to dance faster, work harder, and later, in their darkest moments, to lift their eyes and move forward.

And the phrase also carried a private meaning. They made love for the first time on the banks of a farm pond just over the Oklahoma-Kansas line. They were driving back late from a Saturday night dance in Ashland, Kansas. Jake looked at Willa, she nodded yes, and he stopped the car on a deserted dirt road. He pulled apart the barbed wire strands of the fence while she climbed through. Jake spread out a horse blanket on the dewy ground. Three curious white-faced heifers ambled over. Bullfrogs plopped in and out of the water and joined their bass note grunts to the crickets' trilling mating songs. A coyote yowled and yipped, calling her absent partner. A light breeze brought the scent of fresh-cut alfalfa and damp mud. The moon had set, and Jake and Willa undressed and lay under a black satin sky jeweled with stars. Slowly, as if they had all the time in the world, they explored each other—every soft hollow, hard muscle, and smooth bone—as curious about each other as the three heifers that gazed at them.

Jake's calloused hands lingered on Willa's breasts, marveling at their firm, full perfection.

"What's this?" Willa asked, her fingers probing the deep, ugly scar carved in Jake's left thigh.

"Just an old gunshot wound."

"Somebody shot you! Why?"

"A little mix-up in Dodge City. I'll tell you about it some time."

Willa's hand explored higher and Jake lost control. "I'm sorry," he groaned, wiping himself with the blanket.

Willa laughed. She had never felt so happy or so powerful. She stretched, threw out her arms, lifted her high full breasts and arched her lean brown body. "Come on, Jake," she crooned, just another animal calling her mate, "get with it."

After that moment, Willa and Jake spent every non-working moment together, moving on the dance floor and everywhere else in a paired rhythm that seemed to them as natural as breathing and about as essential. They were inseparable, and everyone called them Willa'n'Jake.

They talked about how much money they'd saved, and they made plans to get married before Christmas. They talked about renting a place north of Enid. About the babies they would have who would help them work the land and be playmates for Charley. About what a smart, good boy Charley was. About Willa's passion for Bob Wills and FDR. About Jake's memories of the 101 Ranch and how much he missed his brothers and how he never really knew his mother. They opened their hearts, and yet their mouths never spoke the words "I love you." They didn't need to. Their bodies and eyes spoke for them.

Jake loved everything about Willa. She had good common sense and was smarter than he was, but he didn't mind. He loved her take-charge attitude. He loved her silky brown skin, huge brown eyes, and her white straight teeth, and he loved that she sensed what he needed before he even knew he wanted it. Willa loved Jake's strong, scarred body and the way he could make her laugh just with a wink or a grin. She loved that he followed her on the dance floor and that he wanted her advice. She loved how hard he worked, and she loved his big, capable battered hands that could fix anything. And she loved how much he needed her. But mostly she loved how he cared for Charley.

No matter how tired they were after a week of work, they spent every Saturday night dancing, and every Sunday afternoon with Charley. Jake taught the boy to shoot and rope, to spear frogs, and to swim and float on his back. While Jake took Charley off on horseback with Joe Savisky to hunt rabbits, Willa hemmed Jake's pants, shortening the left pant legs by three-quarters of an inch so that they wouldn't drag in the dirt or get caught under his boot.

One Sunday afternoon at the Old Freedom homestead, Willa washed dishes under the open kitchen window and listened to Jake and Charley as they talked on the porch.

"Why do you walk like this?" Charley asked, imitating Jake's limp.

"Because my left leg is shorter than my right. Has a piece of steel in it."

"Where?"

Jake sat down next to Charley on the porch. "Right here. Feel it?"

"But why?"

"Well, it's a secret. Can you keep a secret?"

"Sure!"

Willa stopped washing dishes, lit a cigarette, and listened. There were mysteries about Jake. She saw the way he looked at the men who flirted with her at dances. His grin disappeared, his eyes narrowed, and he would step in front of her, and the men would move on. She knew about his trips to Enid for liquor, and while she tolerated his selling liquor, she didn't like it. Even though the Woods County sheriff was one of Jake's customers, it was still illegal and wrong. And she didn't trust fat Senator Drummond, who showed up from time to time in his fancy black car to talk to Jake.

Jake leaned against the porch post. He lowered his voice, but Willa could hear him clearly. The house was quiet except for Doc snoring softly on the couch in the living room and the rustle of Lizzie's newspaper as she read her serial.

"Well, Charley, it was like this," Jake said, his voice low

and rumbling. "It was real early one morning on the Eden ranch. I was on Fortney riding pasture. Joe Savisky had run off somewhere and then I heard him, kind of yelping, not a bay like when he'd treed a coon, but this was different. He sounded worried."

"What'd you do?" said Charley, scratching behind Joe Savisky's ears. The dog lay sleeping at Charley's feet. He opened his eyes when he heard his name and then yawned, as if he'd heard this story before. He rested his snout on Charley's bare right foot and went back to sleep.

"I followed his yelps to over by Wildcat Hill," Jake continued, "and then into that box canyon, you know the one, where we chased that jackrabbit. Anyway, there's a lot of brush and fallen cedars in that canyon and Fortney was slowly picking his way along. Then I saw Joe Savisky. He was on his belly kind of whimpering and looking up at something on the rim of the canyon and so I looked up there too. And then I saw it! It was a big one!" Jake paused and rubbed his left leg.

"What was it?" demanded Charley.

"A big old mountain lion stretched out staring at us with his round yellow eyes. So I reached for my rifle and raised it and that lion raised up too and just watched me. Like he was daring me to shoot."

"Did you?"

"I was just about to pull the trigger and then Fortney shied sideways and the next thing I knew that lion jumped off the canyon right at me. He knocked me off Fortney and my gun went flying. Fortney ran off and Joe Savisky hightailed it

130

after him. So there I was all alone, sprawled on the ground and the rifle was yards away."

"What'd the lion do?"

"He was growling and snuffling, kind of stomping back and forth, whipping his tail, watching me. I started crawling toward my gun, but then the lion did the damndest thing."

"What?" said Charley, moving closer to Jake. "What did he do?"

"He looked at me, then he looked at the rifle. I swear he grinned. Then he padded over to it, his paws were big, about as big around as my hands, and they kicked up little puffs of dust. Then he put his right paw on the trigger, flicked his claws, and pulled. Bang! That bullet hit me right here in my leg."

"Did it hurt?"

"It hurt like hell! But it wasn't bleeding much."

"What'd the lion do then?"

"Well, I guess he thought he'd finished me with one shot. He roared once, but I just laid there real quiet and didn't move a muscle. Then he turned around and limped off down the canyon."

"Why was he limping?"

"I guess he must have hurt his leg when he jumped. After a bit, I yelled for Joe Savisky and Fortney, and they came back hanging their heads and looking all sorry. I tied my bandana around my leg and rode back to the ranch. Mr. Eden drove me to the hospital in Alva. I looked for that mountain lion everywhere, but I never saw him again."

"But why's it a secret?"

"I couldn't tell the old boys back at the ranch that a mountain lion got the drop on me! Promise not to tell? Not even your mother? It'll be our secret."

"I promise!"

Jake stood up. He looked through the kitchen window into Willa's wide brown eyes. He shrugged and grinned. Willa laughed, stubbed out her cigarette, and plunged her hands into the cold dishwater.

"Get with it, Charley," said Jake. "Let's go see if your mama will give us some of her cherry pie."

The last week of July Willa asked Doc and Lizzie to watch Charley so she and Jake could spend a weekend in Tulsa with Arlene Murphy, now Arlene Shelton, who had finally snared a rich husband. Bob Wills and his Playboys were appearing in Tulsa and Arlene promised to take them to the show.

"You sure this is the right address?" Jake asked, as he guided his Ford onto a paved circular driveway.

"It's 2100 South Madison, right?"

"Yeah."

"Well, this is it then."

He stopped the car, and he and Willa got out and stretched, admiring the beauty of the house. The Shelton mansion, a three-story neo-classic red brick house with a green tile roof and white stone pillars, had been built south of downtown Tulsa by Bill Shelton, who made a fortune when the Glenn Pool oil field was discovered. Bill Shelton, Jr. was a chubby, soft-spoken man with thinning hair, ten years older than Arlene. He greeted Jake and Willa politely and then disappeared.

Everything about the antique-filled house, the beautifully terraced grounds, the forty-foot dining room with hand painted murals, the spacious guest bedrooms and marble bathrooms whispered money, no money problems here, no worries about depression or dust storms or drought in this house. As Arlene guided them through the rooms, Willa admired everything, but she could see that Arlene, who looked beautiful in a white summer dancing dress, was unhappy. Her mouth curved into a wide grin, but her eyes didn't smile. She explained that her husband had just been called away on business. In fact, she added, he traveled a lot, while she rattled around in the house. She had a cook and two maids. "What do you do all day?" Willa wanted to know. Arlene said she read a lot, puttered in the garden when it wasn't too hot, and went to the club and lunched with her friends. She joked that she wanted a houseful of kids, but with Bill gone so much she didn't know how she'd manage it. And, she shopped every day. As proof, she showed Willa her large walk-in closet stuffed with dresses and shoes and hats. Arlene put Willa and Jake in separate guest rooms with a shared bath on the second floor.

After a cold supper, Willa and Jake changed into their dancing clothes. Willa wore her black and white sundress with black open-toed heels. Jake changed into his good black pants, hemmed and ironed by Willa, a white western shirt with a black bolo tie, and his good boots, which he'd shined the night before. Arlene drove them the four miles to Cain's Ballroom in her 1938 white Cadillac.

By the time they arrived at Cain's on North Main, a line of people had formed waiting to get in. Arlene took them around the line and knocked on a side door. A bald, heavyset man greeted her like an old friend and led them into the ballroom.

Willa clung to Jake's arm as they pushed through the crowd of sweating dancers. She had been to a lot of dances, but nothing like this. The ballroom was enormous. And the floor was just like she'd heard. She bounced up and down, and the curly wood maple floor moved with her. It was set on springs and made dancing effortless.

Hundreds of people were dancing. All of Tulsa seemed to be there. Men in business suits and ties. Roughnecks in oil-stained overalls and grimy t-shirts, looking as if they'd come straight from the fields. Cowboys in faded jeans and dirty Stetsons. Women and girls of every age wearing flower-splashed cotton dresses, swirled and twirled in the fan-cooled air.

And then, suddenly, close enough to touch, Willa saw them on the bandstand. Bob Wills, at the microphone, handsome and smiling, in his trademark white Stetson and tailored Western suit; Big Leon McAuliffee, over six feet tall and over two hundred pounds, making his steel guitar look small; and the rest of the Playboys, all smiling, all happy. The Playboys always smiled. They never took an intermission. While one of the boys took a break the others kept playing. Bob Wills believed that keeping people dancing kept them from drinking and fighting. If a conflict did break out, he'd raise his fiddle and start playing a sad, slow hymn. Usually the fight ended before he got halfway through it. No one wanted to listen to *The Old Rugged Cross* when they could stomp to *Never No More Hard Time Blues*.

"Take it away, Leon!" Wills called. He caught Willa's eye and winked. Wills's smile and the melody of the steel guitar washed over her, and Willa thought she was going to burst with happiness.

"Get with it, Willa!" Jake shouted in her ear.

They changed partners on the fast dances but always found each other during the ballads. Willa picked up a new dance from a traveling salesman, who taught her the St. Louis version of the Shag. Once in a while, they spotted Arlene in the crowd with a tall, young cowboy.

"Rhythm floating everywhere," Willa sang along with Bob Wills. Rhythm had taken over her body, and she didn't even stop for a cigarette break. Once, Willa saw Jake walk out the door with a fat man in a black suit who looked like Senator Drummond, but Jake soon reappeared, snatching her from her partner and twirling her away.

After Bob Wills played the last song, he and his Playboys lined up at the door and shook hands with everyone as they left the ballroom. Wills clasped Willa's hand in both of his and said, "I was watching you, little one. You're a fine dancer." To Jake, he said, "And you're a lucky man."

"Yes sir," said Jake.

They walked to the car and waited for Arlene. After a

few minutes she appeared leaning unsteadily on the arm of the tall cowboy. Arlene tossed the car keys to Jake. "You two go on home," she said. "I'll see you later."

"Are you sure?" Willa called, but Arlene had already moved away, laughing at something the cowboy whispered in her ear.

Later, they lay in the four-poster bed in Willa's room, too jazzed to sleep.

"Marriage has got to be just like dancing," Jake said, "the man leading, and the woman following."

"But I always lead!"

"I just let you think you do."

"I think marriage is about no lies, ever."

Jake was silent. Willa rolled over, her face close to his. "Don't you agree, Jake?"

"Sure."

"So, what were you doing with Senator Drummond?"

"Oh, he just wanted me to run a little errand for him."

"What kind of an errand? The truth, okay?"

"He gave me some money and papers to take to my dad."

"Why?"

"Some deal they have going on."

"What kind of a deal?"

"There are people Drummond's got to pay off and he can't do it himself. He's known us for years and trusts us. And everybody makes out. Don't worry about it."

"So your dad's paying bribes for Drummond? What if he gets caught?"

"He won't. He's been doing it for years."

"I don't want you doing that. It's not right."

"I'm just helping out a friend. The senator has been real good to us."

"Don't ever lie to me, Jake."

He yawned. "Okay."

"Swear it. Dammit I mean it!"

"Okay, I swear. Now let's get some sleep."

The next morning Arlene's maid fixed a big southern breakfast. The maid said Arlene wasn't feeling well and sent her apologies for not being able to say goodbye.

As they drove away, Willa turned and looked at the Shelton's elegant red brick house. Whenever her mother complained about their shabby old house, Doc always said, "a house doesn't make a home, Lizzie." Willa always sided with her mother, but now she realized that Doc was right.

They took turns driving and napping and got back to Old Freedom at 2:00. Charley was waiting for them on the porch. They drove to the Cimarron and fished with two cane poles. No one caught anything. But it didn't matter. They were together. Willa'n'Jake'n'Charley.

The Price of Gas
Winter, 1938 - January 7, 1939

TIME SLOWED DOWN FOR WILLA. Her mind was clear, and she was curiously calm. She watched her cigarette fall slowly to the floor and worried that she needed to stub it out. She felt Jake's arm push hard against her chest. She braced her legs against the floor. The inside of the car was bright as day. She saw Annie Shaw's hands gripping the steering wheel and Annie's mouth open in a silent scream. She noticed a smudge of bright red lipstick on Annie's front teeth.

It was an ordinary Saturday night. Except Annie finished early with the Gyp Hill Boys and wanted Willa and Jake to go with her to Waynoka to hear a new band called "Spurs in the Heart." Annie had just bought a used Ford and wanted to drive. Jake sat in the middle so Willa could blow her cigarette smoke out the window. They were a half-mile south of Freedom when Annie noticed the gas gauge showed near empty. Instead of filling up in Freedom, where gas was fourteen cents a gallon, she decided to double back to Camp Houston, where she could buy it for eleven cents. They bought twelve gallons of gas and were halfway back to Freedom, just past the spot where the road dipped, when they saw the headlights coming right at them.

Jake had his right arm around Willa, and he threw his left arm in front of her. Annie screamed. "Oh Shit!" and turned the wheel sharply to the right.

Willa heard a horrifying sound of ripping, crunching metal and breaking glass. Then the lights blew out and everything was quiet.

Senator Ed Drummond leaned back and read the *Enid Morning News*. It was just a small article reprinted from the *Alva Courier* on page 16, and easy to miss, but the senator made a daily habit of reading every article in the newspaper. You never knew when a bit of information would come in handy.

Senator Drummond also made a habit of taking care of his people, a network of drivers, shoeshine boys, policemen, and old friends like John Hardesty and his three sons, who served him and helped keep his three-decade political career alive and his whiskey business profitable. Crooked yet kind, he both made and bent the law.

After eating his usual breakfast of four eggs over easy, a slab of bacon, fried potatoes, three pieces of toast, and coffee at the Enid Diner, Drummond brushed toast crumbs off his lapel, straightened his carnation, and buttoned his gray suit over his bulging belly. He waddled to his black Cadillac idling at the curb. Two men in cowboy hats, with faces as hard and as expressionless as fence posts, lounged in the front seat. Drummond settled himself in the back seat. "Boys," he said, "drive over to Martha and Francis's and pick up John Hardesty. We're going to Alva Memorial."

At Alva Memorial Hospital, Lizzie sat in a chair pulled close to Willa's bed. Lizzie was reading the *Freedom Call* aloud hoping that Willa would open her eyes. Willa had been unconscious and non-responsive since the accident four days earlier. Dr. Simmons set both of Willa's broken ankles and taped her broken ribs. He treated her cuts and bruises, probed for internal injuries, but there was nothing he could do about the concussion. "We'll just have to wait and see," he told Lizzie and Doc, who took turns sitting with Willa. For the time being, Charley was staying with Dean and Cissie in Old Freedom.

Every few hours or so, Jake hobbled into the room, his head shaved and bandaged where flying glass had cut it, and his face and arms covered with gashes and scratches and bruises. He looked terrible, but except for two broken ribs and a badly sprained left ankle, he felt okay. He had been released, but he couldn't bear to leave Willa and had sweet-talked the nurses into fixing him a cot in a storeroom. When Willa was alone, he'd sit on the bed, rub her hands and feet, and kiss her cheek, carefully avoiding the bandages and the cuts.

"Get with it, Willa," he whispered in her ear. He spoke to her in his husky, low voice, telling her the news, trying to make her laugh, hoping that she could hear him. He told her about Joe Savisky keeping Charley company at Dean and Cissie's. About Senator Drummond, who'd driven up from Enid. He brought Jake's dad with him and a big bouquet of red roses for Willa. Seeing that Jake wouldn't be able to work at the ranch for a while, the senator offered him a job. He'd just have to spell the boys with driving and keep the Cadillac in good condition. "I told him I had other plans," Jake whispered. "I'm not going to leave you, Willa." Jake didn't tell Willa that Senator Drummond had paid his hospital bill. The senator's generosity always came with a price. But he'd worry about that when the time came.

When Doc and Lizzie asked him about the accident, Jake said he should have been at the wheel, maybe he would have been able to avoid the truck that had veered into their lane. The truck driver said that Annie's car just suddenly appeared in front of him. Annie's father protested that the driver must have fallen asleep. "What was he doing making a grocery delivery at 10:30 at night?" The sheriff couldn't determine who was at fault and said it was an unfortunate accident. What did it matter now whose fault it was? Jake thought. Willa's best friend Annie, who had just turned twenty-two, would never play the piano again. She was buried on Tuesday in the Shaw family plot in the Freedom cemetery.

On Wednesday, four days after the accident, Willa found herself stranded in a vast, gray haze. She felt herself drifting away, disappearing into a bank of cold, distant clouds. Then something called to her, something warm and glowing from deep inside her, and she knew she wasn't alone. Could it be? Oh, I hope so! she thought. She floated away from the clouds toward the warmth, and then she smelled roses. The scent was sweet and very close. She struggled to see through the milky haze. Someone touched her face, cupped her cheek and then stroked her hand. A familiar hand. Jake. Jake was with her in the fog. Willa tried to grab his hand, but she was worn out, too tired to move. Then he pulled her toes and rubbed the soles of her feet. His touch felt wonderful, and then it was gone.

Suspended in the watery mist, Willa floated. Hands, like ropes thrown from a far shore to a sinking swimmer, flew into the mist, caught her and tugged her back and up into the world. Dr. Simmons's hands, smooth and sure and smelling of antiseptic. Lizzie's hands, soft and creamy with lotion that she massaged into Willa's arms and back and legs. And her father's long fingers knotted with arthritis stroked her forehead, cooled her lips with ice, and checked her pulse. And her three sisters' hands—Cissie's quick and strong so like her own, Dilly's nervous and chapped with bitten fingernails, and Ro's plump, soothing hands—thrust through the fog to brush her hair, wash her face, clean her teeth, apply cold cream and lipstick. Heck's lean, hard hands gripped hers and pinched, and then his thin fingers tickled her feet and drummed softly on her arms, beating out a rhythm. Jake's hands seemed always near. Rough and calloused, with swollen oversized knuckles and thick fingers, they pulsed with life.

Eight days after the wreck, Doc gazed out the window of Willa's hospital room into a dark, deserted parking lot. His eyes were red and sore. He rubbed his back, which was stiff from hours of sitting in a hard chair. Everyone else, except for Jake, had gone home depressed and exhausted. That afternoon Cissie brought Charley in to see his mother for the first time since the accident. Charley patted Willa's face and hands and urged her to wake up. "Jake's taking me coon hunting, Mama," Charley told her. "And we're going to shoot some wild turkeys for Thanksgiving!" Then Charley kissed her and said goodbye. Willa never stirred.

Doc turned to look at his daughter. Her breathing was easy and relaxed. The color had returned to her cheeks. Then, suddenly he was furious. "Goddamn it all to hell, Mug, wake up!" He shook her slender shoulder. "Mug! Wake up! We got work to do! You need to get on with your life!"

Willa's eyelids fluttered open. Her brown eyes flecked with gold stared at him, alert and concerned. "Daddy? Why are you yelling?"

Tears filled Doc's eyes, and he turned away so she wouldn't see.

"Is something wrong?" she asked.

Everyone noticed that Willa was different after the accident. There was an air of concentrated purpose and awareness about everything she did, from sewing on a button, kneading bread, mopping floors, or waxing flowers for Annie's grave. Her eyes seemed larger, more searching and more intent. Willa felt the difference, too, but she didn't know how to explain it. She understood, though, that every moment of her life, every beat of her heart mattered, because life was made up of fragile moments, and life could end, as Annie's had, in an instant.

Before she was released from the hospital, Dr. Simmons confirmed her hopes. She was pregnant. She told Jake first, and then she told her parents. She saw them look from her to Jake, wondering, but hesitant to ask. Her father looked disappointed. Before she could say anything, Jake spoke. He lied so convincingly that Willa, for a moment, believed him.

"Sorry," he said. "I guess we should have told you we got hitched. Remember that weekend in October, it was raining to beat all, when Willa and I drove up to visit my Aunt Mattie and Uncle Herman in Kansas?"

Doc and Lizzie said they didn't recall.

"Well, it was a helluva drive, but before we went to see them, I asked Willa if she wanted to stop at the Ashland Courthouse first. She said yes and the judge married us that morning. We've been saving our money and wanted to keep it quiet until we got set up on our own. We wanted it to be right for Charley and have a home for him to go to." Jake grinned his wide grin and winked at Willa.

When she saw the relief on her father's face, and on her mother's, too, Willa was grateful for Jake's lie. Not all lies were bad, she realized, some were good. Necessary stories. Stories that could heal.

On Saturday morning, January 7, 1939, Willa and Jake drove to Ashland, Kansas and made the lie true. Despite her crutches, Willa looked elegant in a long-sleeved cranberry red wool dress with a dropped waist. She wore a matching cranberry wool cloche over her black hair that waved to her shoulders. Jake wore a dark blue suit, borrowed from his brother Jimmy.

"Maybe the suit will bring you better luck than it brought me," Jimmy remarked, when Jake picked it up. Jimmy had been unhappily married for six years to Sally Sneed, pretty and thin with a sweet face but a sour, grasping disposition. Sally cared only about money. Jimmy boxed and worked two jobs, but he never seemed to make enough money for Sally. "I've got Willa," Jake told him. "I don't need luck." Jake slid a plain gold band on Willa's finger. They were declared man and wife by O. T. Landers, Probate Judge, who signed a certificate stating that Jake Hardesty, twenty-one, and Willa Stone, twenty-one, were united in marriage. When Jake gave his age as twenty-one to the judge, Willa didn't say anything. After the ceremony, she asked him why he had cut off two years. He shrugged. "I just thought we should start out the same."

Later, Willa found her old ink eraser from school. Carefully, so she wouldn't tear the paper, she erased the date from the certificate. Then, she looked at a 1938 and 1939 calendar, calculated the days and months, and using the same black ink the Probate Judge had used, she inserted October 14, 1938. She considered Jake's false age on the certificate. She could correct it. But why bother? Maybe he was right.

On the way home from Ashland, perhaps because it was a part of his made-up story, Jake decided to stop at Aunt Mattie's and Uncle Herman's farm and introduce them to Willa. Since he'd run away from them as a boy, he never returned to their place. The few times he'd seen them at Aunt Martha's in Enid, Uncle Herman was cordial; Aunt Mattie cold and indifferent.

It was close to noon, but Aunt Mattie didn't offer them anything to eat or even a cup of coffee. Herman was out at a sale, she said, and she was saving dinner for him. Willa had met Martha and Molly, Jake's other Aunt M's, who had the square Hardesty jaw, were round and white-haired, warm and jolly. Aunt Mattie was also square-jawed, plump, and white-haired, but there the resemblance to her sisters ended. She was aloof and tight-lipped. It was a sunny day, but Mattie had drawn the curtains, and the house was gloomy and dark. Willa excused herself to use the bathroom, and when she turned on the light, cockroaches skittered under the bathtub. Willa's stomach heaved. Fifteen minutes after they arrived, Jake said they had to be on the road. He thanked Aunt Mattie for her hospitality, even though all she had offered was chairs to sit on. Willa shook her limp hand, and they left.

Outside, Willa breathed in the clean January air and held her face toward the sun. "How could you stand living there?"

"Well, I didn't really. I bunked in the barn with the dogs and cows. Much nicer company." Jake laughed at Willa's stricken expression. "Aunt Mattie's always felt sorry for herself, Willa. She and Herman couldn't have any babies. It made her bitter. I feel sorry for her."

"Well, I don't. I know why she doesn't turn on any lights. Her house is filthy. I saw cockroaches in the bathroom!"

Jake reached into Willa's hair at the back of her neck and pinched. "You mean like this one?" he said, holding out his hand.

Willa screamed. And then laughed as Jake showed her his empty hand and pulled her close.

Just Willa

"Let's go home, Mrs. Hardesty."
"But we don't have a home, Mr. Hardesty."
"I do."
"Oh yeah, where?"
"You, Willa. You're my home."

A Pleasant Day
January 26, 1939

"*OLD FREEDOM NEWS*, BY LIZZIE Sharpe

"Well, there's been a lot going on in Old Freedom these past months. So much going on, in fact, that this old lady has been too busy to write her news column. Things have settled down a bit, and I've even found time to take my daily walk and catch up with the serial. Up here in Old Freedom, we're all grateful for the inch of rain we got last week. It sure helped the wheat. Last Sunday at the Doc Sharpe home a good dinner of fried chicken and all the trimmings was enjoyed by all including Heck and Lucy Sharpe, Jake and Willa Hardesty and Charley, and Dean and Cissie Williams and their two boys. Heck and Lucy are living here with us at the home place until their house is moved out from Freedom. Willa and Jake are doubling up with Cissie and Dean until they can take over the farm they've leased north of Enid. So our houses are full up here on the hill. But that's the way we like it. Ro and Arlie Day and their boys, Stub and Nancy Sharpe and their two girls, and John Hardesty and sons Jimmy and Billy were afternoon callers. Ollie and Flo Sharpe visited by phone from Rocky Ford, Colorado. And my sister Pearl and her husband Al Davis visited by phone from Wichita. I didn't hear from my daughters Edith and Effie, but did have long letters from them at Christmas. Everyone enjoyed ice cream and cake to celebrate the January birthdays of Jake, Willa, and Charley. Later, the men played pitch, the women sewed, and the kids were underfoot and running in and out banging the door. It was a pleasant day. I imagine it was a lot like your Sunday. We feel blessed, but like President Roosevelt we're keeping an eye on Hitler."

Days of the Week
March and April 1939

WILLA FLUNG OPEN THE LIVING room windows. The March wind was soft and warm, promising a nice day. Everyone else had gone to a farm sale in Fair Valley. Jake wanted to buy a milk cow and a Deval No. 12 cream separator for Willa. She had stayed at Cissie and Dean's to finish her sewing. They would be moving in two weeks, and she wanted everything to be ready.

Using fabric from flour sacks she had saved and bleached, her mother's embroidery thread, and copying Lizzie's whimsical designs, Willa was embroidering Saturday, her seventh day of the week tea towel. Saturday's towel featured a pink cup with red lips and dark brown eyes wearing black high heels dancing with a blue saucer with bright blue eyes and black cowboy boots. She had just finished Sunday's towel, on which appeared a smiling knife, fork, and little spoon holding hands, surrounded by yellow, black-eyed daisies.

After weeks of sewing, embroidering, and crocheting, Willa had almost filled with sheets and pillowcases, tablecloths, doilies, towels and washcloths, the white trunk John Hardesty made for her. She washed and ironed Charley's old baby clothes, hemmed dozens of new diapers, made a few new gowns, and wrapped everything in tissue to wait for the baby who would arrive, according to Dr. Simmons, around the middle of July.

Willa touched her swelling stomach. It was wonderful to be a married woman and not have to hide her pregnancy. She wondered if it would be a boy or a girl. Charley said he was wishing for a little sister. It didn't matter to Willa or to Jake. They just wanted a healthy baby and were thankful when the doctor assured them that it was too small to have been injured in the car wreck.

Willa felt fine now, although her ankles ached sometimes. Especially when she danced. She and Jake danced for the first time since the accident at the American Legion in Alva to celebrate President Roosevelt's birthday and raise money for infantile paralysis. The Gyp Hill Boys played, and Willa blinked back tears when she saw another young woman sitting in Annie's place at the piano. She was reminded of the accident daily when she brushed her hair and pulled it back at the right temple. A one-inch, jagged scar marked the place where her head had hit the car's doorpost.

Willa finished embroidering the long black eyelashes on the cup's face, knotted the thread, and cut it with her teeth. She stretched and looked out the window at the greening wheat. Soon, she mused, she would be looking out her own window in her own house.

It was good to sit and rest for a moment and just do

nothing. The past few months had been filled with helping Cissie with the cooking and housework and getting ready for their move. When she was able to walk without crutches, Willa found occasional work in Freedom cleaning houses, wallpapering, and ironing. For his part, Jake took any job he could find. He scrubbed cisterns, hauled cattle, built fence, and worked in a gravel pit. She didn't know that he also made two liquor runs to Illinois with his brother Jimmy for Senator Drummond. Jake just said that he was driving for the senator. He didn't consider it lying. He was driving for the senator, but he knew Willa didn't approve of bootlegging, and he didn't want her to worry. Willa did worry and suspected that Jake was running liquor, but when he returned safely and gave her two hundred dollars, she didn't question him.

Willa smiled to herself as she thought about the recent visit of her old teacher Webb Connell. His hair was thinning on top, but he had kept his boyish enthusiasm for trains. Webb stopped by, bringing a bookcase with glass doors, a wedding gift from his mother, who had sold her house in Alva and moved to her other son's farm. Webb was still working for the Santa Fe, but he told Willa that in a few years, he'd probably be a soldier in Europe. "There's going to be a war," he said. "A big one."

Willa admired the Saturday tea towel before she folded it and placed it with the others in the ironing pile. Her mother's designs were amusing and would help make drying dishes a pleasure. As she sat enjoying the breeze from the window and deciding what to work on next, a car turned into the driveway and came to a screeching stop. Willa went to the door to see who it was. It was Dilly, but she made no move to get out of the car. Willa walked to the car and opened the door. Dilly slumped over the steering wheel, sobbing.

"Dilly! What's wrong?"

Dilly, chest heaving, lifted her head and looked at Willa. Tears streamed down Dilly's bruised face. Her lip was split and bleeding, her right eye was swollen shut, her hair was tangled, and her white blouse was ripped and filthy.

Dilly threw herself into Willa's arms and bawled in great, howling bursts. After a while, she calmed down enough to walk with Willa into the house. Reluctantly, she told Willa that Hal had beaten her. "He was drunk," she sobbed.

"Where are your kids?"

"I took them to the boarding house and left them with Alma Ritter. They're okay. He'd never hurt the kids."

Later that day when Jake and Dean returned, they listened to Dilly's story and went to Freedom to have a little talk with Hal. They returned two hours later and said that Dilly could go home now.

"What did you do to him?" Willa asked Jake, as she creamed her face getting ready for bed.

"He was drunker than a skunk. But we sobered him up."

"How?"

"We took him out outside and did to him what he did to Dilly. And we told him if he ever hit her again, he'd end up buried in a canyon somewhere."

Hal never hit Dilly again, but mostly because he lacked the opportunity. After robbing the Square Deal store in Old Freedom of eighty dollars and slugging the clerk with a gun butt, Hal fled. He was soon arrested in Alva and sent to the state penitentiary in McAlester, leaving Dilly with four children and no means of support. Dilly moved in with Lizzie and Doc, took in ironing, cleaned houses, and received two dollars a week from the county relief fund. She was twenty-seven years old, but she looked at least forty. Her unhappiness and loss of beauty seemed a rebuke to Willa's happiness and radiant health.

Still, there was something in Willa's nature that never allowed her to relax completely and accept happiness when it came. Dilly's misery diminished her own joy. Jake's nature was simpler; he shook off adversity, shrugged away doubts, and enjoyed the moment. If she didn't stop herself, Willa often found her thoughts drifting to dire possibilities of what might happen.

"Don't ask for trouble," Jake advised. She knew he was right, but still she worried.

Jake kept his promise to take Charley coon hunting. All through January, every Friday and Saturday night as soon as it got dark, Jake, Charley, Dean and little Dean and Randy, loaded Joe Savisky and Dean's two black and tan coonhounds in Dean's truck, and headed out to hunt coon. Sometimes they drove as far west as the Panhandle to hunt in abandoned farm buildings where coons could find grain and seed that was left behind by suitcase farmers fleeing the dust. Other times they hunted along the river or along creek bottoms, letting the dogs loose to find the scent, and then listening for their voices to change when the track turned hot.

While they hunted, Willa fretted. She tried to sleep, but

she couldn't rest until they returned at dawn, dirty, wet, and hungry. Dean and Jake would carry the sleeping boys into the house and then stretch the hides on the side of the barn to dry.

Jake promised seven-year-old Charley a .22 of his own when he turned twelve. Until then, he said, Charley could make do with a Bowie knife in its own leather sheath that Jake gave him to carry on his first coon hunt. One Sunday morning in early March, when the coon hunting was done for the season, Charley and his cousin Dean decided to play at Indians hunting buffalo. They chased each other through the corrals and in and out of the barn. Then Charley spotted the furry coonskins hanging on the barn. He imagined they were a great herd of stampeding buffalo. With a piercing war whoop, he pulled his Bowie knife from its sheath and stabbed at the hides. Dean yelled at him to stop, but it was too late. Three of the hides, prime coonskins worth six dollars each, were slashed through.

When he saw Jake walking to the barn, Dean ran away. Charley tried to pull the fur over the cuts, but the knife had gone right through the skin. Avoiding Jake, Charley ran to the house and hid in the loft he shared with Dean and little Randy. Jake examined the ruined hides and walked to the house. Cissie had gone up to the home place, and Willa was alone in the kitchen washing the breakfast dishes.

"Charley! Get down here," Jake called, his voice sharp and urgent.

"What's wrong?" asked Willa.

"We'll soon find out," Jake said.

Head hanging, Charley trudged down the stairs.

"Look me in the eye, Charley. Did you cut those coon hides?"

"What?" said Willa, moving toward Charley.

"Go back to the kitchen, Willa. Well? Did you?"

"Yes, sir," Charley whispered.

"Did Randy or little Dean help you?"

"No, sir."

"We worked all night hunting those coons. Those hides are worth about eighteen dollars total. Do you have any money, Charley?"

"I've got fifty cents."

"Well, then, I'll just have to take the rest out of your hide." Jake ripped his belt from its loops.

Willa rushed out of the kitchen to stop him, but he shook his head at her, his eyes cold. "Come outside with me, Charley."

Charley looked at the belt and at his mother's stricken face. "No, I won't!" He ran to Willa and hid behind her.

"Get over here, boy. Now!"

"No, Jake! Leave it be. Can't you see he's sorry?" Willa's heart pounded. Charley's fear made her feel sick to her stomach.

"You're not my daddy! You can't tell me what to do!"

"Did you hear that, Willa? Are you going to put up with that?"

Willa looked down and away from Jake's accusing eyes. Charley was holding onto her dress. No one had ever hit Charley, not even Doc. And she never spanked him with anything but her hand.

"No, I won't put up with it, Jake. I'll punish him. Leave it to me."

Charley peeked out from behind Willa, sniffling, but confident that he was safe from the belt.

Suddenly, Jake lunged. He grabbed Charley and slung him over his shoulder.

"You bet I'm your daddy, boy. And don't you ever forget it."

Willa reached for Jake, but before she could stop him he was already out the door and onto the porch. Why didn't he listen to her? Charley screamed "Mama! Mama!" Willa turned her back, bit her lip and dug her nails into her palms. She heard the lash of the belt, one, two, three, and then four times as Charley screamed. More than anything she wanted to rush out and stop Jake. But she knew if she did, Charley would never consider Jake his real father. But Jake should have listened to her! Not just ignored her like she didn't have any say in what happened to Charley.

Finally, it was quiet, except for Charley's hiccups and sniffles. Willa unclenched her fists and walked out onto the porch, ready to comfort her son, but Jake looked at her and shook his head.

"Give me the knife," Jake said. "You can have it back when I think you're ready."

Charley unbuckled the strap and handed Jake the Bowie knife in its sheath.

"Now, I want you to tell your mother and me that you're sorry."

"Okay."

"Okay, what?"

"Okay, sir. I'm sorry." He looked at Willa. "I'm sorry Mama."

"No, you can do better than that."

Puzzled, Charley looked up into Jake's blue eyes. Jake winked at him and then he knew.

"I'm sorry. Daddy?"

"That's right."

Later in the evening Willa went to the barn and took down the three ruined coon hides. Using her biggest needle and heavy-gauge black thread, she drew the edges together and mended the rips. When she was finished, she tacked the hides on the barn. They wouldn't bring in as much, but they could be sold along with the others.

"You shouldn't have done that," Jake told her. But Willa couldn't help herself. She wanted to make life easier for Charley. She figured an eighteen dollar debt was too high a price for him to pay for a few moments of thoughtless play.

The days and weeks passed, and it was April 1, moving day. Willa's notebook was filled with lists, and she was done with her sewing. She had starched and ironed the tea towels, packed them in the white trunk, and closed the latch.

From now on, she would live her days in her own house. With Jake and Charley and the new baby and the others that would follow. She opened the door and walked outside into the morning light.

"Let's go, Mama!" Charley shouted. "Daddy's waiting."

North of Enid
1939 and 1889

THE CARAVAN LEFT AT 7 A.M. on Saturday, April 1. Willa led the way in Jake's Ford, crammed with kitchen boxes and clothes. Cissie sat beside her, and in the backseat were Charley and Joe Savisky, with his head stuck out the window and ears blowing in the wind. Jake and Dean followed them in Dean's loaded pick-up pulling Fortney and the milk cow in a borrowed horse trailer. Doc and Stub trailed behind in Doc's pick-up stacked with furniture and boxes. Jake and his dad and Doc and Stub had moved the farm equipment, tools, and chickens on Friday.

Lizzie stayed behind in Old Freedom to watch little Dean and Randy. Her contribution to the move was a filled picnic basket and a jug of iced tea for them to enjoy when they arrived around noon. Willa was only moving east about ninety miles, but to Lizzie it seemed a continent. "You write me a letter now and then," she said, as she hugged Willa goodbye. "And tell me all your news. I'll put it in the *Call*."

The route was familiar to Willa. She'd driven it twice with Jake. First, drive east to Alva on 64. About nine miles west of Alva at Devil's Elbow, the land flattens and the familiar red dirt of Old Freedom changes to black soil. Keeping on 64, go through Alva and turn right about seven miles to Cherokee, still on 64, then through Jet and Nash to Four Corners and straight south to Midway. Then three miles east past Kremlin and then turn north on the bumpy dirt road for a mile and a quarter. A right turn, marked by a leaning rusted mailbox with Boyce painted on the side (I'll have to fix that, Willa thought), down a long, deeply rutted driveway lined with elm and mulberry trees. An apricot tree at the end of the driveway. Then home. Two tall American elms on the south side of the house. Two cedar trees, a lilac bush, and several honey locusts on the north. Cement path through the hard-packed dirt of the yard to the front door and around to the cement porch on the west side.

Willa and Jake found the place through Senator Drummond. He introduced them to Helen Boyce, who moved to Enid after her husband died. Her only child, a son, hated farming and went to Kansas City to work in insurance leaving his mother with no tenant and a wheat crop to harvest in June. Willa and Jake rented the farm on a 2/3-1/3 share, giving Mrs. Boyce a third of every crop, except they agreed to harvest the 1939 wheat crop and share it 50-50.

The Boyce place was fourteen miles north of Enid, a city of almost thirty thousand people, the fourth largest in Oklahoma. Pond Creek, seven miles straight north of the farm, had about a thousand people. Just south was Kremlin with a population of one hundred forty, many of them members of the Sedlak family who had emigrated from Bohemia in the 1880s.

Originally the town was called Wild Horse, because it

was near Wild Horse creek, where wild horses liked to water. Railroad officials didn't care for the name, and instructed M. A. Lowe, a railroad executive, to find a new name. Lowe gave the task to his horse-loving daughter. She came up with Kremlin, the name of her favorite saddle horse.

On the west side of town, the Sedlaks' original one-room general store had become a sprawling conglomeration of buildings containing a grocery, a hardware store, a filling station, and a farm implement company. The Sedlaks also owned the grain elevator and the bank. They actually owned most of the town except for the post office and a candy store which was operated by Henry Rathman and his sister, Caroline, the schoolteacher at the one-room Pleasant Valley school just north of town.

Jake knew Kremlin and the Sedlaks well. He and his dad and brothers had always been able to find work with them, either in a store or on one of their farms or ranches. During the 1930s, Rudolph Sedlak took over the land of busted farmers who couldn't pay their notes at his store. When his three sons married, he gave each one a section of land. His middle son, Glen, and his wife Doris owned a farm just south of the Boyce place.

The Boyce farm was the northwest quarter of a section, one hundred sixty acres, with eighty-two acres of wheat ground, forty acres of pasture, ten acres of oats, ten acres of maize, and fifteen acres of alfalfa. Sand Creek, fringed with cottonwoods, ran through the east pasture. The Santa Fe Railroad marked the farm's northern boundary. Outbuildings included a large barn with corrals, hog sheds, a chicken house, machine shed, and garage spread over three acres. A windmill, which pumped their water, was on the east side of the house. Willa was thrilled to discover they even had a phone, on a party line with a switchboard operator in Kremlin. Their ring was two shorts and a long.

The house was one-story, white painted wood. A cement porch with broad steps and a wide, waist-high wall faced west. A screened porch and a washhouse extended off the east side. There were three bedrooms with faded floral wallpaper, a fireplace in the living room, a dining room, a large indoor bathroom, a big kitchen, a cellar, and the promise of electricity in a few years.

Doc and Stub stopped in Pond Creek and bought a fifty-pound block of ice for the icebox so that it could be used immediately. While the men unloaded, Willa and Cissie swept, dusted, scrubbed, and stored. Willa checked carefully and saw no sign of cockroaches or mice. Charley finally decided he wanted the east bedroom off the kitchen instead of the west front bedroom. Willa and Jake took the large middle bedroom with the big closet and set up the crib there. Willa planned to use the front bedroom as her workroom and sewing room.

At noon, everyone took a break to eat the chicken sandwiches, potato salad, and oatmeal cookies that Lizzie had packed. They sat in the sun on the wall of the cement porch away from the brisk March wind. After everyone finished eating, Doc followed Willa into the kitchen.

"Come down to the creek with me, Mug."

Willa stopped spooning left-over potato salad into a smaller bowl.

"You mean right now?"

"This won't take long," he said. Willa grabbed her sweater, and Doc led her out past the barn and into the pasture. "See this good buffalo grass," he said, breaking off a stem. "Now look there."

"Are those wagon ruts? Was it a trail?"

"The Old Chisholm trail. When we brought the chickens yesterday, I recognized it. I came up that trail with a herd of cattle years ago. We grazed and watered the herd at Sand Creek to fatten them up a little before we pushed on into Kansas. There was always good, clean water in Sand Creek."

Willa waited. Clearly he wanted to tell her something. But she knew better than to press her father before he was ready. A cloud passed over the sun, and Willa shivered. Doc put his hand on her arm.

"I was going to live here."

"You mean right here? The Boyce place? Our place."

"That's right. But it wasn't anybody's place then."

"When?"

"Fifty years ago. In 1889. I marked it as a good spot to homestead. Plenty of water, trees, and good grass."

"It's a pretty place. But then something happened?"

"That's right. I never made the run."

"Mama always said tragedy struck and then you ran again in '93."

"And I told you that someday I'd tell you what happened.

I figured since I'd come back to this place maybe now would be a good time."

"Let's sit over here on this cottonwood trunk by the creek bank, Daddy. The work can wait for a bit."

She was worried about her father. He suddenly seemed very old and frail. He was never much of a talker. She knew if he wanted a private conversation it must be something important.

Her father sat beside her on the fallen tree trunk. When his breathing quieted, she prompted him.

"So it was the '89 land rush. Before you met Mama."

"That's right."

"How old were you?"

"I was twenty-four. I was all set to marry Maggie Cole."

"Maggie Cole?"

"She was a banker's daughter from Dodge City. I met her when I signed on with the Comanche Cattle Company. I was the ranch foreman at the headquarters south of Dodge. Maggie and I decided to make the run, file our claim, and then get married. I'd already marked this spot. So we packed the wagon, hitched up the mules, and headed to Caldwell to register."

"Why Caldwell?"

"Well, you could make the run in a couple places, but Caldwell was the closest spot to here. I'd never seen anything like it. Papers said there were more than fifteen thousand people in town. I'd never seen that many people all together. All kinds of people too. Rich and poor and everybody in between. Speculators came from as far away as Philadelphia and New York City. It was so damn hot. There hadn't been rain for weeks. The dust was flying. The stores almost ran out of supplies, and if you wanted a bucket of water, it cost you a dollar. But Maggie and I had a wagon full of supplies and plenty of food and water. Plus we had a plan to beat everybody. Be careful of plans, Mug."

Doc looked down into Sand Creek as if he was trying to find something in the rushing water.

"Go on, Daddy. What was your plan?"

"I had a really fine horse. Smokey. A dapple gray. Half thoroughbred, half quarter horse. It was Maggie's idea that she ride Smokey to the claim site while I drove the mules. I told her no, she'd drive the wagon and I'd ride Smokey. He was my horse. So she argued that she'd use her English saddle which weighed a lot less than my western saddle, and since she only weighed about one hundred ten pounds it would be less of a burden on Smokey. And he'd be a lot faster. And she was a better rider than me. And I couldn't argue with that either. Maggie could be pretty convincing. Oh, I wish you could have seen her, Willa. She was a sight. Funny, after all these years, I really can't remember her face that well, but I'll never forget how she sat a horse. While I waited in line to register, Maggie rode down Main Street on Smokey. People stopped whatever they were doing just to look at them. They looked like a picture in a book, Willa. I bet a lot of those people had never seen a horse like Smokey or a woman like Maggie. She had on her jacket and riding britches and her polished English boots, and she'd tied up her long blonde hair into a knot on her neck and wore one of those English hats. She sat on Smokey like a queen. Smokey was a showy horse, and Maggie loved the attention, too."

"Go on, Daddy. What was the rest of your plan?"

"Well, this here spot is about forty miles from Caldwell. Riding Smokey, Maggie would take the most direct route, ride fast, and beat out any rivals. The only problem was crossing Bluff Creek south of Caldwell. So we scouted the best place for her to cross. The creek was real shallow, but the banks were five to six feet high, which would stop wagons and ordinary horses and riders. A lot higher than these banks. Maggie said Smokey could scramble up the six-foot bank and give her a head start. I didn't like the idea of Maggie riding off by herself, but it was broad daylight, and Maggie was an expert rider. It was a good plan. It was a damn good plan. So I gave Maggie the white flag markers, and we waited for the gunshot."

"Gunshot?"

"That's right. The idea was that everyone, in each of the towns, would make the rush at the same time. Right at noon."

"And the cheating sooners jumped the gun."

"A lot of people, all kinds of bad people, jumped the gun, Willa. Free land is a powerful attraction. So the gun was fired and Maggie and Smokey took off. Now, the plan was that I would head west and cross where the creek's banks were a lot lower, but even though I knew it would slow me down, I wanted to make sure Maggie got up the high bank. By the time I got to Bluff Creek, I saw Maggie and another rider, who was on a big bay horse. He had the same idea. They both made it down the steep bank and were splashing through the water to the other side. The bay horse hit the bank first and then fell back and took part of the bank with him. His rider spurred him, the bay tried again, slid down again, and then balked. So the rider gave up and went off to find a better place to cross. I watched Maggie take her time and ride back and forth, letting Smokey pick his spot, and then when he did, she leaned down on his neck and Smokey scrambled up the steep bank. Just like she promised. When she got to the top, I shouted at her hoping she would turn and look at me before she headed into the open prairie."

Doc shuddered and ran both of his hands through his long white hair.

"What Daddy?"

"It's a terrible thing, Mug. I keep playing it out, over and over again in my head. Years will pass and I never think about it, but then something happens. Like coming here. To this spot. Or sometimes for no reason at all. I just see it all again."

"Tell me."

"Maggie must have heard me because she stands up in her stirrups and waves at me. Then Smokey shies and she almost loses her balance. Then I see what spooked Smokey. It's a man. A big fellow. Tall, heavyset. He's wearing a cap which looks too little for him. He's carrying a big canvas pack. He just comes out of nowhere. He moves closer to Maggie and grabs Smokey's reins. Maggie raises her left hand and shakes her head. Smokey pulls away back toward the creek bank, back toward me, but the man jerks him forward. I can hear Maggie screaming. I grab my rifle and start running. I lose sight of her when I slide down the bank. I run through the water and then half run, half crawl up the bank on the other side. When I get to the top of the bank, I lift my rifle ready to shoot the son-of-a-bitch, but there's nothing to see. Just empty prairie. No Maggie. No Smokey. No man. Then I spot her. She's a ways away. She looks so small. When I get closer, I see she's curled up like a kitten hiding in prairie grass. Her legs drawn up to her chest. Her arms folded in front of her. Blood on her torn white shirt. Her hat's gone. Blonde hair loose and blowing in the wind."

Doc coughed and spit phlegm into the dirt. He took a deep rattling breath. "I've never told anybody this, Mug. Not even your mother. Oh, she knew that I planned to marry Maggie Cole and then she died in the land rush. But not how. You see, it was all my fault. I let her talk me into something I knew was wrong. I never should have let her do it. It should have been me on Smokey. I would have killed that son-of-a-bitch!"

Why hadn't he told anyone? Willa wondered. Why keep it a secret all these years? Maybe it would have helped him to talk about it instead of letting it fester inside. Blaming himself for something he couldn't control. In that moment, Willa made herself a promise. Jake and I aren't going to be like that. We're going to talk about things. Not keep anything secret.

Willa laid her hand on her father's back. "What did you do then, Daddy?"

"Nothing I could do. She was gone. So I carry her across Bluff Creek to the wagon. I turn the mules back to Dodge City. There are so many goddamn prairie fires the whole sky is black. The homesteaders are burning the grass and running off free range cattle. I didn't know it then but it was the start of a range war. The ranchers hated the homesteaders and tried to run them out any way they could. They drove cattle through their claims, burned their dugouts, or just outright gunned them down. There wasn't much law then, so a lot of people went back to wherever they came from. Some of them got sick with dust pneumonia and died. Others were just too worn out to live."

"You didn't give up."

"No. But it took me years to get back on my feet. I didn't give up but I never got over it either. You know people are always saying time heals all wounds. But that's not been my experience."

Doc reached into his shirt pocket and removed a small metal pillbox. He pried open the lid and took out a swatch of long blonde hair curled into a loop.

"I remember that. It was in your medicine box. I used to sneak a look at it. I thought it was the hair of a fairy tale princess."

Doc rubbed the hair between his fingers. "I've mostly forgotten what she looked like. But I'll never forget her."

Doc put the tendril back in the pill box and snapped the lid shut. "Maggie's buried up in Dodge with her folks, but I want to bury this here, next to Sand Creek." Doc's hands shook, and he turned his face away from Willa.

"Give it to me, Daddy. I'll do it."

Willa found a heavy stick and using it as a trowel, she dug a deep hole in the sandy soil, high on the bank of the creek, safe from floodwaters. Doc wiped his face on his sleeve and watched as she laid the small metal box in the hole. Willa filled the opening with earth and patted the dirt smooth. She washed a flat stone in the creek and set it on the tiny grave. She cleaned her hands on the buffalo grass.

Willa and Doc stood for a time, looking down into the clear, swift-moving waters of Sand Creek and then up into the vast blue sky where a few high white clouds drifted. They thought about time and chance; they thought about loss and love. About never giving up. Then they turned their thoughts toward home and all the work that waited for them.

PART TWO

The Hub of the Wheel
1940-1942

"YOU'RE THE HUB OF THE wheel," Jake joked, picking up Willy and Annie, who were racing around Willa's legs while she nursed Frankie and stirred a pot of chicken and noodles.

Willa tried to establish a routine, but she never knew when an animal might get sick, or when Jake might need her to dash into town to get a part for the tractor, or when a storm threatened and she'd have to yank clothes off the line. Or sometimes Jake would quit early in the fields, take an outdoor shower, and say, "Pack up the kids!" And they'd be off to Enid or Alva or Pond Creek or someplace she'd never heard of. To see a man about a used combine or check out a farm sale or sometimes Jake just wanted to ride around looking at the crops, babies on their laps, and Charley and the dogs hanging out the back of the pick-up. Her mother wrote her every week and nagged her to tell her all the news, but Willa didn't have a minute to sit down, much less write a long letter to Lizzie.

The babies, Anne Elizabeth "Annie" born July 13, 1939, John Wyatt "Willy" born April 7, 1941, and Franklin Anthony

"Frankie" born November 19, 1942, kept Willa running from morning to night. Charley loved being a big brother and was her helper. The babies were all delivered at home by gruff old Dr. Duffy, who drove out from Enid and found he had little to do except catch them when they arrived.

After Frankie was born, Dr. Duffy offered to fit Willa for a diaphragm.

"I don't know if Jake would like that."

"Well, Jake's not having the babies, is he?"

"I'll think about it."

In fact, Willa wanted more babies. Maybe then she could get one that took after her. Green-eyed Charley was tall and lanky like Big Charley with her brown skin. Her three other babies all had light skin, blue eyes, brown hair, high foreheads, and the square Hardesty jaw, just like Jake.

The farm was bursting with babies. Walker coonhound puppies (Jake bought a bitch named Queen as a companion for Joe Savisky), baby chickens and geese, Angus calves, and baby Hampshire pigs. Willa soon sold off the coonhound puppies, but she took care of one hundred chickens, raised a flock of geese and stuffed pillows with their down, and helped Jake with the hog operation. She worked with Jake planting and harvesting the wheat, alfalfa, and oats. She milked two cows every morning, separated milk and churned butter, chased after five steers, three cows and their calves, and Night, their yearling black Angus bull, when they escaped from the pasture. She planted and tended the garden, baked bread three times a week, canned fruit and vegetables, drove twice a week to Pond Creek for ice, washed, ironed, and mended clothes, cooked and cleaned.

From time to time, Willa looked at her old schoolbook, *First Course in Home Making*, for tips. She decided Maude Calvert, the author, would need two more volumes to describe all the tasks and unexpected emergencies that cropped up on a farm.

Calvert had no advice, for example, about how to explain death to a nine-year-old boy. One of Charley's daily chores was to feed the pigs. When a Hampshire sow had a big litter with one piglet too weak to battle for milk, he brought the black and white runt into the house and bottle-fed it. A few nights later Willa discovered Charley sitting in the rocking chair holding the baby pig. "It's so cold, Mama." The pig was too weak and died. Charley was devastated. Willa explained that death was part of life and that on a farm something was always dying, and he better get used to it.

"Stop your bawling," Jake told him. "It's just a damn pig. Everything dies. A blade of wheat, pigs, people, everything." Furious with his parents and the unfairness of life, Charley buried the baby pig in the pasture. He never brought another runt into the house.

In her book, Maude Calvert advised simplicity and utility in decorating a room. Advice Willa took to heart. She made simple café curtains for all the rooms and painted the bedrooms a light beige. She painted the kitchen bright yellow with white open shelves and white trim and hung up pictures of President Roosevelt and Bob Wills. She found striped, blue wallpaper on sale in the Montgomery Ward catalog for the dining room and living room, but when Jake helped her hang it, they got into a yelling fight, the first of their marriage, because he had no patience with measuring and just wanted to slap the paper up any old way. The paper ripped, the paste bucket tipped over, so Willa said to hell with it, stored the undamaged paper for drawer liners, and painted both rooms a safe beige.

She kept careful farm records and met with Mrs. Boyce once each year on the first of August to give her the one-third share of the harvest. She balanced the bank statement and kept a running account of their expenses and income in her notebook, but her figures were always off because Jake forgot to tell her about something he'd bought or sold or about a payment he'd received for work. Jake didn't like talking about money or using the checkbook. He preferred cash and always had a roll of bills in his pocket. Willa saved for new linoleum by setting aside some of her earnings from selling chicken and goose eggs to Sedlak's Store. To save money, she started rolling her own cigarettes. She tried to stop smoking but became so snappish that Jake told her to go back to smoking before she bit someone's head off. Cigarettes calmed her down, and they kept her slim. Even after four babies, she weighed just one hundred ten pounds, although her waist had expanded to twenty-four inches.

Charley enrolled at nearby Pleasant Valley School, and once a month the whole family attended box suppers or programs at the one-room school. He became friends with a twelve-year-old neighbor boy to the north, Frank Johnson, and on nice days they walked to school together. On Sunday mornings, Willa sent Charley off with Jake to Sunday school at Kremlin's Christian Church. Jake drank coffee at Sedlak's Store while he waited for Charley to get out of Sunday School.

Jake's dad, John Hardesty, moved in with them in September 1942. He still did some occasional stone carving, but his eyesight had gotten too bad for him to work as a traveling veterinarian. He had been staying with his sister Martha, but he didn't like living in town. Plus he'd acquired a Clydesdale horse as payment of a debt, and he needed a place to keep it. Jake and Willa offered to take him in, and he accepted. Except for a nagging cough, John was in good health. He helped Willa fix up a room in the washhouse and moved in his big wooden trunk and his veterinarian and stone carving tools. John teased Willa about her beloved Roosevelt, which annoyed her, but he would rock the babies for hours or take them for slow, easy rides around the farm on his giant horse. He was especially fond of Frankie, whom he taught to whistle before he could talk.

Every evening, in addition to *Grimm's Fairy Tales* and *Aesop's Fables*, Willa read her children stories from the *Enid Morning News* so that they could learn what was going on in the world. Pearl Harbor came as a shock, but, except for rationing gasoline and keeping ration books for each member of the family, the war seemed far away. It came a little closer, though, when Billy Hardesty enlisted. Unlike his older brothers, Billy didn't receive a farm deferment, but he claimed that he wanted to go to Europe and kick Hitler's ass. Webb

Connell sent a postcard telling Willa that he had enlisted; he hoped to get to Europe and check out their railroads.

The war came even closer to home when the windows of the Japanese Bazaar, a little shop on First Street in Enid, filled with Buddhas and Japanese prints, were smashed with a brick. The shop was next to a shoe repair store where Willa took Jake's boots to be re-soled. She was friendly with the Bazaar owners, an older couple with two married daughters. Mr. Mabuchi told Willa that two young men had burst into his store and threatened him and his wife. "Listen, you Japs," the men said, "we're going to tear this place to pieces if it isn't closed in two hours." Mabuchi's wife called the police, but so far they had made no arrests. "I'm sixty-three and I was twenty years old when I came to this country," Mr. Mabuchi said. "I bought a defense bond just two weeks ago."

Willa talked about the incident with her neighbor Doris Sedlak, who came by several mornings a week to have a cup of coffee and play with the babies. Like her husband Glen, Doris was stocky and solid looking, with pale blue eyes and soft, doughy white skin. She had medium-length light brown hair, which was washed and curled once a week at the beauty shop in Pond Creek. A girl from Kremlin came in twice a week to help her cook and clean, and Doris's smooth hands with bright red fingernails were proof that she rarely scrubbed floors or dug in the garden.

"Glen says," Doris remarked, "that they should run all the Japs out of the country."

Willa stopped kneading bread and narrowed her eyes at Doris.

Just Willa

Willa wanted to tell Doris that she wished she could start a sentence without "Glen says," but she bit her tongue. Glen was a good neighbor, but he was a rich Sedlak and a Republican through and through. He despised Roosevelt. "What would Glen say if they ran all the Bohunks out, too?" popped out instead, and Willa was immediately sorry. Actually, she pitied Doris, who wasn't the sharpest knife in the drawer. Doris lacked for nothing except the one thing she wanted most. A baby. She was ten years older than Willa and desperate to get pregnant. The other Sedlak wives had no trouble having babies and had large families. Willa knew that Doris would give anything to have a baby of her own.

"I'm so bored at home," Doris groaned one day as she held Frankie and watched Willa make cinnamon rolls.

"I wish I had time to be bored," Willa said, but she didn't mean it.

Like Willa, Doris loved to dance and almost every Saturday night, Aunt Martha came to baby-sit and brought her daughter Rebecca to play with Charley, so that Willa and Jake could go dancing in Enid with Doris and Glen. Sometimes Heck and Lucy joined them. Their baby daughter Donna Jean was a month older than Annie.

Willa missed Cissie, Dean, and the boys and talked to Cissie on the phone every few weeks. Lizzie kept her informed about the rest of the family and told her how much Doc missed her. Willa missed them, too, but she felt more like a Hardesty now than a Sharpe. The two hand-tinted portraits (in gold leaf frames she found at a closeout sale in Enid) that hung above the fireplace in the living room were of Hardestys. One was of an unsmiling John Hardesty in a black suit and blue tie, leaning slightly away from his pretty young bride, Maybelle, who was wearing a white, high-necked Victorian wedding dress and an enormous straw hat piled with pink roses. The other portrait was of Billy Hardesty in his Army uniform, his cap at a jaunty angle. He looked like a sweeter, less battered version of Jake. Willa didn't have any portraits of her parents or brothers and sisters, just snapshots that she kept tucked in the big family Bible waiting for her to paste them in an album. She had a coupon for a family portrait at a photography studio in Enid, but Jake said he didn't have time for it, and anyway, he knew what everyone looked like.

Willa considered herself the home manager, and usually Jake followed her lead just as he did on the dance floor, but sometimes he blindsided her with decisions he'd already made. Like the promises he gave to his brother Jimmy and to Senator Drummond. Promises, he said, that had nothing to do with her or the kids. Of course, she knew he was wrong. What should she do? How do you deal with a stubborn, ornery husband without becoming a nag? Maude Calvert's textbook was silent on the subject.

At about 2:00 a.m. on the night after Christmas 1942, Willa woke up. What had she heard? Something. Like a rumble. Frankie was sound asleep in his crib. Jake was snoring softly. She slipped out of bed and checked on Charley, Annie, and Willy. They were sound asleep. Joe Savisky and Queen were curled up on the floor by Charley's bed. The dogs followed her as she tiptoed into the living room. She looked out the west window and saw a large, dark shape, a truck with its lights off, coming down their driveway. She looked again, just to make sure that she wasn't imagining it, and sure enough, it was a truck idling slowly toward the barn. She hurried back to the bedroom and shook Jake awake.

"It's just the senator's boys. Don't worry about it."

Willa straddled him.

"Tell me what's going on!"

"It's a deal I made to help Jimmy. He needs money bad."

"What kind of a deal?"

"A sweet deal. We make a hundred, maybe two hundred a month. I keep a little and give the rest to Jimmy."

"And what do you do for this money?"

"Nothing."

Willa pushed her hand into his chest. "Come on, Jake! What do you do?"

"Just store a little whiskey. For a while."

"Where?"

"In the granary, the one with the trapdoor. Spill a little grain on top and you won't even know it's there."

"That's illegal, Jake! And you know it! What if you get caught?"

"I won't get caught. They only come at night to pick up or to unload."

"You mean this isn't the first time?"

"They were here once before. I was going to tell you."

"You're lying. You're only telling me now because you're caught."

"I forgot about it. It's no big deal. And if someone finds out, I can say I never knew anything about it." Jake patted her butt. "Now, get off me. Unless you want to fool around a little." Jake found her breast and squeezed.

She slapped his hand away.

"No! Why didn't you tell me about this deal? Were you ever going to tell me?"

Jake yawned. "Sure. I said I was going to tell you. I just forgot."

"That's a damn lie and you know it! You didn't forget. You didn't say anything because you knew I'd say no. Remember our promise, Jake? No lies?" Willa pushed herself off Jake and sat on the edge of the bed.

"What are you doing?"

"I'm going to get dressed and go out there and tell Senator Drummond's boys to get off our farm and not come back."

Jake sat up and grabbed her wrist. "No, goddammit. You're going to get back in this bed."

"Shh. You'll wake the kids." She tried to free her wrist but Jake held tight. "Let me go."

"Goddammit, you're not listening. I'm doing this for Jimmy."

"Why can't he store the whiskey at his own place?"

"Think, Willa." He released her wrist and lay back on the pillow.

Willa bumped a cigarette from the half-empty pack on the bedside table. She lit it, inhaled deeply, and blew a smoke ring. Jake was right. Jimmy had lost the Farry farm and couldn't store the whiskey in town at his house or the gas station.

"Say we keep doing this? What's to stop Sally from just getting him deeper in debt?"

"Jimmy's going to hire a lawyer. Get a divorce. But that takes money."

Willa smoked. Soothed by the comforting ritual. Was it the smoke that calmed her down? Whatever it was, whenever she had a cigarette, everything seemed clearer and more manageable. She could manage this. Jimmy just needed to get back on his feet.

"Hear that?" Jake said. "They're leaving. Takes them no time to unload."

Willa walked to the window. At the end of their driveway, she saw a brief flash of brake lights and then nothing. The truck disappeared.

"Come on, Willa. You know we could use a few dollars more a month."

"I don't want any of it! Give it all to Jimmy."

"Okay. Whatever you say."

Willa stubbed out her cigarette and got into bed. He reached for her, but she turned her back and moved to the edge of the bed.

"Don't take it out on me!" Jake said too loudly, and Frankie began to fuss. Willa got up to get him. She sat in bed while Frankie nursed. She studied Jake's wide, strong back and muscular shoulders; his short, thick neck; and square head with its crop of wavy hair. When Frankie was done, she put him back in his crib. She lay awake for a long time smoking cigarette after cigarette listening to Jake snore and thinking. Who is he? Do I really know this man?

The Grudge Match
January 1943

GUARDED BY THE TALLEST OF Senator Drummond's drivers, who stood behind her like a tree wearing a cowboy hat, Willa sat at the door of the building taking the two-dollar admission fee. It was only 8:00, and she'd already collected four hundred dollars. When Jake confessed about his promise to Jimmy, and Willa learned that it was a done deal, she decided that since Jake wasn't going to change his mind, why not make the best of it? And they didn't have anyone else they could trust to handle the money. Certainly not Jimmy's wife Sally. They were separated, but Jimmy still had to pay her bills and support his four children. So Willa packed up Charley, Annie, and Willy to stay with Aunt Martha in Enid, and then she drove with Jake and his father John to leave baby Frankie with Lizzie and Doc at Old Freedom.

When she told her parents why they had come, Doc was furious. "You're all goddamn fools!" he said. "I'm surprised at you, John Hardesty. You're old enough to know better. Everyone in Woods County will be there, including the sheriff, who'll arrest the lot of you."

Just Willa

Jake answered that the sheriff was friendly with both boxers and wouldn't do anything to stop the fight. In fact, he gave his word. Frankie started crying, and Lizzie snatched him out of Willa's arms. Doc slammed out of the house.

The Hilltop Filling Station building stank of gasoline, cigarette and cigar smoke, hair oil, beer and booze, sweat and cheap perfume. Cars and pick-ups spilled out of the parking lot and were lined up along Highway 64. From time to time, when Willa went outside to get a breath of fresh air, she saw Jake slipping pints of whiskey into eager hands, and sliding dollars into his pocket. All under the watchful eye of Senator Drummond, who sat in the backseat of his Cadillac smoking a cigar and dispensing favors, advice, and sometimes warnings.

John Hardesty, who would serve as Jimmy's corner man, was with him in a tiny back room taping his hands and getting him ready for the fight. The match had been cooked up by Jimmy, who saw an opportunity to make some quick money, and he enlisted his friend, Ted Arnett, a popular middle-weight boxer, billed as The Fighting Farmboy, to be his opponent.

At a Camp Houston Dance a month earlier, Jimmy faked a loud argument with Arnett. Then he and Arnett circulated the story that there would be a grudge match to settle their dispute. Since the two boxers wanted to cut out their promoters and split the take between them, they arranged to stage the fight at Hilltop Filling Station, about ten miles west of Alva.

The match excited enormous interest because it pitted

Jimmy, The Phantom of Fair Valley, against the slugging power of Arnett, an excellent middleweight boxer. To give the illegal match credibility, Jimmy hired a local hero, Roy Dunn, a former Northwestern State College wrestling champion who had appeared in the 1936 Olympics, as the referee.

At 9:00 p.m. Roy Dunn announced that the match would be seven rounds and warned the fighters about the rules. Senator Drummond's driver lifted Willa up so she could stand on the table by the door and see the fight. She looked around for Jake but couldn't find him in the crowd that filled every inch of the large machine shed which had been emptied of equipment. Willa felt the same feeling she felt years ago watching Big Charley. She didn't want to look, yet she wanted to at the same time. There was something thrilling and primitive about it, and the crowd became a part of the fight.

Both fighters came out fast and aggressive. The crowd roared and gasped and cheered, vicariously sharing in the action, and applauding the fighters. Arnett had a two-fisted slugging attack. Jimmy bobbed and weaved, trying to find an opening for his quick jabs. Both boxers wanted to avoid the appearance of a fix and fought hard.

By the beginning of the fifth round, Jimmy was cut badly over his eye, and Arnett's nose and lips were swollen and bleeding. The dirt floor turned muddy and slippery and at the end of the sixth round, the exhausted fighters were clinging to each other, barely able to stand.

Willa couldn't watch the end of the seventh round. She

stepped down from her table perch, stared at the wall, and smoked. Time passed slowly. The crowd grew quiet, dispirited by the slow-motion agony. Both men looked spent, and there was no beauty or precision in their punches, just weariness. Still, neither man would give up. When the fight ended, referee Dunn announced that the match was a draw and held up both their hands.

After the fight, John and Willa doctored Jimmy's cuts but could do nothing about Jimmy's dizziness. "You probably have a concussion," Willa warned.

"It'll wear off," Jimmy said, slurring his words. "It always does."

According to Willa's tally, three hundred and thirty men and women watched the fight. She collected six hundred sixty dollars. After paying Roy Dunn a hundred dollars, the two fighters earned two hundred eighty dollars each.

The following week they learned that Doc was right. Sheriff Gillette had attended the match. He leaned against the wall and enjoyed every minute of it. On Monday morning when he returned to work, he sent a letter to each fighter summoning him to appear before the County Attorney to pay a fifty-dollar fine for staging an illegal match. Later, he told Jimmy and Arnett that it was nothing personal, but he had to keep up appearances with the County Attorney.

Jimmy endured and inflicted a savage beating and earned two hundred thirty dollars. The only problem was, he bet a hundred dollars on Arnett to win. During the fight, he forgot about his bet. He felt like a failure. He didn't even know how to take a fall. And one hundred thirty dollars wouldn't come close to paying all that he owed.

Willa was sickened not only by the fight but that it had been for nothing. Never again, she vowed, would she participate in one of Jake and Jimmy's schemes. She had hoped that Jimmy would earn enough from the fight to pay his debts and then they could stop storing whiskey. But Jimmy needed the money now more than ever.

On the Monday morning after the fight, Willa deposited the one hundred fifteen dollars that Jake made selling liquor at the fight, plus two hundred twenty-five dollars that he'd gotten from the senator. She wrote out a two hundred twenty-five dollar check to Jimmy and mailed it. By the size of the roll of bills in Jake's pocket, she suspected that he was holding back some of the senator's storage payment, but he swore he wasn't, so she chose to believe him.

"You worry too much," Jake said, and she knew he was right. If too much meant worrying all the damn time. But how could she stop worrying? The only way to stop the constant worrying chatter in her brain was to keep as busy as possible and soothe herself with cigarettes. She knew that she was becoming a chain smoker. She told herself that spring was on its way and when their workload doubled, she wouldn't have time to smoke so many cigarettes. I'll cut down in the spring, she promised herself.

Night's Work
February 1943

JAKE HAD WORKED AS A cowboy, but he wasn't a cattleman. He knew how to pasture cattle and winterfeed them. He understood that, like people, cattle weren't all the same and had distinct personalities. Jake could dehorn, castrate, brand, and doctor them, but he didn't have the inclination, the resources, or the talent to breed cattle and manage the risk and liability of a large herd. Men like his former boss Henry Eden and Angus breeder Mike Luddington of Alva had the gift and made thousands of dollars raising and buying and selling cattle. They could size up a bull or a heifer with a glance. Recently, both men were experimenting with breeding using artificial insemination, and Luddington bought an Angus bull out of the famous Black Prince of Sunbeam Farms for forty thousand dollars. A registered Angus heifer could bring fifteen to twenty thousand dollars.

"Well, Night," Jake said, as he looped a rope around his bull's neck, "you don't have any papers, but you're a fine-looking animal just the same."

Jake bought the bull as a calf with its mother at a farm

foreclosure sale for eighty dollars. He always bought Angus cattle because of an aversion to horned cattle, maybe because he saw a man gored to death. Something in the Angus calf appealed to him, and he decided not to castrate him. Instead he tried him out as a stud, and as a yearling Night sired three good calves.

Night had a charming, sociable personality. He liked being brushed and petted and handfed and would come when called. Jake reckoned he weighed between sixteen and seventeen hundred pounds. Charley gave the bull his name because he was midnight black, without a speck of white. As a two-year-old, Night was capable of covering up to thirty cows.

Like all Angus cattle in America, Night was descended from four Angus bulls brought to the Kansas prairies from Scotland in 1873 by George Grant. The locals, used to white-faced, horned Herefords, laughed at Grant's black, hornless cattle with their blocky bodies. When Grant crossed the bulls with Texas Longhorns, however, he got sturdy, hornless, black calves able to survive and flourish on the winter range.

It was a beautiful, clear February morning. The temperature had been in the sixties all weekend, and Jake figured that today would be the same. A good day to deliver Night to Glen Sedlak, who wanted to borrow his services. Before breakfast, Jake saddled up Fortney, who was frisky and wanted to run, but Jake kept him to a slow trot. With Night plodding docilely behind, he led the bull to the Sedlak farm.

Glen was waiting for Jake to arrive and waved him into the corral. Glen walked around the young bull, admiring him. "I sure appreciate this," he said. "And come fall, you'll have the pick of the calf crop. Want to sell him?"

"Charley would be mad at me if I did."

Glen opened the gate to the pasture. Jake swatted Night's flank, and the bull swaggered out to meet his harem.

The two men, arms folded, leaned on the fence and watched the bull explore the new pasture.

"Charley's a good boy," said Glen. "He's not yours, is he?"

"Well, I'm not his blood father. But I'm sure as hell his daddy. He's the same to me as my Annie and the boys."

"Blood means everything to my dad. He's always boasting about how many Sedlak grandkids he's got. And looking at me and Doris like there's something wrong with us."

Jake didn't say anything. He and Willa wondered why Glen and Doris didn't have kids. They were both in their early thirties and had been married for nine years.

"This is hard, Jake, but I've got to tell you something. Something private, that nobody else knows, except Doris." Glen worked at a splinter on the top rail of the fence, trying to peel it away.

"Sure."

"Well, Doris and I have been trying to have kids for years and just no luck. So two years ago we went to a doctor. He said Doris was just fine. But turns out I'm sterile, probably from mumps I caught that went down on me."

"That's a damn shame. Why don't you get yourself an orphan?"

"No, that's out. Doris wants a baby of her own and my

dad wants another Sedlak to leave his land to. He helps us when we run short. Hell, I don't even like farming, but if I had a son maybe he'd be good at it."

"Well, I don't know what to tell you," Jake said.

Glen removed the splinter from the rail and began to pull it apart in neat, long strips. "Doris and I've been thinking and talking for over a year now, and we've come up with an idea. Well, I guess it was her idea. I told her that I'd be fine without any kids, but Doris says that she doesn't know how she can live without a baby of her own."

"She sure does love our babies."

"Oh what the hell! I'm going to just say it." Glen swung around and looked Jake in the eye. "We want you to be our baby's father."

"What? Whoa, there!"

"We know you. We consider you a good friend."

"Why don't you ask one of your brothers? Keep it in the family."

"I don't give a shit about that. And Doris wouldn't hear of it anyway. She doesn't like them much. We're not that close with them or their wives. She doesn't want anyone in my family to know. And she's got a point. We don't want there to be any problem with the inheritance. That's why she thought of you. She likes you and trusts you. And so do I."

Jake walked away from Ed into the pasture. Blowing broom weed, which cattle wouldn't eat, had drifted against the fence. Brittle grasses crackled and broke under his boots. He stared at the barren winter earth and thought about Glen and Doris. He thought about his kids and how much he loved them. What kind of life could you have on a farm without kids to help you work it? He turned back and looked at Glen. Doris stood next to him holding a tray with three cups of steaming coffee.

Jake walked back into the corral. "I'll do it," he said, making the decision quickly, the way he made most decisions. Willa turned every decision back and forth and upside down before she made up her mind. But in his experience whatever he decided in the moment usually worked out. "Hell, I'm happy to help you out. But here's the thing. Willa can't know."

"No one will know," said Doris. "Especially Willa."

"That's right," said Glen.

"We'll pay you," said Doris.

"What? Like a stud fee? Hell no to that. I'll do it because I'm your friend."

"Thank you, Jake," Doris said, tears running down her cheeks.

"But here's the deal," Jake said. "After six months, I'm done. No second chances. And not a hint to Willa or anybody. And if you give me a job to do, in addition to, you know, why hell yes, you can pay me for that. And then I'll have a reason to be coming around here, regular like."

The three of them sealed their agreement with a handshake. They drank their coffee. They arranged that Jake would start his new job next Wednesday when Glen would be in Enid all day.

"Well," said Jake, "I better get going." He walked over

to Fortney and got into the saddle. He looked for Night in the pasture and saw him in the distance licking a block of salt, surrounded by his harem.

Jake gave Fortney his head and galloped home. On the way, he worried about his decision. Had he done the right thing? He wanted to help out his friends, but why did they ask him and put him in this spot? How could he say no without insulting them both? Especially Doris. He knew how much she wanted a baby. She talked about it all the time. But he knew Willa would be furious if she found out, and more than anything he feared her anger and disapproval. So the deal was that Willa could never find out.

As he neared home, Jake used a trick he'd learned as a boy shivering in Aunt Mattie's barn. He swept worries about the future and all disturbing thoughts into a dark back corner of his mind. Just brushed them into a heap and left them there. He thought instead about something good and something real. Charley, Annie, and Willy running out to meet him to unsaddle Fortney, cinnamon rolls hot out of the oven waiting for him in the yellow kitchen and the softness of Frankie's fuzzy head nestled under his chin. And Willa in the middle of everything, the hub of the wheel, her full breasts straining against the buttons of her blouse, her brown eyes laughing and snapping, her smoky voice, saying what she said every morning when he came in from chores.

"Wipe your damn feet, Jake. Breakfast's ready. Get with it! We've got work to do!"

All the News
December 20, 1943

"Dear Mama,

Well, everybody's in bed, and I'm trying to get a jump on my Christmas cards. I'm really behind this year. Thought I'd surprise you and write you a letter with the card and tell you all our news. The weather has been cloudy and freezing cold. Would be nice to see some sun this week. Hard to get clothes dry in this weather.

The kids are looking forward to Christmas. Annie thinks she's so grown-up since she'll start school next year. I don't like to brag about my own kids, but she's as smart as a whip. Willy follows Jake and Charley around like a puppy. He said to me the other day, "Damn it, I'm almost three years old!" I had to scold him for swearing, but he's so cute, the spitting image of Jake. Frankie's whistling is about to drive me crazy. I could just wring John Hardesty's neck for teaching him, but that big old horse of his is a good babysitter. The kids sit on him for hours. When Heck and Lucy were here two weeks ago, Annie and Donna Jean played with their dolls and talked up a storm. Wish all of you lived a little closer.

Billy has shipped out from Camp Hoan, New Jersey. He says that he's going to Italy. I haven't heard from Webb in a long time. If you see Mrs. Connell, ask her to give you his address.

I'm looking forward to seeing Cissie and Dean's new little boy. I bet Cissie keeps going until she has the girl she wants. Our neighbors Doris and Glen Sedlak, I think I told you about them, anyway, after years of trying, they had twins just a few days ago. A boy and a girl. Doris's mother was a twin back in Wisconsin so it runs in the family. They each weighed a little over five pounds. I'm afraid Doris will spoil them rotten. Soon as she found out she was pregnant, she started buying baby clothes and toys and new furniture for a nursery. She used to be here three times a week to drink coffee and play with the kids, but she stopped coming. I'm happy that she'll have babies of her own to hold. They're going to move to Enid next year and build a new house. Won't be too handy for Glen working the farm, but Doris is really a town girl.

How's Daddy's arthritis? Jake is fine, working too hard as usual. He still goes coon hunting with Joe Savisky and Queen. He's been taking Charley and a neighbor boy, Frank Johnson, with him. The other day Frank ran up here after his dad whipped him pretty bad. Mr. Johnson was drunk again. Jake wanted to go have a talk with him, but Frank begged him not to. His mother isn't much better. He never gets a decent meal and is so skinny.

There was an outbreak of rabies just north of Enid so we're keeping an eye out. Jake's dad has been no trouble, a big help really, and comes and goes when he likes. And he helps out buying gas and groceries. He said he stopped by and saw you and Daddy when he went to carve the headstone for old Mr. Kasem.

Would you tell Daddy to send me some of his tonic or give it to Heck and Lucy when they come? It's nice of them to bring little Dean and Randy. Charley is looking forward to seeing them. He's been a little peaked lately, tired and run down which isn't like him. I tried to get him to eat some liver, even fried it like chicken with onions. We all love it fixed that way, but he just couldn't stand the taste.

Well, that's about all my news. Oh, you asked about Mrs. Boyce. She says we can stay as long as we want. She said she'd give us the first opportunity to buy the place if she ever decides to sell. It's so hard to save any money, though. Propane is still cheap here.

Love, your daughter,

Willa

P.S. I'm happy about Dilly finally divorcing Hal. It's about time. He was never any good. I won't have time to write anyone else so just pass this letter around if you like."

Charley
January-May 1944

"HURRY UP!" YELLED CHARLEY. IT was cold and windy with a sprinkling of snow on the dead yellow grass. He looked down the railroad tracks lined with reddish-black lava rocks and gravel. It must be about 5:15. The Rock Island Rocket was usually on time. He took off his jacket and wiped the sweat from his forehead.

Dean, twelve, a year older and an inch shorter than Charley, stood next to him. "Now what do we do?" he said.

"Aunt Lucy was yelling at us to get home," said Randy, pushing between them.

"This won't take long," said Charley. "Get out your penny." He took a penny from his overalls pocket and placed it on the center crown of the iron rail. Randy and Dean each laid a penny next to Charley's.

"It's coming! It's coming!" screamed Randy.

"Stand back!" said Charley. "Don't let the engineer see you."

The three boys ran into a shallow ravine south of the tracks and lay on their stomachs and watched as the Rocket roared by.

"Seven cars," said Dean.

"And one dining car. I bet it's going all the way to California," said Charley. "Someday I'm going there."

"Let's go find the pennies," said Randy. He ran to the rail. "They're not here!"

Dean and Randy searched in the dry grass and along the steep and rocky sides of the railroad track. Charley, who had crushed pennies several times with Frank Johnson, knew exactly what to look for and was the first to spot a penny lodged between the ties. He picked it up and held it out for Dean and Randy to see. The force of the train had flattened the penny into a thin sheet of smooth copper, about the size of a quarter.

"Here's another one!" Dean held up a smashed penny.

The boys looked for several more minutes, but the third penny had disappeared. The light was fading. More clouds moved in hiding the setting sun.

"Can I hold one?" asked Randy.

"Here, take mine," said Charley. "I can always make more. But don't tell. You're not supposed to put anything on the tracks. A penny won't hurt, but once, somebody left a clamp on the rail and wrecked the handcar when it came through."

"We'd better go," said Dean, looking up at the sky.

Suddenly, Charley felt tired. "Go on," he said. "I'll catch up." He put on his jacket and followed his cousins back to the house.

Later, Jake nudged Willa when the boys came in from doing their chores. "Charley's dragging."

Maybe it's growing pains, she thought. He was already as tall as she was. His green eyes looked like bright, hot stones in his white face. Willa lay the back of her hand on Charley's forehead. "You're burning up," she said. "How do you feel?"

"Okay. Just tired, I guess."

"Are you hungry? I made a big pot of beef and vegetable soup from the roast we had for dinner. And there's chocolate sheet cake your Aunt Lucy made for dessert."

"I feel funny."

"Funny, how?"

"Kind of cold and hot at the same time."

"The rest of you go ahead and eat," Willa said. "Jake, could you cut the bread? Frankie, stop whistling at the table. Annie, watch him. Lucy, just serve everybody from the pot on the stove. Donna Jean take your mother the bowls." She turned her attention back to Charley, who sat slumped in a kitchen chair, his head in his hands. "Come on, Charley, I'll run a tub. You strip."

"I can do it, Mama. I'm not a baby. I'm eleven."

"I know how old you are. Okay, but I'll be in to check on you."

Willa sat at the kitchen table. Everyone else was eating. But now she wasn't hungry. Her stomach felt off. It was always the same. Whenever one of her kids didn't feel well, she felt sick, too. Just went with being a mother, she supposed.

"Is he all right?" Jake asked.

"I think he just got chilled," Willa said. She got up and filled the glasses with milk, which Lucy had forgotten.

Before she sat back down, she knocked on the bathroom door. "Charley, are you in the tub?"

Charley didn't answer. Willa opened the door and looked in. Charley sat in the bathtub holding a washcloth to his nose and mouth. Blood was dripping from the cloth and turning the soapy water a sickly pink. Willa grabbed the washcloth, wrung it out, and pressed it against his nose. "Hold it tight," she said.

Willa had treated nosebleeds at Dr. Simmons' office. Usually the blood clotted and the bleeding stopped in a few minutes. But minutes passed and Charley's bleeding didn't stop. She called for Jake. They took Charley out of the tub and toweled him dry. "What's this?" Willa said, pointing to bruises on Charley's back and legs and stomach. "Have you been roughhousing, Charley?"

"No, Mama, but I'm sore." Charley said he could walk just fine, but Jake carried him to his bed. John Hardesty brought ice wrapped in a towel for Charley's nose. The bleeding slowed to a trickle but didn't stop.

Willa stayed calm. She didn't want Charley or the other kids to see how afraid she was. "You stay with him, Jake. I'll call Dr. Duffy."

Willa went to the kitchen. When she picked up the receiver, she could hear the familiar voice of Sadie Richey on the party line, probably talking to her sister in Enid.

"Sadie, it's Willa. I need the phone to call the doctor."

"Oh, what's the matter?"

"Get off the phone. I need to call right now."

"Well, no need to be rude. I'll be off in a minute."

Willa hung up the receiver, waited a few moments, and then picked it back up. The line was open. She turned the ringer handle once for Edna Devery, the operator in Kremlin.

"Edna, please get me Dr. Duffy's office in Enid."

"He won't be there. It's Sunday."

"That's right. Call his house."

A minute passed and then another. Finally, a woman's voice said, "Duffy residence."

"I need to speak to Dr. Duffy right away."

"He's eating supper. Who is this?"

"Tell him Willa Hardesty needs to talk to him right now."

Willa waited. Soon, she heard Dr. Duffy's familiar, deep voice. "Willa, what's wrong?"

Willa described Charley's condition, just as she used to describe patients when she worked for Dr. Simmons in Alva. "Take him to Enid Memorial right now," Dr. Duffy said. "I'll meet you there."

"I hate to interrupt your supper."

"I'll wait for you at the hospital. Willa? Do you hear me?"

"Yes. We'll leave right away."

Heck offered to take them to Enid. "I've got plenty of gas. I filled up the tank for our drive back," he said. "Jake and Lucy can stay here and put the kids to bed."

"Is Charley sick, Mama?" Annie asked.

"Yes, a little. Now you and Donna Jean be good and help Lucy. We're taking Charley to see Doc Duffy, who'll fix him up as good as new."

Two days later, Willa and Jake sat in a chilly, small room in Enid Memorial, listening to Dr. Duffy's calm, sad voice. "Charley has leukemia," he said. "A kind of cancer of the blood. We don't know what causes it. He's making too many white corpuscles and they're crowding out and destroying the red ones. No one can catch it from him. There's no cure for it. It's lucky that Heck's blood type was a match. Transfusions help, and we're going to need more donors. I also want to try penicillin injections to head off any infections. Charley's resistance will be low, and you'll have to protect him against colds, and he'll bruise easily."

"Can he come home?" asked Willa.

"You can take him home tomorrow. I'll give you a supply of penicillin, Willa. You can give him his shots. If he feels up to it, he can go back to school. I want you to bring him back next week for another blood test and probably another transfusion. We'll just have to take it one day at a time."

Willa couldn't ask. She couldn't get the words out. She looked at Jake. He understood.

"What are we talking about, Doc?"

"It's a fatal disease. Weeks, a few months. Even lasting six months would be a miracle."

"What if we took him someplace else?" Willa asked. "A bigger hospital, Chicago or St. Louis?"

Dr. Duffy shook his head. "They couldn't do any more for him, Willa, than we're doing. There just isn't any cure. The National Cancer Institute is working on things, like using mustard gas as a treatment, but so far, only transfusions help and that's temporary. Take him home tomorrow. Keep him comfortable and make things as normal as possible. And take care of yourselves. You're going to need all your strength to get through this. That's all you can do."

Dr. Duffy stood up, shook Jake's hand, and patted Willa's shoulder. "I'm sorry," he said. He walked out of the room and closed the door.

Jake stood up. He felt as if he were being smothered. He hated this goddamn gray room. He'd only been in a hospital once, and he'd hated it then, and he hated it now. He hated the antiseptic smell; the white beds all in a row, the unnatural strangeness. He couldn't breathe. He looked down into Willa's face. Her brown eyes were huge and filled with fear and pain. He felt helpless and weak, like he was being punched by a heavyweight fighter who outweighed him by a ton. He reached for her and then bawled like a baby.

Willa didn't cry. She held Jake, patting his back and rocking him, until he stopped crying. As she comforted him, she finally understood the man she had married. Jake wasn't strong. He was weak. He'd never had a mother's love and had been passed around like an unwanted stray. His enormous physical strength and his happy-go-lucky attitude masked his true self, a terrified little boy who wanted his mama.

Willa took a deep breath. She opened her purse and took out her cigarettes. I have to be strong, she thought, for Charley, for Jake, for the babies. Miracles do happen. I'll work hard and make Charley better.

For a time, Charley was better. He walked to school with

Frank Johnson; he fed the pigs; he played with his little brothers and Annie. Joe Savisky kept Charley company day and night. Willa and John Hardesty took turns giving Charley his penicillin injections. As the days passed, Charley tired more frequently. Then it was time to go back to the hospital for another blood transfusion. Aunt Martha and Rebecca brought food to the hospital for them and sat with Charley when Willa or Jake couldn't be with him. He was never alone. On the way home from the hospital one day when Charley felt especially well, Willa took him to the Marquis photography studio and used her coupon to have his portrait taken.

Heck and the other donor matches could only give blood every six weeks, but there was plenty of blood in the hospital blood bank for Charley. Edna Devery, the central operator, had used the general ring to call everyone in the Kremlin community to tell them about Charley's need for blood. Seventeen people proved to be matches and made the trip to Enid to give blood. Lizzie wrote a column in the *Freedom Call* which was picked up by the *Alva Courier*, and Woods County donors drove to Enid to give blood, including Ben Stone, Charley's uncle, whom he had never met. Money donations poured in to help defray the cost of the hospital and doctor bills. Glen Sedlak gave five hundred dollars to the teller at the Kremlin State Bank and asked him to put it anonymously in Jake and Willa's account.

By April, Charley was too weak to return to school. Every day after school Frank Johnson and other students from

Charley's class came by to visit him, and every morning, Willa baked a chocolate cake or cherry pies or oatmeal cookies or cinnamon rolls so they would have something to eat while they drank milk and talked to Charley.

They moved Charley to the daybed in the dining room closer to the kitchen. From his daybed, he could watch his mother cook, help her fold laundry, read his lessons to her, and be a part of everything in the house.

Willa cooked all Charley's favorite foods. Cooking was a balm for her as it was for him. He couldn't eat very much, but he liked to smell everything cooking. As she cooked, she explained what she was doing and why. She fried chickens and made mashed potatoes and gravy. She simmered an old hen for hours with onions and sage and then added thick noodles yellow with egg. She slow cooked pinto beans with ham hocks and made crusty cornbread dripping with butter. She fixed chuck roast so tender it could be cut with a fork. To build up the iron in his blood, she fed him carrots and peas and onions and spinach. Charley's favorite at any time of the day was Willa's bread, hot from the oven and served with butter and sand plum jelly and usually with a juice glass of Doc's tonic. Willa had little appetite, but she forced herself to eat, knowing that she had to stay healthy. Except for the worry lines that appeared around her eyes, her skin glowed, and she looked lean and strong.

She neglected her garden, but it was a wet, cloudy spring, and everyone's gardens were late. Jake planted potatoes in the muddy ground. He put out onion sets, but they all rotted and would have to be replanted.

Just Willa

Willa bought a box of postcards, and when he felt up to it, Charley answered the many cards and letters he'd received. Frank Johnson brought his assignments, and with Willa's help, Charley kept up on his homework. Charley taught Willy to play marbles and he read his comic books to Willy and Frankie. Annie played nurse and learned to take his temperature. Willa could read every expression on Charley's face and understood the plea in his green eyes, so she never spoke of the future or about Charley's dream of going to college and traveling to all fifty states. They both understood that now was the only time he had.

On nice, sunny days, which were rare that April, Jake brought Charley outside to look at the growing wheat and the greening elm and mulberry trees. John took him for a ride on the big Clydesdale. One Sunday, Lizzie and Doc and Cissie and Dean and their boys came for a visit. The boys played Monopoly all afternoon, and Charley bought Park Place and Boardwalk and all the railroads and won the game.

As the days passed and April turned into May, Willa could see that Charley was failing more rapidly. On Wednesday, May 3, she and Jake brought him home from the hospital, where he had received his thirty-second transfusion. On Thursday, May 4 the entire Pleasant Valley School of eighteen students visited and performed their last day of school program just for him. Charley received his final report card, four A's and three B's.

Before sun-up on Friday, May 5, Willa woke to find Joe Savisky's cold, wet nose poking her cheek. She got up without waking Jake and followed the dog into the dining room. Charley looked up at her and smiled. "I told Joe Savisky to get you. Isn't he a smart dog?"

"Yes, he is. Can I get you something, honey?"

"I'm cold, Mama."

Willa pulled another quilt over Charley and tucked it around his shoulders. Then she gathered him up and cradled him in her arms. His head lay on her breast. She could hear his faint, shallow breathing. She held him and rocked him and kissed the top of his head. Just as she had done over eleven years earlier when he was born. On this very same daybed, she realized. Then suddenly in an instant everything changed. His breath was gone. Charley was gone. He just wasn't there anymore. His thin, bony body still lay in her arms, but Charley, the son she loved, had vanished. She lay his head down on the pillow. His eyes were closed, and his face was peaceful. Then the pain hit her belly, a terrible, ripping pain that tore at her so suddenly and so hard it made her cry out in agony. She hugged herself. Shhh, Willa. Strong. Strong. You have to be strong. She kissed the face that both was and wasn't Charley. She lay beside him and held him until she found the strength to let him go. Then she stood up and went to get Jake.

That Friday, by the end of the day, Willa, with Lizzie's help, had made all the arrangements for Charley's funeral, which would be held on Monday at the Christian Church in Freedom. Jake took one look at Charley that morning and fled the house. He called for Joe Savisky, but the dog wouldn't leave Charley. Before Charley's body was taken away, Willa let Annie, Willy, and Frankie see him and say goodbye. She didn't tell them that he'd gone to heaven or that he was at peace or that someday they'd see him again. She simply said that Charley had died of leukemia, and she wanted them to remember him the way he was when he was alive.

"Are you going to die?" Annie asked. "Are we going to die?"

"No. Not for a long time," she said. "Now, Annie, go read to your brothers. I have a lot to do."

She decided that it would be best if Annie, Willy, and Frankie did not attend the funeral, and Aunt Martha took them on Sunday to stay with her in Enid. Willa selected the pallbearers—boys ten, eleven, and twelve years old—and all Charley's Sharpe cousins, except for his fourteen-year-old friend, Frank Johnson. Fossett Funeral Home was in charge and provided the small white casket.

Dilly, who owned a Kodak camera, took a snapshot of the burial service at the cemetery. She stood outside the wire fence to take the picture. The sky was colorless and blank. The young minister, his back to the camera, looked down at the white, flower-covered coffin. Jake's brother, Jimmy, stood next to Jake holding his arm. Jake, wearing a jacket, tie, and white shirt stood with his arm around Willa. His eyes were closed. His hair was thick and curly and too long, since Willa hadn't had time to cut it for weeks. Willa wore a flat black hat, a black suit, and held a white handkerchief in her right hand. Her mouth twisted with grief, she stared at the coffin with eyes wide open and filled with anger and sorrow but no tears. Doc and Lizzie, both in hats and long coats, stood with heads bowed next to Willa. The row of young pallbearers wearing ties and long-sleeved sweaters, all with hands clasped and heads bowed, stood guard over the white coffin. Later, Willa pasted it in the family album next to the obituary that her mother had written for the *Freedom Call*. It was the only photograph she had of Charley's funeral.

A few weeks after the funeral, John Hardesty finished carving the tombstone. He had asked Willa what she wanted, but she couldn't face it. "You decide," she said. "I just can't."

On Decoration Day at the end of May, Willa, Jake, and the three kids drove to Freedom to decorate Charley's grave. Annie had helped Willa make two wreaths of white roses. Willa showed her how to cut and curl the crepe paper, bind the petals together with thin, flexible wire, and dip them in hot wax to preserve them.

It was sunny and warm on top of the hill at the Old Freedom Cemetery. To the north, the Hardesty family could see the Sharpe homestead, and to the south they could see the red bluffs of Freedom. And Charley lay buried in the ground in front of them, in the first row of the cemetery next to the fence. Using metal stakes, Jake and Willy secured the wreaths of white roses in the red dirt, still fresh and raw.

Charley's headstone was a small, rectangular stone of light gray granite with a dark gray border. A sunflower, daisy, and leaf design decorated the two top corners of the stone, a pattern John Hardesty copied from Willa's day-of-the-week tea towels. Centered in the middle of the tombstone were the words he carved deep into the granite.

"Charley"
Charles Luther Hardesty
1933-1944
Our Darling, At Rest

Ants
August 1944

WILLA WAS CUTTING UP CHICKENS at the kitchen sink when she heard the rifle shots. She didn't flinch. It was another hot and windy day. Three months since Charley died. Another day he wouldn't see. The house was quiet. Too quiet, she realized. She rinsed her hands and walked through the house to the west porch.

"Annie! Willy! Frankie! Where are you?"

"Here, Mama," Annie said, between sobs.

Annie sat on the cement wall of the porch with her arms around Willy and Frankie, who were snuffling and sniffing.

Willa kneeled in front of her children. They stared at her with watery blue eyes, running noses, and trembling lips. "Why are you bawling?"

"Granddad shot Joe Savisky!" said Annie, who had turned five in July and was tall for her age. "He said get back to the house. He shot Queen, too."

"The gun went boom, boom!" added three-year-old Willy. His long black lashes were wet with tears, and his face was filthy.

Frankie, who would be two in November and followed his older brother around and copied everything he did, shouted, "Boom! Mama!"

"Well, I'll see about that," Willa said. "Where's your Granddad?"

"In the pasture," said Annie.

"Which one?"

"By the corral."

"Annie, stop crying. You're my big girl. Take your brothers inside. Get their faces and hands washed."

Annie wiped her eyes with her hands. "Okay, Mama."

"And don't touch those chickens in the sink. I'll be right back."

Willa walked past her garden, which John and Jake tended in their rough way when they saw she was neglecting it. She knew she had let things go. She still did her chores, cooked and cleaned and washed, all the essential things, but everything else like cutting the kids' hair or even taking care of her own hair seemed ridiculous. What did it matter if she brushed her hair? She was so tired. Most nights she lay awake listening to Jake snore, wondering how he could sleep so easily with Charley dead and buried. Then the thoughts came, buzzing like flies, and she started worrying about the kids. She went to their beds and bent over them, listening to their breathing. She'd go back to bed and try to sleep, and maybe she would doze for a couple of hours, and then it was time to get up and somehow make it through the day. Just one damn thing after another.

She saw John in the pasture stooped over a shovel. His white hair hung over his ears. He was seventy-one, tall and skinny, but he looked even older. His cough had gotten worse, and he kept a spit can by his bed. He diagnosed himself with dust asthma and refused to see Dr. Duffy. "Hell, man's an animal, too," he argued. "I can doctor myself."

When Willa got closer, she saw Joe Savisky and Queen. They were lying on the ground nose to nose. Each dog had a bullet hole in the head. After Charley died, whenever the two dogs got free, they ran off to hunt for him. She knew where they went. Everywhere Charley had been. The creek bed, the railroad tracks, through all the fields. Willa stayed up late waiting for them to come home. She picked burrs from their coats, rubbed Vaseline into their sore paws, gave them food and water and told them that Charley was gone, but they didn't believe her.

"I had to, Willa. You know how Jake is. He didn't have the stomach for it."

"Where is he?"

"He went to Kremlin to get the propane."

"He did that yesterday. Don't lie to me, John. What was so important that he couldn't help you bury his dogs?"

"He's running a little errand for Senator Drummond in Enid."

"What kind of an errand?"

"He didn't say."

Willa's stomach burned. She had avoided taking her medicine this morning. She hated the chalky taste. Dr. Duffy warned her that she was in danger of a full blown ulcer if she didn't take care of herself. "Why did you shoot them?"

"I thought Jake told you."

"He doesn't tell me a damn thing!"

"They got tangled up with a rabid skunk. I shot the skunk, but they'd been bit. I just couldn't take the chance."

Without a word, Willa turned and left John to dig the graves in the dry, hard ground of the pasture. She thought of the baby pig Charley tried to save. Something was always dying on a farm, she told him. It was true and it was cruel and there was no point to it. No point at all. What was the use of taking one more step?

She crouched down on the ground, arms around her knees. Tiny black ants, piss ants, Jake called them, scurried back and forth, carrying bits of something in their mouths. If she crushed some, she knew the others would keep working, keep living. Did ants grieve? she wondered. Did they miss the ones who were gone? What was the point of all the working and scurrying? At least Joe Savisky and Queen died together. She thought of Charley, dead and buried and gone forever, although from time to time she glimpsed him out of the corner of her eye, and sometimes in the morning before she was fully awake, she sensed him close by. Charley had wanted to live. To go to college and to California. Annie wanted to live. Willy and Frankie wanted to live. Jake wanted to live. The question was, did she want to live? What was the point of all the working and scurrying?

She stood up. Well, she didn't have a choice. She wasn't going to give up now. If the goddamn piss ants could do it, so could she. She walked back to the house and her waiting children.

The White Trunk
1945

THE WHITE TRUNK FASCINATED ANNIE and Willy. They suspected it contained Charley's marbles and games and comic books. They weren't supposed to play in their parents' bedroom, but one Saturday afternoon, when Willa was outside, Annie and Willy, with Frankie toddling behind, tip-toed into the bedroom to stare at the trunk until they got up the giggling courage to open it. Just as they were struggling with the stiff, metal buckles, Willa walked into the room carrying a basket of clothes.

"Don't mess with Charley's trunk!" She pulled Annie and Willy away from the trunk and shook them. "It doesn't belong to you! Do you understand?"

"Yes, Mama," Annie said, hiding her face in her long brown hair. Willy nodded, but he couldn't speak. He'd bit his tongue and it hurt. Frankie grabbed his mother's leg and started howling.

"Stop that bawling!" Willa unwound Frankie's arms from her leg. "Get out of here!" She clapped her hands, and the children scattered like frightened chickens.

Just Willa

Willa slumped down on the bed. She knew what they were after. Charley's baseball mitt. His comic books bound with a rubber band. A leather pouch filled with glass marbles. A metal bank filled with coins. They would have no use for the other items that were precious to Willa. His faded blue pajamas. His last homework assignment, three pages of arithmetic problems. His last valentine. His final report card. A lopsided pink heart with Happy Mother's Day – Love, Charley. A tiny patchwork quilt. Tucked into it was an envelope marked "Charley's first haircut"; inside was a wispy, wheat-colored curl. At the bottom of the trunk rested a blue nylon grave ribbon with "Beloved Son" written on it in glitter lettering. And his obituary from the *Freedom Call*. On the edge of the clipping Willa wrote in pencil Charley's last words: "Mama, I'm cold."

Willa loved her blue-eyed children, but there were times when they seemed like strangers, and she wished she were back in Alva living with Charley in Mrs. Connell's house. Just the two of them with no animals to feed or farm to run and no man to please.

Willa's eyes fell on the basket of clothes to be folded. And there were more clothes to gather from the line. Then ironing and chores to do. She'd have to start thinking about getting supper on the table. There were letters to write to Billy and Webb, who were both stationed in Italy. Too much to do and not enough time to do it. She heard the screen door slam and Jake's laughing roar.

Then Jake stood over her, bringing the scent of hay and

horses. Willy and Frankie boxed at his legs with their tiny fists. He tossed the boys onto the bed. "Get with it, Willa! It's Saturday. We're going dancing tonight."

"I can't go dancing. There's too much work to do."

"Work can wait but the B & M Ballroom can't. Jay and Blanche are meeting us there."

"What'll I wear?"

"Hell, I don't care. Get with it!" He picked up Frankie and swung him onto his shoulders. "Come on boys. Let's go find your grandpop."

Months passed. 1944 turned into 1945, and Willa's life returned to its working routine. She put her grief into the white trunk. She wished she could pack her worries there, too, but she couldn't. "You'll worry your life away," Jake told her, who never seemed to worry about anything. For her part, Willa worried like a devout Christian prayed, daily and with fervor. She sent the kids to Sunday School to get them out of her hair for a few hours, but she didn't care for organized religion. She thought it was wrong to pray for personal benefit. She had never asked God to save Charley. A God that would save her son and let others die was not a God worthy of worship.

Along with the rest of the country, Willa yearned for an end to the war. Every morning in the Enid paper, she read about dead or wounded soldiers. She flinched whenever the telephone rang. No one she knew called unless there was an emergency or bad news. In February, Cissie phoned from the hospital in Oklahoma City to say that Dean had died. Slow-talking, sweet Dean, the father of little Dean and Randy and baby Jack, died of a subdural hematoma in the brain. The year before, Dean was moving cattle when his horse stepped into a gopher hole. He was thrown and hit his head. For months, he'd suffered from blinding headaches, which he treated with aspirin. Then one morning he couldn't speak or walk. Stub and Cissie took him to the hospital in Oklahoma City, but it was no use. Another grave was dug in Old Freedom Cemetery.

In March, Jake received a letter from the Army informing him that his brother, PFC William Hardesty, had been wounded in Italy. Along with five hundred eighty-one other injured soldiers, Billy crossed the Atlantic on the hospital ship *Wisteria*. For weeks, as Billy clung to life in a Long Island hospital, Willa wrote letter after letter to his nurse and his sergeant. The nurse read Billy the letters, but his head injuries were so severe that he was unable to communicate. Pneumonia set in, and Billy died. He was twenty-five. He had served with the Signal Corps in four major battles and was awarded the Soldiers Medal and a Purple Heart. Two days later, President Roosevelt died of a stroke.

Willa heard the news on the radio and was numb. There was too much death. The loss of Billy hit them all hard. All that bad news couldn't be good for the baby she carried, Willa thought. Feeling those stirrings of life, though, gave her hope. Was that why she decided it was time for a new baby? To find hope and the happiness that always seemed just out of her reach? She wasn't sure. She put her diaphragm aside and let her body make the decision for her.

Still, the war was ending, that was clear. She saved Billy's obituary and the announcement of Roosevelt's death. The

President's last words—"I have a terrific headache"—haunted her. She hoped he hadn't suffered too long.

The death of his youngest son broke John Hardesty. Every morning it was Willy's job to wake up his grandfather and empty his spit can. Willy liked telling his granddad that breakfast was ready, but he hated touching the nasty can, filled with brown, foul-smelling liquid.

One early June morning, Willy opened the door to John's room and then stopped. Something was different, but he wasn't sure what it was. "Granddad! Get up!" he called, moving closer to the bed. John didn't stir. His eyes were closed. Willy looked down at the spit can. It was empty. He ran to tell his mother. John Hardesty was buried next to his son Billy in the Enid cemetery.

In August, Jake learned that he was the beneficiary of Billy's ten thousand dollar insurance policy. Every month for five years, the policy promised, a green check for one hundred sixty-six dollars and sixty-six cents would arrive in a brown manila envelope. Jake shared the money with Jimmy. Jimmy and Sally were divorced, and though he still supported her and their four children, she constantly hounded him for more money. She would even sneak into his gas station and steal cash from the register.

Summer ended. Jake sold hogs, sowed wheat, and harvested maize. He didn't tell Willa that while he stopped the liquor storage, he still worked for the senator, mostly doing special deliveries. He figured what she didn't know wouldn't hurt her. And with another baby coming they needed cash.

Just Willa

On October 4, 1945, at Enid Memorial, Willa gave birth to a seven-pound, seven-ounce boy. He was her first baby born in a hospital (Dr. Duffy insisted), and her first brown-eyed baby. They named him Richard Luther.

When Doc and Lizzie visited a few months later, Doc rubbed the baby's head. "Look at this," he said, "like a rock. I'm going to call you Rocky." The name stuck.

To make room for the crib in their bedroom, Willa moved Charley's white trunk into the dining room. She wouldn't let the children open it, but she allowed them to use it in their games. Charley's trunk became the watchtower of their blanket forts, a pirate's treasure chest, a stage for singing and whistling along with the radio, and a brand-new white Cadillac car they drove out of their rutted, dirt driveway, tires squealing and motor roaring, onto the interstate highway.

Making Money
1946

WILLY WAITED ON THE PORCH for the rain to stop. After a downpour was the best time to find nails. Willy was home alone, except for Jake, who was working in the machine shed. Willa, Annie, Frankie, and Rocky had gone to town to deliver eggs and stock up on staples at the big IGA grocery store. Willa's only egg customer was the Enid Diner, who liked her large, farm- fresh eggs. She had twenty dozen to deliver today, and at fifty-five cents a dozen, that would net her eleven dollars. Running money she called it. They would eat dinner with Aunt Martha and would be gone all day.

Jake was replacing a cracked head on the John Deere tractor. He wasn't able to weld the old head, and he ordered a new one from Sedlak's store. Another unexpected expense but essential since the wheat couldn't wait to be sowed. He told Sedlak's to put it on his bill, and in the winter, he'd work in their garage to pay it off.

Except for baby Rocky, the Hardesty children were expected to work to earn their keep. "You don't work, you don't eat," their mother told them. They weren't paid for chores or given an allowance, but they could earn money picking up nails. Jake paid a quarter for each twelve- ounce coffee can filled with rusty #6 and #8 nails. On the farm there seemed to be a limitless supply of nails strewn on the ground or scattered in the weeds. Nails that punctured tires or could give you lockjaw if you stepped on one.

Even though Willy loved going with his mother and the other kids to Enid, he gave up his once-a-month chance because he figured he could collect a lot of nails after the rain. He planned to work his way from the porch, through the yard, to the driveway, and down to the mailbox.

By the time Willy plodded halfway down the driveway, his coffee can was a third full. Moist earth was caked between his bare toes, and his hands and face were stained with the deep red juice of black mulberries. Willy couldn't resist the fruit that hung ripe and sweet from the trees that shaded the driveway. His mother didn't use the berries for pies because they were too juicy, so the kids usually ate them from the trees. Willy put a handful of berries into the pocket of his overalls to eat later. He'd have to be careful not to squish them. He picked up the coffee can and walked in the center of the road, his eyes scanning right and left, searching for nails.

The blast of a car horn startled him. He dropped the can, spilling nails onto the ground. A huge black car streaked with mud and dirt stopped in front of him. Willy had just started the first grade, but he could read the word CADILLAC spelled out on the front fender. He forgot the nails and ran to the side of the car. "Mr. Drummond!" he yelled, jumping up and down.

The back window of the car rolled down, and the fat face of Senator Drummond appeared. "Good morning, John Wyatt."

"I'm Willy."

"That may be true, but your Christian name is John, after your grandfather."

"Yes sir."

"Did your daddy send you out to greet me?"

"No sir. "

"Is he home?"

"He's in the shed working on the John Deere. Everybody else went to town."

"Why didn't you go along?"

"I'm picking up nails. Daddy pays me a quarter for each can."

"Working already? How old are you, John Wyatt?"

"I'm five."

"You're a good, hardworking boy. Would you like to make some more money?"

"Yes sir! I like making money."

"Have you ever seen a silver dollar?"

"Uh-huh. Mama showed me."

The senator held up a silver coin. "You can have this if you do something for me."

"Okay."

The senator beckoned Willy to come closer.

Willy stepped to the open window. So close that he could smell the senator's sweet cologne and see the thready red lines in his eyes.

"What do you want me to do?"

"Not much, but it's real important. Don't tell anyone I was here today."

"Not even Mama?"

"Especially her. It's a secret you can keep with your daddy. Can you do that?"

Willy looked at the silver dollar. His mother had taught him that the worst thing he could do was lie. "Never lie to me," she said. But this wasn't lying.

"Sure! I can do it."

"Good boy. Here's your dollar." Willy opened his red-stained hand and Drummond dropped the coin onto his palm.

Willy buttoned the silver dollar into the top pocket of his overalls. He watched the car drive toward the shed, and then he remembered the spilled nails. He hoped the Cadillac's tires didn't run over them. He picked up the loose nails, dropped them into the can, and headed down the driveway. The sun was just breaking through the clouds. Soon, the ground would be steaming in the hot sun. Willy grinned and ate some mulberries. He was really happy he decided not to go to town. He couldn't wait to show Annie and Frankie his silver dollar. Then he remembered he couldn't tell them where he got it, which meant he couldn't show it off unless he lied. It was a dilemma. Willy pondered his problem as he went back to work picking up nails.

Senator Drummond ordered his driver to stop in front of the open door of the machine shed. Jake heard the car approach, wiped his greasy hands on a rag, and walked out to meet the senator. He didn't know the driver, a Negro man wearing a suit, who got out to stretch and smoke a cigarette.

"So this is the new one," Jake said. "It looks pretty much like the 1942 model."

Senator Drummond opened the back door of the Cadillac, but he didn't get out. He suffered from gout, and he preferred to do his business sitting down. In fact, he bought the new Cadillac in part because of the folding footrest in the back.

"The bumpers are different," the senator said. He patted the backseat. "Get in and talk to me, Jake."

Jake took off his hat and slid in beside the senator. The car smelled of new upholstery and Drummond's heavy cologne.

He passed Jake an envelope. "The boys cleared everything out of the granary in June like we agreed. But we had a little problem at the new place."

"Where's that?"

"The Byford place, east of Oklahoma City. Anyway, the sheriff wanted to make a name for himself instead of making some money. Nine thousand pints of whiskey, smashed and down the drain. Goddamn fool!"

Jake did a quick calculation. At four dollars and fifty cents a pint that was over forty thousand dollars.

"Things are hot around the city right now, and I need a place to consolidate my operation for the time being. Now, here's the plan. My boys will do all the work. They'll put in a conveyer belt to move the cases. Hell, they'll even lay a new cement floor in the granary. You'd get two hundred a month and wouldn't have to do a damn thing except spend the money."

"How many cases are we talking about?"

"Seven, eight hundred, maybe more."

"I don't know, Senator. I promised Willa that I was done with it."

"What are you saying, Jake? Are you the man here or is your wife calling the shots?"

Jake rubbed his aching left thigh. The old bullet wound never stopped throbbing and sometimes a clear liquid oozed from the scar tissue.

"Well, Jake, what do you say?"

Jake looked past the senator at all the work that needed doing. Everything cost more now. Seed wheat, gas, groceries, parts, propane. Mrs. Boyce wouldn't pay for any improvements on the house so they bought paint and linoleum, even a new toilet, knowing they'd never get the money back. With the extra cash from the liquor storage, he could buy a new tractor, help Jimmy pay off his debts, buy Willa something nice. Jake watched Willy running down the driveway toward the car, holding a can of nails. Willy thought a quarter was a fortune, and he was proud of earning it. The liquor money was easy money but unearned. And Jake risked everything for it.

Jake put his hat on and made up his mind. "Thanks for thinking of me, Senator, but I just can't do it. That's the way it is." He stepped out of the car, shoved the envelope in his pocket, and stood by the open door. Willy ran up beside him holding his can of nails.

"Goddamnit, Jake, you've let me down! And after all I've done for you!"

Drummond wasn't used to being denied, and he was furious. "I've known you for most of your life," he said, his voice cold and hard. "Your father, rest his soul, was a good man and a friend. But I'll tell you right now, Jake Hardesty, you'll never be anything but a piss-poor tenant farmer with a crippled leg, scraping by from harvest to harvest on somebody else's land."

Drummond's words fell on him like gut punches. Jake reached for something to hold on to like he'd done so many times in the ring. He laid his hand on Willy's head. "Run into the house and get the senator a glass of ice water, Willy."

"Yes sir." Willy sneaked a glance at the senator. His face was all red. He was really mad. Because his dad had a bad leg? It wasn't his fault.

"Go on, Willy."

Willy ran.

"Your boy should hear this, Jake. He told me he liked making money. He should know that you'll have nothing to leave him or the rest of your kids. You'll work like a dog all your life for somebody else."

Jake waited until he heard the screen door slam and Willy was in the house. He leaned down and looked the senator in the face.

"If you ever talk to me like that again, in front of my boy, those will be your last words."

"Hell, Jake, you know I want what's best for you. You're like a son to me. But you've allowed yourself to be pussy whipped by Willa. Now, she's a fine woman, but she doesn't know anything about making money. I'm offering you a sweet deal here."

"I can't. Willa will find out. The goddamn truck wakes her up. She said she'd run it off herself with the shotgun or call the sheriff if she hears it again."

"Well, that's easy. Make sure she doesn't hear it."

Jake stuck his hands in his pockets. He fingered the envelope filled with cash and the idea just popped in his head. A vision really. A high stack of maize bales. He turned the picture around in his mind. The truck could get off the county road, cross the alfalfa field into the maize patch. It was a half mile from the house. Willa wouldn't hear a thing. It would work. A way around Willa. A way to make both her and the senator happy. A way to put money in his pocket.

Willy ran up to the car. "Sir, here's your water." He gave the glass of ice water to Drummond, who drank it in one long draught.

"Thank you, John Wyatt. That hits the spot. And here's a quarter for your trouble."

"Thank you, sir!"

"Take the glass back to the house, Willy. I need to take a little drive with the senator. I'll be right back and you can give me a hand fixing the tractor. One of these days I'll teach you to drive it and then you can make some real money."

"How much, Daddy?"

"Oh, I don't know. A dollar a day."

Willy walked back to the house and thought of silver dollars piled high, one for every day of the week.

Jake motioned to the driver, who stubbed out his cigarette and got into the car. Jake slid in next to Drummond and slammed the door shut. The Cadillac rumbled down the rutted driveway.

When Willa washed Willy's dirty overalls, she turned out the pockets and discovered a sticky mulberry mess in the right front pocket. She was surprised to find a silver dollar and a quarter tucked into the breast pocket. She scrubbed out the berry stains and set the money aside. When the overalls were dry, she ironed them and put the coins back where she found them. She wondered how Willy got the money, but it belonged to him. If there was something she needed to know, she trusted her son to tell her.

New Words
1946-1947

"Do you want to read Webb's letter with me?" Willa asked. It was the Wednesday after Labor Day. Because it was an unusually hot, muggy day, Annie changed into a playsuit when she got home from school.

As she did every afternoon, Annie picked up the mail from the mailbox. She had grown over the summer, and she didn't need to stand on the wooden crate to open the mailbox's metal door. She was seven and in the second grade. On rainy or snowy days, her dad took her to school in the pick-up. On nice days, she walked a half-mile to the one-room Pleasant Valley School. She took the shortcut along Sand Creek and through the pasture. Next year, when the new school opened in Kremlin, a school bus would stop at the end of their driveway.

Willa believed that all of her children were smart. But as time went by, it became clear to her that Annie was extremely intelligent. She walked at ten months and was talking at a year. When she was three years old, she knew her alphabet, could read simple books, could count and add using her blocks. In first grade, Annie already knew everything that Miss Rathman was teaching, and to keep her from getting bored, Willa encouraged her to read every day and to write letters. For Christmas and her birthday, Annie always received a box of stationery, stamps, and books. She preferred books and puzzles to her doll. Anyway, she had her brother Rocky, a real baby to play with, so she gave the doll to her other brothers, who scalped it.

Willa loved having a daughter. She talked to Annie as if the child were her friend. She consulted with her about what to have for supper, counted on her to settle arguments between Willy and Frankie, and used her as a babysitter for Rocky. Jake adored his pretty, blue-eyed daughter with brown hair and a square jaw just like his. He took her for rides on Fortney and showed her the growing wheat and alfalfa and pointed out the buffalo wallows in the pasture and the traces of the old Chisholm Trail.

Annie tore open the blue airmail envelope with the foreign stamps, unfolded the tissue thin paper and gave the letter to her mother.

"Cara," Willa read aloud, "I've decided to stay here in Rome. The Germans blew up many of the rails and viaducts, and now they all have to be rebuilt. My experience in Naples rebuilding the rails proved to the Italians that I know what I'm talking about. In fact, I'm thinking of writing a book about American railroaders in Italy. Note that my address has changed. I've moved to the third floor of a palazzo (palace or mansion). In a nearby piazza (a town square) there's a wonderful market called Campo dei Fiori, the name literally means field of flowers. You would love all the fresh vegetables and fruits and flowers. I've had a bean and pasta soup here that's almost as good as your ham and beans. They use olive oil for cooking. I'll send you some of it one of these days. Write soon and tell me your news. I heard from Stub that your dad is doing poorly. Webb

P.S. Here's a sentence for Annie. Io guardato con il occhio! (It means I shot him a look — gave him the eye. Io = I, occhio = eye) Tell Annie if she's really interested in learning more, I'll send her an Italian grammar. Va bene? (means Okay.)"

"Okay, Annie. Tell me how many new words you learned."

"What's a viaduct?"

"That's what the dictionary's for. Oh, look at the time. I better start supper. Go see what your brothers are doing."

"*Va bene*, Mama!" Annie ran outside and unlike her brothers, she remembered to close the screen door carefully instead of letting it bang shut.

Annie found her brothers and her father at Sand Creek. The water was shallow near the sandy bank, but in places it formed deep, clear pools. Rocky was sitting on the ground shaping moist sand into pies and loaves, and Frankie and Willy were splashing in and out of the water.

"Come here, Annie," Jake said. He grabbed her under the arms and swung her over the creek, dipping her legs in the water. Annie squealed in delight as the cool water sprinkled her skin.

"Do me, Daddy! Do me!" shouted Willy.

"Me too!" screamed Frankie.

Jake played with his children for half an hour, swinging them over and into the water, making them laugh with pure joy. Rocky took a turn, too, and then went back to his sand pile, lining up his baked goods in neat rows to dry in the sun.

When Willa called them to come to supper, they walked to the house, dripping wet and worn-out. Jake carried Rocky on his shoulders, who had cried when Jake told him he had to leave his pies and loaves behind.

Willa opened the screen door to let them in, took one look, and the words flew out of her mouth. "What's the matter with you? Don't you know how children get polio?" she shouted, furious with Jake for being so stupid and so careless.

"The kids are fine," he said, swinging Rocky down from his shoulders.

"What's polio?" asked Frankie.

"A sickness," Annie said. "It makes you crippled."

"I don't want to be crippled!" said Willy.

"Don't want to be crippled!" echoed Frankie.

"Shut up!" said Willy, shoving Frankie, who pushed back.

"Get out of those wet clothes! Now!" Willa said. The children fled.

"Sand Creek's clean," Jake said, pulling off his boots. "We were just having fun."

"You're nothing but a big, overgrown kid. Go tell the other kids that supper's ready."

The *Enid Morning News* ran polio reports as if they were

reporting the weekly weather. No one knew why, but the danger of polio was greatest during the hot summer months and the disease dwindled in the winter. For weeks after their dip in the creek, Willa checked her children for the polio warning signs of a stiff neck, fever, sore throat, and headache.

The weather stayed unseasonably hot that fall. On the morning of November 19, Frankie's birthday, Willa fried eggs and bacon for Annie and wondered whether she should make a cake or cupcakes for Frankie. The boys were still sleeping, and Jake had eaten earlier and gone off to do chores. She put a plate in front of Annie, who was dressed for school.

"I'm not hungry, Mama."

"You've got to eat something."

"Okay." Annie took a bite of bacon and then spit it out.

"Annie! You know better than that!"

"My throat hurts."

"Let me see." Annie opened her mouth wide. "Your throat doesn't look red." Willa put her hand on Annie's forehead. "You do feel a little feverish, though. Can you touch your chin to your chest?"

"It hurts, Mama."

"Your head or your neck?"

"Both."

The fear hit Willa first in her gut and then spread through her body. She turned away from Annie and poured a glass of milk. "Here, drink this."

Annie took a sip of milk and swallowed. "I told you, Mama, it hurts!"

"I'll be right back, honey."

Willa found Jake in the hog shed. She told Jake to stay with the boys, and she drove Annie to Enid. Dr. Duffy examined Annie and confirmed Willa's worst fear.

"She appears to have polio," he said. "Her chest muscles are already failing, and her breathing is labored. You need to take her to Crippled Children's Hospital in Oklahoma City right now."

Willa called Jake, but he was outside with the boys and didn't answer. She told Edna, the switchboard operator, to keep calling until she got him and tell him where she had gone and why. Something in Willa stiffened and grew fierce. Not this time, she decided. No more.

"Let's go, Annie," she said, taking her daughter's hand. "We've got a lot of work to do and a long way to go."

At the hospital, when Annie was wheeled into the ward and saw the row of green iron lungs with the children's heads sticking out, she was terrified. Gasping, struggling to breathe, she implored her mother to take her home. Willa wiped the tears from Annie's cheeks. "You're going to be all right," she said, making her voice strong and confident. "The machine will help you breathe. You've got to be brave."

Willa sat with her face close to Annie's as she lay in the iron tank, and the technician adjusted the valves. As the machine began to breathe for her, Annie felt the weight on her chest lighten.

"See," Willa said, "isn't that better?"

That night and for the next three days, Willa stayed with

Annie to help her adjust to her new prison. Annie learned to eat, drink, swallow, speak, and laugh to the ba-thump-a, ba-thump-a rhythm of the iron lung.

On the third day, the nurse summoned Willa to take a phone call. It was her old friend from Alva, Carol Ferguson, who lived in Oklahoma City and was now Carol Evinsen, the mother of two children and pregnant with a third.

"How did you know I was here?" Willa asked.

"Arlene called me. Everybody knows. I want you to stay with me."

When Willa left the message with Edna at the Kremlin switchboard, Edna rang a general ring. The neighbors who picked up the call agreed that since the Johnsons lived the closest they should send their son Frank to the Hardesty farm to find Jake and tell him the news. Jake called Lizzie and Doc in Old Freedom, his brother Jim in Alva, and Aunt Martha in Enid. They, in turn, called other family members and friends, and the news of polio, that dreaded disease, whose very name whipped up fear, spread. Everyone checked their children and themselves for symptoms. Heck and Lucy were especially concerned since Donna Jean had spent the weekend with Annie.

Willa racked her brain to figure out how Annie had been exposed to polio. The boys were fine. The dip in the creek couldn't have caused it since it happened too long ago. Was it when she took her to Enid to deliver eggs? Was it someone Annie brushed against at the IGA? Then there was the question that haunted her. Was there something she could have done to prevent it? She talked to the other mothers in the ward and listened to their stories. They were all the same. No one knew why it happened, it just happened.

As the weeks passed and then months, Willa and Annie got used to the new rhythm of their lives. Willa and Jake were relieved to learn that the Infantile Paralysis Foundation would take care of Annie's eighty-six-dollar a day hospital fee while she was in the iron lung and the five-dollar a day hospital fee after that. The hospital told them to pay whatever they could afford, and the Foundation would pay the rest. President Roosevelt had been instrumental in raising money for polio, and Willa said a prayer of thanks to the man who had saved her once again.

Still, Willa worried constantly about money. She scoured her old notebooks looking for unpaid debts she could collect and found several months of work that Jake had done for Glen Sedlak back in the spring of 1943. When she asked Jake about it, he said that Sedlak had paid him, and he'd forgotten to tell her.

"Here," Jake said, peeling off five twenty-dollar bills from the roll in his pocket, "take this. Buy something for Annie or fix up her room." Willa took the money and bought a used hospital bed with an extra firm mattress and a back that could be raised and lowered. She didn't question why Jake always seemed to have plenty of cash in his pocket. She hadn't heard the trucks at night and Senator Drummond hadn't been around, so she believed Jake was out of the liquor storage business. Every moment he could spare from farming and their own operation, he filled in at Sedlak's store or hired out as a farmhand. He had lost weight and was worn down just as she was by worry about Annie.

Every Sunday morning, Jake drove Willa to Midway, where she caught the bus for Oklahoma City to spend the day at the hospital with Annie. At the bus station, either Carol would pick her up or she would take the streetcar to the hospital. Willa bought a box of picture postcards and every day, including Sunday, she wrote to Annie.

A few times, instead of Willa, Jake took the bus to visit his daughter. Willa asked him to go once a month, but he always found some excuse not to. She knew how much he hated hospitals and didn't push him, but still she wondered how a man so strong could be so weak, especially when Annie longed to see him. When Willa missed a Sunday because she had a cold, Carol Evinsen took her place so that Annie wouldn't be without a visitor. In March, the whole family drove down, and Annie was able to stand and wave to her brothers from the window as they played below.

Annie was released from the iron lung in mid-January and her lungs slowly returned to normal. Her right arm and her left arm above the elbow, however, were permanently paralyzed. Every day she received physical therapy and hot pack treatments. At first, Annie hated the smell and itchiness of the wet wool packs wrapped tightly around her body, but the stoicism and discipline she learned in the iron lung helped her to endure. Luckily, she was left-handed and was able to write letters. Annie received cards and gifts from family and friends and from kind strangers as far away as Florida and California.

In early April, Willa drove to the Crippled Children's Hospital for the last time. After picking up wool packs and instructions from the nurses and doctor and packing Annie's clothes and gifts, Willa walked out of the hospital with her daughter beside her. Annie had grown taller in the hospital and her head was almost level with Willa's shoulder. She carried a teddy bear that a woman in Chicago sent her and a box with the letters and postcards that she received. Willa put Annie's suitcase in the back of the pick-up, and she watched how Annie managed her load. Annie set her items on the ground, opened the door with her left hand by standing on tiptoe and flinging her hand up to reach the handle, then she retrieved her bear and the box and placed them inside. She got in and shut the door. Willa took a deep breath. So far so good, she thought.

Thunderstorms threatened as Willa and Annie made the one-hundred-four-mile trip home, and strong winds buffeted the pick-up. Willa held tightly to the wheel. Jake and the boys would be waiting with supper ready. Probably fried potatoes and baked beans, which was all he knew how to cook.

Willa looked at her daughter, who would be eight years old on July 13. Annie sat up straight, thin shoulders back, her left arm resting on her withered right arm, which lay in her lap. She turned toward her mother, her blue eyes bright with intelligence.

"I learned another new word on Sunday, Mama."

"What?"

"Perseverance."

"That's a big word," Willa said. "What's it mean?"

"I forget exactly. But it's something like being able to work hard for a long time."

"We'll look it up in the dictionary when we get home. Okay?"

"*Va bene*, Mama."

Okay, Willa thought. She's not giving up. I'm not giving up. We're going to be okay.

Family Secrets
1947

JAKE HAD TAKEN THE KIDS with him to Pond Creek to get another block of ice for the icebox. Willa sat at the kitchen table drinking a cup of coffee, smoking a cigarette, and enjoying the quiet. It was nine o'clock, and she'd been up since four. Soon, everyone would be gathering at the home place. Except for last year when Annie got sick, they always made the trip to Lizzie and Doc's in Old Freedom for Thanksgiving. But without asking her, Jake bought a live turkey from Breckinridge's. His way of saying they weren't going anywhere this Thanksgiving.

Willa knew he was right; they had their own family now, but she wanted to see her folks, especially her father. She knew Doc would miss her sage dressing and cherry pie, but he wouldn't complain. As his body failed, he fell silent. He refused to talk on the telephone or write letters. She'd have to go by herself, maybe after Christmas when the kids were back in school.

The aroma of the browning turkey filled the kitchen and reminded Willa that she hadn't chopped onions and celery for the dressing. She baked pumpkin, pecan, and cherry pies before she made breakfast. The fresh cranberries were cooked and cooling in the icebox, the light rolls were rising, the potatoes were peeled and waiting, and the bread shredded and seasoned for the dressing. Time to get with it.

She heard the crunch of tires on the gravel driveway and the rattling of a loose muffler. It couldn't be Jake and the kids back already. She went to the door and stepped outside. The sky was blue and clear. It was going to be a beautiful day, sunny and not too chilly. Jim Hardesty got out of a rust-pocked Ford pick-up.

"Hey Jim! Where's your car?"

"Sally has it. Hell, she's got everything else. She might as well have it, too."

"Weren't you and your boys supposed to have Thanksgiving at Aunt Milly's?"

"What was supposed to be and what is are two different things. Do you have any coffee?"

"I sure do. Come on in."

"You're as pretty as a ripe peach, Willa. Is Jake treating you right? If he isn't, just let me know, and the Fair Valley Phantom will kick his ass."

"I can't complain. How've you been?"

"Not so good, Willa, not so good." Jim warmed his hands on the coffee cup, his blue eyes staring off into the distance with the same blank, unblinking stare that Jake slipped into from time to time, as if his mind were a thousand miles away.

Willa studied Jim's thick, brown hair, and square, unshaven face. He looked so much like Jake except for the scars around his eyes, and the nose that was slightly off-center. All that battering in the ring had taken its toll, but he was still a handsome man, and only thirty-four, two years older than Jake.

"So why aren't you at Aunt Milly's?"

"I went to Sally's to pick the boys up early this morning like we'd arranged, but they weren't there. The car was gone, the house locked up tight, no note, nothing. Even the damn dog was gone."

"What'd you do?"

"I called her folks, but they said they hadn't seen her. I called Aunt Milly to see if Sally might have taken the boys there, but she hadn't heard anything. I drove around Alva for a while looking for her, and then I came here." Jim's voice cracked, and his hands shook as he lifted his coffee cup.

"I bet you didn't have breakfast," Willa said, pushing her chair away from the table. "Am I right?"

Jim nodded.

"I'll fry up some eggs and bacon. We won't eat dinner for a couple of hours. Jake and the kids went to Pond Creek for ice." Willa filled his cup. "Here, get rid of that tie."

Jim loosened his tie and gave it to Willa. He took a sip of coffee and smiled. "It's good."

"There's something I've been meaning to ask you," Willa said.

"Not about Sally."

"No. About Jake. And I want you to tell me the truth."

"I always tell you the truth. What is it?"

"I want to know what really happened to Jake's leg."

"He hasn't told you? That sonofagun."

"Just some made-up stories."

"No, I guess he wouldn't. Jake's got a lot of pride."

"So will you tell me?"

"Sure, as soon as you make me some eggs."

"How do you like them?"

"Over easy would be good."

Willa set the plate filled with two eggs, three slices of bacon, and buttered toast in front of Jim. She pulled up a chair across from his and lit a cigarette. "Well?"

Jim took a bite of toast. "I love your bread, Willa. It's been a long time since I've had bread this good."

"You're not going to get out of telling me."

"Okay. Settle down. Let's see. Jake had just started working on the Eden Ranch. I think he was eighteen or nineteen."

By the time Jim came to the end of his story and mopped up the last piece of egg with his toast, Willa was shaking with laughter. "Oh, poor Jake!" She lit another cigarette. "What happened to the dog?"

"I don't know. Probably died laughing."

Jake and the kids picked up the ice in Pond Creek, but instead of hurrying home as Willa had asked, they were taking their own sweet time. Annie, Willy, Frankie, and Rocky loved riding with their dad in the pick-up. Especially since he let them take turns driving. Two-year-old Rocky stood between Jake's legs, holding onto the steering wheel and guiding the pick-up down the middle of the deserted dirt road.

"That a boy," Jake said. "Keep 'er steady. Now, Annie, I'm going to get up a little more speed and when I press on the clutch, I want you to shift it into second."

"I want to do it! She can't do it! She's a cripple!" yelled Willy.

"Am not!" Annie said.

"Are too!" bellowed Willy. He shoved Annie aside and grabbed the gearshift with both hands.

"Whoa!" said Jake. "Steer it over toward the ditch, Rocky. That's good." Jake stopped the pick-up just short of Mud Creek Bridge, turned off the ignition, and pulled Rocky down onto his lap.

"Now, I want to tell you kids something," he said, his voice low and harsh. "And I want you to listen because I'm only going to tell you once. Yes, Annie's a cripple. Don't cry, Annie. There's nothing wrong with being a cripple. Hell, a lot of people are cripples. President Roosevelt was a cripple. I'm a cripple."

"You are?" said Annie.

"Damn right, and I'm proud of it. I'm a survivor, just like you Annie. You beat that damned polio. A lot of kids didn't. So you just keep your head up and your back straight, like your Mama told you. You're smart. A helluva lot smarter than me or your brothers, and you can do anything you set your mind to, including driving a car. And you, Willy, I better not ever hear you say that she can't do something. Are you listening, boy?"

"Yes, Daddy," Willy said.

"Don't you have something to say to Annie?"

"I'm sorry, Annie."

"That's better," said Jake. "Let's get out for a minute. I want to stretch my legs. Anybody need to pee?"

Frankie watched as Jake rubbed his left thigh and then limped across the wooden bridge. "Did you have polio, Daddy?"

"I thought I told you how my leg got hurt."

"No, Daddy, you didn't," said Annie. "I heard Mama say you got shot."

"An Indian shot me," Jake announced. He turned Rocky upside down and balanced him on his head on the iron banister of the bridge. "With an arrow. Almost killed me, too."

"A real live Indian?" said Willy.

"Yeah. With feathers and war paint and everything."

"Oh, Daddy, you're just telling a story," said Annie.

"I've got the scar on my leg to prove it. You've all seen that. Would you believe that I can stand on my head on this bridge?"

"I don't know. I guess if we saw you do it," said Annie.

"That's my girl. Keep an eye on Rocky. Let me know if you see a car coming." The children watched transfixed as Jake tossed his Stetson in the pick-up, tightened his belt, and rolled up his shirtsleeves. He laid his hands on the flat iron railing, measuring its width. He hopped up on the rail, got on his knees, and put his head down on the banister. He gripped the iron rail with both hands, pushed himself up with his arms, and then kicked his legs up into the air. He held himself straight and balanced. "See! Easy as pie." The children stared, wide-eyed. "Well, where's my applause? I can't stay up here forever."

The children clapped and laughed. Jake lowered himself and sat on the rail. "Now do you believe me?"

"Sure, Daddy," said Willy, "but what about the Indian?"

"What Indian? Go get my hat, Willy."

"Stop teasing us!" said Annie. "The Indian who shot you!"

"Oh, so now you believe me, huh?"

"Tell us about the Indian," said Willy, giving his father the hat.

"Whoo! Whoo! Whoo!" whooped Rocky, jumping up and down.

"Okay, I'll tell you, but don't tell your mama. It'll be our secret. You see, she's scared of Indians."

"I don't think Mama's scared of anything," argued Annie.

"You may be right about that," said Jake, "but I don't want to take any chances. Come up here and sit beside me and I'll tell you."

Rocky climbed onto Jake's lap, and the other children lined up along the rail. "It happened a long time ago when I was a little boy, not much bigger than Willy. I was living on the 101 Ranch over by Ponca City with my Dad and brothers. I'll take you there one of these days. Well, every year the ranch had a Wild West show. One of the acts was a big shoot-out between cowboys and Indians. They had a lot of Indians since the Ponca Indians lived right there on and around the 101, but they always needed more cowboys. One year, I think it was 1922, I'm not sure, me and your Uncle Jimmy were asked to work as extra cowboys. They gave us costumes and everything."

"Cowboy hats?" asked Willy.

"Hats, boots, chaps, spurs, the whole shebang. Anyway, we were just supposed to follow one old boy. He'd been in the show for years and knew all the patterns. Now, the cowboys had blanks in their guns, but the Indians used real arrows. So anyway, the day of the show, my horse threw a shoe and they gave me this green filly, but I could ride her okay."

"What was her name?" asked Annie.

"Hell, I don't know. Doesn't matter. Anyway, the show started out in the big pasture. The people watching were in the bleachers or standing on their cars. Jim and me and the other cowboys were riding herd on some steers. At first it was all peaceful like, then the Indians attacked, riding over this little rise as fast as they could. I knew it was make believe, but it was still scary. They were whooping and hollering and shooting arrows high in the air so they wouldn't hit anybody. The cattle got spooked and stampeded like they were supposed to and Jim and some of the other cowboys took off after the cattle, while some other cowboys started shooting at the Indians. I was supposed to ride off with Jim and the others, but my horse got scared and started bucking. I didn't know what to do so I just hung on as best I could. Arrows were flying way over my head, but then my filly bucked so far off the ground, must have been at least ten feet, that one of those arrows caught me right here in my left leg. It went clean through my leg and into the saddle. The good thing was there was no way that filly was going to buck me off now. I was nailed to that saddle like the planks on this bridge."

"Did you cry?" asked Annie.

"Not at first, I just hollered, but later, oh boy, I bawled like a baby. My horse kept bucking, and I rode her, and the crowd was clapping and cheering. They thought it was part of the act. Anyway, one of the cowboys finally grabbed the filly's reins and calmed her down. When he saw that I was shot, he said I'd have to ride to the doctor myself. So that's what I did."

"Where was granddad?" asked Annie. "He could have pulled out the arrow."

"I don't know. I didn't see him until it was all over. Anyway, I rode two miles on that filly, with my leg bleeding and hurting like the devil. They had to cut my jeans off and then pry the arrowhead out of the saddle. Then it took another hour for the doctor to get the arrow out of my leg. They put a steel plate in my leg. If you press right here, you can feel it."

One by one, the children pressed their fingers into Jake's thigh. "Remember, it's our secret," said Jake. "Promise?" The children nodded and crossed their hearts.

"Now, whose turn is it to drive?" asked Jake.

That evening, after the chores were done, supper was eaten, the leftovers cleared from the dining room table, and the dishes washed, Willa got out the cards. "Who wants to play pitch?"

Everybody wanted to play. Jake and Willy partnered with Annie, who had learned how to play cards when she was in the hospital. Willa, with Rocky on her lap, partnered with Frankie and Jim. After a few games when they'd gotten set every time, Willa could see that Jim's mind wasn't on the game. Then it was her turn to deal. She shuffled the cards and then put them back in the box. "We'd better stop," she said. "You kids should be in bed." She picked up Rocky, who had fallen asleep with his head on the table, gathered up the other children and herded them into the bathroom.

"Jake, do you have any bourbon?" asked Jim.

"I think I can find some for you."

Jake poured a shot glass of bourbon and gave it to Jim. "Do you need anything else? There's plenty of pie left."

"Well, I could use some cash."

"How much?

"What have you got?"

"Let's see." Jake pulled a roll of bills from his pocket. "I've got a hundred forty dollars here, and Willa keeps some cash in the buffet drawer." Jake found an envelope in the top drawer of the buffet. He took out the bills, counted them, and stacked them with his roll. "Here. Two hundred ten dollars. It's all we got on hand. On Monday I can get more from the bank."

Jim stuffed the money into his pocket. "Thanks, Jake. I appreciate it. Tell Willa that was the best Thanksgiving meal I ever had. I better get on the road."

"Hell, stay the night. Dad's bed is still out there."

"No, I've got things to do."

Jake walked with Jim to his pick-up. The two brothers shook hands.

"Well, don't be a stranger," Jake said, fake-punching Jim in the gut. "Willa's already bought your damn Christmas present."

"You should buy her a present sometime, instead of making her buy her own."

"Hell, she doesn't mind. That way she gets what she wants."

"You're a lucky man, Jake. So long."

"I'll be seeing you." Jake hit the pick-up door with the flat of his hand as Jim pulled away. "Get that muffler tied up before it falls off!"

The following Monday, Willa and Jake had just gone to bed, when the phone rang. Willa ran to the kitchen and picked up the receiver. She heard others picking up, too. It was unusual for anyone to call after 9:00 at night, and everyone on the party line ran to the phone along with Willa.

"Hello," she said.

"I'd like to speak to Jake Hardesty," a man's voice said.

"He's in bed. This is Willa Hardesty. Can I help you?"

"This is Sheriff Greer, over in Alva, ma'am. I need to talk to Jake."

Someone on the line inhaled. "Yes sir. I'll go get him. And, all of you listening on this line can just hang up now. This is a private conversation." Willa waited. She heard two hang-up clicks, but she knew there were others still listening. Damn nosy busybodies. She went to get Jake.

Just Willa

Willa read and re-read the newspaper accounts and the coroner's report, looking for clues, searching for a reason. On the Monday after Thanksgiving, Jim arrived at Sally's house on Normal Street in Alva about 6:00 p.m. While his sons played in the backyard, he entered the washhouse where Sally was doing laundry. According to Sally, he raised a pistol to his right temple and pulled the trigger. He fell to the floor, blocking the door with his body. Neighbors heard the shot and called the sheriff. When Sheriff Greer arrived, Jim was dead. A deputy found a note in his pocket. Sheriff Greer and his deputies told the coroner's jury that during the last few weeks Jim had talked to them about contemplating suicide, but each time they had talked him out of it. When they'd seen him after Thanksgiving, he told them he was getting along okay now. He'd paid off some debts and seemed to be in good spirits.

Why did you do it? Willa wondered as she laid a bouquet of waxed red roses on Jim's grave. The note he'd left in his pocket didn't have any answers. It said: "Just could not take it. The reason, ask my ex-wife Sally Hardesty." The sheriff, the coroner's jury, Jake, and Willa had all asked Sally why. Sally said she didn't know and didn't stick around for the funeral. She took her sons and left town. No one, including her family, knew where she went.

A week after Jim's death, Jed Randall, a seventy-one-year-old farmer who lived north of Alva shot himself with a .22 pistol. The sheriff found him dead in a coffin he had built himself. Randall left a note saying that his health was so bad he just didn't want to live anymore. That made sense to

Willa, but she couldn't imagine why Jim, a young man with three growing sons, would do such a thing. Had Sally driven him to it, even egged him on? Were his money worries that bad? Willa wanted to know what Jake thought, but he wouldn't discuss it. At Jim's funeral in Alva, when the coffin was lowered into the grave, Jake broke down, and Willa led him to the pick-up. They drove home in silence. When Willa reached out to touch his face, Jake pushed her hand away.

The week before Christmas, the phone rang again, late.

"Daddy walked up to Cissie's, sat in a kitchen chair, and died," Dilly reported. "Mama said he just got up and left and didn't tell her where he was going. He hadn't said a word for weeks."

After Christmas, Lizzie came to stay for a week, but she had gone silent, too. She ignored her grandchildren. When Willa brought her the paper to read, she'd look at it for a few minutes and then set it aside. She sat for hours in the rocking chair in the living room just looking out the window. Her only comfort was the stone egg that she took from the bookcase and placed in her leather Indian pouch. Sometimes she took it out of the pouch and stroked it, murmuring softly to herself.

When she packed her mother's suitcase for the trip back to Old Freedom, Willa returned the stone to its place on the bookshelf. Realizing that the stone was missing from the pouch, Lizzie wailed and cried until Willa put it back. What was it about that old rock? Willa wondered.

Weeks passed. There was work to be done, animals to feed, and children to raise. When Willa tried to talk to Jake about Jim's suicide again, he raised his arm as if he was going to slap her and then stopped himself. "Don't pick at the goddamn scab!" he growled.

But Willa couldn't leave the wound alone. She kept thinking about it. She needed to solve problems, to know the answer, and make a plan. One day while she was hanging clothes on the line, she remembered something Jim told her a long time ago. "Who knows why people do things. It's a mystery," he said. That's bullshit, Willa believed. People did things for a reason.

She reached up to clip a pillowcase to the line, and the wind whipped a wet shirt across her face. Her eyes filled with tears. You never knew when something was going to hit you. She'd have to find a way to live with that.

Sedlak's Store
1948

WILLA WAITED IN THE PICK-UP behind Sedlak's store for Willy to return. She sent him into Sedlak's by himself with the egg order Old Man Sedlak called in at 6:00 that morning. Someone who needed dozens of deviled eggs for a Labor Day picnic had cleaned out his inventory, and he asked Willa to sell him as many eggs as she could spare. She never shopped at Sedlak's unless it was an emergency and preferred to do her trading at the IGA in Enid, where prices were much cheaper.

Old Man Sedlak walked to work from his house across the street, and there were no other vehicles in the back lot. The mechanic's shop where Jake worked part-time in the winter wasn't open yet. Kirkpatrick's welding shop was closed too. He rented the space from Sedlak's and worked his own hours. Trash, broken parts, flat tires, and rusted pipe were strewn against the back of the building. Every six months or so Jake cleaned up the metal and took it away. Last time he made one hundred thirty dollars selling scrap to the junkyard in Enid. Plus Sedlak paid him to haul it away. A nice deal.

Just Willa

Willa thought briefly about going in to check on Willy, but decided that Old Man Sedlak must be taking his own sweet time digging around in the back room for the empty egg cartons. And her hair needed washing, and at eight months pregnant she wasn't moving very fast. Better to stay put and enjoy the cool breeze and the quiet. She lit a cigarette, closed her eyes, and laid her palm on her belly. The baby was quiet. She hoped this one was a girl. Ever since Rocky was born, Annie had begged for a sister. But that wasn't the only reason Willa had given in. She wanted a girl too. This one would be the last, and she told Dr. Duffy she wanted her tubes tied. The boys, of course, wanted another brother. Jake said he didn't care as long as it looked like him. Willa already had a girl's name picked out except she hadn't told Jake or anyone.

She opened her eyes and checked the back door of the store. Still no sign of Willy. Just as she decided to go fetch him, the back door opened and Willy backed out balancing a tall stack of empty egg cartons in his arms. The burden wasn't heavy, but it was awkward. He turned around and struggled to see where he was going and keep the load balanced. Just like efficient Willy to try to carry all the cartons in one trip. Although he'd still have to go back and shut the door.

Amused, Willa blew smoke rings out the window and watched his careful progress. She figured that he had a seventy-thirty chance of holding onto the cartons. At seven, he already considered himself grown-up, especially since Jake had taught him to drive the tractor.

She looked away for a moment to crush out her cigarette in the ash tray.

"OWW!" Willy shouted.

By the time she turned to look, all she could see were egg cartons lying in the dirt and Willy and another boy rolling around on the ground. She opened the pick-up door and climbed out. Willy smacked the boy in the face with his closed fist.

"Willy! Stop that!"

Her shouted warning stopped Willy's arm in mid-flight but he still straddled the smaller boy who struggled beneath him.

"He tripped me, Mama!"

"I don't care! Get off him, pick up the egg cartons, and go sit in the pick-up!"

"Yes, ma'am."

Willy did as he was told.

Willa stood over the smaller boy who was rubbing his eyes and whimpering.

"Well, get up," she said.

The boy stood up and wiped his nose with his hand.

"Lift up your head, boy, and look at me. I'm Mrs. Hardesty. Who are you?"

The boy tucked his chin into his chest and mumbled something.

"What's that? What's your name?"

"Jerry."

"All right, Jerry. Do you have a last name?"

"Sedlak. Jerry Sedlak."

"Glenn and Doris's boy? And you have a twin sister Janice?"

"Yes, ma'am."

"How old are you?"

"Almost five."

"I remember. You were born right before Christmas 1943. Stop crying, Jerry. I'm not going to hurt you. Although you should be punished for tripping Willy. Why did you do that?"

The boy shrugged his shoulders and turned away.

"No! You're not getting away that easy."

Willa moved closer, kneeled down, and put her hands on the boy's shoulders. He lifted his face and looked at her.

Willa gasped. The baby chose that moment to give her a sharp kick.

For a long moment, Willa and Jerry stared at one another. Jerry's sweeping dark eyelashes framed bright blue eyes swimming with tears. Dirt and what looked like Hersey's chocolate were smeared around his mouth and square jaw. A jaw with a tiny cleft. A small dimpled flaw. Sawdust and dirt covered his curly hair. Two stray curls drifted onto his dirty forehead.

Willa squeezed his shoulders.

"Oww! That hurts!"

Willa stood up. Was she going to throw up? She clenched her teeth. She stared at the boy who wouldn't meet her eyes.

"Tell me. Why did you trip Willy?"

"He's mean."

"Go on."

"He said if I ate candy bars and drank Cokes all the time my teeth would rot!"

"Well, he's telling you the truth. Where's your mother? Does she let you eat candy at six o'clock in the morning?"

"Uh-huh."

"What about your Grandpa?"

"I can have whatever I want! It's my store!"

"Where's your sister?"

"She's with Mama. Can I go now?"

"You should go wash your face. But first I want you to say you're sorry to Willy. Can you do that?"

"I'm not sorry! He's mean! He hit me! You're mean too!"

The boy stuck out his tongue and ran into the store, slamming the door behind him. Willa walked slowly to the pick-up and got in beside Willy.

"Here's the money for the eggs, Mama."

"Just hang onto it until we get home." She tousled her son's curly hair. He needed a hair cut again. "Are you okay, Willy?"

"Sure. He didn't hurt me. He's just a little spoiled baby."

"Do you know him?"

"Yeah. I've seen him a couple times at the store. Daddy said I should stay away from him and Janice."

"Did he tell you why?"

"I guess 'cause they're town kids." Willy thrust out his arm toward the steering wheel. "Mama! Watch out! You almost hit that mailbox!"

By the time they got back to the farm, Willa had her thoughts in order. First, she would find her 1943 notebook and check some dates. The question was, what then?

A Rainy Day
1951

"IF YOUR TONGUE GETS DRY," Willa advised, drink some water. "Or just wet this sponge and use it." Ellie sat on the kitchen floor pasting S&H green stamps into the booklet. Willa was saving the stamps to redeem for a set of the new Mel Mac dishes. The kids seemed to drop a piece of Fiesta every other day, and it would be nice to have a complete set of brand-new lightweight dishes that wouldn't break. In addition, pasting stamps was a good, rainy day job for Ellie, who missed her brothers and sister while they were at school.

Willa opened the back door and looked outside. It was pouring. Just in time, too, since Jake finished sowing wheat yesterday. Jake was in the garage tuning up their old pick-up, which they planned to trade in for a new 1951 Chevy pick-up. She checked the big advertising calendar she'd gotten free from Sedlak's store hanging to the right of the back door. Willa used it to keep track of birthdays, doctor appointments, school events, garden plantings, and their hay-baling schedule. Today was empty. Alfalfa season was over, feed season hadn't started yet, and for once, except for regular chores, Willa had a free day.

While she waited for her bread to rise, Willa sat at the kitchen table and sorted through a stack of snapshots and school photos she had tossed in a shoebox, separating the ones she wanted to place in the family album. Many of the pictures were two and three years old.

Willa studied a picture Heck had taken on Easter Sunday, 1949. Her mind drifted back to that day. Heck and Lucy had invited everyone to their house in Old Freedom for dinner and an Easter egg hunt. Heck had a new camera, and after the egg hunt, he decided to take family portraits. By the time he got to them, it was almost 4:00, and the kids were worn out. It wasn't a very good picture, but it was the only one Willa had of her whole family together. She placed a tiny black photo corner on each edge of the photo.

Bored with her job on the floor, Ellie pulled herself into a chair beside Willa and looked at the picture.

"Mama, that's you."

"Me with frizzy, long hair. And who's this?" Willa asked, pointing to Annie, who stood beside her on Willa's right, wearing her striped, cotton Easter jumper and the same frizzy hair-do.

"Annie Bananie!" said Ellie.

Those store permanents were an expensive mistake, thought Willa. She had to trim Annie's hair and cut her own to get rid of the fried, broken ends. Annie grew hers out so she could wear it in a ponytail, but Willa kept hers short. If you glanced quickly at the photograph, Annie's right arm looked normal, not limp and withered. Jake said she babied

Annie. Maybe she did. Annie liked to dust and straighten, but she hated washing or drying dishes and making her bed. Willa didn't push her. She'd rather Annie spend her time reading. So far Annie never received anything but A's on her report cards, and Willa wanted her to finish high school and go to college and be able to support herself.

Ellie jabbed at the photo with her finger. "Daddy, Silly Willy, Bad Frankie." Jake stood on the left side of Willa, smiling slightly and squinting into the sun. He never seemed to take a bad picture. His arms were around Willy, who stood in front of him, grinning the same grin. They both wore starched blue shirts and khakis. Willy had really taken on a lot of responsibility, helping with the younger kids and working with Jake in the fields like a man. Frankie, who would be nine in November, lounged in front of Willa, wearing a devilish smile and his old overalls. He'd ripped his good pants on the Easter egg hunt roughhousing with Dilly's boys, Bud and Leo. Frankie was a talker and a charmer. Always smiling and buttering you up to get an extra piece of pie or money for a comic book. Like Willy, though, he was a hard worker and could be trusted to keep a straight furrow when he plowed.

"Now, Ellie, who's this pretty baby?" Willa asked. In the photo, she held six-month-old Ellie high in her arms. With her large brown eyes, long, dark eyelashes, brown skin, and compact muscular body, Ellie was a miniature version of her mother. Except, Jake pointed out, she had the square Hardesty jaw. Jake adored the baby, whom he nicknamed Snooks. They all doted on the new arrival, with the exception of Rocky, who resented Ellie and the attention she got from their mother.

"That's me!" crowed Ellie.

"And what's your name?"

"Snooks."

"Your real name."

"Eleanor Sharpe Hardesty," Ellie recited.

"And who were you named after?"

"Eleanor Roosevelt."

"Why?"

"Because we have the same birthday!"

"When's your birthday?"

"Mama! You know! It's October 11. I'll be three!"

And Rocky, who had just started first grade, would be six on October 4. Where had the time gone? Willa wondered. It seemed like only yesterday when Ellie was born. So tiny. Five pounds and six ounces. She was perfectly plump and healthy, but Dr. Duffy insisted that she stay in an incubator until she gained ten ounces. At Willa's insistence, Dr. Duffy tied her tubes. They really couldn't afford any more children.

Willa poured herself another cup of coffee and lit a cigarette. She felt slightly guilty about sitting around doing nothing, but she had worked like a dog for months, and she deserved a moment of rest. This was nice, spending time with Ellie. She'd hardly seen her all summer.

Last year, when Billy's Army insurance check ran out, she and Jake started a custom hay baling business. Mrs. Boyce hinted that she was looking to sell her farm in a few years, and to buy it they needed a substantial down payment.

Jake bought another used tractor and two used balers from Sedlak's. Jake wanted to hire a man to work with him, but Willa said no, they couldn't afford it. Besides, she could drive a tractor better than any hired man. They taught Willy and Frankie to work as a baling crew, and with all four of them working, they needed to hire only two extra hands.

In a season with plenty of moisture, alfalfa could be cut and baled three, even four times. They had plenty of work, cutting and baling straw and alfalfa, and harvesting maize in the fall. In addition to her fieldwork and running the house, Willa took care of the bookkeeping and collected the money. At first, Jake would say just pay us when you can, which meant they were paid months later or not at all. "You want everybody to like you," Willa told him, "but being liked doesn't pay the bills." If customers didn't pay promptly, she hounded them until they did.

Jake ran one baling crew, and Willa the other. They hired Dilly's nineteen-year-old son, Leo, and Charley's old friend Frank Johnson, as extra hands. They still had to farm their own place which meant that sometimes Jake and Leo plowed most of the night, slept for a couple of hours, and then started baling in the morning. Willa hired her sister Ro's daughter, Lorraine, to live in and help with the cooking and housework. Every morning Willa got up at 5:00 to fix breakfast, start a batch of bread and cinnamon rolls for tomorrow's meals for Lorraine to finish, and pack field lunches and jugs of water. By 6:30 a.m., chores were done and breakfast eaten. As soon as the dew burned off, they could start baling.

Willa drove the tractor for her crew, Frank Johnson blocked, throwing the iron block plates that separated the hay into bales, and Willy hand tied the bales with baling wire. Willy and Frankie didn't have the strength yet to throw the heavy blocks. On Jake's crew, Frankie drove the tractor, Jake blocked, and Leo tied.

At a time when tractor gas was nine cents a gallon, they earned seventeen cents a bale. If they put the bales in the barn, they got an extra ten cents a bale. The work was filthy and exhausting and sometimes dangerous. Summer heat in Oklahoma often reached between one hundred and one hundred ten degrees. Sitting on the iron seats of the baler was like sitting on a hot stove. Willa told the boys to heap alfalfa or straw on the seats before they sat down. She could stand up while she was driving the tractor, but there was nothing she could do about the searing heat of the engine that was blown on her from the radiator fan. Their eyes burned constantly from the flying chaff, and all of them had dust coughs. Once, when the baler's beater got stuck, Jake kicked it to get it started again, something he warned his sons never to do. His boot got caught, and when the boys started to help him, he ordered them not to move. If he hadn't been strong enough to pull himself out, he could have lost a leg. The beater did tear up his boot and rip off the heel.

***

Willa's reverie was broken by Ellie's giggles, which brought her sharply back to the moment. "Mama! Look at me!" she exclaimed. She held Willa's cigarette between her fingers and was sashaying around the kitchen.

"Put that down, Ellie! You'll burn yourself."

"Wanna smoke!" Ellie put the cigarette to her lips and blew.

"No, you don't. Give me that." Willa carefully pried the cigarette from Ellie's grip and stubbed it out. "You're not going to smoke." She pinched her daughter's soft, plump cheek. "Sit down beside me and let's work on these pictures."

Willa picked up the Easter photograph again and examined her face. Well, she hadn't changed much in two years. Every night and morning she slathered a layer of Pond's Cold Cream on her face and hands. She was thirty-four and didn't have any wrinkles yet. Out in the field, she tried to cover up completely. She wore a straw hat and kept a bandana wrapped over her face, but the sun and the dirt seemed to get through anyway. When she came home from baling, she washed off the dirt, towel dried her cropped hair, and pushed it into place with her hands. Then it was time to eat supper, do some accounting, make phone calls to schedule jobs, wash clothes or iron, maybe find time to read the paper, and then fall into bed. The next morning, she started all over again and continued the same schedule until late October or early November. There had to be an easier way to make money.

Willa looked at her daughter and made the same vow

she'd made for all her children. "You're going to college. You'll never have to work in the fields for a living. I'll make sure of that."

Ellie grabbed the photo out of her hands. "Why's Rocky lying down?"

"Oh, he was throwing a fit."

"Why?"

"Something or other. I don't remember." Actually, Willa remembered exactly why Rocky flung himself to the ground kicking and screaming. He wanted to stand in front of Willa. When Frankie pushed him away, Rocky demanded that Willa hold him. She'd said, "No, I'm holding the baby." Then, Rocky exploded. Heck tried to jolly him out of his fit with no luck.

So there they all were, frozen in time. Dilly and Cissie never bothered ironing overalls or jeans for their boys, but Willa prided herself on keeping her family's linens and clothes clean and ironed. In the picture, their clothes, except for Frankie's faded, old overalls, looked clean and pressed. It was too bad you couldn't see Rocky's face, Willa thought, just the back of his head and the back of his blue shirt and khakis. At least you could see his new brown shoes and striped socks. One of these days, she'd get everybody together and have another picture taken.

As she studied the photo, Willa realized there was something else wrong with it. The gaping hole behind Willa and Annie. Emptiness. Charley would be eighteen now. A tall, young man with green eyes, reddish-brown hair, and a big smile. She could see Charley so clearly. He had his arm around her shoulders, and then he was gone.

"Are you sad, Mama?" Ellie asked, patting Willa's face.

"Yes, honey."

"Why?"

Willa led her daughter into the living room. "See those pictures above the mantel?"

"Uh-huh."

"The one on the left is your Grandpa and Grandma Hardesty, Daddy's parents. They're both dead now. And the one on the right is your Dad's brother, Uncle Billy. You know, like Uncle Heck is my brother. He was killed in the war. And the little boy in the middle is your oldest brother, Charles Luther. He died of leukemia when he was eleven."

"What's leukemia?"

"It's a very bad disease."

"Like polio?"

"No, it's a lot worse than polio. Annie got better, but Charley didn't."

"Why?"

"He got very sick. Then one day he said he was cold and then he died."

"Like my kitten?"

"Yes."

"Frankie squashed my kitten! I hate Frankie!"

"No, you don't hate Frankie. It was an accident. You shouldn't have been playing with your kittens on the back steps. You've got to learn to pay attention. Now, get in there and finish those stamps for me."

Ellie ran into the kitchen. "Can I let Tippy in, Mama?" she asked, standing at the back screen door.

"Is he wet?"

Water flew as Tippy shook himself.

"No."

"Okay. Let him in."

Ellie opened the door wide, and a medium-sized black dog with erect, pointed ears, four white feet, white chest, and just a tip of white on his black tail walked into the kitchen. He looked at Willa with his intelligent, dark almond eyes as if to say, well, I'm here now. What do you want me to do?

As near as they could tell, Tippy was a fox terrier-shepherd mix. Willy and Frankie found him as a puppy down by the mailbox where somebody had left him. He was the same age as Ellie, but he watched over her like a serious old uncle. In the winter, he slept with Frankie, who let him under the covers, but he didn't play favorites. When any of the kids hit each other, Tippy got between them and growled and snapped until they stopped. He loved to hunt rabbits with Jake and the boys, but he was also content to sit in the kitchen while Willa worked or follow Ellie around as she played in the yard. He rarely barked, but when he did, they knew something was wrong. Anyone who visited regularly or anyone he had met, he didn't threaten. He bit the substitute mailman on the leg when he walked up to the house without being introduced. And he held on until Willa ordered him to stop. He was loyal and obedient and fearless, except for thunderstorms, which terrified him. As soon as he heard thunder, he whined to be let into the house where he hid under Willa and Jake's bed.

"You should have been in our family picture," Willa said, wiping his wet coat with a rag. Tippy sat and thumped his tail and gazed longingly at Willa.

"Oh, I know what you want," she said. "I saved it for you." She unfolded the oleo wrapper she had left on the counter and put it on the linoleum floor.

When the electric lights flickered and then went out, Willa got down a propane lamp from the top shelf of the pantry. Ellie sat cross-legged on the floor pasting S&H stamps in the book. Tippy put his right paw on the oleo paper to hold it steady, and then with a bright red tongue, he delicately licked the smear of yellow oil left on the waxed paper.

As the rain pounded steadily on the roof, Sand Creek filled with rushing water. The driveway and dirt road in front of the house turned into a muddy, rutted river. Standing water transformed the wheat fields into a shallow lake. Willa thought about the grains of wheat Jake had planted that would swell and burst through the soil into a soft blanket of green.

As Willa sat in her yellow kitchen in the glow of the lamp, with the family album open in front of her and her baby girl at her feet, that feeling returned. What was it? An overwhelming feeling. Not happiness, just sadness and other feelings, too, hope, fear, anxiety, dread, and the joy she felt sharing this moment with Ellie. Too many emotions, a fullness of emotion that was too much, even frightening.

And at the center of it a wound that refused to heal. An infected boil that she knew she should lance but couldn't bring herself to do it. Instead she tried to ignore it, but it was always there. Poisoning her feelings for Jake. She had always prided herself on speaking plain and telling the truth, so why couldn't she speak? Was she afraid of what she might hear? Of course Jake would lie to her. Was that why she remained silent? She didn't want to force him into a lie? Or maybe he wouldn't completely lie. Maybe he would concoct some bullshit explanation for what he did. She imagined it so many times. Glen and Doris wanted babies and Jake was their prize stud. According to her records, Jake wasn't paid a dime for it. He said he'd worked for cash building fence at the Sedlaks, but she never saw the money. She didn't give a shit about the money. The thought of Jake in bed with Doris made her sick to her stomach. Sometimes she wondered if they kept it a secret from Glen, too. But no, they were all in on it, except her. Did they think she couldn't understand Doris's hunger for babies? Didn't Jake understand that it wasn't the fact that he'd been unfaithful, it was that he lied to her? His lie meant they didn't have a true marriage, a real marriage. Which meant her whole life was a lie. Why did the three of them lie to her? It was humiliating when the evidence was right there for all to see. Jerry Sedlak was the spitting image of Jake and as like to Willy and Frankie as steps on stairs.

Willa pressed on her stomach. She imagined the poison seeping slowly through her body. No, it was just her goddamn ulcer. She had forgotten to take her medicine that morning. She got up and opened the refrigerator. She poured about two tablespoons of the chalky liquid into a glass and swallowed.

Just Willa

"Can I have some, Mama?"

"No, child. You don't need it." And Willa thought as she watched her sturdy daughter working away at her task, you'll never need it. There won't be any poisons in your life because I'll make damn sure your life will be different from mine. You'll go to college and get married or not, have babies or not, and you'll do whatever you want to do. Whatever will make you happy. Most of all you'll get as far away from this farm and this life as you can. There's no happiness on a farm.

Willa turned to her work. She had discovered that work was the best remedy for keeping the poison contained and all those disturbing, unsettling feelings at bay. She moistened each of the four photo corners with the sponge and pressed the Hardesty family portrait into the center of an empty album page. She closed the album. It was time to punch down the bread dough for its second rise.

A Piece of Glass
1952

WILLY AND FRANKIE TOOK ADVANTAGE of the substitute school bus driver and jumped off at the corner, using the short cut across the Hardesty pasture instead of spending an extra half hour on the bus. Annie could have gone with them, but she didn't mind riding the bus. She was twelve and in the sixth grade and much too grown-up to run through the pasture and risk getting her socks and shoes covered with cockleburs. By the time the bus stopped at the Hardesty driveway, the sun was hidden behind heavy gray clouds.

Annie walked down the long driveway, amusing herself by skipping between the deep ruts. Before she went inside the house, she decided to get a drink from the rain barrel, which sat under the eaves. She took the ladle from its hook, raised the lid, and dipped it into the soft rainwater. She took a drink and some of the water splashed onto a piece of glass sticking out of the ground. She put down the ladle. She pried up the glass and the sharp tip pricked her thumb, drawing a pearly red drop of blood.

Annie sucked the blood away. She poured water over the glass to wash off the dirt. The smooth, clear glass, in the triangular shape of an arrowhead, was about two inches thick and three inches across the widest part, and surprisingly heavy. She lifted the glass up to her eyes. Strange. She couldn't see through it.

That can't be, she thought. She looked through the glass again, this time through her left eye, keeping her right eye closed.

Then she did see.

Buried deep in the glass a huge empty plain stretched flat into the distance. There seemed to be no division between the plain and the dirty black sky. It was a desolate landscape of weeds, thistles, and barren, rocky ground. A fierce hot wind blew. A wind Annie could taste, gritty, metallic and raw.

She pulled the glass away. Her heart was pounding.

She examined the glass, which fit neatly into her left palm. It looked ordinary. She took a deep breath and held the glass up, this time to her right eye, and looked again. There. She sighed with relief. Through the glass she saw their familiar dirt-packed yard with tufts of burnt yellow grass. And the warped wood of the storm cellar door.

I'd be safe in the cellar, Annie thought.

But she didn't move. She pressed the glass to her left eye and stared again into that same barren plain. Then she saw something that terrified her. Two huge tentacle-like clouds appeared in the dead black sky and moved slowly toward her.

The pressure of the glass hurt her cheek, but she didn't feel it. She was lost in the glass. Her vision split and her world cracked in two, and when it did, only the dark world inside the glass was real.

Everything familiar, the barn with its stacks of baled hay, the hog sheds, the lopsided mailbox at the end of the driveway, and the screen door of the house, everything had vanished and been replaced by a desolate world ruled by those churning clouds that blew ever closer.

"Annie!" Willa called, through the open kitchen window. "Stop lollygagging! Get in here and set the table!"

Annie yanked the glass away from her eye, and the dark world disappeared. She shivered. "I'm coming, Mama." She slipped the glass into her pocket. That night, safe under the covers of her bed and before her mother turned out the light, she looked through the glass again. She saw nothing. It was just a piece of glass.

Still, the glass had a strange, shimmering beauty. She held onto it, smoothing it with her thumb. The next day, she carried it with her to school. At night, she slept with the glass, and during the day, she kept it in her pocket, where she could stroke it. In time, she forgot about her peculiar vision, and that dark world didn't return. As the weeks and months passed, the hard edges of the glass softened, and it resembled an oversized teardrop.

One day, while they were eating supper, Annie placed the glass next to her plate. When Annie wasn't looking, Ellie snatched the glass and tucked it under her leg.

"Ellie," Willa warned. "Give it back."

"It's pretty! I want it!" said Ellie.

"Well, find your own glass," Willa advised. "This one belongs to Annie."

Playing Around
1954

"YOU SMELL GOOD, MAMA," ELLIE said, breathing in her mother's jasmine scent. Jake and the three boys had given Willa the purse-sized perfume for Mother's Day. The saleslady said that the ten-dollar price might seem high, but it was the best you could buy. The four Hardesty males pooled their money and bought Joy.

Almost every Saturday night, Willa and Jake washed off the dirt and went dancing at the B & M Ballroom in Enid. There, they would meet their friends, Jay and Blanche Clark, who lived in Waukomis, and Lloyd and Mae Malloy, their neighbors to the south, who were renting Glen and Doris Sedlak's farmhouse.

To reward Frankie and Willy for their work on the baling crew, Jake and Willa often treated them to a Saturday night outing. The boys dressed up in khaki pants and well-ironed shirts, combed and oiled their hair, and tried to look fifteen and sixteen instead of twelve and thirteen. With a dollar in their pockets, they walked from the B & M parking lot, down Randolph Street, across the Square, to the Cherokee and

Sooner theatres. Before going to the movies, the boys dashed over to Kress's and bought a half-pound of hot salted Spanish peanuts. After seeing a movie at each theatre, they sauntered down the street, paused to look in the dirty windows of the pool halls, and then went upstairs to Sanford Kunkel's Drugstore and watched duckpin bowling. Around 1 a.m., they ran back to the parking lot to meet their parents. On the way home, Jake always said, "I'm starving," and they stopped at Polly and Peggy's Café, where they devoured bacon, eggs, hash browns, and buttermilk pancakes with hot syrup.

Willa and Jake looked forward all week to Saturday night and seeing their friends. Blanche and Jay were almost fifteen years older than they were, and their two children were grown and married. Jay, a good-looking man with thinning, gray hair and a receding hairline, was a snappy dresser who always wore a white Stetson. Blanche was a heavyset, bleached blonde from Kansas City with a big, brassy laugh. They owned a section of wheat ground and raised Brahmas for rodeo stock on the side. Lloyd and Mae Malloy were both in their early thirties. Lloyd, quiet and reserved except on the dance floor, had a good job with Carrier Oil Company and drove to Enid to work. Willa was particularly close to Mae, who was cute and freckled, with a beguiling Irish brogue. Lloyd and Mae had one child, Peggy, who was nine, a few months older than Rocky.

One Saturday night, Glen and Doris Sedlak showed up at the dance. Glen nodded hello, but Doris kept her distance, speaking only to her Enid friends, and they left early after dancing just one dance. When Mae told Willa about seeing the Sedlak twins in Enid, slouching around drinking pop and eating candy bars, looking all sickly with bad teeth, Willa listened but didn't comment. From time to time, Willy and Frankie picked up odd jobs around Sedlak's on weekends, and Old Man Sedlak even trusted the boys to move tractors for him. He didn't care two pennies about his twin grandkids. Willa wanted nothing to do with the Sedlaks or their twins. She insisted that her children stand up straight and say "Yes sir," and "No ma'am." Pop and candy bars were rare treats. Her children didn't have cavities. Sometimes Willa wondered if Jake forgot what he had done. She still felt the wound; it would always be with her, but Jake seemed to forget the past as soon as it happened. He lived only in the moment. What would it be like to be married to someone she could talk to? Someone to share her worries about the future and even the day-to-day problems of living. Jake shrugged away problems like water off a duck's back. Nothing seemed to penetrate his cheerful demeanor or his faith that the world was a kind place filled with friendly people.

On Sunday mornings, Jake dropped the kids off at Kremlin's First Christian Church. Their Sunday School teacher was Caroline Rathman, the first and second grade teacher at Kremlin Grade School. If the Hardesty children missed Sunday School, Miss Rathman dashed off a postcard to Willa reminding her to be sure and send the children next Sunday.

Willa didn't need any urging to send her children to church. She loved Sunday mornings when the house was empty and quiet. "I wish it could be like this all day," she said to Jake.

"Good idea," he said.

After dinner one Sunday, Jake surprised Willy by tossing him the keys to the 1951 Chevy and saying, "Why don't you take the kids over to the show at Pond Creek?"

"You mean it?"

"Sure," Jake said. "Stay off the highway, though. Take the county road. And bring some ice home."

Willy looked at his mother.

"It's okay, Willy. You're a good driver. You're in charge." Willa tapped Frankie on the head. "You understand, Frankie? Got that, Rocky and Ellie? You mind Willy and Annie."

Pond Creek, if you traveled on the county road, was a little over seven miles from the farm. The ice plant, a few blocks from the Pond Creek Picture Show, was at the end of Main Street, on their way home. They always needed ice. The new electric refrigerator's freezer compartment held only two trays of ice cubes. Whenever there was a storm, the power shut down for a couple of hours, so they kept the wooden icebox in the kitchen as a back-up.

Jake watched Willy drive the car carefully down the driveway. Then he fiddled with the radio until he found KCRC.

"Hey good lookin'," he sang along with Frankie Laine. "What you got cookin'? How's about cookin' something up with me?"

"Oh, Jake, it's so hot," Willa said.

"I'll keep you cool." He grabbed her around the waist and danced her into their bedroom.

Willa sat on the bed, pulled her blouse over her head, and shut down her brain. The music helped. Transporting her to a time when she was young and in love and eager.

Jake turned on the small electric fan. "I'll be right back."

Jake went into the kitchen, opened the refrigerator, and shook a few cubes of ice from an ice tray and put them into a glass. Then he walked into the bedroom and looked down at Willa. She was naked. She lay on her stomach and her brown skin gleamed with sweat. The hot air blowing from the fan ruffled her short, dark hair.

He placed a cube of ice in his mouth. With his lips holding the ice, he traced a pattern from her neck to her waist, curving over her hips, and down her thighs to her toes. Willa shivered in delight.

"Turn over," Jake said. He stripped off his shirt and pants and shorts. He put another ice cube in his mouth.

When the kids burst into the house three hours later, they found their parents sitting in the kitchen drinking iced tea and reading the Sunday papers. It didn't dawn on Willy why his parents allowed him, a thirteen-year-old boy without a driver's license, to drive his brothers and sisters to the show on Sunday afternoons.

Pond Creek's picture show never featured the really good movies, like *High Noon*, that played at the Sooner and Cherokee theatres in Enid. Pond Creek offered B-movie westerns and occasional horror movies. When they got to the show, the kids separated.

Unless he saw a friend from school, Rocky sat by himself in the back corner of the theatre. Frankie had little interest in movies. Going to the show was an opportunity to talk, especially to older people, who doted on the good-looking boy with the big blue eyes and lopsided grin. Frankie learned that if he hung around the concession stand someone would buy him a pop or a bag of popcorn.

Willy and Annie enjoyed the movies and sat together in the middle of the theatre. Ellie started out sitting with them, but after the cartoons had finished and the movie started, she fidgeted until Willy let her run up and down the aisle. Once in a while, a movie held all their interest, maybe because it was set in Oklahoma Territory with characters like Billy the Kid and the Sundance Kid. They all liked *Return of the Badmen*, starring Randolph Scott, their favorite western hero.

One Saturday afternoon, Frankie and Rocky were acting out a movie. Frankie was Billy the Kid, and Rocky imagined himself as the sheriff. Ellie begged to play, too, so Frankie installed her in the cellar as a combination banker and barmaid. Her job was to serve drinks (water in shot glasses) and stand guard over stacks of money (cardboard egg carton dividers).

The Hardestys used the cellar only when tornados threatened or when they needed to get canned goods that Willa stored there. The cellar was chilly and dark. One bare light bulb left a small circle of light on the rough cement floor. Shadows hung in the corners and there was a dank, musty odor of wet wool and cardboard.

Ellie waited in the cellar for her first customer. In her imagination, the cellar transformed into a big western saloon with swinging doors and a long mirror behind the bar. Instead of bare feet, overalls, and t-shirt, she wore high heels and a low-cut red dress with ruffles. Ellie polished the two shot glasses and watched out of the corner of her eye for spiders.

Finally, Ellie heard whistling and boots scuffling on the steps. Frankie, no, it's Billy the Kid, she thought, wearing a black cowboy hat pushed back on his head and a pair of six guns, swaggered up to the bar. He said he was thirsty and asked for a whiskey.

Ellie filled a shot glass from the water jug. The Kid drank and asked for another shot. As Ellie leaned over to pour his drink, the Kid grabbed her short brown hair and demanded money.

"No!" Ellie shouted. The Kid twisted and pulled her hair until it hurt. "Stop it!"

"Give me the money, and I'll stop." Ellie handed him the stacks of money she had hidden under the bar. He stuffed the bills inside his shirt. He pushed her away and knocked the shot glass off the bar. It shattered on the cement floor. Then he ran up the steps and into the yard.

Since Ellie didn't have a gun belt, she had placed a metal six-shooter, an old one she borrowed from Willy, on the floor behind the bar. She grabbed the gun and ran after the Kid, not minding the broken glass as it pierced her bare feet. At the top of the cellar steps, Ellie waited for her eyes to adjust; the sunlight was blinding.

Ellie ran around the house, holding the gun in front of her. Then she saw him. Billy the Kid. He leaned against the cottonwood tree, laughing and waving the stacks of money.

"Bang! Bang!" she shouted, pointing the gun directly at him and pulling the trigger. He didn't fall and held the money over his head, grinning in triumph." Bang!" Ellie hollered. Furious that he wouldn't fall dead, she ran toward him and threw the metal gun as hard as she could. It smashed into his forehead right above his left eye. Then he fell. Hard.

"I got you. You're dead. You're dead. You're dead," Ellie chanted. She stood over him. Blood poured out of a gash on his forehead. His eyes were closed. His face was sickly white.

Rocky ran up beside her. "Did you kill him?"

"I shot him, but he wouldn't die."

"I'm going to get Mama."

"No! Don't tell!"

It was too late. Rocky had already left. Ellie ran to the barn and climbed the rope into the hayloft. She hid there, wondering if seven-year-olds could go to prison.

Willa was cutting out a new wool skirt for Annie when Rocky burst into the kitchen shouting that Frankie was dead and Ellie had killed him.

"Where is he?" Willa asked. She followed Rocky outside.

They found Frankie groaning under the cottonwood tree holding his head in his hands. Willa examined the cut.

"Well, I think you'll live," she said. "Go into the kitchen and put some ice on it. Rocky, find Ellie and tell her to get into the house."

Ellie worried Willa. Her daughter seemed to have trouble distinguishing between what was real and what was play. Later, as Willa picked glass out of Ellie's feet, Ellie argued that she hadn't thrown the gun at Frankie, she had hit Billy the Kid, who deserved to be shot. Working with Dr. Simmons trained Willa to handle most family emergencies, but he did not give her an antidote for an out-of-control imagination. All she had was a well-stocked medicine box.

Just like her father, Willa kept a wooden box filled with aspirin, iodine, salves, ointments, alcohol, Doc's cough remedy, hydrogen peroxide, Campho Phenique, laxatives, tape, and bandages. Underneath the sink was the hated enema bag with its long rubber syringe. "I think your bowels might be stopped up," Willa would say when one of her children complained of a stomachache. The Hardesty children learned to keep their complaints to themselves. They rarely missed school. If they were sick, or pretended to be sick, there was always the chance they would have to endure an enema.

Willa's medicine box got plenty of use. The kids were always into something and had the scars to prove it. After supper on the day Ellie knocked out Billy the Kid, the whole family sat around discussing their various scars. Willa showed the scar on her temple and the scars on her ankles from the car wreck. Jake had the deep scar on his thigh, and there were three new ones on his upper arm from Willa stabbing him with the turning fork when he pinched her leg while she was cooking breakfast.

Ellie, who was sitting on her father's lap, touched the three white marks. "Poor Daddy!" She had missed the scene since she hadn't been born yet. "That was mean, Mama."

"That's right, Snooks," Jake said, winking at Willa.

"Your daddy shouldn't have been playing around," said Willa.

Rocky pointed out the white puncture scars on the back of his left hand. When he and Frankie were fishing with pitchforks in Sand Creek, Rocky stuck his hand in the way just as Frankie was spearing a big Appaloosa catfish. Willy rubbed a scar on the side of his head, which you could feel with your finger, but his hair had grown over the scar. When Willy was five, his cousin Leo swung him on a rope around the grain silo too hard, and Willy slammed his head into the metal, giving him a gash and a concussion. Ellie traced a tiny white line above her lip where Rocky crashed his metal airplane when she was eighteen months old. Annie's skin was flawless except for a white dot of a scar on the top of her foot where Ellie spilled a spoonful of hot fudge. No one mentioned Annie's useless right arm, which trumped any scars that her brothers and sister might show.

Before Ellie's gun throwing, Frankie complained that he didn't have any good scars. He touched the bandage above his eye. "Do you think I'll have a scar?"

"Probably," Willa said. "It was a deep cut."

"But once I almost died, didn't I, Mama?" Frankie said.

"Well, when you were three, you came pretty close."

Frankie had mixed candy and marbles in his pocket and instead of candy, he swallowed a marble. He had begun to turn blue when Willa grabbed his heels, turned him upside down, slapped his back, and the marble popped out. Frankie kept the marble in a small wooden box in his dresser drawer.

All the Hardestys had scars. But there were some scars so deep and so mysterious that they were never discussed. Those scars hid wounds that would never heal. Rocky had a wound like that buried deep in his chest. Often he forgot about it, but sometimes it ached so much he couldn't bear it. Then he'd run to Willa, throw his arms around her neck, and breathe in her jasmine scent. She'd laugh and ask, "Who's my only brown-eyed boy?"

"Me, Mama," Rocky would answer. "Me."

Everybody's Fault
1955

"MONKEY ON A GRINDSTONE!" BOB Randall shouted from the back of Jake's pick-up as it rattled down Highway 64 to Enid. Bob, a thirteen-year-old who lived on a farm west of the Hardestys, was tall and skinny with crew cut red hair and a loud, boisterous manner. Willy and Frankie stood next to Bob, clinging to the sides of the cab to keep their balance. They echoed Bob's cry, yelling, "Monkey on a grindstone! Monkey on a grindstone!" as they closed in on and then passed a Negro boy in overalls and bare feet, pedaling a bicycle in the rough gravel on the side of the highway. The boys kept yelling and waving at the Negro boy as the pick-up slowed, turned right onto a dirt road, and then stopped with a lurch.

Jake turned off the ignition. "Rocky, you stay here." He jumped out and slammed the door.

"Why'd you stop, Daddy?" Frankie asked.

"You boys get down right now," Jake snapped. Willy and Frankie started to speak, but Jake raised his hand. "Shut your damn mouths! Get down here. Not you, Bob. You stay right where you are. You're not my boy, and even though I'd like to, I can't whip you."

Willy and Frankie stood at the back of the pick-up facing their father, who ripped his heavy leather belt from his khaki pants. Willy, fourteen and a year older than Frankie, looked Jake in the eye, pressing his lips together to keep from trembling. Frankie, arms folded, looked away, trying not to cry. Seeing his boys like that, slim, blue-eyed, with thick curly brown hair, square jaws, and broad shoulders, made Jake feel like he was looking at younger versions of himself, but where had they learned to talk like that? Not from him, that was for damn sure.

"What the fuck do you think you were doing?" Jake said, shaking his head in disbelief.

Shocked, both boys hung their heads and looked down into the weedy, overgrown ditch. They never heard their father use that word. He cussed all the time, but never that word.

"Look at me!" The boys raised their heads. Jake waited until he could look directly into their eyes. "Why were you shouting at that Negro boy?"

"I don't know," Willy said.

"Bob started it," Frankie offered.

"Well, Bob's a chickenshit Randall. You're Hardestys. And you should know better. Lean against the pick-up."

The boys turned their backs on Jake and braced themselves against the tailgate. Jake folded his belt in half, held the buckle in his right hand, and whipped each boy several times. Willy and Frankie cried out in pain and embarrassment. From the corner of his eye, Willy saw the

Negro boy, legs pumping frantically and head bowed, make a wide detour around the pick-up as he biked toward Enid.

Jake threaded his belt back through the loops. "Well, you boys can forget about going to town."

On the way home, Jake and Rocky were silent, but when Jake turned left at Kremlin and headed to their farm, he spoke. "Don't ever let me catch you pulling a stunt like that, Rocky. A Negro boy is just like you, no better, no worse."

Rocky looked at his father and then turned away to glance through the window at his brothers riding in the back of the truck. Frankie's eyes met his, and the older boy scowled and made a face.

"So, Rock," Jake said, "did I ever tell you about Tuffy Burgess, a boxer out of Texas? He was as black as a Hershey bar, the blackest Negro I'd ever seen. And a damn good boxer with a snaky right hand, but he couldn't beat your Uncle Jim."

Rocky didn't say anything. He didn't know any Negroes. He never knew what to say to his father. Whenever he asked to do something, his father always said no. Like today, when he wanted to ride in the back with his brothers and Bob, his dad said "Hell, no." Rocky looked out the window at the wheat stubble in the fields.

What was wrong with the boy? Jake wondered. He tried to talk to him, but Rocky was so damn quiet and secretive. Every once in a while Jake caught a look in Rocky's eyes that reminded him of his father. The boy was going to be tall and skinny like John Hardesty, too, even though he had Willa's brown eyes and brown skin.

Just Willa

By the time they dropped off Bob at the Randall's farm, Jake's anger had worn off. When they got home, Willy and Frankie saddled old Fortney and rode to their camp on Sand Creek; Jake went to the machine shed to work on the John Deere; and Rocky went to the house to find his mother.

Willa was in the kitchen. When she saw him, her face lit up, and she sang a song that he loved. "Can you make a cherry pie? Rocky boy, Rocky boy? Can you make a cherry pie, charming Rocky?"

For the rest of the afternoon, Rocky stayed close to his mother in the kitchen. He watched her roll out the pie dough until it was smooth and round. Then she laid the thin crust over the thick cherry filling heaped in the pie tin. She trimmed the extra crust and set the pieces aside for him to brush with butter and then dust with cinnamon and sugar and bake in the oven. The taste of the flaky, golden-brown strips of dough with just a touch of sweetness was heaven. Almost as good as the cherry pie.

Working in the kitchen with his mother, Rocky was happy. He forgot about his father and his brothers, and how they made him feel left out and unwelcome. Rocky was wrong about them but it wasn't his fault; it was nobody's fault; or maybe it was everybody's fault. It was just the way things were.

Five years earlier, in 1950, when Willy was nine, and Frankie was eight, they and their friend Bob Randall, helped by Jake, built a camp on Sand Creek near the cement bridge. They used a tarp for a tent, gathered stones for a campfire, and on late summer and fall weekends, the boys camped out. Willy and Frankie saddled Fortney, packed their bedrolls and a water jug and food bag along with Willy's .22. They'd meet Bob and stay overnight or sometimes for two nights. Jake checked on them from time to time, but the boys were allowed to be on their own and do as they pleased.

When they rode home, filthy and exhausted and smelling of wood smoke, they told Rocky about how much fun they had at the camp. Rocky begged to be allowed to join them for a weekend. Willa said, "Absolutely not, he's too young," but Jake said, "Let the boy go. Tippy can go, too. He'll take care of him." It was late October. Rocky had just turned five.

It had been a wet fall, and when the boys arrived at Sand Creek on Saturday afternoon, the creek bed was filled with rushing water. They unpacked their supplies and arranged their camp. Willy unsaddled Fortney and turned him loose to graze, knowing that the old horse wouldn't stray far. Tippy, his nose to the ground, patrolled the campsite. Rocky wanted to shoot, so Willy taught him how to load the .22 bolt action rifle, set and release the safety, aim, and shoot. Rocky used the cement bridge to support the rifle. He listened carefully to Willy's instructions, and after a few shots, he hit a can.

"Stop shooting," Bob called. "I'm hot. Let's go swimming."

"It's not deep enough to swim," Willy said.

"Maybe for baby Rocky it is," said Bob.

"I'm not a baby!" shouted Rocky.

"Don't call him a baby," Willy said.

"Oh, yeah, and who's going to stop me?"

Willy grabbed Bob and threw him in the water. Bob caught himself and sat down on the sand bottom of the creek.

"This feels great!" yelled Bob. "C'mon in, you big Hardesty babies!"

The Hardesty brothers splashed into the creek, ignoring Tippy, who barked a warning from the bank. All afternoon, the boys splashed and played in the water. Then thunderheads moved in and covered the sun, and the air grew cool. The boys ran up on the bank and stripped off their wet clothes. Willy built a fire, and they hung their jeans and shirts on branches to dry. For supper, they ate fried chicken, bread and butter, and cherry pie that Willa had made.

Rocky, his clothes still slightly damp, went to bed first. With Tippy stretched out beside him, he lay close to the fire to keep warm. The next morning, the boys woke up with the sun, cooked breakfast, and planned where they would go to hunt rabbits.

"What's wrong with you?" Willy asked, looking at Rocky, who had not moved from his bedroll.

"My throat hurts," Rocky said.

"Here, eat some of this egg," Frankie said.

"I'm not hungry."

"Well, you've got to eat something," Willy said.

"No, I don't."

"Maybe you should go home, little baby," said Bob.

"Don't call me a baby!" Rocky screamed, his face red.

To prove that he wasn't a baby, Rocky got up, forced

down some egg and a drink of water. Throughout the day, he lagged after his brothers and Bob as they tramped along the creek and through the pasture. Tippy, torn between hunting rabbits and his concern for Rocky, ran back and forth, sometimes hanging back with Rocky, and then racing off in search of a rabbit. Finally, when it was time to pack up and go home for supper, Willy and Frankie walked and let Rocky ride Fortney back to the house.

Willa and Jake were outside standing in the yard, wondering if they should check on the boys, when Fortney trotted up the driveway with Rocky slumped in the saddle. Jake went to meet the horse. When he reached for Rocky, the boy fell into his arms. Willa ran to them.

She touched Rocky's forehead. "He's burning up! Get him inside."

Jake carried Rocky into the house and laid him on the daybed. Willa stripped off his clothes and wrapped him in a blanket. "I'm cold, Mama," he said, shaking with chills. Willa's heart clenched. She ran to get another blanket and the thermometer. Rocky's temperature was one hundred two, then climbed to one hundred three, and he continued to shiver. "I think we should take him to Dr. Duffy," Willa said.

Willa called Mae Malloy to come over and look after the kids while she and Jake drove Rocky to Enid. Dr. Duffy diagnosed Rocky with pneumonia and admitted him to Enid Hospital. For the next ten days, Rocky hovered between life and death. Willa rarely left his bedside. Her mother took the bus from Freedom to Enid and stayed a few days at the hospital. Rocky woke up one morning and looked into the soft brown eyes and brown, wrinkled face of his Grandma Lizzie. She held his hand and told him he was going to be fine.

Unlike Jake, whose temper flared suddenly and then burned itself out, Willa's anger took time to build. As she sat by her child's bedside, she thought about what had happened, and her anger stirred into a steady flame. When Rocky was finally out of danger and they brought him home, only then did her anger burst into a hot, consuming rage. A rage she turned on Jake as they lay in bed on a cold December night.

"It's all your fault!" she snarled, her voice low. She spat out the words slowly and clearly. "You should never have let him go down to the creek. Why are you so goddamned stupid? You know nothing about taking care of children! About raising children! I listened to you and I let him go! We almost lost him, Jake. I couldn't bear it. Never again! Never again!"

She continued to berate Jake, who lay silent beside her, taking his beating. He loved his boys. He just wanted them to have fun, to be cowboys, to enjoy being outdoors, to live as he had as a boy, on his own, taking care of himself. Although maybe Willa was right, he thought. What did he know about raising kids?

From then on, Jake was extra careful with Rocky, not roughhousing with him the way he played with the two older boys. If Rocky needed punishing, he let Willa handle it. Willy and Frankie, who felt guilty and terrified that Rocky would die, sensed that Rocky was weaker and needed protecting, and they, too, pulled back, not including him in any activities where he could get hurt. Rocky felt their abandonment keenly and spent more time with his mother. He felt uncomfortable and tongue-tied around his father.

Sometimes Rocky took his anger out on Ellie, who adored him and followed him around like a puppy, constantly wanting attention. Rocky would tease her and then push her away. When Peggy Malloy, who was the same age as Rocky, came over when her parents played cards with Willa and Jake, she joined Rocky in teasing Ellie and called her a big baby.

Ellie didn't whine or complain. She knew a better way to get back at Rocky. She ran to her father. Jake would pick her up, and she'd sit on his lap while he played pitch. Once in a while he let her hold his cards. From time to time, she'd reach up and rub the rough stubble on his jaw.

"You're my girl, Snooks," Jake would say, giving her a tiny taste of his bourbon. "You're my tough little girl."

Feeding Tramps
1956

TIPPY SAW THEM FIRST AND started barking. Two men were walking down the driveway. The taller one, who had a scraggly black beard and long black hair hanging over his ears, pushed an old motorcycle with a battered cardboard sign hanging from the front saying "Knives Sharpened." He wore faded denim pants and a denim shirt with the sleeves rolled up. The other man, about a head shorter and dressed all in gray, took short, quick steps to keep up with his companion.

Willa and Rocky were working in the garden southeast of the house trying to keep ahead of the weeds and grasshoppers. They were both sweating in the muggy heat. "Go see what Tippy's up to," Willa said.

Rocky walked to the front yard and saw the men. They were about halfway down the driveway now, and Tippy's barking had gotten louder and more threatening. Rocky hurried back to the garden to tell Willa.

Willa stood up slowly. Her back was sore. Too much kneeling and lifting. "Where's Willy?"

"I think he's in the garage."

"Run tell him tramps are coming."

"Okay, Mama."

Willa washed her hands with the hose. She whistled for Tippy, and they both went into the kitchen and waited. Willa looked in the refrigerator, thinking about what she could give the men. She could heat up the leftover pot roast, potatoes and gravy, and add some bread and butter, sand plum jelly, and sliced tomatoes. That was the best she could do. Jake had eaten the last piece of pie this morning before he and Frankie left for Perkins.

"Ellie! Annie! Where are you?"

"In here, Mama," Annie said from the living room. "We're reading."

"Well, stay there. We're going to have some company."

Ellie ran into the kitchen. "Who, Mama? Who's coming?"

"Just some hungry tramps."

"I want to see them! Can I see them? Can I?"

"It's may I and you don't need to see them. They're just men."

"But why are they hungry?"

"Because they don't have jobs."

"Why don't they have jobs?"

"How should I know? They're down on their luck, I guess."

Several times a year, Willa fed tramps, who either walked in or jumped off a Santa Fe train that ran through their pasture. She'd seen the X carved on the post at the end of their driveway marking their farm as a good place to get a meal. Willa had learned to stop asking them to work for food. Most

298

tramps just wanted a quick meal and to move on down the road.

Tippy growled and the black fur on the back of his neck bristled. Through the window above the sink, Willa saw two men walking up the sidewalk toward the screened porch. She looked toward the garage. She could see Rocky peeking out from behind the doorframe. Willy, holding his .22, darted into the doorway, waved to her, and quickly stepped back.

The knock on the screen door was no more than a few taps, but Tippy started barking and pawing at the kitchen door.

"Tippy, that's enough," Willa ordered and the dog quieted but stayed alert and listening.

"Ellie, go back to the living room. Take Tippy with you. Stay with Annie."

"No, Mama, I want to see the tramps!"

"Do as I tell you!" Ellie would turn eight in October. The older that girl got, Willa thought, the more she back-talked. With Tippy padding behind her, Ellie went into the living room. Willa opened the kitchen door and stepped onto the screened porch. She checked quickly. Yes, she'd remembered to latch the screen door. The two men smiled at her, displaying yellow, broken teeth. Their clothes and faces were caked with dirt as if they'd been working in a field all day.

"Howdy, ma'am," the shorter man said, swiping at the dust on his filthy gray pants.

The taller man with the black beard just nodded. He stared at Willa intently.

His gaze made Willa uncomfortable, and she wished

she'd changed out of her shorts and skimpy halter-top.

"How do you do," Willa said. "You must have had quite a day. Did you come off the train?"

"No, ma'am," the short man said. "We walked from Pond Creek, got caught first in the rain, then the hail, and then the dust started blowing."

"It's been a nasty day all right. I bet you're hungry. I could bring you some food."

"That would be wonderful, ma'am," the shorter one said.

"You can wash up at the windmill. There's a hose there."

"Thank you, ma'am," said the shorter one, who seemed to be the spokesperson.

While the men were washing up, she fixed their plates, giving each man two slices of her homemade bread with butter and jelly since she didn't have any pie or cake for dessert. She poured two big glasses of iced tea. She put everything on a tray and carried it to the screened porch. She unlatched the screen and set the tray on the steps. She closed the door and relatched the screen.

Shaking their hands in the air to dry them, the men walked to the back steps. When they saw the food heaped on the two plates, with stainless steel cutlery, and folded paper napkins, the men stopped and stared.

"Is something wrong?" Willa asked.

"No, ma'am," the spokesperson said. "It's just been a long time since we've had a meal off a plate."

"That's too bad. I'm sorry I don't have a table for you.

But you're welcome to sit here on the steps and eat."

The men sat down. Willa went back into the kitchen and closed the door. She ran soap and water in the sink and scrubbed the dishes that had held the leftovers. As she dried a bowl, Willa glanced out the kitchen window. Ellie was standing by the rope swing hanging from the cottonwood tree. She sneaked out through the front door, Willa thought.

Willa opened the kitchen door and went onto the porch. The taller, bearded man still sat on the steps eating, but the man in gray, the spokesperson, walked toward Willa holding his clean plate.

"That was delicious, ma'am. Thank you." He handed his plate to Willa, and took off down the driveway.

"Aren't you going to wait for your friend?" Willa called.

In reply, the man just waved his hand. Willa watched to see which way he would go at the end of the driveway. He headed south. Maybe he was going to Enid.

Willa turned to see if the other man had finished. He'd left his clean plate on the step and was walking toward Ellie, who had climbed up the rope and was now swinging back and forth.

"Ellie!" Willa called. "Get in the house. I need you to help me."

"Okay, Mama," Ellie said, using her toes to hold on as she climbed down the rope.

Before she could get to the bottom, the bearded man grabbed the rope and swung it back and forth. "Hey, stop it!" Ellie yelled.

Willa put down the plate and ran toward the swing. "You there! Take your hand off that rope!"

The bearded man looked at Willa. Something in his eyes was off, like that crazy white cow they had for a while that tried to gore Jake. The cow finally calmed down when Jake dehorned her, but they sold her anyway. The man let go of the rope. Ellie slid to the ground and headed for Willa. As she ran by him, the bearded man grabbed Ellie's ponytail, jerking her to a stop. He picked her up and held her in his arms. Ellie started screaming and kicking. The man never took his eyes off Willa.

"You're a cute little girl," the man croaked, in a strange, rusty voice, "but if you don't stop that screaming, I'll snap your neck like a chicken."

Ellie, who had seen her mother snap the head off a chicken many times, stopped screaming. Willa moved toward the bearded man.

The man put his hand around Ellie's neck and spoke in the same rusty voice. "I wouldn't do that, lady."

Willa froze. Willy, where was Willy? Then she saw him. He was running into the yard. About fifteen feet behind the bearded man, he stopped and raised the rifle, pointing it at the man's head. "Put down my sister," he said. Willy's voice was deep, like his father's, and it held a tone that Willa had never heard in her son's voice. He sounded old and experienced, more like fifty than fifteen.

The bearded man, his right arm gripping Ellie tightly around her waist and his left hand circling her neck, swiveled around and eyed Willy. "Hey, I know you," he said. "You're the one who wouldn't trade your old horse for my motorcycle."

"If you don't put down my sister," Willy said, "I'll shoot off your goddamn ear."

For a long moment, the bearded man held Willy's eyes. Willy's blue eyes never blinked.

The bearded man laughed a raspy laugh. "Fuck you, little boy!"

Willy's finger squeezed the trigger. There was a loud pop.

Ellie screamed. The bearded man dropped her and grabbed at the side of his head.

"You shot me! You fucking shot me!"

"I told you I was going to shoot off your goddamn ear."

Willa scooped up Ellie.

The bearded man swiped at the side of his head, which was streaming with blood. "Hey, I was just fooling around," he said. "I don't want no trouble."

Willy didn't move. He continued to sight down the rifle, keeping it pointed at the man's head.

"Get!" Willa said. "And if we ever see you around here again, we're calling the sheriff." The man backed away, keeping his eyes on Willy, who stalked closely behind him. He stopped to get his motorcycle and then pushed it up the driveway. Blood poured down his neck, turning his denim shirt black. At the end of the driveway, he turned to look back. Willa, Ellie, and Rocky waited in the yard, keeping watch. Ten feet behind him Willy motioned for him to keep moving. Willy still had his finger on the trigger of the .22.

When the man disappeared down the road, Willy lowered his rifle and joined the rest of his family in the yard.

Ellie was the first to speak.

"Mama, I wet my pants."

"Well, you'd better change them," Willa said, hugging her daughter. "Because you're going to get a whipping. I'll teach you to mind me!"

Later that night, Frankie leaned over from his top bunk and looked down at Willy. "What if he hadn't put Ellie down? Would you have killed him?"

"Hell, yes."

"But what would Mama say?" Rocky asked, from his twin bed against the other wall. "If you killed somebody, I mean."

"Who do you think told me to go to the garage with my .22 anytime a tramp shows up?"

"Daddy didn't tell you?"

"No, Mama did. She said if a tramp ever tried to get into the house or hurt any of us, I was to shoot the sonofabitch. I just did what she told me."

A Cold Draft
1957

WILLA SAT AT THE KITCHEN table hemming the full skirt of the black silk dress Cissie and Dilly had given her as a combination Christmas and birthday present. Sleet bounced against the kitchen window. She could feel a draft coming from somewhere. Where was it? She rolled up an old towel and wedged it against the back door sill, which helped a little. According to the radio, a river of frigid air was flowing down from Alaska putting all of Oklahoma into a deep freeze. Jake said the barn thermometer read three degrees this morning. They needed moisture, some snow for the wheat, but so far all they'd gotten was a little icy sleet.

Willa was feeling her usual January blues. Last Tuesday her fortieth birthday had come and gone. As usual, Jake didn't buy her anything. She baked a chocolate cake, and when they came home from school, the kids helped her blow out the candles. The boys gave her a card, Annie wrote her a poem, and Ellie made a card with a drawing of their farm and signed it "Snooks and Tippy and all the animals." It had been just another birthday. Jake would turn forty-two tomorrow, although he claimed he'd be forty.

Funny, she didn't feel forty; she still felt the same as she had in her twenties. She didn't have any gray hair yet, and her face was unlined, and, thanks to Pond's cold cream, soft and smooth. Her hands, though, were so worn and battered, they looked like they belonged to a sixty-year-old. Slowly but surely, she was changing, getting older. Nothing she could do about that.

Times were changing, too, and not for the better. With Eisenhower and Nixon voted in for another term, it didn't look good for farmers. Wheat prices were down. They gathered around the radio last year and listened as Adlai Stevenson warned of the danger of putting Republicans in charge of farm policy again. Especially when Ike was being led around by that no-good Richard Nixon.

They had rented the Spore place west of Kremlin last year, one hundred sixty acres of wheat ground and double the work, but then came the drought, the high price of seed wheat and gas, the upkeep of their machinery, and their income hadn't doubled; they'd barely held their own. With custom hay baling, Willa's egg money, and extra cash Jake brought in selling scrap iron, buying and selling a few cattle, and working at Sedlak's garage on Saturdays in the winter, they got by. Willa knew that times could be and had been worse.

Willa stood up to stretch. She lit a cigarette and looked out the window. The sleet had stopped, but it was still gray and cloudy, and the wind was blowing like the dickens. She heard the slap of cards on the coffee table. The kids were playing pitch. She listened for a moment. Annie and Rocky were partners against Willy and Frankie. Willy was attempting to teach Ellie how to play, but she couldn't sit still and ran around looking at everyone's cards.

It was nice they enjoyed playing together. It didn't happen often. They were good kids. She and Jake had tried to raise them right. They didn't have many rules. Work hard, tell the truth, be clean and kind, don't feel sorry for yourself, pay attention. Most of the time, they behaved themselves. Willa and Jake matched the kids' chores to their talents. Willy, who'd be sixteen in April, was calm and sensible, although he liked being the boss a little too much. An excellent driver and a good mechanic, Willy could be trusted with any farm job involving machinery. He'd made All-State as catcher on the baseball team last year and played starting point guard on the basketball team. He was smart, but his grades didn't show it. He worked just hard enough to get B's and C's. Said he didn't want to do any better than the other boys. When Willa pointed out to him that he needed to make more of an effort if he wanted to go to college, he just shrugged. He needed to start thinking about the future instead of fixing up that old car of his and going to see his girlfriend.

Then there was Frankie. Although he was only fourteen, he was too handsome for his own good. Always running off to see some girl or talking on the telephone. People took to him immediately. He was a talker, a wheeler-dealer, who liked to go with Jake to sales and on cattle buying trips. Willy called him a bullshitter and maybe he was. Willa didn't know who he took after. No one, in her family or Jake's as far as she knew, was like Frankie. He was a hard worker, though, and good with animals. He liked feeding, dehorning, castrating, and doctoring. If you got a splinter, Frankie was the one to dig it out. When he sliced off the big wart on Ellie's arm with his jackknife, Willa put her foot down. Frankie claimed he had sterilized the knife blade with a match. Ellie was fine, but sometimes Frankie's confidence in his own abilities was overblown.

Rocky was quiet like John Hardesty and her own father. He was methodical with a remarkable memory. Like her, he could figure in his head and keep track of all the cards playing pitch. He taught himself chess out of a book and played with Annie and once in a while with the old men at the pool hall. He could beat both his brothers at table tennis, but he was only a mediocre baseball and basketball player. Except for Annie, her kids enjoyed kitchen work, but Rocky had a real knack for cooking. He was the only one who would risk getting wasp stung and help her pick sand plums for jelly. He could be moody, though, and quick to start an argument, particularly with Jake. She had to whip him a few times when he was too rough with Ellie. Like the time he ran her down with his bike on the gravel road. Ellie had sneaked into the house trying to hide her scraped and bloody arms and legs. "Rocky said he'd kill me if I told," Ellie finally whispered, after Willa threatened to whip her if she didn't tell what happened. Her two youngest were so damn stubborn. Ellie should have moved out of his path, but there was no way she would give in to her older brother. When he was whipped for running over his sister, Rocky didn't flinch. He was getting too big to be whipped now anyway. Willa worried more about him than about any of the other kids. He seemed to take life too hard.

Annie, who would be eighteen in July, never gave Willa a bit of trouble. Maybe having polio and spending all those weeks in an iron lung had given her an appreciation of good health that no one else had. It was hard to know. They never talked about it. Annie was cheerful and normal, and according to her teachers and her test scores, maybe even a genius. She adored Elvis Presley, joined his fan club, and started a scrapbook filled with his photographs and newspaper clippings. She had girlfriends, but so far no boyfriends. That worried Willa, and she knew it bothered Annie. She liked Dean Baxter, a boy ahead of her in school, but he had another girlfriend. Annie had never been asked out on a date. Once in a while she went to movies with a group of friends. Maybe college would be different for her. Annie would graduate next year and planned to go to the University of Oklahoma. With her perfect grades, she was assured of getting a scholarship.

Eight-year-old Ellie had Jake wrapped around her finger, and, Willa had to admit, she babied her, too. Ellie could manipulate her family into getting her what she wanted. She was a good girl, though, and never missed a day of school, but she disappeared for hours into a book and had to be nagged to do her chores. While everyone was working in the fields, she ran around the pasture by herself acting out stories with Tippy. Sometimes her imagination got the best of her. When Mrs. Rathman showed the Bert the Turtle movie about the atomic bomb, it was all Ellie could think about for months. Convinced that they were going to be bombed by the Russians any minute, she organized half of her class into a watch group to look for enemy planes. One day a blimp floated over during recess while Ellie stood watch on the top of the monkey bars. The whole class gathered as the cigar-shaped blimp hovered in the sky over the school and then disappeared in the distance. When she got home, certain that the atomic bomb with its bright blast of blinding light would come at any moment, she insisted on taking a jug of water, a bucket, toilet paper, and canned goods to the cellar. Willa let her prepare her little bomb shelter. It couldn't hurt anything. For all she knew, maybe the Russians would drop a bomb. Anyway, it was easier to let Ellie do what she wanted than try to fight with her.

Did I ever have that much energy and determination? Willa wondered when she looked at her daughter hustling around on some imagined errand. Except for Ellie's square Hardesty jaw and her light brown hair, Ellie looked like Willa did as a girl. A small, straight nose, brown skin, big brown eyes, even a round brown beauty mark on her left ankle like Willa's. Of all her children, Willa worried least about Ellie. She was tough, but she was little, and everybody, even Rocky when he wasn't tormenting her, watched out for her.

As Willa worked the needle and thread in and out of the black silk of her dress, she listened to the progress of the pitch game. Annie and Rocky seemed to be winning. No surprise there. They were sure being good today. Playing pitch and so far no arguments about the score or whose turn it was to deal. There. The hem was finished. Willa knotted the thread and cut it. She hung the dress on a hanger next to its matching silk jacket with white satin collar and cuffs. The dress had a scalloped V-neck and three-quarter length sleeves, elegant and sexy at the same time. Too bad she didn't feel much like going out tonight. The roads would be terrible, but Jake insisted that they couldn't let Jay and Blanche down. They hadn't seen their friends for a couple of months.

Willa stubbed out her cigarette and plugged in the iron to press her dress. She still had to do her nails, take a bath, and fix her hair. Supper, just leftover beef stew, could be warmed up whenever the kids were ready. She and Jake were meeting Jay and Blanche at the B & M parking lot and then going out for a bite to eat before the dance.

Later, on the drive to Enid, Highway 64 was a sheet of ice, just as Willa predicted.

"Be careful! You're following too close!" she said, bracing her hands against the dashboard as the car skidded.

"Would you like to drive?" Jake snapped.

After that, Willa was silent, gripping the armrest and staring at the slick, black road ahead, wishing she had never agreed to go out.

When they arrived at the B & M, they saw Jay's Oldsmobile idling by the entrance. Jake pulled up beside the car. Willa rolled down her window.

"Blanche ran in to go to the bathroom," Jay said. "Something needed fixing on her dress. Could you go in and help her, Willa? Jake can park your car. We'll take ours to Polly and Peggy's. No reason to take two cars."

"Okay," Willa said, opening the car door and stepping carefully onto the pavement. The wind was bitter cold against her legs. She held her coat around her throat and walked quickly to the door. When she got inside, she turned right to go to the ladies room. The door of the ballroom opened and Blanche stuck her head out.

"Willa!" she called. "Come here. You've got to see this!" And then Blanche closed the door and disappeared.

Curious, Willa opened the door. The ballroom was pitch black and silent. Behind her, Willa felt Jake's hand on her back pushing her. Why had he come in? she wondered. "Blanche?" she called.

Then someone threw a switch, and the lights blazed revealing a room full of people with colorful bandanas over their faces, looking like well-dressed bank robbers. "Surprise! Surprise!" they shouted. "Happy Birthday! Happy Birthday!"

Willa felt as if someone had knocked the wind out of her. What was going on? She turned to look at Jake, who was dancing a little jig. Jay stood beside him waving his white Stetson. Then Blanche was kissing her cheek and rubbing off the red lipstick mark with her handkerchief. People pulled off their bandanas and rushed toward Willa.

Cissie and her husband Vernie Knox. Had they come all the way from Amarillo? Willa wondered. Then Dilly with her husband, Mike Dixon, as homely as Hal had been handsome, but an electrician with a good steady job, and he loved her. Jessica, Dilly's daughter with her husband Gene; her brother Stub and his wife Nancy; Heck and Lucy; Frank Johnson with his pregnant wife Melba; Aunt Martha and Francis with their daughter Rebecca and her husband; Lloyd and Mae Malloy; their banker Henry Thompson; and other neighbors and friends from Kremlin. And Carol Evinsen, who hadn't aged a bit and looked as thin and pretty as she had in college, had driven in with her husband from Oklahoma City. As flashbulbs popped, blinding her, Willa smiled, but she was overwhelmed and disoriented. Even after everyone hugged her and wished her happy fortieth birthday, she still couldn't believe it was real.

Jake spun her onto the dance floor as the band played *Kisses Sweeter Than Wine.*

"Surprised you, huh?" Jake whispered in her ear.

"Shocked is more like it."

"Jay and Blanche and your sisters helped. Hell, they did most of it," Jake admitted.

"I can't believe you kept it a secret! Did the kids know?"

"Sure. Why do you think they were being so good today?"

"Even Ellie?"

"Yep."

Willa looked around the dance floor of the B & M. They'd rented the place just for her. A party just for her. It had been nineteen years since her last birthday party on the home place, when she was twenty-one and Charley was five. She'd given birthday parties and was planning a family reunion for her mother this August when Lizzie turned eighty, but she hadn't imagined that anyone would surprise her. It was strange and unsettling not to be in charge. She watched Cissie and Mae and Blanche fill the punch bowl and set out platters of sliced ham and roast beef.

Later, after she blew out the forty candles on the three large sheet cakes and opened her presents, Willa walked to the front of the room to the band's microphone. "I don't know what to say, except thank you everybody for this surprise party. Thank you so much for coming out on these dangerous icy roads on such a bitter cold night. I wanted to stay home, but I'm glad I didn't! Tonight I feel forty years young."

"You look thirty!" Frank Johnson shouted. Everyone laughed. Frank turned red. He'd had a crush on Willa for years.

"Play something, Mug," Stub called.

Nobody had called her Mug for a long time. A wave of sadness swept over her. She missed her father so much. "I don't know, Stub. I haven't played since the Camp Houston dances."

The drummer rolled his drums, and the bandleader motioned to her to come up on the stage. Willa took off her jacket and sat down at the piano. Somebody in the crowd wolf-whistled. "Do you play any Bob Wills?" she asked.

"Hell, yes," the bandleader said. "How about *San Antonio Rose* for our little rose from Freedom, Oklahoma. Hit it, boys!"

After Willa chorded a few numbers, Jake pulled her back onto the dance floor. Willa danced with him and with all the men, and even danced a jitterbug with Dilly. At 2:00 a.m. the dance floor was empty except for Jake and Willa. Everyone else, including the band, had gone home.

Willa was exhausted. Her feet and ankles were killing her, and her throat was starting to feel scratchy as if she might be getting a cold, but she didn't want the night to end. Jake held her in his arms. His lips nuzzled her neck. She leaned against him, moving to their own special rhythm, feeling the same yearning she felt when she'd first danced with him at Camp Houston in 1938.

Jake slipped his warm hand inside the V-neck of her dress and cupped her breast. "Ready to go home, brown eyes?"

"Yeah. Take me home."

A few months later on a Sunday afternoon in late April, Willa sat at the kitchen table smoking a cigarette. She had ironing to do, but first she wanted to clean out her purse. The window and back door were open to let in the warm breeze. The kids were at the movies in Pond Creek, and Jake had gone outside to work in the garden. Tippy started barking, and Willa heard the crunch of tires in the driveway. She looked out the window and saw a blue Buick. Then Glen and Doris Sedlak stepped from the car. Tippy continued to bark, and the Sedlaks waited by the gate, not daring to open it and walk through. What in the world were they doing here? Willa hadn't seen them in years. Her stomach knotted.

Through the window, Willa saw Jake walk over to meet them. He quieted Tippy and opened the gate. Jake shook

Glen's hand and nodded at Doris, who stood slightly behind her husband. Glen began to talk. He held a large piece of paper in his left hand. Willa couldn't hear what he was saying, but whatever it was, it wasn't good. Jake's fists were clenched. Glen continued to talk and showed Jake the paper. Jake looked at it, then punched it away and said something. He held the gate and gestured for Glen and Doris to leave. Glen spoke, and stuck out his right hand toward Jake. Jake didn't move, didn't take his hand, just spit out a few words, and glared at him. Glen put his hand in his pocket. He and Doris got in the Buick and drove away. Jake banged the gate shut. He turned and saw Willa in the kitchen window. He walked slowly toward the house.

Willa met him at the back door. "What was that all about?" Jake looked strange, almost as if he was in shock.

He sat at the kitchen table. "Fix me a glass of iced tea."

Willa brought the iced tea and sat down. She lit another cigarette. "Well?"

"They're goddamn, lying, backstabbing sonofabitches."

"The Sedlaks? Why?"

"And nice Mrs. Boyce? She's a dirty goddamn liar, too."

"What did Glen say to you?"

"He asked if they could look at the house before they took possession. Wanted to see if it needed fixing up before they rented it. Like we'd gotten it dirty or something. Instead of putting our own money into it to fix it up."

"What? Took possession?"

"That's right. Glen and Doris Sedlak are the new owners

of the Boyce place. Brought the contract to prove it. Of course they won't live here."

"That's not right! Mrs. Boyce said she would let us have the first chance to buy when she was ready to sell. We shook hands on it."

"Well, she lied, didn't she. So much for a person's word. Glen knew we had a deal with her! Hell, everybody knew it! We've been here for eighteen years. But he went behind our back, worked on Mrs. Boyce and her son to make his own sweetheart deal. He said he paid more than she asked for. Goddamn right he did!"

"Glen's got his own place. Why does he want this one?"

"Because they hit oil six miles east of here. But I'm sure Glen didn't tell Mrs. Boyce that. He said the farm was next to his and he wanted it for his boy Jerry to farm. So the Sedlaks could farm together."

"That boy doesn't know the first thing about farming."

"Hell no. Another goddamn lie."

And Jerry's not even a Sedlak! Willa screamed the thought but kept her mouth shut. Jake must never know that she knew his secret. She knew her husband. Jake was weak and easily manipulated. More than anything he wanted to be loved and to please. He didn't have a selfish bone in his body and lacked the imagination to understand that others might be motivated by greed or ambition or naked self-interest. Jake gave the Sedlaks the children they yearned for, and they betrayed him. She reached out and took Jake's big calloused hand.

"I'll fix this. I'm calling Mrs. Boyce."

Jake pulled his hand away and cracked his knuckles.

"Too late, Willa, it's a done deal. Contract's signed. We have to move right after harvest. Our lease is up August 1. Glen said no hard feelings, it's not personal, just business."

"What'd you say?"

"I told him he was a greedy lying sonofabitch and he and his whole goddamn family could go straight to hell."

"But where will we go? There's no house on the Spore place. What about the kids? And school? Annie will be a senior."

"I don't know."

They sat in silence. Jake finished his iced tea, put his glass in the sink, and then slammed out the back door. Willa crushed out her cigarette and lit another one. She reached for her purse. It was the new leather bag, hand tooled with her initials and a floral design, that her sisters and brothers had given her for her fortieth birthday. It had a matching leather checkbook cover and wallet, also hand tooled with her initials and the same floral design. It was a handsome bag, the nicest she'd ever had. She turned it upside down and dumped the contents on the table. Checkbook, wallet, cigarettes, matches, lipstick, comb, coupons, small bottle of Jergen's hand lotion, handkerchief, tissues, some loose coins, a half-filled book of green stamps, emery board, pocket calendar and notebook, address book, two pens, and a black velvet case holding her compact.

Willa took the compact out of its cover. The compact was about four inches in diameter, perfectly round, and made of sterling silver. "Solid silver," Jake said, when she unwrapped it. Jake told her he and the kids had ordered it last July, over six months before her fortieth birthday. The silversmith in Enid helped them create the design, which he engraved onto the case. Two hearts entwined with WH on one heart. A loose bouquet of leaves and flowers, tied with a ribbon, shaded the hearts. A simple curving line made a border on the front and back.

Willa admired the gleaming silver compact. She would never have bought something so extravagant for herself. She opened it and looked into the mirror. Willa Hardesty, forty years old, with five kids, and soon to be homeless, stared back. Her eyes filled with tears. Her lips trembled and her chest ached.

As she stared into her own wet eyes, suddenly Willa smiled at her nonsense. She was acting just like Ellie, making faces at herself in the mirror. She put on a fresh coat of lipstick, blotted her lips on a tissue, and snapped the compact shut. She had too many things to do to waste time feeling sorry for herself. She picked up a pen and opened her 1957 notebook. Time to make a list. The first item on that list was to call Mrs. Boyce and give her a piece of her mind. Item number two—find a new home.

Mrs. Boyce
1957

WILLA DECIDED THAT THE BEST time to call Mrs. Boyce was on Sunday morning at 8:00 a.m. before the older woman got dressed and started her day, which always included a long lunch at the country club after church. That time of the morning their party line would be free and Willa could speak openly and without interruption. The boys were outside with Jake doing chores, and Annie and Ellie were still sleeping.

There was no changing Mrs. Boyce's mind; she knew that. The contract was signed. But maybe she could find out why Mrs. Boyce had broken her word to them. They'd never missed a payment even in the years when the wheat crop had been ruined by hail. More than anything, Willa wanted to know why. Was it money? Simple greed? Mrs. Boyce had more money than she knew what to do with.

Willa got out her address book and found the number. She lit a cigarette and took deep calming drags. She dialed the Enid number.

"Hello?"

"Mrs. Boyce, this is Willa Hardesty."

"Oh!"

"Is it as hot there as it is out here?"

"Yes, I think it's going to be a warm day."

"On days like today you must really enjoy your air-conditioning."

"Yes, I do, Willa. It's a blessing. I can't take the heat like I used to."

Willa drew smoke deep into her lungs and then released it slowly.

"I just want to know one thing, Mrs. Boyce. Why? You promised me and Jake that we would have the first chance to buy your place. We've scrimped and saved for years and we have the down payment. Then you up and sold it to Doris and Glen Sedlak. They already have a farm! Why did you go back on your word?"

Willa listened to silence on the other end of the phone.

"Mrs. Boyce? Are you there?"

"I'm here, Willa. I suppose I should have spoken to you first, given my reasons. But I've always liked you Willa. We've never had a bad word in all the years you've been my tenant. And if it was just you, well, things might have been different. And Glen made an offer that I knew you couldn't match."

"But at least we should have been given a chance! And what do you mean, if it was just me?"

"I suppose I shouldn't say anything to you. Glen said I shouldn't since he was sure you knew all about it."

"Knew all about what?"

"What your man did for years!"

"Jake? What did he do?"

"Ran liquor out of my farm, that's what! According to Glen, I might have been liable if he'd been caught. I didn't want a man like Jake buying a farm that belonged to my father, God rest his soul, who never touched a drop of liquor in his life."

"What you're saying is a damn lie, Mrs. Boyce!"

"There's no need to swear, Willa. You ask Jake about it and see what he says. Glen says he kept the stash hidden behind a stack of maize bales."

"No! I'm not going to ask Jake because we don't have a stack of maize bales, and Glen Sedlak is a liar who will say and do anything to get more land. Did Glen tell you about the oil they discovered just a few miles from your place? Did you hang on to your mineral rights? I bet you sold those too. You broke your word to us, Mrs. Boyce. We shook hands and made an agreement and you reneged on it. That's the truth. If you had doubts about Jake or how we were running things, you should have come to us. What you did was shitty and small, Mrs. Boyce. And you're going to have to live with that."

Willa lay the phone carefully in its cradle. She crushed out her cigarette in the ashtray. Her stomach burned. She walked into the kitchen and took her ulcer medicine. Then she told Annie and Ellie to get dressed for Sunday School and set the table. She made pancakes, fried eggs and bacon, and poured juice. They all sat down to breakfast. Willa served everyone and watched them eat, and no one noticed that she ate nothing. She sipped her cup of coffee, and refilled plates.

Just Willa

After breakfast, Jake loaded the kids in the pick-up and drove them to Kremlin. She knew he would wait for them, drinking coffee at Rathman's. Willa slipped on her boots and walked outside, where Tippy was waiting for his morning scraps. She fed him and gave him fresh water. Then she walked across the yard and into the pasture. How far was it to the maize field? About a half mile she figured.

She heard a bark, and Tippy raced toward her. He looked up at her with his wise old eyes. Yeah, I know, Tippy. We sold all the maize bales. I've lost my mind. But I have to know. When they reached the maize field, there was nothing to see. Just a field of maize. There used to be a huge stack of bales at the edge of the field, but that was years ago. Could Jake have hidden liquor there? Maybe. The truck could have come from the road across the alfalfa field. She wouldn't have heard a thing.

Jake promised her that he would have nothing to do with Senator Drummond and running liquor. Had he kept his promise? She couldn't ask the senator. Last year Drummond choked to death while eating a steak sandwich in the back of his car. His funeral and subsequent burial in his 1954 black Cadillac instead of a coffin attracted national headlines. But she could ask Jake. He would be home soon.

Willa whistled for Tippy. By the time they got back to the house, Willa was dripping with sweat. "You know what I'm going to do, Tippy? I'm going to take a cool bath and then I'm going to make some iced tea."

Later, after the kids left for the movie at Pond Creek, Jake read the newspaper at the kitchen table. Willa fixed them each a glass of iced tea and sat down across from him. He still moved his lips when he read, Willa observed. When they first got married, she had helped him with his reading. Writing was another matter. He still couldn't write much more than his own name. He claimed not to see a reason for it. All he needed writing for was to sign checks or contracts. He never wrote letters. Who would he write to? Besides, he said, if something needs writing you can do it for me, he told her.

"I called Mrs. Boyce this morning."

Jake looked up from his paper but kept his finger on the page to mark his spot. "Yeah. Did you give her a piece of your mind?"

"I did. But she gave me a piece of hers too."

"What was that?"

"She told me the reason why she reneged on selling her place to us."

"She did?"

Willa studied Jake's blue eyes. Those wide blue Hardesty eyes fringed with long dark lashes that seemed so clear and honest.

"She said she couldn't sell to you because you ran liquor and stored it on her farm."

Jake blinked and looked away, flinching as if she might reach out and slap him.

Willa felt drained. She had no anger. She felt nothing. Just empty. What was the point of talking to this man? He wasn't her partner. He was a stranger who lied to her. He lived with her, but she might as well be living alone.

"You want to know how she found out?" Willa asked.

Jake didn't move.

"Your friend Glen Sedlak told her. He wanted her land so he stabbed you in the back. What gets me, Jake, is that you told Glen but you didn't bother to tell me."

"Dammit Willa, that was years ago! I didn't tell Glen. He saw the truck once and figured it out."

"What else have you lied about, Jake? Anything else you want to tell me?"

"How do you think we paid for our baling operation? For Christmas presents for the kids? Gas money to go to Freedom?"

"I guess liquor money paid for all that. Well, was it worth it, Jake? We just lost the chance to have a place of our own! To have something to leave to our kids! And now we've got nothing ahead of us but working like dogs and starting all over again! Piss-poor tenant farmers! That's what we are! Nothing but piss-poor tenant farmers!"

Jake stood up, knocking over his glass of iced tea. He limped to the back door then stopped and stared at the Sedlak calendar hanging on the wall. With a roar from his gut, a sound that Willa had never heard him make before, he punched the calendar, over and over again, with both fists, until the paper shredded and fell to the floor, and still he kept punching until the wall gave way, and still he kept punching until he was hitting nothing but a cloud of plaster, and still he kept punching, until finally his bad leg gave way and he fell to the floor. He lay there, down for the count, a man who had fought himself and lost.

Willa plucked a towel from the hook by the sink and sopped up the spilled tea. Then she got out the broom and dust pan. She stood over her husband.

"Get with it, Jake. Help me clean up this mess."

PART THREE

On the Edge
1960

Willa lay awake and listened to the quiet noises of the night. Jake's steady breathing from across the bedroom. The curtain blowing in the breeze. An owl hooting in the pasture. The constant chirp of crickets. The rustle of wind in the wheat. The rattle of the rotating fan in the living room. The creak of the daybed springs. A sliver of light flickered underneath the bedroom door. Ellie. Reading under the covers with a flashlight. She was going to ruin her eyes if she kept that up.

Willa longed for sleep. She was exhausted. It was unusually hot for the middle of May. And there was no shade around the house. They'd moved only seventeen miles from Kremlin to Carrier and were now a few miles closer to Enid, but it was like living on another planet. It was almost three years since they left the Boyce farm. But she still couldn't get used to it. It was the trees. Most of all, she missed the trees.

The Carrier place, one hundred sixty acres rented from the family of old Solomon Carrier, who had founded the town back in the land rush of 1893, had few trees, no mulberry, elm, or honey locust, and not even one fruit tree. Wheat fields, not trees, bordered the long, curving driveway as if the land was too precious to waste on something as frivolous as a tree. A windbreak of cedars grew west of the house, one scraggly cottonwood shaded the north chicken house, and a few cottonwoods lined the draw in the pasture. That was it. The yard had cement sidewalks and hard packed dirt, with here and there tufts of sunbaked yellow grass. They had one hundred thirty acres of wheat ground and thirty acres of good grass pasture. But the soil was rich, better than the Boyce place. When they were forced out of the Boyce farm, they were lucky to find a place so quickly with a two-story farmhouse and modern outbuildings.

Thinking about Mrs. Boyce again just made her angry. I've got to get to sleep, Willa thought, shutting her eyes tightly, but she couldn't shut down her brain. Jake fell asleep as soon as his head hit the pillow.

Willa couldn't stop worrying about the future and thinking about the past. She missed her old friends and neighbors, especially Mae and Lloyd and their pitch games. She and Jake rarely went dancing anymore. Without Jay and Blanche, it wasn't fun. Hard to believe that Jay was dead and buried. What a horrible, freak accident. Jake helped dig Jay out of the load of oats that had tipped over on him. No one knew how it happened. Blanche was lost without Jay and moved to Kansas to live with her son. Jake bawled like a baby at Jay's funeral, but then he moved on, seemingly untouched by the loss. The same thing happened when he put Fortney down. He shot the old horse, burned the body in the pasture, and never mentioned it again. The past didn't seem to exist for him, but Willa worried about the past. She worried about everything, turning her fears over and over in her mind, imagining the worst that could happen, never satisfied, never happy.

Everybody adapted well to the move except her. Annie thrived at Carrier High School. She joined the debate team and traveled all over the state. She earned perfect grades, was valedictorian of her class, and was now a sophomore scholarship student at the University of Oklahoma. Willy and Frankie were good-looking and outstanding athletes, which assured them of being popular, especially with the girls. Rocky and Ellie seemed to have declared a truce and shared their favorite science fiction books.

Their neighbors were friendly and welcoming, and their social life revolved around high school basketball and baseball games. Usually, Jake sat with the men on the stage at the basketball games. Willa sat with the women in the bleachers, and then worked in the lunchroom at half time selling slices of pie that she had baked.

Willa turned onto her back, lifted her cotton nightgown, and pressed softly on her stomach. The burning wasn't so bad tonight. Dr. Duffy told her she might be getting another ulcer, and he prescribed a different chalky liquid to coat and calm her stomach. What she really needed was something to calm her mind. She couldn't stop herself from making lists in her head of things to do. The more tired she was, the harder it was to get to sleep. She tossed and turned in Ellie's single bed while Jake snored across the room in Annie's hospital bed. Frankie and Shirley, since they were newlyweds, slept in the double bed in Jake and Willa's room. Rocky was asleep in his upstairs bedroom, Annie was in her twin bed in the dorm at O.U., and Willy stretched out on an army bunk somewhere in Germany, close to the East German border.

She tried to talk Willy out of joining the Army, but when he graduated, he signed up for three years. "I want to go somewhere and see something besides wheat," he said. His steady girlfriend, Joanie Adams, a hardworking, pretty redhead, enrolled in nursing school in Enid. Willy was with the 543rd Engineering Company. In his last letter, he said they were building Quonset huts for the infantry. They were on constant alert, he wrote, in case the Russians tried anything. When he got leave, he wanted to travel through France and Italy. Willa sent him Webb's address in Rome.

Willy will be all right, Willa assured herself. He'll come home and maybe he and Joanie will get married. Joanie was a sensible girl, who fit in well with the Hardestys. She didn't mind Jake's teasing, and she didn't wait to be asked to wash dishes or help clean up—she pitched in.

"You can't live their lives for them," Jake told her, when she fretted about the kids. Willa knew he was right, but it made her sick when she thought of the waste Frankie had made of his life. Only seventeen, he was a married man with a baby on the way. She warned both Willy and Frankie when they started dating to look out for themselves, to be careful. She'd had such hopes for Frankie. Several colleges offered him basketball scholarships, and he said he wanted to be a veterinarian, just like Granddad Hardesty. Well, that wasn't going to happen now. She couldn't help blaming Shirley Hanson, who was almost two years older than Frankie.

Shirley's family lived on a farm outside Lahoma, a small town about ten miles south of Carrier. Shirley hated living on a farm and rebelled against her strict, religious parents. After she graduated from high school, she moved in with a wealthy divorced woman in Enid. She took care of the woman's children, drove her new Buick, and wore her clothes. It seemed to Willa that Shirley learned to want things. Expensive things. Jewelry and fancy clothes and cars.

A few months ago, Willa drove with Frankie and Shirley to Ashland, Kansas, where a judge married them. Since Frankie was seventeen, Willa had to give her permission. Next week, when Frankie graduated, he and Shirley planned to move to a tiny garden apartment in Enid. Frankie found a job as a salesman with Prudential Insurance Company. She knew Frankie would make a good salesman. He could charm the bark off a tree and then sell it back to the tree as new and improved bark. Like Jake, he made outrageous bids playing pitch, but he was lucky and often won. That was Frankie's problem, Willa thought, everything came easily to him. Handsome and smart, he was a star in high school, admired by teachers and students. But then he'd been dumb and careless. Well, I was dumb too, Willa thought. I shouldn't judge anybody else.

Willa tried, but she just couldn't like Shirley; however, anyone who was male adored her. Jake couldn't take his eyes off her, and Rocky followed her around like a lovesick puppy.

I'm just jealous, Willa thought. Shirley was stunning. Her beauty seemed out-of-place and improbable confined in their shabby farmhouse. Frankie was up at 6:00 a.m. to do chores before he went to school, but Shirley stayed in bed until 10:00. She floated around the house in a filmy "peignoir," her name for nothing more than layers of fluffy pale pink ruffles. She moved slowly, gliding like the model she imagined herself to be. More than anything, she reminded Willa of a self-satisfied, lazy cat.

She makes me feel short and old and unattractive, Willa thought. Dried up and over-the-hill. Willa fanned the sheet and shook off her self-pitying thoughts. Enough thinking about Shirley. Let her enjoy her honeymoon. It isn't her fault she's beautiful. She'll lose her figure soon enough. And when the baby comes in November, the honeymoon will be over.

Willa lay on her side and looked out the open bedroom window. The moon had set and the stars were out. The sliver of light gleamed under the door. Time to tell Ellie to turn out the flashlight. Willa tiptoed out of the bedroom into the living room. Light glowed under the sheet that Ellie had pulled over her head.

"Ellie," she whispered.

Ellie clicked off the light and poked her sweaty head above the sheet. "I'm almost done," she pleaded. "It's *The Martian Chronicles*."

"How many more pages?"

"Less than ten."

"Okay, you can finish."

"Thanks, Mama." Ellie tugged the sheet over her head and flicked on the flashlight.

Willa went to get a drink of water from the jug in the refrigerator. The ticking of the round, stainless steel wall clock that she'd gotten with green stamps sounded loud and metallic in the silent kitchen. She'd never noticed how noisy it was. Why in the world had she wanted such a large, loud clock? From her leather purse on the counter by the back door, she took out a pack of cigarettes and her lighter. She slipped on Frankie's loafers and went outside to the screened porch. Tippy thumped his tail in greeting, then curled up and went back to sleep.

Willa walked into the front yard and looked at the sky. She smoked a cigarette and tried to settle her mind. Bright bands of brilliant white stars filled the heavens. Ellie said aliens lived in the stars. Sometimes Ellie pretended that she was an alien sent to observe Earth. Right now, I feel like an alien, Willa thought. Unable to sleep, unable to stop worrying and fearing something she couldn't name, something she couldn't control. "Don't ask for trouble," Jake advised. "It'll come soon enough." Easy to say, Willa thought, inhaling smoke deep into her lungs, harder to do. She heard the screen door open and then close softly.

Ellie, barefoot and her skin as dark as an Indian's against her white t-shirt and panties, padded up beside her, rubbing her eyes. She was eleven and would soon be taller than Willa. "What are you doing?" she asked.

"Just looking at the stars."

Ellie followed her mother's gaze and yawned a huge yawn.

"I finished the book, Mama. I'm a Martian. We're all Martians."

"Sure, honey."

They stood looking up at the stars while Willa finished her cigarette. "Mama?

"What?"

"Will you sleep with me?"

Willa didn't ask why. Ellie was lonely too. "I guess this once."

Willa stubbed out her cigarette. They went into the house, and Willa lay beside her daughter on the daybed. The iron daybed where Charley was born and where he died. Ellie fell asleep almost immediately. Willa pushed Ellie's damp hair behind her ears and listened to her daughter's slightly raspy breathing. She tried to imagine Charley as an adult. Would Charley have joined the Army instead of going to college? Would he have gotten a girl pregnant when he was only seventeen? What would his life have been like? What would her life have been like if he had lived? Would he have remained her perfect, beautiful boy? Questions without answers buzzed around and around in her mind.

Finally, as the stars winked out and the sky turned black, Willa drifted off to sleep and dreamed. When she woke, she was smiling. It had been a good dream. She tried to remember it, but she couldn't. It was so close. Something happy and light as a butterfly perched on the edge of her mind. No matter how hard she tried, she couldn't quite grasp it. Still, it was nice to know that it was there.

Going to Hell
1962

"DEAR MAMA, SORRY THIS MOTHER'S Day card is so late. I'm enclosing some snapshots. Jake, Rocky, Ellie, and I drove to Norman for Annie's graduation. She graduated summa cum laude. That means with highest honors. The first college graduate ever in the Sharpe or Hardesty family. I put the announcement in the Enid paper. Make sure you put it in the *Freedom Call*. You could include one of the snapshots I took of her in her cap and gown. She's taking some courses this summer and then will start her job as a speech therapist in the Wichita schools. We paid the down payment on a brand-new Dodge Dart for her with push button controls. We're so proud of her. But she just acts like it's nothing big. Isn't little Charley cute? They surprised me with the name. Another Charles Luther. He stays with us on the weekends because Frankie and Shirley go out a lot. Shirley's turned out to be a good mother. I wouldn't be surprised if they had another baby real soon. It still makes me sick that Frankie didn't get a chance to go to college. But he's ambitious and still young. Looks like we're moving to Kansas.

Bye for now, Love, Willa and all"

Willa laid down her pen and rubbed her aching fingers. She lit a cigarette, one of the new Belairs. The menthols really do have a cleaner taste than Raleighs, she decided, although it didn't feel like she was breathing any easier.

She wondered how Jake was getting along with Aunt Mattie. He was helping her move into the house she bought in Protection. At Herman's funeral, Mattie looked old and shrunken. After the funeral, Mattie begged Jake to come run her farm. She promised him that he would inherit the land when she died. Jake said yes immediately. Mattie owned four hundred acres of wheat ground with eighty acres of pasture. They would farm on a 2/3-1/3 share, giving her a third, and she would supply the house and the farm machinery.

Willa was furious that he didn't consult her. But Jake wouldn't budge. He gave his word and what's done was done. Willa conceded that they were barely scraping by on the Carrier place. Without her work at the egg factory in Enid for six months, they wouldn't have been able to afford the down payment on Annie's new Dodge Dart. Everything cost more now, but their income stayed the same. She'd just have to make the best of it.

Willa addressed the envelope and sealed it. As she took her notebook from the kitchen drawer and began making lists, her stomach burned. She was out of her ulcer medicine. She'd put that on the list, too. Maybe Dr. Duffy could help her find a new doctor in Kansas.

Just Willa

Two months later, with Tippy beside her on the front seat and Ellie sulking in the backseat, Willa turned into the driveway of Mattie's farm. Willa didn't blame Ellie. The whole family was sulking. No one was happy about the move to Kansas. Willa took for granted that she would always be an Oklahoman. She was enormously proud that her father was one of the original founders of Oklahoma. She would never consider herself a Kansan.

It took them about four hours to drive the one hundred thirty-five miles from Carrier. When they arrived at Mattie's place, the sky was cloudy; it was cool for August with a nice breeze from the east. Jake and Rocky would arrive later in the loaded pick-up, and then Rocky would drive Jake back for the last load. Jake warned her that the house was filthy, and Willa wanted to clean it before they moved anything in.

Set back a quarter mile off Highway 160 between Protection and Ashland and surrounded by flat wheat fields, the white frame house with a large fenced yard looked solid and imposing. A screened porch wrapped around the front of the house, shaded by two tall elm trees. The back door opened onto a cement porch that led to a neglected kitchen garden. There was a new clothesline in the side yard, a two-car garage with a propane tank behind it, a large red barn, corrals, and a new metal machine shed.

The back door was not locked, and Willa, with Ellie and Tippy trailing behind, walked into the house. The air was stale and smelled like dirty socks and dust. Willa left the back door open to let in some fresh air. Jake was right, the house looked like it hadn't seen a broom or a dust rag in years. The hardwood floors were dirty and worn, but would be all right once they were cleaned and waxed. The back door opened into a large, square room with three big windows on the east wall. Mattie had left her mahogany dining table with eight ladder-back chairs. The living room was rectangular and about twenty feet long with windows on the north and east. It would be bright and sunny when the windows were washed. There were three downstairs bedrooms along the west wall with a bathroom between two of them, and a laundry chute to the basement. Upstairs there was a large finished attic and a storage closet. The basement, where she would put her washer, ran the full length of the house and had a cellar door that led outside. The kitchen, at the back of the house off the dining room, was a long, narrow room with built-in cabinets, a fairly new stove and refrigerator, and a sink under a window at the west end. All the rooms, including the kitchen, had the same ancient green paint on the walls, as if Mattie had bought gallons of it sometime during the 1930s.

"Go get the cleaning supplies, Ellie, and the vacuum cleaner and the mop out of the car. We'll start in the kitchen."

Willa opened the window over the sink. Dead flies littered the sill. The rust-stained white porcelain sink needed a good scrubbing. The countertops were filthy with layers of grease, dirt, and food. The stove, a recent-model white Magic

Chef, was grimy with burned on grease and dirt. She opened the refrigerator-freezer, a two-door Frigidaire. It was foul, but at least it was empty and running. The stove would be the hardest job, so she decided to start with it. She turned on the front burner and as the flames shot up, three cockroaches, at least an inch long, scrambled across the stovetop and dove under a back burner. Willa's stomach turned. She hated dirt, but cockroaches were worse than dirt, spreading disease and filth on everything they touched.

Cockroaches. Years ago when she visited here with Jake on their wedding day, she saw them in the bathroom. The house must be infested with them. How could Mattie have stood it? Willa wondered. Her eyes couldn't be that bad.

Ellie plodded into the kitchen lugging a bucket filled with rags and cleaning supplies, a mop, and a broom.

Willa lifted the two back grates from the stove, and a covey of cockroaches rushed across the stove and then scattered under the burners and behind the cabinets.

Ellie screamed. She dropped everything and ran. Willa picked up her purse from the dining room table and followed her outside. Ellie was holding onto the fence and vomiting her breakfast.

"Get in the car," Willa said, handing Ellie a tissue to wipe her mouth. "We have to buy a bomb."

They drove ten miles west to the hardware in Ashland and bought five cans of insect spray and two powerful bug bombs. Harry Glenfield, who had owned the well-stocked store for thirty years, walked them to their car. Harry was old, with sparse gray hair and shaky old man's hands, but he still liked to flirt, and his voice was loud and strong. "These bombs will kill every damn roach you got, no matter how big they are," he boomed. "If they don't, I'll come out there and stomp the sonsabitches to death myself."

For Ellie, their move to Kansas would always be associated with cockroaches and the Clutter killings. Even after the house was scrubbed, the rooms painted, the floors cleaned and waxed, the windows washed, and not a roach in sight, Ellie imagined the brown greasy insects skittering across the stove, or heaped in dead piles on the dining room floor where her mother had swept them, and her stomach heaved. When she was alone in the house at night, she locked all the doors, barricading herself in her room with Tippy, watching the headlights of the cars on the highway, fearing that any minute the two vicious killers might escape from prison and show up to rob the house and shoot her dead, just like they had killed that poor Clutter girl and her family in Holcomb.

For Jake, Kansas offered an opportunity to change. If truth be told, he didn't really care about owning land. He would have been content to stay on the Carrier place for the rest of his life. But he knew owning land mattered to Willa and to his boys. He saw how they looked at him. Especially Willy. Working Aunt Mattie's land would be a way to leave them something. And prove to Willa that he could be more than a piss-poor tenant farmer.

At the same time as her parents were moving to Kansas, Annie was moving to her new home, a furnished apartment on Riverside Drive in Wichita, one hundred fifty-five miles northeast of Mattie's farm. Annie's two roommates at OU, Linda Billings and Jill Stainton, helped her with the move. Annie had persevered and achieved Willa's highest ambition, a college diploma, and now she had a good job with the Wichita school system as a speech therapist. She owned a new Dodge Dart, a set of Samsonite luggage, and several new suits and dresses for work. She was looking forward to her new life on her own.

After Linda and Jill left, Annie was alone in her new one-bedroom apartment. She'd never had a room of her own. She walked around the furnished apartment, admiring how she'd arranged things. A nook in the living room with a bookcase, a small desk, and a wooden chair would be a good place to work on her lesson plans. Since she wasn't much of a cook, she didn't care that the kitchen was pretty bare, but she could have cereal for breakfast and most lunches she would eat out. There was a diner two blocks away where she could grab a cheap meal. It would be nice living next to a park and be surrounded by trees.

Annie brushed her teeth, washed her face, and decided to write her mother before she went to bed. She described her new apartment, assured Willa that she was almost finished with her thank-you notes, and asked about their move to Kansas. Her mother was a good correspondent, and Annie knew that she could count on a letter at least once a week.

She got into bed and felt herself surrounded by gifts. Her Sharpe aunts had given her three sets of sheets, matching pillowcases, two pillows, and two pink bedspreads, a heavy one for winter and a lighter one for summer. Her Sharpe uncles' gift was a new clock radio. She checked to make sure she had set the alarm. She was tired from the exertion of moving, almost too exhausted to sleep. The glow of the streetlight bathed the room in a soft light. She listened to the cars drive by and remembered that she needed to get a map of Wichita to practice driving the routes to all the different schools where she would be working. Since she was still an inexperienced driver, that thought made her anxious.

And as she always did when she became nervous or afraid, Annie craved the piece of glass she kept close. She placed her paralyzed right arm across her stomach and reached into the pocket of her pajamas and found the glass. She stroked it, the smooth edges and teardrop shape as familiar as her own face, until she became calm. Finally, she fell asleep with her arms folded over her heart.

Willa stood at the sink at Mattie's place smoking a cigarette. She was worn out, her feet and ankles ached, and she was almost too tired to stand. She wanted nothing more than to sleep, but when she got into bed, Jake reached for her breast. She slapped his hand away. When he persisted, she grabbed her cigarettes and left. The last thing on her mind was having sex. She tried to push down her resentment, but it kept bubbling up. She couldn't remember the last time she'd wanted to make love. She'd done her duty, but she wasn't sure she even loved Jake anymore, a man who lied to her and betrayed her and moved her to Kansas. She couldn't understand why he was still attracted to her. After six kids her breasts sagged, and she gained ten pounds, mostly around her middle. White hairs had appeared, and soon she would have to color her hair or just go gray.

A cold nose nudged her leg. She looked down, and Tippy stared up at her with his dark almond eyes. "Hey there. You're depressed, too, huh." She patted his back and scratched his chest where he liked it. "Let's go sit on the steps."

Tippy leaned against her as she smoked what she told herself would be the last cigarette of the day. They listened to the night sounds—a coyote howled, something rustled in the grass—but there was nothing to see in the darkness. There were no stars, just clouds, and the only light was the glow of Willa's cigarette.

Protection
1962-1963

AFTER DROPPING OFF ELLIE AND Rocky at the red-brick high school to enroll for classes, Willa drove three blocks onto Protection's Main Street. While she was waiting for the kids, she planned to do some exploring. It was a pretty little town with lots of trees set in a valley between Bluff and Cavalry creeks. The road sign said Pop. 800.

Willa parked the car in front of the only department store. Maybe she could find some fabric on sale to make Annie a winter suit. A bell tinkled as she opened the door and walked into the fan-cooled air. She was dressed in black pedal pushers, a sleeveless white cotton blouse, and her comfortable, well-worn black flats. Willa rarely wore dresses, preferring the ease and comfort of pants, and she knew that she still looked good in slacks. When the Sharpe family photo was taken at her mother's eightieth birthday party, Willa had worn a white shirt and tailored pants with her western leather belt while all her sisters had chosen the same style of shapeless floral print dress that Lizzie wore, as if saying we're middle-aged now; we've resigned ourselves to being dumpy. At forty-five, the youngest of the Sharpe sisters, Willa wasn't ready to give up quite yet.

As she examined a bolt of blue plaid wool, Willa felt eyes appraising her. Three women, about her age, rummaging through a sale rack of summer dresses, were whispering and glancing at her. Despite the late August heat, the women wore dresses with petticoats and stockings and heels. Willa smiled at the women, but they moved to another sale rack and continued their whispering. Well, that's not very friendly, Willa thought. The fabric prices seemed much higher than Enid's, and since there wasn't a clerk in sight, Willa decided she had seen enough.

Willa walked out into the sun and waited for a moment to allow her eyes to adjust. A heavyset man, wearing gray coveralls and a Farmer's Co-op cap, got out of a pick-up across the street and headed toward the café. The man stopped behind Willa's car. Chewing on a thick wad of tobacco, he scrutinized the bumper sticker and then spat a stream of tobacco juice. He pointed at Willa, who was opening the car door to get inside. "Kennedy, huh?" he grunted, and then spat again. "Goddamn Oklahoma trash, why don't you go back where you came from?"

Too shocked to speak, Willa watched the man disappear into the café. She walked to the back of the Chevy. Yellowish-brown tobacco juice was spattered on the chrome bumper, on the Oklahoma license plate, and on the red, white, and blue Kennedy for President bumper sticker. Brown juice dribbled down JFK's head and eyes and onto his wide grin and white teeth. What kind of a place is this, Willa wondered, where people spit on your car?

Willa got into the car and sat for a moment. She was shaking and unnerved, but she was angry, too. She lit a cigarette. To hell with Protection, she thought, I can do my trading in Ashland and Dodge City. She drove to the high school and parked in the shade of a tree. She found some tissues in the glove box and while she waited for Rocky and Ellie, she cleaned the plate and bumper sticker. But no matter how hard she scrubbed, the ugly brown stain remained on Kennedy's forehead and eyes.

Rocky wanted to drive home, and Willa was happy to let him. When they turned onto 160 and headed west, Rocky found KOMA on the radio. Gene Pitney was singing *Only Love Can Break a Heart*. Willa studied her tall, skinny son. He stared straight ahead at the flat, two-lane highway, his wavy, dark hair too long and falling in his eyes. He chewed the inside of his cheek and looked worried about something. Sensing that she was examining him, he frowned and turned the radio louder.

She knew Rocky had his own problems. He'd left his friends and a girlfriend behind at Carrier. She stubbed out her cigarette and lit another. Willa thought about the spitting man. The Hardestys, the Sharpes, and their friends, Democrats all, were thrilled when Kennedy beat Nixon. She and Jake watched the debates at Floyd and Mae's, and it was clear that Kennedy was the better man. Too bad others couldn't see it.

Willa checked on Ellie. She was stretched across the back

seat reading a novel with her skirt hiked up and her bare feet hanging out the window.

"Ellie, put your feet down."

Without taking her eyes off her book, Ellie moved her feet until they were resting on the edge of the back window, but not over it.

"Ellie!" Willa warned. Ellie sighed a dramatic sigh and slammed her feet to the floor. Willa knew that whatever had happened at the high school wasn't pleasant for Rocky and Ellie. Willa's visit to Protection wasn't pleasant either, but there was no reason she had to tell anybody else about it. While she yearned to know what Rocky and Ellie were thinking and feeling, she respected their privacy; she rarely intruded on their private thoughts. She had been raised to get on with life without complaint, without whining, and even though it was a lesson she and Jake never consciously taught, it was one lesson their children absorbed.

Rocky and Ellie's introduction to Protection High School was humiliating. At Carrier, everyone knew who they were, the younger siblings of popular Annie, Willy, and Frankie Hardesty, which assured them of their own importance and popularity. Here they were outsiders.

Mr. Brown, the assistant principal and assistant coach, didn't bother to introduce himself to the two Hardestys. He's looking at us, Ellie thought, as if we're alien scum. Short, with a thick, muscular body and no sign of a neck, Brown stood and barked questions at them. When he learned that Rocky didn't play football and didn't want to learn to play football, he shook his head in disgust. Like most Kansans he looked down on Oklahoma, which was filled with too many Indians. "It will be a lot harder here than in your little Oklahoma school," he said, which proved he didn't bother to look over their transcripts. Ellie, a straight A student, was furious. Her parents taught her to be polite, so she smiled and nodded. Teachers always liked her, and she knew this man would too, eventually.

Knowing he had to last only one year at Protection, Rocky didn't bother being polite. He yawned, looked at his shoes, and slumped in his chair while the man talked. He did straighten up when Brown commented on their dark skin and asked if they had any Indian blood.

"Yeah, we're full-blooded Cheyenne, fresh off the reservation," Rocky muttered. Ellie jabbed him with her elbow, but Brown was already out the door and headed to the football field. The school secretary stopped talking on the telephone for a moment and shoved information packets at them. Rocky and Ellie exchanged a grimace. They were enrolled. It was going to be a long year.

During their first year in Kansas, the Hardestys lived in the same house, but they existed in different worlds, similar only in their unhappiness. At Willa's urging, Jake rented two quarters of farmland in addition to the four hundred acres that he farmed for Mattie. He bought cattle and put them on wheat pasture. His day began early and ended late.

Every week, Aunt Mattie summoned him for questioning, and he stood in front of her like a schoolboy giving a report.

Willa helped Jake with the farming and flung herself at the house, cleaning and scrubbing, painting, and laying linoleum, as well as making clothes for Ellie and Annie. She avoided Protection, shopped for groceries in Ashland, and made a monthly shopping trip to Dodge City, which was sixty miles northwest.

Rocky drifted silently through his classes, did all his homework in study hall, and then he spent a couple of hours after school at the pool hall playing cards and chess with the town's old men. On the weekends, he either worked with his father or found work with other farmers. He dated a rebellious sophomore girl, who found his dark, serious demeanor, outsider status, and slim, handsome face attractive and dangerous.

About halfway through the year, Mr. Brown phoned Willa and asked her to meet him in his office to talk about a problem with Rocky. None of her children had ever been in trouble in school, and Willa was worried. Rocky was earning B's and A's in his classes, and when she asked Rocky if had done something wrong, he said he couldn't think of anything. Since girls weren't allowed to wear pants in school (a stupid rule Ellie and Willa despised), Willa dressed for her meeting in a navy blue wool dress, stockings and heels. Willa waited while Brown wedged himself into his chair.

"Do you know that Rocky goes to the pool hall after school?"

"Yes."

That answer seemed to fluster Mr. Brown, who shuffled through his papers.

"You said there was a problem with Rocky?"

"Well, his grades are fine. Good, in fact."

Willa stared at Mr. Brown and wondered why she was here. She had work to do. She had been piecing a baby quilt for Frankie and Shirley's new little girl.

"We don't think it's a good idea that Rocky spend his time at the pool hall."

"Why?"

"It's just not healthy for him to be there."

"My son's in perfect health."

"Well, there's been some talk in town, and it doesn't look good for the school."

"The school day ends at 4:00, right?"

"Yes, for those who don't play sports and have practice."

"Well, Mr. Brown, I can't see how it's any of your business what Rocky does after 4:00." Willa stood up. She needed a cigarette desperately.

"I'm sorry you feel that way, Mrs. Hardesty. We've also noticed that he doesn't attend either church or Sunday school. Frankly, we're concerned. Rocky seems troubled and we're worried about his soul."

Willa wanted to slap the man across his fat, white face. Instead she took a deep breath, imagining that it was smoke filling her lungs and calming her. "And I'm sorry, Mr. Brown, that I drove all the way here to listen to you butt into something that's none of your business. My son will do whatever he wants after school, and you don't have anything to say about that. Is that clear?"

Mr. Brown started to speak, but Willa was already out the door and searching in her purse for her cigarettes.

Rocky continued to frequent the pool hall. By temperament a listener not a talker, he relished the old men's stories, and he liked challenging them at chess. He figured they were part of his education, too.

Ellie, an avid reader of science fiction and Annie's Jane Austen novels, knew that she had moved to a strange world with its own customs and culture. To learn how to live in that world, she would need allies. For years, she had successfully manipulated her family, and she was adept at getting what she wanted. In two months, she had her allies. A girlfriend and a boyfriend. The girlfriend was Elise Edwards, a green-eyed, conventional girl from an old Protection family who longed to be wicked, and Stewart Hubble, a good-looking farm boy, whose parents raised quarter horses and hunting dogs. Stewart's father, Steve, had become a coon-hunting buddy of Jake's. Once, when Stewart picked her up for a date, Ellie saw her father slip him a ten-dollar bill. She was mortified, but she didn't say anything. It was just his way. He was always saying he remembered what it was like to be young.

Still, like the rest of her family, Ellie was unhappy. She wasn't sure why; maybe it was the atmosphere of Aunt Mattie's house, which was sparkling clean yet gloomy. And, Ellie knew, no matter how hard she tried, she was still an alien in a town run by powerful women's clubs, which her mother did not belong to and would never be asked to join, and an outsider at school, where everyone had known each other since first grade.

By the fall of 1963, with their first year in Protection behind them, the Hardestys had improved their circumstances, but their unhappiness continued. Rocky moved back to Oklahoma, where he attended college in Tahlequah and worked part-time at a restaurant. Annie enjoyed spending part of her summer visiting her former roommate Jill Stainton in San Diego, but she returned to the Wichita School system apprehensive about another year. Jake was pleased because the wheat crop had been good, but Aunt Mattie had become more involved with church work and more demanding. With the house in order, Willa planted a garden, but her ulcer flared up, and she couldn't seem to stop worrying, mostly about money and Annie. She couldn't put her finger on it, but something was off with Annie.

On a late November morning, Jake and Willa were driving back from Enid after selling a load of scrap iron. They stopped and had coffee and pie with sweet Aunt Martha, who had invited Floyd and Mae to surprise them. It was good to see their old friends. As they visited, they listened to KCRC on the radio. The announcer broke in and said that the President had been shot. Something broke inside Willa. She cried so much she got the hiccups. She cried all the way home until her throat was raw and sore. It was horrible, beyond sad. Kennedy was young, younger than she was, and filled with so much promise. She thought of the spitting man and his hatred for Kennedy. How could someone hate that much?

That weekend, Annie drove home unexpectedly from Wichita. She arrived babbling and in tears. She kept talking about voices telling her to do things, bad things, and she raved about a storm in the glass. Willa kept her away from Jake and Ellie, put her to bed, brought her supper on a tray, and wouldn't let her watch the television coverage about the assassination of President Kennedy. By Sunday afternoon, Annie calmed down. She blamed her behavior on menstrual cramps and insisted she was well enough to drive back to Wichita. Willa watched her go. She made Annie promise to call as soon as she got to her apartment. She waited for the call, smoking cigarette after cigarette. Annie did call, but her voice sounded strange and tight.

After spending Monday watching Kennedy's funeral on television, Willa and Jake went to bed. Willa lay awake and listened to Jake snore. She got up to get a drink of water and then looked in on Ellie, who had her light on.

"That's a long book," Willa said. "What is it?"

"It's Rocky's." Ellie held up the worn paperback. "*Stranger in a Strange Land*."

"Well, don't stay up too late. You've got school tomorrow."

Willa sat in the dark at the dining room table finishing her cigarette before she went back to bed. Her mind swirled with images of the past days. Annie's wild hair and distraught face as she ran to the house. Jackie Kennedy in her bloodstained suit, head bowed and lost, standing by LBJ in the plane. The black horse in the funeral procession, who looked as if he wanted to run.

We live near a town called Protection, Willa thought. But there's no protection anywhere. Not for President Kennedy, not for Annie, not for any of us. She crushed out her cigarette. At least she could try to sleep. As she walked past the back door on the way to the bedroom, she heard scratching and then a soft whining. Tippy. She'd forgotten to feed Tippy. She'd made scrambled eggs for supper, and there weren't any table scraps. He must be starving.

She opened the door and the black dog stepped into the room. He waited patiently, ears pricked, looking up at her with sad eyes. "I'm sorry, Tippy. How about some bread and butter and milk?" Tippy thumped his tail.

Well, at least I can feed the dog, Willa thought. And tomorrow there's more work. I'll make breakfast and do the laundry and ironing that didn't get done this weekend, and I'll finish that wool jacket for Ellie. I'll write letters to Mama and Cissie and Webb. And one to Annie, too.

Willa slid into bed beside Jake, warming her cold feet on his warm legs. She shut her eyes, but she couldn't shut down her brain. She made mental lists of what she had to do, but her mind kept seeing the bumper sticker and the ugly brown stain that she wasn't able to remove. Maybe I should have tried harder to clean it, she thought, as she drifted off to sleep. Maybe there was something I should have done.

The Daily Soaps
1965

WHERE WAS ELLIE? SHE ALWAYS snatched the phone on the first ring. It was 5:30 p.m. She couldn't be at school. Jake was probably watching the news and ignoring the phone like usual. Okay, three more rings and I'm hanging up.

"Hello?"

"Ellie! Where the hell were you?"

"In the bathroom. Oh, I'm out of hairspray and Kotex. Daddy! It's Mama!"

"No! I don't want to talk to him. I want to talk to you."

"Hey, shouldn't you guys be on the road?"

"That's what I want to talk to you about. Annie's been invited to a lunch tomorrow. A shower for the English teacher who's getting married."

"Okay. Mama. I've gotta go."

"Where are you going?"

"To the game! Friday night football, duh. I'm a cheerleader! Elise is picking me up any minute."

"Ellie! Wait. Annie and I won't be coming home this weekend. There's plenty of food in the freezer and you can get by a week without laundry. But I remembered, was I supposed to bake a cake for you for something tomorrow?"

"It's the stupid senior class slave auction. Can you believe it? It's 1965 and Protection High School has slave auctions! Thank God we don't have any Black people! Elise's mom is hiring us to clean her house so that creepy old guy who always buys the girls won't get us."

"What about the cake?"

"Elise is here! Bye, Mama."

"Wait, Ellie. Tell Jake I called."

But it was too late. Ellie was gone. Off to town. To live her life. Well, she couldn't blame her. Had she been any different? Last year Willa found an invitation to a Kayette Mother-Daughter Tea stuffed in the drawer of the phone stand. The date already passed. Willa wondered if Ellie went by herself or just skipped it. She was going to talk to Ellie about it, but then she had to get Annie ready to go back to Great Bend, and she'd forgotten. Jake said he and Ellie were doing fine and not to worry. Still, she worried. And she felt guilty. Mostly because it was nice being on her own with Annie and not having to deal with Jake's bullshit day in and day out, and Ellie ignoring her. At least Annie needed her.

Since late 1963, during the week, Willa lived with Annie, first in Wichita, which Annie called the City of the Witch, then in Great Bend, another city on the Arkansas River, just over 100 miles from home. Annie was lucky to get the Great Bend job. Driving to the eight different Wichita elementary schools had been too much for her. Now, she just did her speech therapy at Great Bend's two junior high schools. During the school year, Willa helped Annie cope with the stress of her job by spending her day cooking, cleaning, doing laundry, and running errands as well as sewing for both her daughters.

Every weekday, Willa stopped to watch two soaps. *As the World Turns* from 11:30 to 12:00 and *The Edge of Night* from 2:30 to 3:00. For an hour a day, she escaped into the slow-moving, black-and-white worlds of Oakdale and Monticello, peopled by well-dressed, attractive characters with never-ending problems. While she watched, she sometimes ironed or pieced a quilt, so the hour wasn't entirely wasted. It was one of the few times when the knots of worry in her stomach and in her head loosened. In the evening, she made supper and told Annie what had happened in Oakdale and Monticello. Annie would listen for a time, and then she told Willa about her world, about teachers who were conspiring against her, about locked doors, and missing papers. On especially bad days, Annie heard voices coming from the silent, blank screen of the television. During the night, Willa woke to Annie screaming in fear, pursued by a predator she could never name. Willa gave her a glass of warm milk and soothed her back to sleep. Annie seemed to have no problems when she was working with her students on their speech therapy, and so with Willa's help, she kept her job, paid into Social Security, and saved some money. Willa and Jake decided that Willa should continue to stay with Annie until she could manage on her own.

Willa and Annie drove home every Friday for the weekend

and drove back to Great Bend on Sunday afternoon. Annie enjoyed driving her Dodge Dart and seemed happiest on the road. At home, Willa paid bills, listened to Jake complain about Aunt Mattie, did the laundry, cleaned house, cooked meals, and tried to talk to Ellie. But Ellie was usually out at a school event or on a date. When Ellie was home, she mostly kept to her room reading, surfacing only to eat and do chores.

Willa looked at the clock. Where had the time gone? If they were to get to the movie on time, they needed to eat supper soon.

"Annie?" Willa knocked on the bedroom door. Annie's room had twin beds, but Annie valued privacy, so Willa slept on the living room sofa, making and unmaking her bed every day.

"Come in, Mama." Annie was at her desk looking at the Great Bend paper.

"Did you decide what movie you want to see, Annie?"

"We have three choices, Mama. Lee Marvin in *Cat Ballou,* Jimmy Stewart in *Shenandoah,* and Janet Leigh in *Psycho.*" Annie laughed. But it was the good laugh. The one that said yes I know you think I'm crazy and I may be crazy, but I'm not stupid.

Still, Willa measured her words. Anything could set Annie off. Last September they watched Miss Kansas win the Miss America pageant, and Annie threw a huge fit. Cursing the women in their bathing suits as sluts and whores until Willa turned off the television and forced Annie into her bedroom until she calmed down.

"Well, that's an easy choice," Willa said. "I like Jimmy Stewart. And we have time to grab a bite at the drive-in before the movie."

The phone rang. Who can that be? "Annie, go get your coat."

Willa picked up the phone. "Hello?"

"It's me," Jake growled.

Willa's stomach dropped. Jake never called her. "Is everything all right? Ellie?"

"I wanted to wait until she left to tell you."

"Tell me what."

"Aunt Mattie stopped me at the Co-op today. Wanted to introduce me to my sister."

"Who?"

"Yeah. My sister. Some woman, blonde hair all stiff and sprayed up, was driving Mattie around town. A widow who said her name was Gladys Hardesty Rorke. Aunt Mattie said that Gladys had moved in and would be helping her oversee the farm operation."

"What'd you say?"

"Nothing. Aunt Mattie was still talking. She told me that if I wanted her land, I got to join her church like Gladys did and go with her every Sunday. I told her I never had a sister. My dad had three sons and that was all. I told them both to go to hell. Told her I didn't want her land or anything to do with her ever again."

"What did Mattie say?"

"I didn't wait to find out."

"Oh my God. I can't come home this weekend. I'll call Mattie."

"Don't bother. There's nothing you can do about it. It's done." Jake slammed down the phone.

"Mama? Is everything okay?"

Willa closed her eyes, took a deep breath, and put down the phone, willing herself to stay calm. "Yes, Annie. Everything's fine. Go start the car. I'll be right out."

This is the shits, Willa thought. I'm living in a goddamn soap opera, and I can't turn it off. She grabbed her coat and gloves. How long did they have on the farm? Surely Aunt Mattie wouldn't kick them out before harvest.

Willa's World
1967

IN MAY, ANNIE FINISHED THE school year at Great Bend and was hired for another year. While they were packing to go home for the summer, Annie started screaming and crying. Yelling at the voices to shut up, to stop hurting her. But the voices didn't stop.

Why now? Willa thought, as she faced her red-faced stranger of a daughter. "Annie! This is no time to have a fit. The car's packed. Let's go home."

"I'm not going anywhere with you, you bitch! I don't know you! Get out of my house!"

Willa had no choice. She called an ambulance. The next day she committed Annie to Larned State Hospital.

When the doctors at Larned examined Annie, they gave her voices and her fears a name. Schizophrenia, they called it, speaking the name slowly, reverently. Schizophrenia. "What causes it?" Willa asked.

"It's a brain disease," they said. "No one knows what causes it. It attacks young women like Annie, sometimes without warning. It's no one's fault. It just happens. There are drugs we can try, and we'll give her therapy."

"Will she get better?" Willa asked.

"Maybe, maybe not," the doctors said. "We'll do our best."

Their words were little comfort for Willa, who couldn't accept their answer. Doctors found a vaccine for polio, but it had been eight years too late for Annie. Life was so unfair. Aunt Mattie agreed to let them stay through another harvest, but then they had to move. But where would they go?

It shamed Willa to have others know about their problems, but when the Hubbles found out that Jake and Mattie had a falling out, they offered to rent them their small three-bedroom farmhouse, a mile and a half from Protection. The Hubbles had struck two oil and gas wells and moved into a large house in town. No one had lived in their farmhouse for several years. In June, after harvest, Willa and Jake moved out of Aunt Mattie's place into the Hubble house.

Once again, Willa cleaned and painted someone else's house. The Hubble place was all right, the rent was cheap, but it wasn't hers. She resigned herself to never having a house of her own.

Willa wanted to lash out at Jake and say I told you so, but how would that help? She'd given up the dream of inheriting Mattie's four hundred acres a long time ago. Jake prided himself on being able to get along with anybody, but he hadn't been able to get along with Mattie. He wouldn't talk about it. Just pushed it out of his mind like it never happened. Jake didn't like rehashing troubles, "picking at scabs," he called it. She knew Jake had seen Janice Sedlak's wedding picture in the *Enid Morning News*. She married one of the Morris boys and lived in Coldwater. Then, Jerry Sedlak's obituary and photo appeared in the paper. The first Enid resident to be killed in Vietnam. What was Jake feeling, she wondered, about the marriage of his daughter and the death of his son? Did he feel anything at all? There was no way of knowing and no point to asking. So she didn't ask, and he didn't mention it. Willa bought a sympathy card and sent it to the Sedlaks and signed both their names. She knew what it felt like to lose a son. Work and constant movement were Jake's answer to everything. That and coon hunting and cattle sales and shooting the breeze for hours at the Protection Co-op with some old boy he barely knew.

One September afternoon, Willa watched *The Edge of Night* and then turned off the television. She sat with her sewing basket on her lap. The house was quiet except for the rumbling, dripping water cooler in the living room window, and the ticking of the kitchen clock. There were no trees around the Hubble house. It was over ninety outside with no breeze.

She lit a cigarette and wished she had someone to visit with over a glass of iced tea. She thought about calling her sisters, but Cissie and Dilly had their own troubles, and she didn't want to bother them with hers. Both had gone through menopause and prepared her for the hot flashes and weight gain. Jake never seemed to age or change. Even his hair looked good with a few streaks of silver. Hers had turned an ugly gray which she colored dark brown every few weeks. The kids were gone now, out in the world. Tippy was gone too. She found him one morning, laid out like he was sleeping. He'd been a good companion, never any trouble, but she didn't want another dog.

Willa picked up the teardrop of glass that she kept in her sewing basket next to the thimble. She closed the basket and put it on the end table. When they moved into the Hubble place, they bought a new sofa, two new living room chairs, and an end table. There were brown plaid cushions on the western style wood furniture. It was the first new furniture she'd ever had, and they were still paying it off.

She and Jake were past fifty, starting over and going into debt to buy farm equipment. At least there were the two leased quarters to farm, and cattle prices were looking good. Ellie's student loans and her job took care of her college expenses. They didn't need much to live on. They would get by.

She looked at the teardrop of glass in her hand. Here she was feeling sorry for herself when who knows what Annie was going through right now at the hospital. She wished she could talk to Annie, but Annie was lost to her. The doctors said it wasn't Willa's fault, but she kept searching for a reason. Did she do anything wrong? Was there something she could have done?

Willa visited Annie at the state hospital once a month, but Jake refused to go with her. He hated hospitals and swore he'd never set foot in one again. He didn't believe in mental illness and thought Annie should just snap out of it and get back to work. On her last visit, Willa tried to find her beautiful, brilliant daughter in the face of the pale puffy-faced stranger who sat hunched and stiff on the hospital bed. Her thick, long hair hung in an unwashed, uncombed rat's nest. Willa washed her hair and combed out the tangles. This quieted Annie for a time, but then the stranger was back. Rocking back and forth and talking to voices only she could hear. Annie moved her fingers frantically over the piece of glass. When Willa asked her if she could look at the glass, if she could hold it, Annie shook her head no and curled her fingers protectively around it. Willa reached out to touch Annie's hand, and Annie pulled her hand away and thrust the glass into her mouth. She bit down until the edges of the glass cut into her lips. Blood trickled slowly down her chin. Shaking uncontrollably and wailing like a lost calf, she glared at Willa. Willa ran for help. It took the efforts of a nurse, two orderlies, and the injection of a powerful sedative to force Annie's jaw open. The doctor gave Willa the glass and told her not to give it back to Annie.

Willa held the glass up to the light and remembered the last coherent words Annie spoke to her. "I'm trapped, Mama. I'm trapped in the glass," Annie said, her voice unexpectedly calm and her blue eyes wide with fear and a terrible knowledge.

Willa turned the glass in her hand. Maybe it was the glass, she thought. Maybe if I had taken it away years ago, maybe this wouldn't have happened.

The back door banged open, and Jake limped into the house.

"What the hell are you doing sitting in the dark, old woman?" He flicked on the kitchen light. "What's for supper?"

"It's not time yet, old man."

"Hell, woman, it's after five." Jake ruffled her short, dark hair. "What's wrong with you?"

That's a good question, Willa thought. What's wrong with me? Better ask what's wrong with the world. She got up to put the sewing basket away.

Jake washed his hands, opened the refrigerator and took out leftover ham and scalloped potatoes to warm up. He'd gotten used to rustling up supper for himself and Snooks. He missed Ellie. He liked her boyfriend Stewart Hubble, but he'd seen they were getting a little too serious. So one night, he and Ellie had a talk. He fumbled around and finally said, "If you play with fire, Snooks, you're gonna get burned." Ellie laughed at him.

"Don't worry about me, Daddy. I know what I'm doing. I'm not getting pregnant. I'm going to college and getting as far away from here as I can. Maybe I'll never get married."

Jake remembered that was the same night Ellie asked about his bad leg. He almost told her the truth, but then she asked if he'd really been a bootlegger and her eyes lit up with excitement. So he made up a story about being chased by the Woods County sheriff, who shot out his tires and then shot him in the leg when he'd tried to run. Hell, it could have been true, if the sheriff hadn't been one of his customers.

Jake poured Willa a cup of coffee. "Have you heard anything from Snooks? I wonder how she's getting along on those crutches."

"She said she'd call if she had any problems."

"Seems like everyone I run into wants to talk about it. I

tell them what I told her, if she'd listened to me, nothing would have happened."

Jake shook his head. It made him sick every time he thought about it. Two weeks ago, they went to the Protection Rodeo. Ellie and Stewart were sitting on the hood of the Chevy next to the arena fence. During the bronc riding, Jake warned Ellie to move away because some old bronc could fall against the post and crush her leg against the fender. Ellie didn't pay attention to him, and sure enough, that's exactly what happened. A horse bucked off his rider and fell against the post just as Ellie turned away saying something to Stewart. The fence post smashed against her. Ellie screamed and grabbed her leg. Dr. Gibson, Protection's doctor, who was at the rodeo said the leg wasn't broken, but the calf was badly bruised and battered. He prescribed aspirin, put an elastic bandage around her calf, gave Ellie a pair of crutches, and told her to keep off the leg as much as possible. The next day Ellie's calf was swollen and black and blue, but she insisted she had to get back to work in Wichita. Since it was her left leg, she could drive all right.

Jake set up the TV trays, and they ate supper while they watched the news. Willa was washing the dishes, and Jake was reading the paper when the phone rang. As usual, Willa's stomach jumped. A phone call usually meant bad news. Her first thoughts went to Annie.

"Hello," Willa said.

"Mrs. Hardesty, this is Barbara Congdon."

Willa heard noise in the background and an intercom.

Willa had met Barbara when she came home with Ellie for Easter. A farmer's daughter from Fredonia, Barbara was a tall, pretty girl with long, wavy brown hair. She and Ellie roomed together in the dorm, and they decided to stay in Wichita and work during the summer. They found a one-bedroom apartment near the park for only eighty dollars a month. Barbara worked for an insurance company, but after years of reading Perry Mason and Ellery Queen novels, Ellie was determined to work for a private detective. She called every agency in the Wichita Yellow Pages, and to her great amusement, she found a job as a secretary for a private detective, unbelievably named Mason, who worked out of his home.

"Barbara, what's wrong?"

"Ellie passed out in the tub tonight. I called an ambulance, and they took her to Wesley Hospital. Can you come to Wichita?"

"I'll leave right now. Where's the hospital?"

"It's on Hillside. Just turn left off Kellogg, you know 54, onto Hillside. You can't miss it."

"Tell Ellie that I'm on my way."

"Just hurry. Please hurry."

Willa hung up the phone. Jake looked at her face. "It's Snooks, isn't it?"

In less than fifteen minutes, Willa packed a bag and was on the road. She took 160, the faster but lonelier Medicine Lodge route instead of the well-traveled 54. Between Coldwater and Medicine Lodge, the highway passed through a desolate landscape of sagebrush, cedars, and deep canyons. If the car were to break down somewhere on this stretch, it could be hours before anyone found her.

Willa kept the Chevy at a steady seventy miles an hour. Wind whipped at her face through the open window. She gripped the wheel with both hands and chastised herself. Foolishly, she had thought Ellie was safe. That she didn't have to worry about her baby girl. All through high school, while Willa was staying with Annie, Ellie took care of herself. She made good grades and was always winning some award or starring in the school play.

Willa tried to remember if she ever told her how proud she was of her. But there was all the trouble and worry with Annie, and she didn't have much time for Ellie. "Please don't let me be too late," Willa whispered.

The doctor who came out to talk to Willa and Barbara was short, with a round, boyish face. "Mrs. Hardesty?" he said, holding out his hand. "I'm Dr. Rollins. Ellie's going to be okay. As I told Barbara, though, we almost lost her. If Barbara hadn't called the ambulance when she did, those blood clots could have gone to her lungs. She'll be here until the swelling goes down and those clots disappear."

All the strength, all the fear that kept Willa steady and upright, left her. She knew what happened when a blood clot traveled to the lungs or the brain. She sank into a chair. Barbara grabbed her hand.

"May I see her?" Willa asked.

"She's asleep now, but you can go in."

Willa followed the doctor down a long hallway and into a small room. He drew back the drape. Ellie lay on her back. A compression bandage was wrapped around her left leg. Willa heard the whoosh of the pump that would help keep the blood circulating. "Is it all right if I stay with her tonight?" Willa asked.

"Sure. Just lie down on the other bed if you want to sleep."

Ellie was in the hospital for six days. Willa stayed with Barbara in the apartment, fixed their breakfast and supper every night, washed and ironed, and cleaned. She went to the hospital every day, and every day she and Ellie watched Willa's soaps on the small hospital overhead TV. Willa filled Ellie in on the history of both shows, and Ellie, too, became hooked on the intrigues in Oakdale and Monticello. Barbara came after work, and then she and Willa went back to the apartment.

Before they went to bed, Willa worked on a wardrobe of doll clothes she was making for her two granddaughters, while Barbara crocheted a sweater for her brother's new baby. As they worked, they talked. Willa discovered that she could talk to Barbara about anything. She told her about Big Charley, about Charley's leukemia, about Annie's mental illness, about Rocky's volunteering for Vietnam which broke her heart. He hadn't even talked to her about it. Just enlisted. Willa told Barbara about her fears and her pride in her children. About her hopes for Ellie. She talked about menopause and about how her body had betrayed her. She shared all of her troubles. Her own personal soap opera. She listened as Barbara confided the ambivalence she felt about her engagement to her high school sweetheart, who was in the Air Force. He wanted to get married next year, and she'd have to quit school. Maybe she was too young to get married. Fears she hadn't confessed to her own mother. They agreed not to tell Ellie about her brush with death. "What good would it do?" Willa said. More than anything, she wanted Ellie to be happy, unshadowed by fear.

When Ellie was released from the hospital, her left leg was weak and withered. She would have to use crutches for another month before she started physical therapy to build up her muscles. For the next few weeks, Ellie stayed home on the farm with her leg propped up on pillows, pouting because Willa hadn't allowed her to stay in Wichita with Barbara. Ellie followed the fate of the Clutter killers in the newspapers, and she devoured Capote's *In Cold Blood* in two days and one sleepless night. But every day at 11:30 and 2:30, Willa turned on the television, and she and Ellie drank iced tea and watched the soaps. Jake started coming in early for dinner, and he got hooked on *As the World Turns*.

Willa tried to talk to her daughter, the way she talked with Barbara, but most of the time Ellie kept her nose in a book or was on the phone and didn't seem interested in conversation. Why is it, Willa wondered, that I can talk to Barbara but not to Ellie? Willa overheard Ellie tell Jake that she was going to break up with Stewart, but Ellie had never said a word to her. They both avoided talking about Rocky. When a letter came from him, they studied the exotic names,

Phan Thief, Bang Son, Chu Lai, and then watched the evening news dreading that those names might be mentioned.

When it was time for Ellie to return to Wichita State in late August, she couldn't wait to go. She had nothing in common with her mother, and she felt trapped in the small farmhouse. After years of making her own decisions, she was irritated by Willa's meticulousness and control. And Willa had grown impatient with Ellie's sloppiness, sleeping late, and her nagging about smoking. Jake and Willa packed Ellie's car, checked the tires, filled the tank with gas, and told their daughter goodbye.

"Don't drive too fast," Jake warned, kicking the car tires. "This Corvair is a piece of shit."

"Daddy! It's cute. And it only cost five hundred dollars."

"That's about four hundred ninety-nine dollars too much," Jake said, grabbing Ellie and kissing her on the cheek.

"Call when you get there," said Willa.

"I will." Ellie threw her crutches in the back seat. "Don't worry, Mama. All will be well in Willa's World. Hey, Mama, that could be your soap." Ellie lowered her voice and mimicked the television announcer, "And Now! Willa's World brought to you by, by what, Mama? Who's your sponsor? Belair cigarettes?"

"Don't be a smart mouth, Eleanor Sharpe Hardesty, or I won't give you this fried chicken and cherry pie." Willa hugged Ellie tight. She wanted to tell Ellie she loved her. She wanted to tell her to be safe, but those words didn't seem big enough for what she was feeling. So, she hugged her again, and then she let her go.

Just Willa

Willa stood with Jake in the dusty driveway and watched as the green Corvair rattled down the dirt road.

"I think that muffler has a hole in it," Jake said. He put his arm around Willa's shoulders. "We're alone again," he said, fondling her breast. "Want to fool around?"

The Secret of Sappa Creek
1970

Minister Stevens nodded at them, and the Beagley twins and the Hepner sisters stood up. The popular quartet sang at most funerals in Freedom. The four young women wore matching red velvet dresses and red satin headbands and moved with well-practiced assurance to the front of the church.

Willa sat dry-eyed beside Jake in the second pew filled with Hardestys. She wasn't able to zip up her good black dress, so she settled on black wool pants, a white blouse, and a black jacket. It was a pleasant fifty-three degrees, unusual for late December, and she hadn't bothered with a coat. Willa placed her purse on the floor and looked down the pew. Annie, wearing her old navy blue suit, sat on Willa's right, where Willa could keep an eye on her in case the voices started talking to her and telling her to throw a fit. So far Annie had been quiet. The new medication seemed to be working, although she gained about ten pounds.

Willa had directed Ellie to sit on the other side of Annie and help keep watch. Wearing a black and white mini-dress, black tights, and black boots, Ellie looked sixteen instead of twenty-two. She leaned against Mark Shanahan, her tall, blue-eyed husband, who sported a thick, curly blond Afro. Willy and his new wife Kayla, who was a few months younger than Ellie, sat next to Mark. Kayla seemed like a nice person, Willa thought, but nothing special. Although she did have beautiful, long hair which she ironed straight.

After Willy and Joanie divorced, she moved back to Enid with little Brad and Lou Ann. Willa missed her daughter-in-law and the grandkids. She wrote Joanie several letters, but she hadn't heard a word back from her. Willa didn't ask Willy what happened, and she didn't plan to. If he wanted to tell her, he would.

At the end of the pew, looking as if they had stepped out of a fashion magazine, were Frankie, Shirley, and their three children: Charley, ten; Alison, six; and Emmett, three. Shirley wore a low-cut black sheath dress and pearls, and a black hat with a large, swooping brim. She was the only woman in the church wearing a hat, and as far as Willa could tell the only woman with frosted hair. If Rocky had come to the funeral, he would have found a way to sit next to Shirley. Willa imagined him in his grubby, patched blue jeans, work boots, and stained leather jacket, his hair too long and hanging into his eyes and down his back. Ever since he'd returned from Vietnam, Rocky had gone quiet. He was always listening, though, smoking one cigarette after another. He flew home for Christmas, but returned to New Haven the day before his grandmother died.

Willa leaned against the back of the pew and closed her eyes. When Heck called to tell her that their mother was dead, she was not surprised. Lizzie had been failing for months. Willa felt Jake fidgeting next to her, tugging at his tie and stretching his left leg, trying to get comfortable on the hard bench. He hated churches almost as much as he hated hospitals.

Willa looked around the church crowded with Sharpes and their relatives and friends. Yesterday she and Cissie wrote their mother's obituary and counted Lizzie and Doc's descendants. They had three sons, Ollie, Stub, and Heck, who were present with their families; and four daughters, Ro, Dilly, Cissie, and Willa, who were there with most of their children; plus Lizzie's daughters Effie and Edith, who sent flowers, but weren't able to travel from Missouri and Canada in time for the funeral. Lizzie had fifty-two grandchildren, twenty-three great grandchildren, and seven great-great grandchildren. Six of her oldest grandsons were the pallbearers.

The singers stood quietly on the platform as the pianist played the opening chords of the hymn. The girls began to sing *Beautiful Isle of Somewhere*, and Willa felt as if someone were squeezing her heart. She hadn't heard the old hymn in years. The last time she heard it, her mother was singing it as she walked down the driveway of the home place on her way to gather news for her column. Lizzie lived for ninety-two years, yet, Willa realized as she looked at the closed coffin covered with flowers, what did she really know about her? She was born in 1878 in Kansas to John and Laura Allen. Her older sister Pearl preceded her in death. Lizzie wrote poetry, newspaper columns, and thousands of letters. She read stacks of books, enjoyed crocheting and beading, taking long walks, and visiting with her neighbors. What else did she know about her? At the moment, Willa couldn't think of a thing. She'd never been close to her mother. The only memory Willa had of being alone with her was the time Lizzie took her to Blue Springs on the train. The truth was Willa always felt closer to her dad. Doc had died twenty-two years ago, but she still missed him.

Willa glanced at Ellie, who like Jake was fidgeting and restless. Ellie was turning her new wedding band and diamond engagement ring around and around on her finger. *What will Ellie feel when I'm gone? Will she sit dry-eyed like me? Thinking about all she has to do after the funeral instead of mourning my passing?*

Annie lifted her head and looked straight into Willa's eyes. Willa blinked, embarrassed. She felt as if Annie could see exactly what she was thinking. Annie smiled a tiny smile, and for a moment, Willa glimpsed her daughter's sweet, sane self. Annie ducked her head and the moment was gone. Today, for whatever reason, Annie was behaving herself. But the stress of smiling and making small talk would exhaust her, and Willa knew that tomorrow she might have a schizophrenic episode and rant and rave for hours. Annie, who had minored in psychology in college, charted and noted each of her fits, as she called them, on a calendar in her bedroom. Despite what the doctors and Willa told him, Jake persisted in believing that Annie could control her fits, and he had no patience with her outbursts. "Snap out of it," he would growl. Sometimes Annie would listen to him, the voices would subside, and she would grow calm. More often, though, Annie would scream that she didn't know Jake. He wasn't her father. He was a stranger and had no right to tell her what to do.

Later, after the burial in Old Freedom Cemetery and cake and coffee at Heck and Lucy's, Willa stayed on at the home place with her sisters to sort through Lizzie's things. Everyone else hurried back to jobs and their lives. Jake left the car for Willa, while he and Annie drove back to the farm with Ellie and Mark, who would then drive to their apartment in Wichita.

Before she went inside the house to join her sisters, Willa lingered on the porch smoking a cigarette. When she finished, she buried the stub in the dirt to hide it just as she always did when she was at the home place. Of course, she'd never been able to keep a secret from Doc. He was always able to see right through her. As she was about to go inside, a new 1970 bright blue Mustang convertible pulled into the driveway. The driver honked. A slim, white-haired man wearing jeans and a blue sweater got out of the car. He removed his sunglasses.

"*Buon giorno, cara,*" the man called.

"Webb!" Willa shouted. She walked to him and held out her hand. He grabbed her, wrapping his arms around her in a tight embrace.

"Let me look at you," he said. "Still pretty as ever, but you've let your hair go white."

"You should talk! After Ellie's wedding this summer, I stopped coloring it. So, you heard about Mama?"

"I had to be in Wichita this morning, so I couldn't make it to the funeral. I'm sorry, Willa."

"Well, they said she didn't suffer. She just went to sleep. So have you moved back? What are you doing here?"

"I decided I wanted to ride some American rails again and get to know my nieces and nephews. I'm living at the ranch now, but mostly I've been traveling."

"Your letters and cards have been a big help to Annie. Seems like all she does anymore is read and write letters."

"I wish I could do more. So, how's Jake and the rest of your family?"

"He's good, everybody's good."

"And, you, Willa, how are you?"

Perhaps it was the note of concern in Webb's voice or the gentle kindness of his gaze as he looked into her eyes, or maybe it was just the force of memory, an image she had of a little girl cracking eggs in a cold classroom that caused the knot to untie in Willa's chest. A flood of feeling overwhelmed her, and she felt her throat swell and her eyes fill with tears. How long has it been, she wondered, since anyone wanted to know how I'm doing?

Willa turned away from Webb and walked to the back of the Mustang. She stood looking down the hill where the school had been. Her heart was racing. She took a deep breath and exhaled. So many years. They'd gone by so fast. Where had the time gone?

Willa heard the click of a lighter. Webb handed her a lit cigarette.

"Why don't we sit in my new car for a bit?"

"I should go in and help my sisters."

"They can wait."

Webb opened the passenger side door, and Willa slid into the bucket seat.

"Pretty nice, huh?" Webb said, sitting beside her and gripping the four-speed gearshift. "I feel like a real American now."

They sat in the Mustang, doors open, smoking their cigarettes. Webb looked south toward the red bluffs over the Cimarron and thought about how good it was to be home, in the place where he was born and raised. Willa looked inward, thinking about her early dreams of going to high school and college and becoming a teacher like Webb. It had been a long time since she thought of herself, of what she wanted. Her children always came first. What would it be like, she wondered, not to have children? To get up and go whenever and wherever you wanted to?

"What's it like?" she said aloud.

"What?"

"Not being married. Not having children."

"I don't know. I don't know anything else."

"Do you ever get lonely?"

"Sure. What about you?"

Willa lit another cigarette. Yes, she was sometimes lonely, even surrounded by Jake and a family. They took her for granted, but that was nothing unusual. That was most wives' and mothers' lives, a life she had accepted. What if she had gone to high school and college? Could she have left the country like Webb and lived among foreigners where no one needed her?

Willa sank into the bucket seat. She drew smoke deep into her lungs and exhaled slowly. She thought about the day before Ellie's wedding last August when she gave the quilt she had made to Ellie and Mark. "Thanks," Ellie said, and then grabbed another gift to unwrap. "Wait," Mark said, stopping Ellie's hand. "Look." He picked up the quilt, which had taken Willa six months of work to complete. He unfolded it, examined it, and marveled at the intricate, interlocking star pattern of blue, pink, yellow, and green prints and solids set against a white background. The free form design came to Willa in a dream so vivid and clear that when she woke up the pattern was etched in her mind as if it had always been there. Mark pointed out and counted the precise, tiny stitches, twelve per inch. His engineer's mind appreciated the craftsmanship and artistry required to fashion such a beautiful and functional piece of work. Willa could see the understanding dawn in Ellie's eyes as she looked again and saw the quilt for what it was. It was a wedding quilt crafted from fabric left over from years of spring and summer clothes that Willa had made for her. A quilt that contained her own history. "It's beautiful, Mama," Ellie said. "Thank you."

Thank-yous were few and far between for most mothers, Willa realized, trying to recall when she ever thanked Lizzie for anything. A life without her children would be unbearably lonely. Willa knew they were a part of her. She couldn't imagine life without them. It would be like living without her own beating heart.

"So, Willa? Cat got your tongue?"

"I'm sorry, Webb, my mind was a thousand miles away. I forgot what you asked."

"Never mind," he said, patting her shoulder. "I'm just glad you have some time for your old teacher."

"You're not much older than me." Willa stubbed out her cigarette in the ashtray. "It's funny, but I don't really feel that I've gotten older, inside, I mean."

"I think in my head I'm still about thirty-five," said Webb. "Until I look in a mirror, of course."

A cloud passed over the sun. Willa buttoned her jacket and glanced at her watch. "It's getting late. I better go in. If you're ever up our way, Webb, come and see us. You still owe me a bottle of that Italian olive oil."

"I'll bring it first chance I get."

Willa got out of the car and waved goodbye to Webb as he drove away. She picked up her purse from the porch and went inside the house. Cardboard boxes, some half-filled and a few sealed with tape, lay scattered on the living room floor.

Ro appeared from the bedroom carrying a pile of sheets and pillowcases in plastic wrapping. "Would you look at this? She never even opened the packages."

"Daddy never let her buy anything," Dilly called from the kitchen, "so after he died she was making up for it."

"That's because Mama didn't know how to handle money," Willa snapped.

"Oh, stop it, you two," said Cissie, rolling quilts together and tying them with twine. "Let the dead rest in peace."

The sisters worked quickly and efficiently, boxing the household items to be given away and then sorting Lizzie's clothes into a pile for the Salvation Army and another pile to be thrown away.

"Look at this," Dilly said. "Who's that with Mama?"

Ro took the photograph and looked on the back. "That's Aunt Pearl. It says she was eighteen and Mama was sixteen when this was taken."

"Well, they don't look a thing alike," Dilly said. "Look how dark Mama is. But she's so pretty."

"Just like all of us," said Ro.

"Dark or pretty?" asked Cissie. "I'm dark, except for my hair, what's left of it, but I'm sure not feeling pretty." She took the photo from Ro. "Isn't it funny, though, how none of us took after Daddy."

"I take after Daddy," Willa said.

"But you look nothing like him, Mug. You look just like Mama and the rest of us."

"Here's Grandpa and Grandma Allen," said Dilly, holding up a photo in a small gold frame. "They look so young, all starched and shiny. It must be their wedding picture. Why don't you take it, Willa? You're the youngest."

"Let me see," said Willa. "Huh. They both have blue eyes." She tucked the portrait into her purse.

"Who's this man with all the blond hair?" asked Cissie, showing them a cameo photo on a gold chain. "It was in

Mama's jewelry box."

"He's a handsome devil," said Willa.

"Maybe he's Mama's old flame," said Cissie, "you know, Effie and Edith's father."

"I thought they had different fathers," said Dilly.

"You're right; they did," said Ro.

"How do you know?" asked Willa.

"I don't remember. Something Mama said once."

"There," said Willa, labeling a box filled with crocheted doilies, embroidered tablecloths, and knitted shawls. "Is that everything?"

"I brought her things from the nursing home," Dilly said. "I threw her old purse away."

"Let me see," said Willa. Dilly handed her a shoebox.

Willa rummaged through the box. "Not much here. Poems and papers. She was always working on a poem. This looks interesting. Wasn't Sappa Creek where Mama's folks lived?"

"Yes," said Ro. "On a farm not far from Oberlin."

"So, what does it say?" asked Cissie.

"I'll just read it," said Willa. "It doesn't look finished though. 'The Secret of Sappa Creek, by Lizzie Sharpe.' John and Laura and little Pearl hiding in the tall corn, hiding from the Cheyenne, fleeing the cavalry. Cheyenne going to the Black Hills, Cheyenne, Running for their lives, Saving? She's crossed some words out. It's hard to read. Leaving a baby, a dark-eyed baby wrapped in a blanket, hidden all alone in the muddy creek bank, waiting to be found, waiting to be saved."

"Well, that's interesting," said Dilly. "Is Mama saying she was an Indian baby?"

"No!" said Ro. "It's just a story she's making up."

"Well, it would explain this," said Willa. She held up a beaded leather pouch. "Remember this?"

"We'll never know," said Cissie, sealing a box with masking tape. "There. That's the last one."

"If no one minds, I'd like to keep it," Willa said. No one minded, and Willa slipped the beaded buckskin bag into her purse. Inside the pouch she could feel the stone egg that her mother had given her and then taken back.

When Willa arrived home at 10:30 that night, Jake and Annie were asleep. She found a note on the kitchen table from Ellie saying that before she and Mark left she made sure that Annie took her pills. Willa warmed some milk to settle her stomach. It had been a long day. Her head and ankles ached, and she was exhausted. Her heart was racing again. She sat down to drink the milk and make her list for tomorrow. Annie had to be at the Mental Health Clinic in Greensburg by 9:30, and while Annie was with her therapist, Willa could do some grocery shopping and pick up the tractor part for Jake at Greensburg Implement. Willa rubbed her dry, sore eyes. She needed to make an eye appointment, too. Maybe the doctor could give her something to stop the itching.

She yawned and reached into her purse for a last cigarette before she went to bed. She pulled out her Belairs, the buckskin pouch, and John and Laura Allen's portrait. She lit a cigarette then opened the pouch and took out the familiar smooth stone. It would make a good paperweight. She studied the beaded leather pouch. Lizzie always kept it close. It was fine Indian beadwork. All the red, yellow, blue, and white seed beads were still intact, and the leather was soft and supple. She weighed the empty pouch in her hand. I wish I'd asked Mama where she got it, Willa thought. Maybe her Indian mother left it with her.

Willa took a deep drag on her cigarette and filled her mouth with smoke. She blew a perfect smoke ring and then another and another. She put down the pouch and picked up the Allens' portrait and searched their solemn, young faces. Her mother never talked about her parents, and Willa knew nothing about them except that they survived the last Indian raid in Kansas. Willa breathed smoke deep into her lungs and then blew three perfect smoke circles. She watched the rings climb and revolve, so beautiful in their fragile symmetry, and then in a moment they were gone, dissolving into floating wisps of smoke and then disappearing completely into the still air.

Hardesty, Inc.
1976

"Dear Ellie,

Here I am late again with your anniversary card. Thanks for all your news. It was good to hear from you finally. Nobody seems to write letters anymore. I know you've been busy with teaching and your move. Jake got a kick out of how much you paid for your house. Said you could have bought a farm for $42,000! That does seem like an awful lot for a house, even in Connecticut. Our mortgage on the 160 acres we bought is $47,500. $4,125.25 comes due every year in August. I told Jake you and Mark wouldn't join us on the land and cattle business. Frankie has all his money tied up in his deals, but Willy and Rocky both said yes, so we're calling it Hardesty, Inc. Jake didn't want to, but I reminded him how we ended up with Aunt Mattie, and we got a lawyer to draw up the agreement. Everybody agreed that Jake and I would run the daily operations of the farm and cattle business, and Willy and Rocky will be silent partners since they have their own businesses. We made our wills and everything. I want you to know that I asked the lawyer to put in a clause that if anything happens to me that I give up my part of the land so that Annie will be taken care of. It's just a request, not legally binding. Which worries me, but because of Annie's Social Security, she can't have any income or property. Annie is back home again, so write to her at our new address in Sitka. The Kinsley boarding house didn't work out. The psychiatrist who runs it didn't hire any nurses, and she wasn't taking her medication. When I moved her out of there, Annie threw a fit and had to go back to Larned for 10 days. She was there a week when she called & asked me to bring her car & her money to her. A man she met wanted her to go to California with him. I went up there and told her all he wanted was her car and her money and then he would dump her somewhere. Turns out I was right. This man is in and out of the hospital. So that's one reason she can never be on her own as she would give away all her money. We don't mind having her here. She keeps herself busy writing letters and poems, and she helps me around the house sometimes. Yesterday I took her shopping in Ashland. I bought Jake 5 pr. of Levis. They're hard to get now. I could have let the old gal at Warren's lose $31 & some cents if I had wanted to. I told her three times to figure out the bill again & finally told her of her mistake. I could figure it better in my head than she did on her machine—guess I should have let her cheat herself & gotten 3 Levis for free—Ha. It's supposed to be around 106 degrees today. I helped Jake build fence this morning when it was cooler, and I just canned 10 pt. of zucchini relish and 18 qt. of sweet lime pickles. I picked my vines clean of cukes &

squash. Willy said he told you all about the Sitka Social Club. It's a big success. No wonder. There's nowhere else to eat on 183 for 50 miles. The parking lot is packed every day. Annie sits on the front porch and makes lists of the different kinds of trucks. Mud trucks from the oil fields, salt haulers from Cargill down by Freedom, hazardous waste haulers from Waynoka, and all kinds of cattle and feed trucks. Cars mostly come later when the private club is open. So far most of his local customers are from Ashland, a few from Protection, although it's about half way between the two. I make 4 pies most days, and Willy says they're all gone by 10:00. Our Sitka house is ok. Three bedrooms on one floor. Since we moved in the population is 7. Well, I guess it's 6 now since Delores Harper passed last week. They're on the other side of 183 across from us. Quint called and wanted me to come over. The old woman just up and died on me he said. I waited with him until the doctor and the funeral home came and took Delores away. I stripped the bed, washed the bedding, and then made his bed again. He said Delores was 67. I thought she was older. The Sitka water is no good, so we have to haul water in for drinking. Just remembered you asked for my cherry pie recipe. Next time I make it, I'll write it down and send to you. Well, I'm pooped and my eyes are itching. Better close now & figure out what's for supper. Bye now & hope you had a nice anniversary. Love, Mama

P.S. Annie asked me to enclose her card too."

"Dear Ellie and Mark, I sit at the table in Sitka, Kansas after a glass of milk and write you to wish you a happy belated anniversary. I was in Ashland yesterday afternoon doing my shopping with our mother. It keeps me hopping. It was very quiet in Ashland. No buzz buzz of gossip, just noise of cars pulling up or leaving. As for leaving, I am as without flight as a bird with one wing. Love, your sister, Annie"

A New Year's Resolution 1980

"Ellie, I can't understand why you don't like him." Frankie laughed. "He's an actor. You love actors."

"No. He's a movie star and a terrible actor. Except when he's telling lies! I can't believe that you voted for him! Hardestys are Democrats!"

"Of course, I voted for Reagan. So did Shirley. And Willy and Kayla. Millions did. Most of the country in fact. Anybody with brains did. What? You want four more years of inflation and high interest rates?"

"That's because all you guys care about is money. Wait and see. You'll be sorry."

"He says he's going to make America great again," Mark said, pouring more bourbon into his glass. "When exactly was that?"

No one had an answer.

"Give him a chance. He'll be a great president," Willy offered. "What do you think, Mom?"

"Well, I voted for Carter but I wanted Ted Kennedy to beat him in the primary."

"Why?"

"Kennedy says everyone should have good health care. Not just rich people. Insurance costs so much and it will be a couple years before Jake and I can get Medicare."

"Kennedy's a socialist," said Willy.

"Well, they called Roosevelt that too. And worse. He saved us during the Dust Bowl. I don't know what Annie would do without her Social Security Disability."

"Are we going to play pitch or not?" Rocky said. "Annie, be my partner. I want to teach Kerry how to play."

This was the first time they had all been together in ten years. The last time was right before Mama's funeral, Willa realized. No one had changed that much. Frankie and Shirley still looked glamorous and rich. Frankie was a bullshitter, but when had he become such a braggart? Talking about his deals and the money he was making. He wasn't raised like that. Their kids were home in Oklahoma City. Willa wished their oldest Charley could have come, but he was twenty now, a pilot for Frankie's company, and he wanted to be with his friends on New Year's Eve. Willy and Kayla seemed to have energy to burn. Raising Wyatt and little Willa, running Willy's restaurant, and interfering in the farm and cattle business, which pissed Jake off. She needed to remember to get a picture taken before they all left. Who knew when they would all be together again? "Time is really slipping by," Jake had said the other day, when the free 1981 calendar arrived in the mail. Sometimes days slipped by so fast that a month disappeared in a blink. Before you knew it, another decade had flown by.

Annie was wearing her new black velvet pants and top that Ellie and Mark gave her for Christmas. Kayla had washed and set Annie's graying hair and convinced her to put on some lipstick. She looked nice. "Kayla, may I have some wine?" Annie asked.

Kayla looked at Willa who shook her head no.

"Sure, you can," Frankie said. "It's New Year's Eve." He took the bottle from Kayla, poured a wine glass half full of white wine, and gave it to Annie. "Mom, are you playing?"

"No, not right now." Should she take it away? Annie took a tiny sip of white wine. Well, she would keep an eye on her. A little bit couldn't hurt.

Willa watched as Rocky pulled Kerry onto his lap. She was a cute Irish girl from Massachusetts with a funny accent and a cloud of frizzy strawberry blonde hair. It was nice to see Rocky happy and enjoying life.

Willa leaned back in her chair. Did she dare have a cigarette? She glanced at Mark. He looked at Ellie, who was leading Willy's three-year old Wyatt and toddler Willa Suzanne into the bedroom. Mark smiled. Reading her mind. He took out a Marlboro and walked over to Willa and lit both their cigarettes. They each took a deep drag and relaxed.

"Thanks," Willa said. Leave it to Ellie to find a tall husband. Ellie hated being short. Maybe she figured that by marrying someone taller than anyone else in the family, she was tall by proxy. Mark was smart too, and Willy, Frankie, and Rocky admired him. He designed helicopters for Sikorsky, but as a teenager, he cowboyed on a ranch near

Garden City, Kansas and could talk cattle and hunting with Jake. Mark always tried to draw Annie into the conversation. Unlike her brothers and Jake, who talked around her as if she weren't even there.

Right now, playing pitch, everyone was laughing and getting along. As usual, Rocky and Annie were winning. Jake always over-bet his hand.

"Hey, Mom, how about some dessert?" Frankie called.

Willa stubbed out her cigarette. On the way to the kitchen, she unbuttoned her tight new pants. She should have told Shirley to get her a size fourteen. The print top, though, fit just right. Who cleaned the kitchen and put away the food? Not Ellie. She was still trying to get the kids to sleep in the bedroom. Rhinestone rubber gloves lay by the sink. Shirley. Well, that was nice. The kids hadn't let her help with dinner either. Willy brought over prime rib from his restaurant and bottles of wine and bourbon. Frankie and Shirley contributed scalloped potatoes. Ellie and Mark made a green salad, and Rocky and Kerry spent the afternoon making the *petits fours*.

Willa nibbled a *petit four*. The combination of sponge cake and butter cream filling was delicious. Light and rich at the same time. Rocky had a real gift. After he graduated from the Culinary Institute, he opened a restaurant in Miami.

Willa placed the last of the *petits fours* on a tray. She lit another cigarette and admired the beauty of the tiny cakes. They were individually iced and decorated with tiny balloons and "1981" in various colors. She'd never had time to decorate cookies or cakes, but with his training Rocky could do everything so fast. She looked at the clock. It was 11:45. Almost time.

She heard Jake holler, "So the salesman lifted his head and said, 'Shut the damn door!'" There was a roar of laughter and a few groans. Willa chuckled. How many times had she heard that stupid joke? She did a quick calculation. At least three times a year. One hundred and twenty-three times. On January 7, which was their real anniversary, not October 14, the date she had made up so that Annie wouldn't be an early baby, she and Jake would be married forty-one years. Annie would turn forty-one in July.

"Shut the damn door! Shut the damn door! Why don't you all shut the damn door!"

Was that Annie yelling? Oh no! thought Willa. She's having a fit!

When she got to the living room, Annie was standing by her chair, waving a wine glass. "Everyone shut the door on me! You all did! Left me in the Crippled Children's Hospital and then in the Larned State Hospital!"

Shirley closed the magazine she was reading. "Annie, calm down." She patted the sofa. "Come sit by me."

"Sit by you? You're a whore! Look at you. All that makeup and dyed hair. You're nothing but a whore."

"You're upset, Annie," said Kayla. "Why don't you go to your room?"

"Get away from me! You're a whore, too. You just want to shut the door on me. Like Willy shut the door on Joanie and Brad and Lou Ann! You're all dirty bastards and sonsabitches! Shut the goddamned door! Shut the goddamned door!"

As Willa reached for Annie, Willy grabbed a glass of water from the coffee table and threw it in Annie's face.

Shocked, Annie dropped the empty wine glass.

Willa gasped. "Damn you, Willy, why did you do that?"

Willy shrugged and looked down.

Ellie ran into the living room. "Annie, what's wrong? Why is your face all wet?"

"Who the hell are you?" Annie screamed. "I don't know you!"

Annie glared at her family. Her face was red with rage and dripping with water and tears. She yelled, "SHUT THE DOOR. SHUT THE DOOR. SHUT THE GODDAMNED DOOR."

Willa threw her arm around Annie's waist. "Time to go to bed, Annie. Time to take your pills."

Ellie grabbed Annie's good hand and held it.

Together they pulled Annie toward her bedroom. Ellie opened the door. Annie stopped yelling, turned, and stared at her family, who looked back at her in stunned silence. She spoke in a low, guttural snarl. "I don't know any of you. I'm shutting my door on all of you. I want to go back to Larned State Hospital. I'm packing my suitcase. I never want to see any of you sonsabitches ever again."

She glared at Ellie, who was holding her left hand. "Let loose of me!" she growled. Ellie let go and took a step back. Willa shoved Annie into her room. When Ellie tried to follow, Annie yelled, "Get out! I don't know you! Get her out of here!" Ellie looked at her mother, who shook her head. Willa closed the bedroom door.

An hour later, Willa went outside. She stood on the front porch. The cold air felt good. Her heart was racing. She hadn't done a lick of work all day, and she was still worn out. She was exhausted thinking of the drive tomorrow. Did she have enough gas in the car? It would take hours to get the paperwork done, Annie settled, and then the two hours' drive home. What if something happens to me? she thought. Where would Annie live? Who would take care of her? Jake was helpless where Annie was concerned. Willy and Rocky had their own families and lives. Frankie the same, and all he cared about was wheeling and dealing and making money. Ellie and Mark had been married for ten years, and she was tired of nosy people asking her when they were going to start a family. Maybe they didn't want a family. There was nothing Ellie could do about Annie. She lived too far away. There was nothing anybody could do. Annie was her child and a mother's responsibility never ended. I'll find a place for her next year, Willa vowed, that will be my New Year's resolution.

She heard the door open behind her. Mark came out and stood beside her. He took off his leather jacket and draped it around her shoulders.

"I brought your cigarettes. Smoke?"

Willa sighed. "Yes."

Mark lit her cigarette and then his own.

"Everyone's gone?"

"Yeah. They said to tell you goodbye. Frankie and Shirley plan to stay all night in Dodge and then go on to Colorado for their ski trip. Charley's flying in some high roller clients to meet them. Rocky and Kerry have a flight leaving out of Wichita early in the morning."

"What's Ellie doing?"

"She's in bed. Upset that Annie kicked her out. Did Annie go to sleep?"

"She was in bed when I left her. But not asleep. She finally calmed down when I gave her the glass."

"Oh, the teardrop. Yeah. I tried to go to sleep, too, but Jake's snoring like a chain saw! It comes right through the wall. How do you stand it?"

"After forty years, you get used to it."

They finished their cigarettes. An empty tractor-trailer rumbled by on 183, deadheading south. A lone coyote called in the distance.

Willa looked up at Mark. "Long day tomorrow. What time is your flight?"

"We'll stay a couple extra days. Ellie and I will drive you and Annie up to Larned."

Willa exhaled, her breath fogging in the cold air. She leaned on her son-in-law. "Thank you," she said. Her eyes flooded with tears.

Everything Changes
1985

IT TOOK WILLA OVER THREE years to find a place for Annie. In December 1984, Annie moved to the Lifecare Rehab Center in Haviland, a small town about fifty miles northeast of Protection. The nursing home for the elderly had expanded its care to treatment of the mentally handicapped, and, in exchange for Annie's monthly Social Security check less thirty dollars a month spending money, Annie received supervised medical care and planned activities.

When she helped Annie move in, Willa was surprised by how many people her daughter knew from her stays at Larned Hospital. Through Annie's eyes she glimpsed another world inhabited by mental patients, most of them in their forties and fifties, a floating population hidden from the rest of the world, neglected and sometimes forgotten by their families. Willa assured Annie that she would visit her often. She emphasized that the Center was her home now, but she would still have her bedroom on the farm when she visited.

Willa's relief that Annie was taken care of was overshadowed by loss. In 1977, as soon as she turned sixty-five, seemed like everyone started dying. Her half-sisters Effie and Edith, Ro, Ollie, Stub, and just last year, Heck, and then right before Christmas, Cissie died of a heart attack.

"I just can't believe she's gone," Willa wrote to Ellie. "I can't believe any of them are gone. It all happened so fast."

Willa's remedy for grief was always work, but now she didn't need to work so hard. After the 1984 harvest, when she and Jake moved to their new home three miles south of Protection on farmland purchased by Hardesty, Inc., she stopped making pies for the Sitka Social Club. A local contractor, with the help of Rocky, who brought Kerry and his three sons, worked during the summer and renovated the house according to Willa's specifications. A guest room and a master bedroom, both with walk-in closets; a large, sunny bedroom for Annie with a half bath; two bathrooms, one near the backdoor for Jake when he came in filthy from the fields, and another between the master bedroom and the guest bedroom. A laundry room with space for Willa's sewing machine and quilt frames. The living and dining rooms had nubby oatmeal-colored wall-to-wall carpet. Rocky designed a modern eat-in kitchen that was painted yellow with white cabinets. For the first time in her life, Willa owned a dishwasher.

Willa helped Jake measure terraces, build fence, and move cattle. Afterwards she was exhausted. Keeping Wyatt and little Willa for a weekend wore her out. She didn't feel up to cleaning metal and had to push herself to work in the garden. She'd never felt so tired. When she went to Dr. Hudson in Buffalo for a check-up, he said her blood pressure

402

was way too high. He told her to stop smoking and gave her Visken to take twice a day. The medicine made her feel a little better, but she still felt worn out.

When Frankie called to wish her "Happy Sixty-Eighth Birthday," he put Shirley on the phone to say hello. Willa told Shirley she was feeling poorly and had her usual January blahs. "When I'm feeling like that I get my hair done," Shirley said, "or buy some new clothes, and I feel like a new woman." When she hung up the phone, Willa thought about what Shirley advised. Shirley was certainly an expert on hair and clothes. Maybe she was right.

A month later, Willa made an appointment in Dodge City to get a permanent. The beautician shaped her hair into soft, silver white curls that framed her face. At the mall, where she bought a pretty red blouse, she spotted a sign in a jewelry store advertising free ear piercing with the purchase of 14K gold earrings. She never allowed either Annie or Ellie to get their ears pierced, but earrings would look nice with her new hairdo. She wished she had taken Shirley's advice a long time ago.

On Thursday morning April 11, Willa woke up late, around 7:30. Jake had gotten up earlier and left to build fence on the quarter they wanted to use as wheat pasture.

She dressed in her favorite pair of black polyester pants with the stretchy waistband and a black and white checked cotton blouse. When she went into the kitchen, she noticed that Jake hadn't taken the letters she wanted him to mail, but, as usual, he'd made a pot of coffee. She'd forgotten to tell him to pick up bread from the restaurant. She could go over and get some herself or call Willy and have him bring a loaf by, but he wouldn't take his break until 3:00, and meanwhile they wouldn't have any bread for dinner. Well, it's easy enough to make some, Willa thought.

Before she started, she poured herself a cup of coffee and admired her house. Jake had left the back door open and the morning sun streamed in. It was going to be a fine day. A good day to work in the garden. At Christmas, Mark had helped her hang all the pictures. The gold-leaf framed portraits of Charley, Jake's folks, and his brother Bill were in the living room above the sofa with the kids' high school graduation photos. She and Jake never tired of looking at the pictures on the south wall of the kitchen. Kerry made photo collages of all the grandkids and another collage with old Hardesty family photos that she had gathered from everyone. There was even one of Tippy, guarding the five kids on the Boyce place.

Rocky designed a special marble pastry counter for making bread and rolling pie dough that was just the right height for her. Willa poured herself another cup of coffee and gathered her ingredients for bread. It felt good to be back in the familiar relaxing rhythm of bread making. She didn't have to think, and her mind was quiet. Her hands knew exactly what to do. She kneaded the dough until it was warm, pliant, and smooth. She put it in a greased pan, turned it once, then covered it with a tea towel and set it on the table in the warm sun. She lit a cigarette and picked up last week's *Freedom Call*.

The pain hit her like a gunshot. A sudden, blinding blow

to her head that struck all at once. Willa stumbled and almost fell, but she held onto the paper. In a moment of blazing white clarity inside the dark, bloody chaos that was spreading through her brain, she realized what was happening.

She worried that she wouldn't have time to do what she needed to do. She looked around the kitchen. There. By the phone. She grabbed a pencil and scribbled across the front page of the *Call*: Head hurts something awful. And then there was no time to write anything more. She couldn't make her right hand work, and the pencil scrawled a long line on the paper. She dropped the pencil and paper. She had to get to the bedroom. Jake would be home in a few hours, and she didn't want him to find her sprawled on the kitchen floor.

Around noon, Jake walked into the house, banging the screen door behind him. He tossed his hat on the hook. "Hey, old woman! I'm starving." He waited for the usual answer, I'm right here, old man. He heard nothing. The room was silent except for the loud ticking of the clock. He looked around the kitchen. On the table, there was a coffee cup with red lipstick stains on the rim, an ashtray with a burned down cigarette, and a bowl with bread puffing up beneath a towel. There was nothing cooking on the stove. He stepped over the newspaper and pencil lying on the floor. Queasiness gripped his gut.

"Willa?" He walked through the dining room and into the living room, peered into her empty bathroom and then went into their bedroom.

Willa lay on her back, half-on and half-off the bed, as if she was trying to lie down and then changed her mind. Jake stood, shocked, looking at her face. Her eyes were closed, and her skin was the color of dry, blowing dust. Her breath was loud and raspy, and her cheeks puffed in and out as she struggled to breathe.

How long did he stand there? Later, when Willy asked him, Jake couldn't say. It seemed like forever, and it seemed like a second. Finally, he reached down and touched her forehead. She was burning hot. He tore himself away and limped to the phone in the kitchen. Then he realized that without his glasses, he couldn't see the goddamn numbers, and he didn't know where his glasses were, and even if he had them, he didn't know what numbers to call. Whenever he needed to make a call, Willa always dialed the number. He saw his pick-up keys on the table, snatched them up, and shaking with fear, he drove to Kayla and Willy's. They would know what to do.

That afternoon, at Coldwater Hospital, Dr. Jennings spoke to Jake and Willy. "It was a massive cerebral hemorrhage," she said. "There's nothing we can do."

"What about taking her to Wichita, to Kansas City, somewhere other than this piss-ant hospital!" Willy demanded.

The doctor looked wearily at him. Then she repeated her phrases as if speaking to a slow child. "Her brain is filled with blood. She's paralyzed and unresponsive. Her pupils are fixed and dilated. It's just a matter of time. Twenty-four to thirty-six hours at the most."

The only sound in the room was Willa's loud, rasping breath. Every breath seemed an immense effort.

"Why is she breathing?" Willy asked.

"Her respiratory system's still working," said Dr. Jennings, "but soon it'll give up."

Jake collapsed into a chair at the end of the bed with his left hand resting on Willa's right foot. Willy went off to make the necessary phone calls. Frankie drove in from Oklahoma City that evening. The next day, Frankie's son Charley picked up Ellie and Mark and Rocky at the Oklahoma City airport and flew them to Coldwater in the small company plane, just beating a thunderstorm that had moved into the area.

Incapable of sitting still in their dying mother's room, her children created tasks. Frankie discovered that if he held Willa's jaw open with his hands, her breathing was easier. When Frankie grew tired, Ellie took over, then Rocky, then Willy. Every once in a while a nurse entered to check Willa's vital signs. They turned her and tried to find a position to make her more comfortable. They spoke to her occasionally, saying her name, telling her they were there. When her body temperature started to rise, they placed cool cloths on her forehead, and the nurse brought in more ice to pack around her. From time to time, they smoothed ice across Willa's dry, parched lips. They knew their efforts were futile, but still they did it, wanting to do something, and the routine felt peaceful, and the work necessary somehow.

Jake sat helpless and shattered. He slumped beside Willa holding her hand. He looked at his kids with empty, lost eyes, as if he didn't know who he was anymore.

They stayed with Willa through the night, listening to

her rough breath. Through the open window, they heard the pounding of the rain and the crackling of thunder. Finally, the rain stopped, and the sun rose. The hospital began to wake up. There were sounds of people walking down the hallway, carts rolling, doors opening and closing, and the smell of food. Ellie walked down the hall to the bathroom again. What a time to have diarrhea, she thought. When she returned to the room, Willy said, "Go get some fresh air."

"Are you sure?" Her mother lay on her right side. Her breathing sounded like heavy snoring. Frankie placed some ice into Willa's open mouth and held it there, letting it melt.

"Can I get anything?" Ellie asked.

"We're fine," Willy grunted, looking at his father sleeping in the chair beside the bed. Rocky stood, as he had most of the night, staring out the open window. Mark had gone with Charley to bring Willa and Jake's car to the hospital, and Kayla was at home in Protection with the kids.

Ellie walked down the long hallway to the side entrance. She passed a nurse who smiled at her sympathetically. At the side entrance there was a concrete patio and some lawn chairs. She walked outside and stretched. The morning air smelled like fresh-cut grass. A door slammed behind her. One of the nurses was taking a cigarette break.

"That's really something, isn't it?" the nurse said.

"What?"

The nurse pointed to the west. "I've never seen anything like it," she said, crushing her spent cigarette into the dirt. "Well, back to work."

Just Willa

Ellie looked up. The rainbow curved across the sky. A platonic ideal of a rainbow or maybe a copy of the one Noah saw, arching triumphantly across the clouds. Bright arcs of radiant color. Violet, indigo, green, yellow, and red. It was as if the rainbow had caught up all the colors in the world and flung them shimmering across the sky. And like a reflection in a still pool there was a faint hint of another rainbow behind it. Ellie imagined rainbow after rainbow stretching into infinity. She stared in disbelief at this sign in the sky. She wanted to scream at God. She wanted to rip Him from the heavens and slap His face for playing such a cruel joke, for displaying such magnificent beauty that her mother would never see.

That morning, still furious, Ellie drove ninety miles an hour to Haviland to get Annie. The day before she'd talked to Annie's psychologist, who had prepared Annie. Ellie found her sister calm and in control. Annie said that a voice told her last week that her mother would soon be changing.

Ellie helped Annie pack. She picked up enough medication for a week from the nurse, and then they drove to Coldwater. Willy met them at the steps of the hospital. Ellie searched his eyes. Willy nodded.

Annie asked if she could be alone with her mother. Everyone else left the room, and Annie sat by Willa, head bowed, and spoke to her.

At 2:15 p.m. on Saturday, April 13, surrounded by family and with Jake holding her hand, Willa raised her head off the pillow, lifted her chin, and then, suddenly, she stopped—just stopped working.

Were they all feeling what I'm feeling? Ellie wondered, as she gripped her mother's ankle and doubled over in pain. It felt like something was being torn from her gut. Horrible, excruciating pain. Ellie was stunned. She'd never experienced grief before and hadn't known that it was first felt by the body and then by the mind.

The Hardestys returned to the farm. Jake took care of his cattle, and then came home and sat silent in his recliner as his children planned the funeral. It was set for Tuesday at 11:00 a.m. in the Christian Church in Freedom.

Ellie ordered hundreds of bedding plants from her old high school friend Elise and her husband, who owned a nursery in Protection. Mark and Rocky built three large flat wooden boxes and painted them white to hold the plants. Ellie and Mark separated the flowering bedding plants into individual foil-wrapped packets of tiny blue violas, pink petunias, yellow and purple pansies, white dianthus, and used various greens as accents, including chives, thyme, mint, and small spikes of asparagus fern.

Willa's family and friends filled every pew of the small white church. Willy covered the closed bronze coffin with the king-sized quilt Willa had made him. When Jake walked down the aisle to take his seat, he stopped in front of the coffin, took off his black Stetson, and placed it on top of the quilt.

The service was short. Frankie's minister gave a brief sermon about Willa's relish for hard work and her devotion to her family. The Beagley twins and the Hepner sisters, wearing matching navy blue linen dresses, sang *In the Garden* and *In the Sweet Bye and Bye.*

At the end of the service, Willy stood up. He took a deep breath and then spoke clearly and without tears. He said Willa's nine grandchildren would be passing out spring bedding plants at the door.

"Farmers know everything changes, everything dies," he said, using the words he'd heard his parents say many times. "A blade of grass, a sheaf of wheat, the people you love. Mom knew that life didn't last, and she never wasted a minute of hers. She wouldn't want you to waste your time mourning her. She'd tell you to Get With It! And all of you know that if Mom told you to do something, you'd damn well better do it." There was a small ripple of laughter.

Willy paused and looked at his two brothers and two sisters, then into the wrinkled, brown face of Aunt Dilly, the last of the Sharpe sisters, and finally into the ravaged face of his father, so like his own. "Mom would tell you to find a nice, sunny spot, dig a hole, then put these spring plants in the ground, and water them in good. Then she'd tell you to get back to work and enjoy the time you have left."

The day after the funeral the Hardestys returned to their homes and went back to work. Mark flew home to Connecticut, but Ellie stayed on for a few days with Jake and Annie. Ellie wrote thank-you notes to everyone who sent flowers or donations to the Leukemia Foundation. She took the gifts of food and dozens of flower arrangements to the Protection nursing home and to the hospital.

One day Webb Connell came by the house to visit with Annie and to give Ellie a packet of Willa's letters. "I thought you might want these," he said. "I knew your mother for fifty-seven years."

Willa had left the house immaculate, but still Ellie vacuumed and mopped, Annie dusted, and they packed up their mother's clothes to give to the Salvation Army. They didn't touch the white trunk that sat in its usual place in the bedroom. Ellie did some mending that Willa hadn't finished. It was comforting to use her mother's sewing kit, to take up her needle and continue the stitches that Willa had begun. On the ironing board in the sewing room, Ellie found the seventh day of the week tea towel that Willa had promised to send her to go along with the six others she had mailed earlier.

Ellie cooked for Jake and Annie and herself, and she was a good cook, but none of it tasted like her mother's cooking. Never again would they savor Willa's food. Tender chicken with yellow egg noodles, raisin-filled cinnamon rolls, crispy fried chicken, and fresh ham with red-eye gravy. No more homemade bread and cherry pie.

Ellie pasted extra-large numbers on the phone that Jake could see without his glasses. She printed a card with everyone's telephone numbers in big, block letters and put it under Willa's stone next to the phone. She made sure he had enough food and that his clothes were in order. Willa had left enough supplies in the pantry and bathroom for several months.

While Ellie and Annie busied themselves in the house, Jake stuck to his usual routine, working every day, doing his chores, but he couldn't sit still, always needed to be moving, and spent hours driving back and forth to town to drink coffee with Kayla or to sit at the community table at the Sitka Social Club and watch people come and go.

Ellie and Annie decided to go through Willa's jewelry box to find costume jewelry to give her granddaughters. When they opened it, they saw the beaded buckskin bag on the top shelf.

"This bag was Grandma Lizzie's," said Ellie. She stroked the soft leather. "There's something inside." She opened the pouch and shook it. The glass teardrop fell into her hand. "Look, Annie! It's your glass! Did you know Mama had it?"

"Yes."

"Well, you should take it, the pouch, I mean, since you're Anne Elizabeth named after Grandma Lizzie."

"Mama named me after her best friend Annie who died in a car wreck."

"Who?"

"Annie Shaw. She could play the piano."

"Really? I didn't know that. Anyway, here's your glass."

"No. The voices say you're the keeper of the glass now."

"Are you sure?"

Annie nodded her head.

"Okay. Thanks, Annie." Ellie dropped the glass into the pouch and pulled the strings tight. They sifted through the jewelry box, setting aside a few necklaces and bracelets. At the bottom of the box, Ellie spotted a newspaper clipping. She unfolded it and read aloud:

"Youth, Shot in Leg, Recovering. Nineteen-year-old Jake

Hardesty had gone to the chicken house on the Eden ranch, near Fair Valley, where he works, to dispatch a dog caught sucking eggs. In chasing the dog around the chicken house, the gun became entangled between Hardesty's legs and was discharged. The charge took effect in the femur of his left leg, blowing out about two inches of the bone. The charge missed the artery. There was no one at home at the time and Hardesty saddled a horse and rode two miles to the home of W.A. Graves, who brought him to Alva General hospital. Physicians removed the wadding and slugs of the .410 charge. None of it had gone entirely through. Today he was reported resting fairly well."

"Oh my God! Daddy told me he was shot running whiskey! Did you know about this, Annie?"

"He told us an Indian shot him with an arrow. But I never believed him."

"I can't wait to show him this. This is too funny."

"No! You can't!"

Surprised at the vehemence of Annie's tone and not wanting to provoke a fit, Ellie thought for a moment. "Well, it is pretty embarrassing. A cowboy shooting himself in the leg. I can't wait to tell Willy."

"No! You can't tell anybody."

"Why not? What difference does it make?"

"It makes a difference to Daddy, and Mama knew it. That's why she never told us."

"Well, okay, maybe you're right. But I wish I could ask him how he got on the horse with his leg all shot up."

Ellie folded the clipping and tucked it inside the leather pouch. "There. Are you all packed and ready to go, Annie?"

"Yes, I'm ready. I don't want to be late."

"Maybe one of these days you can come visit us in Connecticut. Unless you're afraid to fly like Mama."

"Mama flew."

"No, she didn't. She was terrified of planes."

"She flew in a plane. Charley took her."

"Frankie's Charley?"

"They flew on Valentine's Day. It was a present."

"Mama didn't tell me!" Ellie said. And then it hit her. There was so much she didn't know about her mother. And now she could never ask. For as long as she could remember, she pictured her own death in a tornado or of various diseases or in a car accident, and she had imagined sudden deaths of others in her family, like Rocky shot down in a helicopter in Vietnam and her father crushed under an overturned tractor. But never, not even once had she ever imagined her mother's death. Her imagination had failed her there. "Was Mama afraid?"

"No. She liked flying with Charley. They ate cherry pie in the air. They flew to Freedom and back. She told me that from above the land looked like her quilt blocks."

Annie glanced at her watch and then checked it again. "It's time to go now, Ellie. We have to go right now. Are you driving me or is Daddy?"

"I don't know where Daddy is. I'll take you."

Up in Smoke
1985

"HEY! HEY! ANYBODY HOME?" THERE was no answer. Where the hell was Ellie?

Jake pulled off his boots and looked around. There was a note next to the phone under the rock but he couldn't read it without his glasses, and they were in the bedroom, and he didn't want to go in there. He wandered through the empty house. From the living room to the kitchen to the dining room and back to the living room. He sat in his recliner for a while and then got up to take a piss. He thought about driving to Sitka, but he'd sat there all morning, and there was nothing to do there except listen to people feel sorry for him.

I'll read the paper, he decided. Sit in the kitchen and read the paper. But he needed his glasses, and they were in the bedroom. He sat in the recliner for a time and maybe he dozed a little. Then he got up his nerve and walked to the bedroom and opened the door. He took off his socks and tossed them in the basket in the closet. He'd asked Ellie to give away all Willa's clothes except for one thing. Her new red blouse. There it was hanging all by itself.

The rage hit him harder than he'd ever been hit in the ring. Like a sledgehammer to his whole body. Fury at Willa. Goddamn her! How could she leave him so alone and lost? He howled in agony at the empty red blouse. Goddamn you, Willa!

He caught a glimpse of himself in the door mirror, and he didn't recognize himself. Who the hell was that old man staring back at him?

His white hair bristled straight up from his large, square head. His face was worn and dark from the sun and as cracked as old leather. His thick hands were liver-spotted and pitted with scars. His bare feet looked more like talons than human feet. He clenched and unclenched his fists, boxing the air at an unseen adversary. Then he let out a bellow like a gutshot bull. He ripped the red blouse off the hanger and threw it on the bed. He limped into the living room and smashed the bookcase glass with his fist, and, blood dripping from his hand, he grabbed the big black Bible and stacks of photograph albums and scrapbooks off the shelves. He went back into the bedroom and tossed everything on the bed. Then he tied the ends of the quilt together, making a large bundle. He grabbed Charley's white trunk by its metal handle. He took Willa's lighter from the bedside table and put it in his pocket. On the way out of the house, he picked up the brown rock. Willa liked to hold it when she was talking on the phone. What good was it now? Then dragging the laden quilt and the white trunk, he limped out of the house, across the dirt-packed yard and into the dry pasture.

Out-of-breath, his face flushed, and his denim shirt wet with sweat, he staggered across the pasture, finally stopping at the shallow hole used to burn dead animals. He pushed and kicked everything into the pit. The last to go was Willa's goddamn old rock. He reached into his pocket for the lighter. The bone dry albums erupted first. Soon the pit was filled with flames and smoke.

Perhaps he would have stood there forever, if Ellie hadn't seen the smoke.

She ran across the pasture. "Daddy, what the hell are you doing?" She grabbed his arm and tried to lead him away, but he moved closer to the fire, taking her with him.

Afraid that Jake would throw himself into the fiery pit, Ellie pleaded, "Daddy, please, come home!"

Jake turned to her, his faded blue eyes glistening with loss. "Get with it, girl. Home's gone."

Epilogue
Holding On

IN JANUARY, 1991, ALMOST SIX years after Mama died, I flew to Wichita and then drove to Dodge City to visit Daddy and his new wife, Cindy. I had a mission. To assume responsibility for Annie. To accomplish that, Daddy had to agree to sign over his right to administer her Social Security, which paid for her care plus thirty dollars a month spending money. In her will, Mama left me thirty-five hundred dollars, which was the money she saved for Annie over the years. She asked me to take over the account and pay the taxes. Mark and I put the money into a CD and let the interest accumulate. Every Christmas Annie joined Mark and me on our visits to his folks in Garden City. In the summer, I would stay in Protection for a week and take Annie with me to Freedom to see Aunt Dilly, Aunt Lucy, and our cousins. Annie didn't like her roommate at Haviland and longed for a change. I decided to move her to the nursing home in Protection, where Willy and Kayla lived and where we knew the staff. The home had expanded their services to include younger people with mental illness. Freedom was only forty miles away, so her cousins could visit more easily. Also, she would be able to have a private room.

After Daddy remarried, there were disputes over money, and Hardesty, Inc. dissolved. Daddy no longer spoke to Willy and Rocky. I tried to be a peacemaker, but failed. Cindy discouraged calls or visits from any of us. Daddy would talk to me on the phone if I called but he hated using the phone and never called me. Annie told me that Cindy gave her only five dollars a month in spending money instead of the thirty dollars she was allotted. Once in a while Daddy and Cindy stopped to see her in Haviland, but months would go by before she talked to them. Annie needed someone she could count on. I told my brothers what I wanted to do, and they agreed.

Daddy and Cindy lived in senior citizen housing in Dodge City. Their second-floor apartment opened onto a long balcony that wrapped around the front of the building. I knocked. Cindy cracked open the door. I'd only met her a few times, but I was struck again by how thin she was. Her dyed black hair was piled high, and she wore an enormous amount of eye make-up. "Oh," she said. "It's you."

Daddy sat in an armchair with his stocking feet on a hassock to the left of the door. "Daddy, it's me," I said. He turned his head, but he didn't stand up. "Well, Snooks," he said, "get in here out of the cold."

Cindy stepped back, and I took off my coat and put it and my purse on the sofa. I sat on the hassock and looked at Daddy. His hard muscle had turned to fat. He was always a big eater, but now with no farm or animals to take care of, he didn't have anything to do except sit in a chair, read the paper, watch television, and eat. I could feel Cindy's eyes boring into me. I kept my eyes on Daddy.

I visited with him a while. Telling him my news, and then getting to my point. "It's my turn to look after Annie," I said. "It's what Mama would have wanted. I'm already buying her clothes and looking after her hair and dental appointments. It's too much responsibility for you and Cindy. All you have to do is sign a paper. I can take it to the Social Security Office today."

I placed my hand on his knee, and he put his hand over mine. I waited. Then, Cindy erupted. She opened the door, letting in a blast of cold air. "No! Get out! Get out now!" She picked up my coat and purse and tossed them out on the balcony.

I stared at Daddy. I was scared. His face was unreadable. What would he do? He didn't look at Cindy or change his expression. His rough warm hand never left mine. His voice, though, was cold and hard. "Cindy," he said, "get Ellie's coat and purse and bring them back inside. Now."

I couldn't look at Cindy, but she did what he asked. When my things were back in place on the sofa and Cindy had slammed the bedroom door, Daddy patted my hand and said, "Snooks, where's that paper? I'll sign it."

And just like that, the Hardestys had a new hub. Annie pulled us from our separate paths and bound us together. We would revolve around Annie now.

Daddy died in 2001, and Annie died two years later. When I cleaned out Annie's room at the nursing home, I boxed her papers and shipped them to Connecticut. I found dozens of poems and stories, the postcards Mama sent to her at the Crippled Children's Hospital, and notebooks filled with records of her fits and symptoms.

My sister had secrets too. In a large Whitman's Sampler box, I found almost a hundred cards and letters, dating from a sympathy card in April, 1985. They were all from the same person. A stranger, I thought, until I read her letters. Janice Sedlak Morris. Our half-sister.

I remember the last time I spoke to Mama. I called on Monday, the day after Easter, a week before she died, to tell her that she had a credit at the Protection Greenhouse to buy plants for her garden. I had forgotten to send an Easter card and felt guilty. I don't know what else we said, but I remember the joy in her voice when she answered the phone. "Ellie! Jake, it's Snooks!" That's what I hold onto. That and Mama's stone egg which I dug out of the ashes.

ACKNOWLEDGMENTS

So many generous people all across Oklahoma and Kansas, friends and family members, former neighbors, and strangers walked with me through pastures, drove with me down country roads and through small towns, and shared their memories and stories. I'm so grateful for their time and countless kindnesses.

The Freedom, Oklahoma museum, the *Freedom Call* newspaper, and Freedom ranchers Tana and C. R. Nixon and Donita Luddington were especially helpful. Members of the Probst and French extended families offered information and inspiration.

I'm grateful to Jim Barker, a writer, historian, and beloved columnist at the *Alva Courier* who shared his vast knowledge of Oklahoma with me. Alyssa Vaughn and Veronica Redding of the Oklahoma Historical Society provided insight and material. Thanks also to Gail Kay, Dewayne Herd, Steve Herd, Anne Christopher Lousch, Marge Harmon, and Barbara McGinnis. Dave Webb, writer, historian, and teacher, shared his knowledge.

Two decades in the making, this novel has gone through many drafts. Daniel Menaker introduced me to Sam Douglas, who pointed the way forward. Sandra Katz and Alison Sheehy read every draft, and their comments and belief sustained me. Thanks to Philip Spitzer, Lukas Ortiz, and Carol Mann, I kept working and revising.

Fellow writers and kindred spirits, Connie Congdon, Brian Kellow, and Leslie Stainton, challenged me with their understanding and encouragement of my work, making me laugh and cry and rewrite, often at the same time. I'm so grateful to artist Sue Rollins, my steadfast "cuz," who designed the cover.

I'm appreciative of the perception and expertise of my editors, James Taylor, G. B. Crump, and R. M. Kinder. My wholehearted thanks.

With joy and love, I thank Tom Sheehy. This book would not have been possible without him.

About Helen Sheehy

Helen Sheehy grew up on tenant farms in Oklahoma and Kansas. She's worked as a dramaturg, written a theatre textbook, and biographies of theatre pioneers Margo Jones, Eva Le Gallienne, and Eleonora Duse. Sheehy taught theatre and acting in a university, and most recently, in a maximum-security prison. After spending years writing non-fiction, Sheehy turned to her earliest love, telling stories. *Just Willa* is her first novel. She lives in Hamden, Connecticut.

Find Helen Sheehy online at: **helensheehy.org**

www.ingramcontent.com/pod-product-compliance
Lightning Source LLC
Chambersburg PA
CBHW051310190726
48290CB00001B/95